S0-BMW-227

Rapture's Tempest

ROMANTIC TIMES PRAISES BOBBI SMITH, NEW YORK TIMES BESTSELLING AUTHOR!

WANTED: THE HALF-BREED
"Smith fulfills her title of 'Queen of the Western Romance' in this fast-paced, suspenseful offering."

LAWLESS, TEXAS
"Readers will be entertained and find themselves cheering for the good guys in the final shootout."

HIRED GUN
"Nobody does a Western better than Smith. *Hired Gun* is about a man...depending on no one and nothing but his wits and his gun. Finally he meets a woman who demands more of him...."

DEFIANT
"The talented Smith is in her element out West. This novel is fast-paced and filled with adventure and tender feelings...a very beautiful story."

HALFBREED WARRIOR
"Smith is the consummate storyteller. The pacing is quick, with snappy dialogue moving the story forward at breakneck speed."

BRAZEN
"As sexy and gritty as [Smith] has ever written."

HALF-MOON RANCH: HUNTER'S MOON
"Bobbi Smith is a terrific storyteller...wonderful characters, good dialogue and compelling plot will keep you up all night."

FOREVER AUTUMN
"*Forever Autumn* is a fast-paced, delightful story."

LONE WARRIOR
"Fast paced, swift moving and filled with strong, well-crafted characters."

EDEN
"The very talented Bobbi Smith has written another winner. *Eden* is filled with adventure, danger, sentimentality and romance."

MORE ROMANTIC TIMES RAVES
FOR STORYTELLER OF THE YEAR BOBBI SMITH!

THE HALF-BREED
"Witty, tender, strong characters and plenty of action, as well as superb storytelling, make this a keeper."

BRIDES OF DURANGO: JENNY
"Bobbi Smith has another winner. This third installment is warm and tender as only Ms. Smith can do….Ms. Smith's fans will not be disappointed."

BRIDES OF DURANGO: TESSA
"Another wonderful read by consummate storyteller Bobbi Smith….Filled with adventure and romance, more than one couple winds up happily-ever-after in this gem."

BRIDES OF DURANGO: ELISE
"There's plenty of action, danger and heated romance as the pages fly by….exactly what fans expect from Bobbi Smith."

WESTON'S LADY
"Bobbi Smith has penned another winner."

HALF-BREED'S LADY
"A fast-paced, frying-pan-into-the-fire adventure that runs the gamut of emotions, from laughter to tears. A must-read for Ms. Smith's fans, and a definite keeper."

OUTLAW'S LADY
"Bobbi Smith is an author of many talents; one of them being able to weave more than one story….Ms. Smith creates characters that one will remember for some time to come."

THE LADY & THE TEXAN
"An action-packed read with roller-coaster adventures that keep you turning the pages. *The Lady & the Texan* is just plain enjoyable."

RENEGADE'S LADY
"A wonderfully delicious 'Perils of Pauline' style romance. With dashes of humor, passion, adventure and romance, Ms. Smith creates another winner that only she could write!"

INNOCENT PASSION

Jim thought he was dreaming when he opened his eyes and saw the ivory-bodied goddess coming toward him. Held captive by his intoxicated state, he lay still, letting his gaze roam over her.

"Who are you?" he managed to whisper, the thrill of this midnight illusion making coherent thought impossible.

Delight was scared. She hadn't thought he would awaken—not yet. Her lack of experience frightened her, but she wanted to be with him...needed to be with him.

"I've come to love you, my captain," she replied, her voice as soft as a gentle breeze.

"Then tease me no longer, my beauty," Jim responded, slowly extending a hand in her direction.

The blackness of the night surrounded them as their bodies touched intimately for the first time. His mouth descended to hers slowly, sensuously opening her lips to him and drawing her life from her in a devastating kiss unlike anything she'd ever dreamed.

"What pleases you beauty?" he asked between short, breathless kisses.

"Your touch pleases me, my captain," Delight replied, without thought. "As I hope the gift of my love pleases you."

Delight couldn't control the urge to move against the hardness of Jim's muscled body, and he was thrilled at her uninhibited response. "Not so fast, little one." He slowed her with gentle hands as she twisted erotically beneath him. "Let's go slowly—together."

"I'm yours, forever, my captain, to do with as you will...."

Other books by Bobbi Smith:

WANTED: THE HALF-BREED
LAWLESS, TEXAS
HIRED GUN
DEFIANT
HALFBREED WARRIOR
BRAZEN
BAYOU BRIDE
HUNTER'S MOON (HALF MOON RANCH)
FOREVER AUTUMN
LONE WARRIOR
EDEN
WANTON SPLENDOR
SWEET SILKEN BONDAGE
THE HALF-BREED (SECRET FIRES)
WESTON'S LADY
HALF-BREED'S LADY
OUTLAW'S LADY
FORBIDDEN FIRES
RAPTURE'S RAGE
THE LADY & THE TEXAN
RENEGADE'S LADY
THE LADY'S HAND
LADY DECEPTION

The Brides of Durango series:

ELISE
TESSA
JENNY

Writing as Julie Marshall:

MIRACLES
HAVEN

BOBBI SMITH

Rapture's Tempest

LEISURE BOOKS NEW YORK CITY

This book is dedicated to the Walton Clan, one and all—
Margaret, Tim, Mary, Julie, Aimee, and Randy and to
the brave and gentle men and women of the St. Charles
Fire Protection District, St. Charles, Mo. Thanks!

A LEISURE BOOK®

November 2008

Published by

Dorchester Publishing Co., Inc.
200 Madison Avenue
New York, NY 10016

If you purchased this book without a cover you should be aware that this book is stolen property. It was reported as "unsold and destroyed" to the publisher and neither the author nor the publisher has received any payment for this "stripped book."

Copyright © 1985 by Bobbi Smith

All rights reserved. No part of this book may be reproduced or transmitted in any form or by any electronic or mechanical means, including photocopying, recording or by any information storage and retrieval system, without the written permission of the publisher, except where permitted by law.

ISBN 10: 0-8439-6051-5
ISBN 13: 978-0-8439-6051-8

The name "Leisure Books" and the stylized "L" with design are trademarks of Dorchester Publishing Co., Inc.

Printed in the United States of America.

10 9 8 7 6 5 4 3 2 1

Visit us on the web at www.dorchesterpub.com.

Chapter One

Wearily, Delight de Vries parted the heavy velvet drapes and stared bleakly out into the darkness of the cold January night. The wind was strong out of the northwest, promising yet another winter storm, and it howled in protest as it cut a chilling path down the snow-packed, deserted streets.

Though soft lights shone invitingly from the unshuttered windows of the other houses on Lucas Place, Delight felt none of their warmth. For a moment, she almost wished herself away from here . . . away from the cold and dark . . . away from the pall of sickness that hung over her home. But duty and love banished the thought forever. Her mother needed her.

For the better part of a week now, she had been nursing her mother through a very serious illness, and it seemed as if all of her efforts were for naught . . . Clara de Vries Montgomery had shown little improvement. She was not doing well.

Turning from the frigid, night-shrouded landscape, Delight let the curtain fall and returned to her vigil at her mother's bedside. Curling once again into the high-backed wing chair, she pulled a warm knitted afghan about her and waited. Her eyes lovingly traced her mother's pale features, hoping for some sign of life renewed, but there was no change. Clara lay quietly, her breathing shallow and labored.

Dr. Freemont had just left a short time before, and he had had little to offer in the way of encouragement. He had, however, given Clara a more potent sleeping potion in hopes that she would rest more peacefully. And, so far, Delight had to admit that her mother was less fretful. Maybe, in the long run, sleep would be the best medicine for her.

But for Delight, the feelings of uselessness that assailed her as she waited in this emotional limbo were almost intolerable. She was tired of hearing "only time will tell." She wanted some proof that her mother would get better. Patience was not one of her stronger virtues.

Sighing her frustration, Delight leaned her head back. Closing her eyes, she hoped a short rest would improve her worrisome outlook. Soon, Martin, her stepfather, would return, and her hours of lonely waiting would be at an end.

Odd, she thought, that Martin had been so supportive during Clara's illness. Before, for some reason, she had always felt uncomfortable around him. . . . But his gentle forbearance these past few days had helped her to endure the tense, nerve-racking hours of waiting, and for that she would be ever grateful to him. Finally, as the clock struck ten, she dozed off, sleep erasing all of the cares and worries that beset her.

His dark eyes ablaze with illicit desire, Martin Montgomery stood silently in the doorway of the master bedroom. A triumphant leer curved his too-full lips as he gazed upon Delight, asleep in the chair by the bed. It was going to work! All of his careful planning was finally going to pay off!

Not wanting to awaken Delight just yet, Martin hesitated, taking the time to observe her as she rested. His gaze caressed her, lingering on her sleep-flushed cheeks and the glory of her silken, raven hair. It had come unbound as she slept and now fell about her shoulders in a cascade of soft curls. How he longed to bury his face in its seductive loveliness. Martin felt the familiar tightening in his loins as he imagined having Delight, willing, in his arms. With an effort, he fought down the urge to take her then and there. It would be soon, but not yet. He could wait another hour or two. . . .

Schooling his features into a mask of concern, he entered the room, "Delight?"

Delight came awake slowly.

"Has there been any change?" he asked softly, his tone reflecting just the right amount of worry.

Delight looked up and smiled tiredly. "No. None. But I think she is resting more comfortably."

"I only hope the new medicine the doctor left is doing some good," he said with measured uneasiness. Then, turning to face her, he offered her the tray he carried with a small pot of tea on it. "I've brought you some tea . . . I thought you might need it."

"Thank you, Martin." Delight greatly appreciated his thoughtfulness. "Dr. Freemont said the medicine should help Mother to sleep all night, but as sick as she's been . . . I was afraid to leave her alone."

"I understand." He was solemn. "But I'll stay with her now. You go ahead to bed." He smiled warmly at her.

"I think I will lie down for a while since you're back . . . I just can't seem to keep my eyes open anymore," Delight finished the last of her tea and set the cup and saucer aside.

"It is late. It's after eleven already." Martin took her arm solicitously as she rose from her chair. "I'll call you if there's any change."

"All right." Her smile was tinged with fatigue as Martin escorted her the short distance to her bedroom. "I can't begin to tell you how much your help has meant to me these past few days . . . I don't know what I would have done without you."

"Nonsense." Martin dismissed her words abruptly, irritation flaring. Gratitude was the last thing he wanted from her. "I love your mother. You know that."

With warm affection, Delight reached up and kissed his cheek. "Well, good night. And please, call me if you need anything," she told him as she entered her room.

"I will," he answered and then murmured under his breath as she closed the door, "Don't you worry about that . . . you'll be the first to know when I need you."

Pausing in the hall, Martin listened anxiously to see if she was going to lock the door. When no telltale click of the bolt came, he smiled wickedly to himself and returned to his wife's bedside.

With an unsteady hand, Delight lit the small lamp on her bureau and then sat down heavily on the fleecy softness of her half-tester bed. She felt uncomfortably warm all of a sudden, and with sleep-clumsy fingers tried to unbutton the bodice of her high-necked gown. After struggling in frustration for what seemed an eternity, Delight gave up the arduous task and lay back, savoring the welcoming comfort. She wanted to undress—to take off her shoes and really relax, but for some reason she couldn't manage to keep her eyes open. Surrendering to the inevitable, Delight rolled to her side and, brushing an errant, tickling curl from her cheek, fell quickly into a deep, dreamless sleep.

With a click that seemed to echo loudly through the bedroom, Martin closed his timepiece and put it back in his vest pocket. Damn, but it had only been twenty minutes! Glancing at his sleeping wife, he smiled to think how convenient her illness was. For months, he had tried to figure a way to be alone with Delight, and now Clara had given him the perfect opportunity. At last, he had Delight right where he wanted her.

The knock at the bedroom door startled him and he looked up, almost guiltily, as Sue, Clara's maid, came in.

"How is she doing, Mr. Montgomery?" Sue asked with genuine concern.

"She's been resting quietly since Dr. Freemont gave her the new medicine."

"Good." Glancing at Martin, she inquired, "Can I bring you anything?"

"No, I'm fine Sue. But thanks." Martin smiled benevolently, wanting the woman to go on to bed.

"Then I'll be retiring for the night, sir."

"Fine. I'll see you in the morning."

Martin breathed a strained sigh of relief as Sue left the room. Now, he was certain. For the rest of the evening there would be no further interruptions. Nothing could go wrong. *Nothing!*

Rising, he paced the floor. As soon as he was sure that the double dose of Clara's sleeping potion that he'd put in Delight's tea had taken effect, he was going to make her his.

The fire of desire that was burning in his soul for Delight was reflected plainly in his handsome, swarthy features. Stopping at the foot of the bed, he stared at Clara, cursing the fates that had forced him to marry her those long months ago. At the time, marrying the wealthy, older widow Clara de Vries had seemed the easy way out . . . and Martin did pride himself on always handling things expediently. Money had been his main motive, and Clara certainly had enough of that. She had pleased him in bed, too, for a while. For what she had lacked in youth, she had made up for in enthusiasm. It was only when Delight, Clara's much-adored daughter, had returned from school back East that Martin had discovered, much to his surprise, that she was closer to twenty than ten. Clara's child was not the little girl he had expected. She was a young woman in full bloom. Delight was graceful and gorgeous, with hair as black as night, and fair, flawless skin. He had wanted her from the first time he'd seen her. His only problem had been finding the time to be alone with her. And now . . . well, tonight was the night.

Martin's eyes raked over his wife's colorless features as she lay inert beneath the heavy bedclothes. Clara's illness had aged her, and she looked even older than her thirty-eight years. Angry for having tied himself to her, he turned his back on her and quit the room. He could bear it no longer. He was going to Delight.

Like a man possessed, he strode down the hallway, not stopping until he stood before Delight's closed door. With as much restraint as he could muster, Martin carefully turned the silver-plated knob and pushed open the heavy six-panel oak door. He held his breath as it swung silently to one side. The door had been the last tangible barrier between him and the prize he coveted. Now, nothing stood in his way. He grinned, evilly . . . triumphantly . . . as he paused to savor the thought. A tremor of anticipation shook him as he realized the object of his desire lay not ten feet from him—vulnerable and ready.

No longer would Delight be only the substance of his dreams. From this moment on, she would be his.

Stepping into the room, Martin closed the door behind him and approached the bed. His breathing was labored as he stood over her. Asleep, Delight seemed even more beautiful, and he couldn't stop himself from reaching out to touch her. Hesitantly, he stroked the black satin of her hair, rubbing the lustrous strands sensuously between his fingers. It was as soft as he had thought it would be, and with that touch came the rush of forbidden passion that he had been controlling with some difficulty for a long time.

In the beginning, he had honestly tried to fight the desire he'd felt for her. But soon, living in the same house and seeing her every day had become too much for his meager self-control. Martin had always lived his life by one rule and one rule only—if you want it, take it. And he definitely wanted Delight.

The fact that she was an innocent, trusting him completely, meant nothing to him anymore. He was driven by lustful demons. Demons who would settle for no less than full possession of Delight's ample charms.

Turning away, Martin moved to lock the door and then hurriedly stripped off his jacket and cravat. He slipped into the bed next to her. With trembling, questing hands, Martin turned Delight to him. When she stirred only briefly, he waited, holding himself in check. But the moment passed. The potion had taken effect! Thrilled that Delight offered him no protest, he quickly finished unbuttoning the bodice of her gown. She lay limply beside him, unresisting as he parted the material and pushed it off her slim shoulders. The sight of her bosom, so full and round, pressing against her chemise encouraged Martin even more. Dipping his head, he pressed hot, wet kisses down her neck and across the tops of her barely concealed breasts.

Delight came awake slowly, as if from the bottom of a deep pool. Blinking, she tried to focus . . . to remember where she was, but her mind was so foggy that serious thought was impossible. She almost drifted back to sleep and would have save for the shocking sensation that jarred her back to reality.

Delight twisted in violent surprise as a strong masculine hand slid beneath her skirts. Eyes wide with fright, she finally recognized the man who loomed over her.

"Martin?" Her voice was broken as she tried to understand what was happening.

Mistaking her husky tone for passion, he ceased his caresses for a moment and smiled down at her.

"Yes, my precious. Lie still and everything will be fine," he soothed.

His tone was soft and coaxing, and she almost relaxed trustingly against him. But as he moved, Delight felt the coldness of the night upon her bare flesh and she started in surprise to discover that her clothes were in disarray.

"Martin! What are you doing?" She panicked, trying to free herself.

"Hush, sweet. You're mine now, as you always will be." He was fumbling with her skirts as he sensed her growing agitation. "I'll take care of you."

He held her forcefully as she tried to squirm from beneath him.

"Let me go! Are you crazy?" She was scared and disgusted by his unwarranted assault. "No, Martin! No!"

"Yes, Martin, yes," he spoke, ready at long last to claim her.

Tears fell unheeded as Delight sobbed brokenly, sure that at any moment he would violate her. It was only the muffled cry from the master bedroom that saved her from that terrible fate.

Martin froze . . . waiting . . . his body tense with unreleased passion.

"Martin!" Clara's call held him immobile. "Martin, I need you. . . ."

With a violent curse, he threw himself from the bed, knowing that if she was lucid and he failed to answer her call, she might ring for a servant.

"Wait here," he ordered tersely. Then, recognizing the fear in Delight's eyes, he threatened, "Don't move. If you do, there'll be hell to pay!"

Delight lay on the bed unmoving as he stormed about throwing on the rest of his clothes.

"I'll be back," were his final words as he left to see to his wife.

Sprawled on the bed like a broken, lifeless doll, Delight didn't stir. It was only when she heard him enter his own bedroom that she spurred herself to sluggish action. Her arms were leaden as she pushed herself up and off the bed. Staggering dazedly, Delight leaned weakly against the wall. She had to get away. There was no doubt in her now active mind that Martin would return, and when he did . . . swallowing nervously, she moved to the door and peeked out into the hallway. Although there was no sign of him, the door to the master bedroom was ajar and Delight knew she would have to use the servants' steps. With thought to little save escaping Martin, she fled her room.

The chiming of the mantel clock in the front parlor as it sounded the quarter hour startled her as she made her way furtively down the narrow, curving stairway. Breathless in fearful anticipation of being discovered, Delight hurriedly buttoned her bodice. Racing as silently as possible through the kitchen, she paused only long enough to grab Sue's cloak. With shaking fingers, she unlocked the bolt and fled the only home she'd ever known.

Delight knew not what awaited her in the blackness of the frigid winter night, but surely any fate would be better than submitting to Martin's lecherous advances. Clutching the cloak about her, Delight ran out into the shadowed darkness of the back alley.

Panting, straining to breathe in the bitter night air, Delight paused in the narrow passageway to listen. When she was certain no one followed closely, she leaned heavily against the rough-hewn siding of the shanty. She was safe . . . for the moment. Drawing an agonized breath, she pushed herself upright and struggled on. There was only one place she could go, and she wasn't sure how long she'd be able to stay. Rose's house was bound to be one of the first places *he* would search.

A sense of peace welled inside of her, temporarily easing her feelings of panic, as she thought of her friend Rose O'Brien.

It had hurt Delight when she'd returned home and found that Rose was no longer in the family employ, but Martin had assured her that Rose had only left because she'd gotten a better job. Delight had visited her at her home several times since her return, but their conversations had been strained somehow, and she had had no idea why.

A sudden thought of Martin caused Delight to shiver with disgust as drug-clouded memories of his hands and mouth upon her continued to assail her. She wanted to bathe . . . to scrub every reminder of his slimy touch from her body. She felt dirty—soiled—and she wondered if she would ever feel clean again.

Hurrying onward, Delight was relieved to see a soft light shining from Rose's window. Hiding momentarily, she watched the street to make certain that Martin wasn't already there, waiting. When she finally felt it was safe to venture forth, she moved quickly to the deeply shadowed door and knocked softly.

"Rose?" her voice was hushed yet full of panic. "Rose, it's me . . . Delight. Please . . . open up!"

"Delight?" Rose questioned, her voice muffled through the door.

"Yes, Rose. Please . . . let me in!" she pleaded, glancing nervously down the deserted street.

The moment the door opened, Delight rushed inside and quickly pushed it shut behind her. She took the time to slide the bolt back into place before turning to her friend.

"Thank you," she breathed in relief. "Oh, Rose, thank you."

"Delight . . . what's wrong? Why are you here? It's practically the middle of the night!" Rose demanded.

"I had to leave. . . ."

"It's not your mother? She isn't . . . ?" Rose had heard that Clara de Vries was ill.

"No, no," Delight hastened to reassure her. "It's nothing like that. . . ."

"Then what?"

A noise sounded outside and Delight jumped guiltily.

Her eyes wide with fear, she spoke, "I've got to get away . . . will you help me?"

Rose looked at Delight, her confusion evident. "Of course, I'll help you. But what's happened? Are you sure you don't want to go back home?"

"No!" Delight exclaimed, her tone desperate. "I can't go back."

"Well, sit down. I'll get you a hot cup of tea and then we can talk," Rose instructed as she moved to put the kettle on her small stove.

Delight nodded mutely and somehow, with numb fingers, she managed to unfasten Sue's cloak.

"Let me take that." Rose took the wrapper and looked at it questioningly. "Why this isn't yours."

"No—it's Sue's—I had to—um—borrow it," Delight tried to explain, but she started to shiver uncontrollably as the shock of the past hours became a reality to her.

Rose hung the cloak on a peg by the door and hurried to pour the hot tea into the mismatched and chipped china cups.

"Here you are." She handed Delight the soothing brew and watched the trembling of the young girl's hands worriedly. "Are you still cold?" Rose sat down beside her and took back the cup. Setting it aside, she took Delight's hands in hers and rubbed warmth into them.

"It's not the cold," Delight finally spoke, her voice quivering. "It was Martin."

Rose was stunned. How could he? Rage shook her. It had been bad enough when she'd been forced to quit her job at the de Vries home. Martin Montgomery had made his intentions toward her clear shortly after marrying Clara, and the only way for her to retain her virtue was to leave their employ. She might do scullery work and take in laundry and mending, but she was no whore! No matter what that filthy man had thought.

Delight was not so unaware that she didn't sense the change in Rose.

"Rose? What's wrong?" She was concerned at her friend's pale, stricken features.

"Nothing. Nothing at all. Tell me what happened. How can I help you?" Rose's concern was real.

"Did you know that Mother has been ill?"

"Yes," Rose responded sympathetically.

"Well, I've been nursing her. She was so weak. . . . And Martin was helping, too. . . ." Delight frowned as her concentration faded. Why couldn't she think straight? Surely, she wasn't that tired. Rubbing her forehead in a gesture of confusion, she continued, "I'm sorry, Rose . . . I can't seem to remember. . . ."

Rose, wise to the ways of men like Martin Montgomery, asked gently, "Did you have anything to drink earlier?"

"Why—yes. Martin brought me a hot drink before I went to bed."

Rose nodded, "Just relax and take your time. I'm sure it'll all come to you as your mind clears."

Delight lay back against the sofa, closing her eyes. Again she shivered with revulsion as she remembered his touch, and she looked at Rose quickly, a wildness in her eyes. Her voice was low and laced with determination when she spoke. "I've got to leave . . . to get away. This will be the first place he'll come, and then he'll force me to do those awful things again!"

"Did he take you, Delight?" Rose questioned gently.

Delight, her eyes cast downward, shook her head. "No."

Rose breathed a sigh of relief and said a quick prayer of thanks. "Good."

"It was so close. Thank God, Mother called out for him and he had to go to her. But he told me not to move or he'd do something terrible to me. . . ."

"Darling, you did the right thing. If you had stayed, something terrible definitely would have happened to you."

"He was like a crazy man."

"I know," Rose said flatly.

"You do?"

"Why do you suppose I quit working for your mother?"

"Martin told me that you'd gotten a better job."

"If I had, do you really think I'd be living like this?"

For the first time, Delight was aware of her surroundings. She'd never noticed before. On her previous visits, she'd been so glad to see Rose that she'd paid scant attention to the furnishings in the small two-room home. But now, it struck her glaringly.

The wind picked up just then, rattling the poorly fitted windows. Both women looked up startled.

"Rose, I'm so sorry . . ."

"Don't be. I can take care of myself. I always have. It's you we've got to worry about. How quickly do you think he'll come after you?"

Delight could feel her sanity slowly returning, and she looked up at Rose, a plan forming in her now-clearing mind. "I'm not really sure. It all depends on Mother. If she fell back asleep right away, he could be here at any time. But if she's restless, we might have until morning."

"We can't take the chance. Whatever we're going to do, we have to do now."

"I've got an idea," Delight began.

Rose listened intently as the younger woman explained.

A half an hour later, Rose stood back, staring in disbelief at Delight.

"If I didn't know. . . ." She shook her head in amazement as she circled her, studying every angle.

"It's the only way. Martin will never expect this." Delight managed a smile, feeling better now that she had bathed and taken charge of her life. "Do you think I make a good boy?"

"Yes—but your hair . . ." Rose surveyed Delight's short-cropped curls. "It was so beautiful."

Delight ran a hand through what was left of her long, silken hair and shrugged. "It'll grow back."

"Well, I'm just glad those boy's clothes fit you. It was a stroke of luck that I even had them. I mended them for a woman, but she never came back to claim them."

"Thank you, Rose," Delight told her in earnest and hugged her tightly. "I'd better go now. Martin might show up any minute."

"Delight," Rose stopped her. "Think about what you're doing."

"I have. There's nothing else for me to do but run," she responded sadly. "At least until Mother's well. Check on her for me, will you?"

"Of course. And you'll be back?"

Delight nodded, "As often as I can."

"You're welcome to stay here, you know, once it's safe."

"I know. And I will. I promise."

"Wait!" Rose halted her exit again. She took a small knotted handkerchief from under her mattress. "Take this. It's not much, but it'll help some."

"I can't take your money, Rose."

"You most certainly can, Delight de Vries. You'll need it." She put the gift in her hand. "Now, go with God, and *please* be careful."

Delight hugged her again quickly and then squared her shoulders bravely. Leaving the warmth of Rose's protection, she faced the cold night unflinchingly. There could be no turning back. Not now . . .

Chapter Two

"Are you sure you're doing the right thing?" Ollie Fitzgerald asked his captain and friend, Jim Westlake.

Jim looked up quickly from his seat at the desk in his cabin, and, noting his first mate's anxiety, he replied reassuringly, "Of course. Don't tell me you're going to change your mind now?"

"It's not *my* mind I'm worried about!" Ollie snapped, irritated at Jim's lighthearted approach to so serious a decision.

Jim grinned easily. "It's time. You know how everybody's been after me to do this."

"But shouldn't you think about it a little longer?" his friend argued.

"What for?" Jim countered. "I know everything I need to know about her. She's beautiful and she says she's in love with me. Isn't that enough?"

Ollie snorted derisively and commented cuttingly, "Sometimes, Jimmy, beauty is only skin deep."

For a moment, Jim Westlake seemed angry, his expression hardening, but then he masked it behind his usual easygoing facade. "Enough said, Ollie. I have proposed and Annabelle Morgan has accepted. We're going to announce our engagement at a ball the Saturday after we get back from this trip."

Ollie slowly shook his head. "You know I just want what's best for you. Do you love her?"

Jim was put off by his astute question. His mind raced. Love—Annabelle? He cared for her . . . found her attractive and enjoyed her company . . . but love? Jim knew the truth. No, he did not love her.

Jim had been in love with only one woman in all of his thirty-odd years, Renee Fontaine, and she had married his brother. There was no bitterness in having lost her to Marshall, simply resigned acceptance, but he was determined never to allow himself to fall in love again. He would marry now because he felt that it was time.

Forcing himself to lie, he answered, "Yes, I do."

Ollie sensed Jim's hesitation, but let it go, "Have you told your family?"

"This afternoon," Jim affirmed.

"Good. I take it they were happy about it."

"All except Renee." Jim chuckled. "She had another friend lined up for me to meet. The girl had a unusual name, too. . . ." Frowning, he tried to recall the name of the young woman whose praises his sister-in-law had been singing before he had told her the news of his engagement. "I know—Delight . . . that was it."

"Delight?" Ollie smiled.

"Yes, Delight de Vries. Renee said she was very attractive, but I told her she was too late. I'd already made my choice."

"I bet they were in shock."

"Only for a little while," Jim laughed. "Mother seemed most pleased, and I think Father was just glad that my 'wayward' days are coming to an end."

"What about you? Are you glad to give up your freedom?"

Jim was thoughtful for a long moment. "I really don't see that there will be that much change in my life. You know how busy we are."

"Does your fiancée understand about your work? She knows you're going to have to travel with the boat, doesn't she?"

"We've already discussed it, and Annabelle is very understanding."

"Good." Ollie was relieved. Jim was one of the best steamboat captains on the Mississippi and he didn't want to lose him. His business expertise was needed on the long trips between St. Louis and points south. "Well, I think a celebration is in order. What do you say we go to Harry's and raise a few?"

"Excellent idea," Jim agreed.

The noise level in the seclusion of the smoke-filled back room was deafening as the men who were gathered there assailed one another for being totally ineffectual in their quest to help the Cause. Fists slammed the tabletop in anger as tempers grew heated, and it was only the sharp knock at the locked door that prevented some of them from coming to blows. Shocked into silence by the unexpected intrusion, they stood poised for flight as the pounding came again.

Gordon Tyndale, the unofficial leader of the small covert group, stood and walked to the door with slow, deliberate steps.

"It's Nathan, Gordon." The voice was muffled by the closed portal.

Gordon smiled weakly in relief and quickly unlocked the door. The men behind him gave a collective startled gasp as an unknown Union major entered their midst, and their hands reached nervously for their sidearms.

"It's all right," Gordon told them. "He's one of us."

When Nathan Morgan followed the Yankee into the room, they relaxed a little, but their expressions grew even more guarded and skeptical when a woman, wearing a heavy cloak that hid her features, came through the door.

"Gentlemen." Captain Wade MacIntosh spoke confidently to the frightened men.

"Wade, Nathan." Gordon greeted them warmly. "Thank you for coming."

"It was important that we come. We have news that I'm sure you'll be interested in," Nathan replied, ushering the mysterious female into the room before closing and bolting the door behind them.

"You have news?" Gordon was indeed surprised.

"Good news," Wade affirmed.

"In case you haven't met before," Gordon turned to face the group, "this is Nathan Morgan." He introduced the older man first. "And this is Captain MacIntosh."

A murmur of approval ran through the crowd. They had heard that there were other Southern sympathizers in St. Louis, but they had never had the opportunity to meet them before.

"It's an honor."

"Thank you." Nathan returned their warming welcome. "I'm sure you're wondering what Captain MacIntosh is doing here, but let me reassure you. He is as loyal to the Cause as all of us. In fact, in many ways he is more so."

"Nathan," Gordon interrupted, concerned about the identity of the woman standing so quietly by the doorway. "I don't believe we've had the pleasure of meeting your other companion."

Nathan smiled and turned to extend his hand. "My dear, the gentlemen would like to meet you."

Moving gracefully forward, Annabelle Morgan lifted the concealing hood, revealing her identity to the room full of men.

"My daughter, Annabelle." Nathan introduced her.

"But Nathan!" Gordon was outraged. "You know women aren't allowed here."

"Gordon." Nathan spoke sternly to his acquaintance. "Annabelle is the one with the news. I trust you will extend her every courtesy?"

Gordon blustered momentarily and then managed to get control of himself. "Please, have a seat." He gestured expansively, and the three visitors sat at the front table. "And now, if we may continue?"

"I want to know what *he* is doing here," one of the more hostile men challenged, glaring at Wade.

All eyes turned to the Yankee.

"Wade MacIntosh is a very good friend. He has family in Mississippi and is most anxious to be of service to us."

"Really?" the man sneered. "And how will you help us, Captain? By turning us in?"

Wade pinned the fat little man with a glacial glare, his ice blue eyes freezing the next derogatory comment that he was about to make. The man swallowed nervously as he sensed MacIntosh's barely contained fury.

"Your name, sir?"

"I am Elroy Lucas," he managed.

"Mr. Lucas." Wade spoke, his jaw rigid with leashed anger, "if I had wanted to stop your meager activities, I could have turned you over to the proper authorities weeks ago and made myself into an instant hero."

"But you're a Yankee!" Elroy spat out, and several other men murmured in agreement.

"I may wear a Union uniform, Mr. Lucas. But my heart is with my heritage," Wade began, wanting the issue clear with these men from the beginning. "And besides, can you think of a better place to get accurate information about troop movements and payroll shipments than within the ranks of the enemy army itself?" His statements won over all opposition, even Lucas's.

Nathan spoke up, wanting to get on with what he had to tell them. "Wade has been checking on all the payroll shipments coming through the city."

"You have access to such sensitive material?" Arthur Brown was surprised.

"Not directly, but there are ways," Wade informed them.

"Well, tell us what you've found out," Brown insisted.

Again, all attention was directed to the tall, broad-shouldered man in the Yankee uniform.

"All my sources indicated that the Westlake Steamship Line has the present contract."

"Contract for what?" Lucas demanded.

"Elroy, please, let Wade finish. Wade—" Nathan invited him to continue.

"Thank you, Nathan. The contract to ship the army's payroll south."

"But I thought you said that Miss Morgan had the news?" another man questioned.

"She does, and she'll tell you in just a moment. I wanted to let you know what we have been doing and how we came to be involved in this situation."

"Is the payroll in greenbacks or gold?"

"Usually gold, but at this point either will do for our purposes."

"What can we do to help?" Gordon asked, glad at last to have some idea of how to help the South.

Wade and Nathan smiled at his enthusiasm. "Annabelle, if you'd like to address the men, now?"

"Yes, Father." Rising from her seat, she faced the room full of men. "Gentlemen. I am, as you know, Annabelle Morgan."

The men were courteous, but openly doubtful of her ability to help them. For she was, after all, only a woman. Beautiful though she might be—and she *was* beautiful, for her silver-blond hair set her apart from the crowd and her petite figure was, no doubt, the envy of many women of more statuesque proportions—Annabelle was an unknown quantity to them, and they listened to her attentively.

"When my father and Captain MacIntosh were discussing ways to get information about the gold shipments, I offered to help them. They, like you, were skeptical of my help, but I think I've won their confidence and I hope I can convince you, too, of my sincerity, and competence."

Her businesslike manner was a shock to some of the men, who were used to subservient, submissive females, but they held their tongues, knowing that Nathan Morgan was a powerful, influential man.

Annabelle took a moment to survey their expressions before continuing. Pleased that there was no overt disapproval of her, she went on.

"When the subject of the gold first came up, I was intrigued. We all know how the South is suffering. And it seemed to me that this would be the best, most direct way we could help. With gold the necessary supplies and arms could be purchased. And with that kind of help we can defeat the Yankees and drive them from our homeland!"

Her statements drew a cheer from the group and she paused until they were once again quiet.

"Captain MacIntosh has been instrumental in locating the information I needed. And once I knew who was in charge it was a simple matter." She smiled warmly at Wade. "As of this afternoon, I am the betrothed of Captain James Westlake, the owner and captain of the steamship *Enterprise*. The *Enterprise*, by the way, is the boat that carries the bullion south."

The men regarded her with open admiration.

"Don't you feel you're sacrificing yourself?"

"There is no sacrifice too great for the Cause!" she returned.

"Hear, hear!" they cheered her.

When they had quieted, she continued, "I don't have everything we need yet, but I'm sure I will before too long."

"We don't have a lot of time, you know. Vicksburg could fall at any moment, and, if Vicksburg goes, I'm afraid all is lost." Another man spoke his worries out loud.

"I have Captain Westlake's complete trust and admiration," she told them confidently. "I see no problem in getting the final pieces of information we need . . . when the gold goes, how big the guard is, and how much is actually being carried. If you will give me your complete trust, then I solemnly promise you that I will do everything in my power to provide you with the necessary facts. After that, it's up to you."

The men sat silently as she concluded and returned to her seat by her father.

"Gentlemen? Do you agree this is a risk worth taking?" Gordon asked. When they gave their approval, he turned to Annabelle and Nathan. "We support you fully, Miss Morgan, and we appreciate your sacrifice for the Cause."

Chapter Three

Despite the lateness of the hour, the streets along the riverfront were busy. Delight, effectively disguised as a youth, made her way through the milling crowds of rowdy riverboatmen trying desperately not to attract undue attention to herself.

From the upper windows of the bawdy houses, ladies of the night called out lewd invitations to the passing deckhands, tempting the men who were passing by with explicit accounts of their prowess and promising them a rollicking good roll for a nominal fee. At another time, Delight would have stared in astonishment at this bold open haggling, but right now she was so exhausted that she paid little attention.

Delight thought she was doing an admirable job of keeping panic at bay until a raucous voice above her singled her out.

"Hey, laddie! Tasted a good woman yet?"

At Delight's mumbled husky, "No," the prostitute laughed loudly.

"Then come on up, sugar. I can teach you at lot! I'll keep you warm, too!"

Nervous, Delight hurried on, trying to ignore the ribald comments the whore yelled at her.

Ducking into an alley, she slumped against the rough brick wall. Berating herself, she wondered what she'd been thinking of when she'd come down to the wharf . . . how could she have forgotten that it was the roughest part of town?

Exhausted and cold, Delight determined it was time to find a place to spend the night. Hauling herself upright, she shoved her hands deep into the pockets of the patched, almost too-small boy's jacket she wore. She had barely left the safety of the dark gangway when she heard two leering, conspiratorial voices.

"Hey, Archie! Look what we got here!"

Archie chortled to his companion, "What ya hidin' out in the dark alley for, boy?"

Delight froze momentarily at their verbal assault and then started to flee, but the drunken roustabouts were too fast for her. A hamlike fist grabbed her and threw her back against the side of the building.

"Let me go!" she hissed. "I ain't done nuthin'!"

"Listen to that high voice, Sam," Archie smirked. "Why the kid's voice ain't even changed yet!"

"Must be a young un," Sam deduced. "Ya got any money, kid?"

He loomed over her threateningly. "Gimme your money. Archie and I done run a little short."

"I ain't got no money," Delight lied, hoping they wouldn't find Rose's coins hidden in her shoe.

"Well, let's jes' check them pockets, Sam, and see what this little guy's got that we can use."

"NO!" The protest was out before she could stop it. Twisting furiously, Delight squirmed and kicked, trying to break free. "Let me go!"

But the men only laughed, snarling, victorious laughs, that enraged her even more.

"Help!" she yelled as loudly as possible, struggling in helpless frustration.

"Hold still!" Sam commanded, giving her a tooth-rattling shake.

"NO! Let me go!" She finally managed to kick out and her foot made contact with Sam's shin.

Grunting in painful surprise, the drunk loosened his hold momentarily, and that was all she needed to break free. With a burst of speed, she fled the scene. And, running as if the devil himself was chasing her, Delight darted out into the main street, dodging horses and carriages in her quest for safety.

"Where'd he go, Sam?" Archie bellowed.

"That way," Sam pointed, and they followed her down the street in hot pursuit.

The snow was beginning to fall in earnest as Jim and Ollie left the stifling smokiness of Harry's saloon. They paused only briefly to catch their breath in the frigid winter air before heading back to their home—the steamer *Enterprise*. It was then that the young boy, running at top speed with his head down and not looking where he was going, collided full force with Jim, jolting them both.

Delight looked up into a pair of warm brown eyes, as strong yet gentle hands helped to balance her. "Hold on there, boy. What's your rush?"

"Sorry," she mumbled, remembering to keep her tone husky.

"There he is! Get him, Sam!" Archie's strident shout reached Delight.

Looking back nervously, she tore herself free from the big man's steadying grip and dashed down a nearby gangway.

Jim and Ollie exchanged quixotic glances before stepping forward to block the path of the two drunken louts.

"Two on one's a little unfair, don't you think, Ollie?" Jim folded his arms across his broad chest and glared at the two rowdies.

Ollie shifted his stance defensively. "I sure do. What do you two want with the boy?"

"He done robbed us!!!" Archie lied.

"And he attacked me!" Sam embellished.

"I find that a little hard to believe," Jim taunted, eyeing their bulk. "Get out of here and leave the boy alone or I'll make sure you never work on this riverfront again."

"Sez who?" Archie challenged drunkenly, swaggering bravely forward.

"Me," Jim replied quietly, and he was ready when the roustabout swung at him wildly.

With cold precision, Jim's right upper cut laid Archie low as a stunned Sam looked on.

"You were leaving?" Jim asked sarcastically.

Sam jumped into action and helped Archie to his feet. He guided him away, and they both glared resentfully over their shoulders at Jim and Ollie.

"Nothing like a little surprise to stir up your blood," Jim grinned, turning, but he was surprised to find that Ollie had disappeared down the heavily shadowed passage in search of the youth.

Following, Jim heard their voices ahead of him in the darkness.

"You can come out now," Ollie was saying in a reassuring tone. "The captain and I took care of them."

The sound of a creaking crate was followed by the boy's respectful reply. "Thank you, sir."

"You're welcome, son. But what are you doing down here? This is no place for a youngster," Ollie scolded him, judging his age to be no more than fourteen or fifteen.

"I found that out, sir. I'll be going now."

Jim somehow sensed the youth's nervousness as he joined them. "Where are you going? Home?"

"I don't have a home. I take care of myself," Delight replied bravely.

"Well, it doesn't look like you're doing too good a job," Jim said sarcastically, staring at the boy's dirt-streaked face. "What's your name?"

Delight panicked—a name! Grasping for an idea, she blurted out, "Del Murphy."

Jim studied the boy thoughtfully. "You need a job, Del Murphy?"

For the first time that night, hope flared within her. "Yes, sir!" Delight answered eagerly. Then, feeling Jim's eyes upon her, she shifted uncomfortably. The man had the most piercing gaze . . . it was almost as if he could see right inside of her . . . as if he knew her most intimate secrets.

"What do you think, Ollie? I do still need a cabin boy."

"He's a little on the skinny side, but I guess he'll do." Ollie voiced his opinion, feeling a certain empathy for the youth. It was rough to be alone in the world. Especially in the wintertime.

Delight looked back and forth at the two men, trying to judge their thoughts.

"All right. But one question first." Jim was serious and he drew the boy's full attention. "Murphy—did you steal anything from those two men? I want the truth."

Standing straighter, her chin tilting in pride, Delight looked him in the eye. "No, sir. I've never stolen a thing in my life."

"You've got yourself a job. But Murphy . . ."

"Yes, sir?"

"If I ever find out that you've lied to me . . ." Jim threatened.

Delight nodded nervously, all the while wondering what she'd gotten herself into.

"Yes, sir. I understand," Delight answered quickly when she realized that he was expecting a reply.

"Good. You'll be working for me on my steamer, the *Enterprise*. I'm Jim Westlake, the captain, and this is Oliver Fitzgerald, my first mate. We run from St. Louis to New Orleans when the river's open, but right now we can only get a little south of Memphis."

"Yes, sir," she replied.

Delight was dumbfounded at the discovery that Jim Westlake was one of her rescuers, and she wondered if her life could possibly get any more complicated. Though she had never met him in person before, she was friends with Renee West-lake, and Renee had spoken often and proudly of her brother-in-law Jim, who captained a steamboat. Groaning inwardly, Delight braced herself for the arduous task ahead . . . keeping her identity concealed.

"Well, let's get on back to the boat and warm up," Ollie encouraged.

"Let's go, Murphy." Jim and Ollie led the way down the snow-trodden street.

Delight found it remarkably easy to keep up with them in the snow without the cumbersome weight of her skirts and petticoats. Hurrying along behind, she concentrated on the rhythm of their manly gait and tried to imitate their purposeful strides. She knew that if she could successfully master their walk, she'd be able to fool anybody from a distance. But close up—well, she'd worry about that later, although she was sure her disguise was pretty effective, for neither man had given her more than a second glance.

Chapter Four

The furious pounding on the door brought Rose upright in her bed, and, clutching her quilt about her, she ventured into the sitting room.

"Open up, Rose," Martin ordered arrogantly. "I know she's in there."

"Martin? What do you want?"

"I want to talk to you."

"Why?"

"I'll tell you as soon as you let me in."

"Just a minute," she called out, stalling, not wanting to face him in her present state of undress.

"Well, hurry it up or I'll break the damn door down."

Lighting a lamp, she pulled on her dress and fastened it quickly, knowing full well that Martin could very easily force his way in. Girding herself, she went back to admit the hated man to her house.

As soon as Rose had slid the bolt free, the door was slung violently open, crashing against the wall. Stepping into the room, his manner overbearing, he glanced around, searching for some sign of Delight. When he could find no trace of her, Martin directed his attention back to Rose, surveying her worn dress and work-reddened hands.

Smirking at her obvious poverty and glad that she was suffering, Martin faced her squarely. "All right, Rose, where is she?"

"Who?" Rose's innocent answer did sound convincing, but Martin didn't hesitate in his purpose.

"There's no point in playing games with me. We both know she came here and—"

"Who came here?" Rose cut him off in agitation.

"Delight," Martin responded through gritted teeth, growing angrier by the minute.

"Delight, here? No, Martin. I haven't seen her," she maintained steadily, not retreating from his obvious anger.

"Don't lie, Rose. She had nowhere else to go."

"Obviously, she did, because she didn't come here." Sensing his barely restrained violence, she countered, "Go ahead and search the place if you don't believe me."

"I don't believe you, Rose. And I think I *will* take a look around." Stalking past her, he explored the back room.

Rose's blue eyes were frosty with dislike when he returned to her. "Did you find her?"

"No, but—"

"Then get out of my house, Martin Montgomery, and don't ever come back," she ordered, unafraid of this spineless man, who preyed on helpless women.

Martin, recognizing her disdain, decided to put the

smart-mouthed wench in her place. With lightning speed, he grasped her wrists and wrenched her closer to him.

"I'll go when I'm ready," he sneered, enjoying her struggle to free herself from his painful grip. "But remember this moment. Rose. For I could have you right now, if I wanted you." Then, with seemingly little effort, he shoved her away. "But I don't want you. You're old and you look it." He let his critical gaze sweep over her, taking in her tired features and her too-thin body. "No. You don't have to worry about that. No self-respecting man would ever want to have anything to do with you."

"Get out," she seethed, rubbing her bruised wrists. Rose was furious that he'd been able to manhandle her so easily.

Indolently straightening his coat, he looked at her coldly once again. "Tell Delight that I'm looking for her and that I won't quit until she's back home where she belongs." Then, turning on his heel, he was gone, the only reminder of his visit the livid welts on Rose's arms.

As the sound of her father's footsteps ascending the staircase echoed into the study, Annabelle smiled invitingly at Wade.

"I thought he'd never leave," she complained sensuously.

"If you'd marry me, we wouldn't have these problems."

Wade's words sounded lighthearted, but Annabelle knew that he was serious.

"Wade—" she began, her tone brooking no comment, "we've been through this before, and you know how I feel about marriage. Let's just enjoy the relationship we have."

Wade didn't respond as he poured them both a brandy and carried the crystal snifters back to her. He had loved Annabelle for a long time now, and he would never give up hope that one day she would change her mind about marriage. He didn't know why she never wanted to wed; he just knew that it was the one subject she absolutely refused to discuss with him.

"For you." He handed her the liquor and sat down easily beside her.

Taking the goblet with both hands, Annabelle swirled the potent liquid, warming it with her palms. "Thank you."

Their eyes met and locked as they both sipped the heady brew. Silently, Wade admired her delicate beauty, marveling that such a fragile-looking woman could be such a formidable foe. He was glad that they were working for the same side in this war.

"How did I do?" she asked.

"You were magnificent."

"Good. I do detest pleading my case before those imbeciles, but we really will need their help with this one."

Wade nodded his agreement. "They're all we have. I wish I could tell you that they'll be there when we need them, but, apart from Gordon Tyndale, I don't think there's a real man among them."

"I had that impression, too. The war's been going on for three years now, and not once have they taken any action."

"Well, under our direction, that's all going to change."

Raising her glass in a toast, Annabelle spoke, "To the Cause. May it never die."

As their glasses met, their fingers touched, and thoughts of the war faded from their minds. Wade took her snifter and put it on the small table with his, then, without speaking, he took her in his arms and kissed her deeply. Passion, long suppressed, flamed to life as Annabelle strained against him.

"My darling." Wade spoke breathlessly as they broke apart. "I love you."

He bent to kiss her again, not caring that her father slept upstairs, not caring that the door was open and anyone could have walked in on them. When he was in Annabelle's arms, nothing else mattered . . .

"Annabelle?" He spoke softly when he ended the kiss, but his expression was worried.

"About Westlake."

Always aware of Wade's thoughts, Annabelle was instantly alert to what was coming, and it irritated her. She knew that

Wade loved her, but he had no right to feel that he had any claim on her. Why couldn't he just accept it?

"I don't want to share you, Annabelle."

She met his gaze without wavering. "I have no intention of marrying Westlake."

"God, I hope not."

"But what about you?" She quickly distracted him. "Are you still going through with your plans?"

"You mean courting his sister?"

She nodded.

"I think it's important. That way, if for some reason you're unable to get the information out of Jim, we'll have another option."

"That's a good idea. You'll have to let me know how you're doing."

"Just be careful. Remember, I'm an engaged woman now. Whenever you stop by, it will have to be to see my father."

"I'll remember." Giving her one last devouring look, he left to return to duty. But the fact of her engagement to Westlake haunted him. Wade couldn't shake the feeling that, somehow, he was losing her. And worst of all, he didn't know what to do to prevent it.

Chapter Five

Delight followed the two men across the slippery cobblestones of the riverfront and up the slush-covered gangplank. On the main deck, the captain stopped abruptly, and she skidded to a halt behind him.

Jim motioned Ollie aside. "Take care of Murphy. There's no need for him to start work until he's had something to eat and some sleep. Fix him a cot in your room for now and he can move into my cabin tomorrow."

"Fine, Jim," Ollie agreed.

"I'll need you again about eleven."

"All right. We'll see you then." He turned to Delight. "Come on, Murphy. Let's go get some sleep."

Delight watched as Jim Westlake strode off down the deck, and the female in her couldn't help but admire the proud, confident way he carried himself. She remembered well what Renee Westlake had told her about him. In her opinion, Renee had been too modest in her description of her brother-in-law. To Delight, Jim was her knight in shining armor. Tall and powerfully built, with dark eyes that could warm your soul, he was certainly handsome enough. He had rescued her from a fate worse than death, and for that she would be eternally grateful to him. Her musings were interrupted as she realized that the older man was waiting for her, and Delight fought to keep from smiling. What if Mr. Fitzgerald had known her real thoughts?

"Are you coming?"

"Oh—yes, sir!" She hurried after him.

"Murphy, there's something you need to know," Ollie began, his tone earnest.

"Yes, sir?" she replied nervously.

"My name's Ollie. Use it."

"Yes, sir . . . I mean—uh—Ollie, sir."

"No, no," he laughed, leading the lad on to the companionway. "The captain, now he's a sir, but I'm just Ollie."

Delight grinned at him as she finally began to relax a little. But her relief was short-lived as he led her up to the texas deck and into his own small cabin.

"You can sleep in here with me for now. The captain says that you can move down to his cabin later on."

"Sleep?" Delight eyed the single bunk with trepidation, her heart sinking. "Here?"

"Sure," Ollie continued. Oblivious to her distress, he began to undress.

Delight stifled a groan of misery. Now what? Just as she was about to bolt and run, he stopped unbuttoning his shirt and moved to pull a cot out from beneath his bunk.

"Here's your bed. There are blankets in the chest." He indicated a big wooden chest near the door.

"Thanks." She breathed more easily for a moment.

But once again, her relief was short-lived as Ollie unbuttoned his trousers and let them drop. Turning away lest he see her blush, Delight gave a prayer of thanks for the woolen long-johns that had just saved her from a quick lesson in male anatomy. Busying herself, she made the bed, and then, with her back still to Ollie, she shed the coat and shoes Rose had given her. Lying down, she quickly pulled the covers up to her chin.

It was only when Ollie turned out the lamp that she looked over toward him again.

"Ollie?"

"Yes, Murphy?" his voice was good-naturedly gruff.

"Thank you."

"You're welcome, son," his reply came. "Get some rest. We've got a lot to do in the morning."

Turning over, he was soon fast asleep.

Rest did not come easily to Delight, as she lay reviewing the events of the past day . . . events that had changed the course of her life forever. She shivered as she remembered the two drunks chasing her, and she wondered what would have happened to her if Jim Westlake hadn't come to her aid. But the outcome didn't bear thinking about—especially if she wanted to get any sleep.

Rolling to her side, she thought briefly of her mother. It had hurt her to leave, but there had been no help for it. Delight only hoped that she would understand when she found out. Tired of worrying, she thought instead of Renee Westlake and the many times they'd talked at various parties and balls. But even these distracting thoughts couldn't keep her from the looming recognition of Jim Westlake as a man and the certain knowledge that, under normal circumstances, she would have been attracted to him. But then, these were not normal circumstances. In fact, after her ordeal with Martin tonight, Delight wondered if she'd ever feel that way about a man again.

Struggling to keep her thoughts away from that trauma, she tried to imagine what her life was going to be like on board this steamer. Keeping to her disguise was going to be the most difficult part. She had no doubt that she could do the work . . . but just how long she could carry off playing a boy . . . well, that was another matter.

Finally, her exhaustion overpowered the shock of the past few hours and she slept, her dreams filled with a nerve-racking chase that ended in the safety of an unknown pair of strong arms.

Delight was relieved to find that Ollie was already up and gone when she awoke the next morning. Relishing the privacy, she took the few minutes to complete her toilet and to try to smooth some of the more stubborn wrinkles from her loose-fitting trousers and flannel shirt. Peering into the mirror, she paused before the washstand to skeptically survey her appearance.

Delight's biggest worry was that someone would see through her disguise, and she frowned at the thought. Glancing at her reflection, she was pleased to note that the frown hardened her features, making them seem less feminine. Determined to maintain that look, she practiced several expressions until she felt she had it right. Then, running her hands through her tangled mop of curls, she slipped into the too-tight boy's coat and headed out to face the blustery day.

As luck would have it, the first person she came face-to-face with was none other than Jim Westlake.

"Morning, Captain," she greeted, keeping her eyes humbly downcast. She didn't want to take any chances at this stage of the game.

"Murphy," Jim acknowledged as he passed by on his way up to the pilot house. "Ollie's waiting for you in the saloon."

"Yes, sir," she replied respectfully and started down the companionway to the lower deck.

The morning passed in a blur of activity for Delight. Struggling to maintain her boyishness, she spent all the time with Ollie learning everything she could about her new job. It pleased her to find out that, as the captain's cabin boy, her duties would be more varied and more exciting than the usual cleaning work.

Finally, as midday approached, Ollie and Delight paused for a moment in the bar.

"You seem to have caught on quickly, Murphy. That's good."

"Thanks, Ollie."

"Just remember, though, that the captain is the boss. If you take care of your work and get it done on time, I can guarantee you'll be well treated. The captain is a fair man."

Delight nodded, "I'll do my best."

"Good. You'll be paid on the first of the month. As the captain's cabin boy, you'll be making three dollars and twenty-five cents per month."

Her eyes widened. She hadn't even considered that she'd actually be making money. While it wasn't much, maybe her future wouldn't be so bleak, after all.

"Murphy . . ."

The sound of Ollie's voice dragged her away from her thoughts.

"Yes, Ollie. Sorry." She hung her head in a good imitation of youthful embarrassment.

Ollie watched her pensively for a moment, wondering at her thoughts, and Delight, feeling his gaze upon her, quaked inwardly with the fear of being discovered.

"Tell me about yourself." Ollie felt a protectiveness toward the youth they'd rescued and he was curious to know more of his background. "How old are you?"

"I'm fourteen," she lied, not eager to offer any more.

He sensed Murphy's hesitancy and smiled, "It's been rough for you, has it?"

"Yes," she affirmed. "It has."

The past twelve hours had changed her entire life. Gone was the security of her loving family. She'd found out the hard way what kind of a man her stepfather really was, and that knowledge left her uncertain as to whether she could ever return home again. She was still distressed at having left her mother, but there was no way she could have stayed . . . not with Martin wanting her as he did.

The opening of the Grand Salon door and the laughter that followed drew her attention, and she looked up to see the captain striding toward them with a Union officer at his side.

"Join me in a drink, Mark," Jim was saying to his companion as they entered the bar.

"I will. It's been one long morning."

"What's wrong?" Jim recognized the tension in his friend's manner.

Captain Mark Clayton flashed Jim a warning glance, not willing to speak openly in front of Ollie and Delight.

"It's all right, Mark," Jim assured him.

"You're sure? Who's the boy?"

"Del Murphy, my new cabin boy." Jim dismissed the boy as insignificant. "Murphy, bring us two beers."

Ollie went behind the bar to draw the brew for the men, and Delight quickly served them, hoping to bring as little attention to herself as possible.

"Beer?" Mark questioned, knowing Jim's usual drink was scotch.

"It's too early for anything heavier . . . and besides, I haven't been to bed yet."

Mark grinned. "One of these days you're going to have to stop this wild lifestyle of yours."

"I think I'm at that point," Jim admitted.

Mark almost choked on his swig of beer. "You're what?"

Shrugging, Jim looked at him, his expression serious. "It's not enough any more. I feel it's time to settle down."

"You're tired of being the most sought-after bachelor in town? I didn't think I'd live to see the day. Who's the lucky woman?"

"Annabelle Morgan."

Mark gave a low whistle in appreciation of Jim's success. "I don't believe it! She's the most beautiful woman in town."

"I know," Jim said smugly.

"You're amazing." Mark shook his head in disbelief. "There are men who have been after her for months. And you're the one to finally win her hand. Well, just remember to throw your castoffs in my direction. I'll be glad to help them recover from their broken hearts."

Jim laughed. "You know you love Dorrie."

"I know that and you know that, but Dorrie . . . well, she's got different ideas."

"Giving you trouble again, is she?"

"You'd better believe it. She's so afraid of being hurt. You know how devastated she was when Paul was killed."

Jim nodded, remembering well his sister's sorrow after the death of her fiancé.

"Just give her time. She'll come around."

"Lord, I hope so."

They fell silent for a moment, enjoying the beer and each other's company.

"So you still haven't told me what's troubling you," Jim prodded. "Is there a problem with the next shipment?"

"No—not yet," Jim replied. "We're all set to go. Be ready to leave some time after midnight tonight."

"Why so late at night?"

"Things are growing more dangerous by the hour."

"This sounds ominous." Jim tried to keep his tone light, but he recognized Mark's very real concern.

"It could very well be. We'll be doubling the guard from now on."

"All right."

"And, I want to know if you hire any new men. We both know it'll take an inside job to get the bullion."

"I know. But don't worry about the boat. Murphy there is the only new crew member and I doubt he's capable of stirring up any trouble." Jim eyed the skinny youth with little interest.

"Well, take it for what it's worth. Just keep your eyes open and let me know if you see or hear anything suspicious."

"I will," Jim assured Mark.

"We've been lucky so far. If the weather holds up North, the river may remain ice-free for another few weeks."

"You'll never hear me complain about that," Jim grinned, grateful that his steamer hadn't been threatened yet by the hull-crushing floes of ice that plagued the Mississippi every year about this time.

"I've got to get going. If I hear any news about the shipment I'll get in touch; otherwise, I'll just see you late tonight."

"We'll be ready."

When the two men stood and left the bar, Delight finally let herself relax, and Ollie noticed her obvious relief.

"Murphy? Anything wrong?"

Delight jumped nervously at his inquiry. "Oh, no, Ollie. There isn't anything wrong."

No, she thought, not anything—everything is wrong. Oh Lord, why of all the steamboat captains on the Mississippi did Jim Westlake have to be the one to rescue her? And then, to find out that he had dealings—both business and personal—with Mark Clayton! Delight could only gird herself and try to stay out of their way. For, though she hadn't met Jim before, she most certainly was acquainted with Mark. They had been introduced after her return to St. Louis and had danced and flirted casually at numerous parties since then.

"Well, let's get back to work. Later, we'll have to go up to the captain's cabin and get your sleeping quarters ready."

"I'm going to sleep with the captain?" Her tone was incredulous.

Ollie was puzzled for a moment, but then shrugged Murphy's reaction off, attributing it to youthful nervousness around the captain. Ollie wasn't overly concerned, for there were many on board who held Jim in awe.

"There's a small room with a connecting door to his cabin. You'll have a cot in there. So you'll be close by if he needs you."

"Oh." She trailed after him as they left the Grand Salon and looked worriedly about, hoping they wouldn't run into the captain and Mark again. When she was sure the coast was clear she was relieved, and she hurried to keep up with Ollie on his way up the companionway to the texas deck.

Chapter Six

Cold, wet, and totally thwarted, Martin approached his home. He had never considered the possibility that he wouldn't find Delight, and now he was faced with the awesome prospect of explaining her absence to both Clara and Sue. How could he make it seem plausible that she would pick up and leave home in the middle of the night? As he trudged up the unshoveled walkway, idea after idea occurred to him, but, just as quickly as they came, he discarded them. Whatever story he used would have to be totally believable, and something that couldn't be readily disproven.

Pausing on the porch to knock the snow from his boots, Martin unlocked the front door and let himself in. At another time the warmth of the house would have seemed inviting, but this morning it felt stifling . . . almost as if he had just walked into a trap from which there was no escape.

Using the boot jack, he pulled off his sodden boots and stepped into the waiting pair of dry shoes that were kept nearby.

"Mr. Martin! I was so worried!" Sue appeared in the foyer, startling Martin.

"Sue . . . you surprised me." He forced a smile as he explained his nervousness.

"I'm sorry. It's just that I overslept, and when I did get up I couldn't find either you or Miss Delight."

Latching on to her admission of being late, he said, "Then you didn't hear us leave?"

"No, I didn't," she told him confusedly as she took his coat.

"Good. We tried to be quiet, but we were in such a rush."

"What happened?"

"We got word last night from Clara's sister-in-law Faith that Joe had been wounded," he lied.

"Oh, no." Sue knew how fond her employer was of her only brother.

"Yes. Faith wanted to travel to be with him, but she couldn't leave the children. So she sent the message asking Delight to come at once to help her with them for a while." Martin was surprised at how easily the tale came to him. It was so perfect. "Delight didn't want to leave Clara, but I convinced her that we could take care of her now that she was improving."

"Of course. And you know how much Miss Clara loves Joe. She would want Delight to go."

Martin nodded, his expression a good rendition of concerned fatigue. "How is my wife this morning?"

"She's still sleeping. The medicine seems to have done her a lot of good."

"Good. Tell Cook to fix my breakfast. I'll eat and then try to get some rest."

"Yes, sir." Sue hurried off to do his bidding, leaving Martin to his thoughts.

Pacing the dining room, Martin was still furious. Damn her! Here he was caught in a web of lies all because of that stupid chit! He only hoped that no word came from Faith or Joe during the next few days. Surely Delight would return by then. After all, where could she go? Rose was her only friend, and Rose knew what would happen to her if she tried to protect Delight.

Running a hand nervously through his hair, he tried to relax . . . to get himself under control. But his body was tense with a mixture of unreleased passion and fury. One day he would get even with Delight for the agony she had caused him. Never again would he be outwitted by her. Never!

Sue brought his meal and Martin ate sparingly. He was anxious about telling Clara the story he'd invented and hoped that she was as gullible as Sue.

It was near noon before he headed upstairs. Pausing at the master bedroom, he looked in to find that his wife was stirring. Entering quietly, he stood by the bed waiting to see if she would awake. When her eyes fluttered open, Martin smiled down warmly at her.

"Good morning, darling." His tone was warm with pseudo-affection.

"Martin." A weak smile came to her lips. "I'm so glad you're here."

"I've been with you most of the night."

"Thank you." Her voice was weak as she reached out a shaking hand to take his. "You must be so tired. . . ."

"A little, but it doesn't matter. What matters is that the medicine the doctor gave you seems to be working."

She nodded slightly, "I did sleep well last night . . . except for that one time I had to call you."

"I know. It's after noon already. Do you feel rested?"

"No. I'm so faint."

"You haven't eaten in so long, it's no wonder. I'll call Sue and have her prepare you some broth. Maybe that will help."

"Thank you."

Martin patted her hand before leaving the room to give Sue her instructions. When he returned, he gave her another dose of the medicine and sat beside her on the bed.

"Is Delight here?"

"No." He paused, wondering if he should tell her the story now or wait until she was feeling better. Martin was certain of one thing . . . she couldn't be put off for long. "She's been called away."

"The hospital?"

"No. I'm afraid it's more serious than that."

"What happened?" A spark of worry showed in her eyes.

"We got a message last night from Faith."

"Not Joe!?"

"No . . . he's not dead."

"Thank God."

"He has been wounded, though, and Faith wanted Delight to come stay with the children so she can go to be with Joe."

"Good," Clara sighed. "I'm glad she went. Faith needs her more than I do. I have you. . . ."

"Yes, you do," Martin agreed, hiding the bitterness in his voice.

As Sue entered the room with the broth, Martin excused himself, telling her that he was going to get some sleep. Once alone in his room, he was more furious than ever with Delight. Now he was condemned to a life alone with Clara. Before he'd met Delight he could have managed it . . . maybe even enjoyed it. But now . . .

How could his carefully laid plans have been ruined? He had hoped to keep Delight with him. He had been confident that she would stay and never tell her mother of their intimacies. But what if she returned and she did tell Clara? Where would he be then? If Delight came back, bent on revenge, his only hope was that Clara loved him enough to think that her daughter was jealous. It was a long shot, but right now it was the only positive thought he had. And, while he didn't relish spending the rest of his life tied to Clara, the alternative at this time was decidedly more unattractive. His rich wife had provided him with a comfortable lifestyle, and she had to be placated if he wanted it to continue.

Stretching out on his bed, he tried to rest, knowing that at any moment Delight could show up and destroy his existence. Tense and frustrated, he lay unmoving, wondering what the future held for him.

Chapter Seven

Delight was nervous as she followed Ollie down the texas deck. Hunching her shoulders against the cold, she waited tensely as he knocked at the captain's cabin door.

"Come in," Jim called, and Ollie quickly did as he bid.

"We're ready to get Murphy's bed set up, if you don't mind, Captain," Ollie said, explaining the interruption.

"No. Go ahead." Jim waved them on about their duties.

Turning his attention back to the books spread out before him on his massive desk, Jim went on with his figuring, totally ignoring the presence of the older man and his new cabin boy. He had put off the work too long, and, although he was more than tired, the final entries had to be made this afternoon.

Ollie, anxious not to disturb his captain while he was busy with the books, quickly took Delight into the small room that would be her quarters.

"Well, this is it," he told her in quiet tones.

"Thanks, Ollie." Delight was surprised and pleased by the little cubbyhole, for it would afford her some much-needed privacy.

He nodded. "We'll be leaving port later tonight, so plan on getting to bed early. You'll be working more closely with the captain tomorrow, and he can be very demanding."

"I know," she grinned at him in what she hoped was a boyish fashion. "I heard him today."

"Well then, you've got an idea of what to expect."

She nodded, "I'll be fine, Ollie. Really." The female in her wanted to hug the dear, sweet man. He'd been very kind to her all day, and at this point in her life that kindness had meant everything.

"All right. I need to speak with the captain for a minute." He started out the door and then stopped. "I'll see you later."

With that, Ollie was gone, and Delight was alone in a safe place for the first time since she'd awakened that morning. She longed to undress and bathe and snuggle under soft, comfortable covers, but there was no chance of that. When she heard Ollie leave the cabin, she opened the door and looked out at Jim Westlake, who was working diligently at his desk.

"Captain?" she asked timidly.

"What is it?" he growled, aggravated by the intrusion.

"Is there anything I can do for you?"

He looked up, rubbing his neck wearily. "Yes, please. Coffee might be just the thing."

"Right away, sir."

Since she still was wearing her coat, she left the cabin without hesitation and made her way unerringly to the crews' galley. Within a few short minutes she was back with a pot of the strong, hot brew, but to her dismay Jim had already fallen asleep. Delight stood hesitantly in the doorway, not quite sure what to do. Should she awaken him so that he could finish his work or just let him sleep? It was obvious that he was exhausted, and she felt a strange urge to help him somehow, but it was not her decision to make whether he was to rest or not. He had ordered the coffee, so with no further hesitation she made a lot of extra noise as she shut the door and then moved to set the tray on his desk.

"Here's your coffee, sir," she announced loudly.

And Jim, startled back to wakefulness, glowered at her for a minute. His piercing, knowing glare unnerved Delight, and for a moment she was almost afraid that he had discovered her secret.

"Will there be anything else, Captain?" she questioned, her manner jittery.

"Yes." He paused.

Delight was sure that all was lost. Biting her lip, she made ready to confess all.

When he spoke again, she had to fight to keep from smiling, her relief was so great. "Find Ollie and have him take you into town to get a decent coat. That thing is about two sizes too small."

She swallowed and let her breath out slowly, "Yes, sir. I'll do that."

"In fact, get a change of clothes, too. If you're going to work for me, you have a responsibility to maintain a decent appearance."

His tone was so cold and disinterested that for some unknown reason tears stung her eyes. She knew it was silly, but he had hurt her feelings. He thought she looked ugly!

"Yes, sir."

"And Murphy . . ."

"Yes, sir?"

"Take a bath."

"Yes, sir." Delight was crushed, but she could not allow herself the luxury of emotion. A fourteen-year-old boy didn't cry just because his captain ordered him to take a bath!

"Good. Get going; there's not a lot of time left. We'll be pulling out right after midnight."

And so dismissed, she left the cabin in search of Ollie.

Jim, however, poured himself a mug of the potent steaming stimulant and leaned back in his chair to try to wake up. Draining his coffee, he got a refill and then settled back over the ledgers. He was frowning in concentration when a distracting thought taunted him. Glancing up across the room, he eyed the small tintype he kept on the shelf above his bunk. Getting up, he crossed the room and took the likeness in the palm of his hand. The face smiling up at him tugged at his heart. Renee . . .

Jim sighed. It was over. In fact, it had never been. She had been totally honest with him about her feelings, and she had not been in love with him.

A sardonic grin that seemed almost a grimace twisted his lips. Renee was the one and only woman he'd ever had deep feelings for, and she'd been beyond his reach. Could he find happiness with Annabelle? Happiness was all relative, Jim decided, and, placing the picture back on the shelf, he returned to his books.

Delight found Ollie busy at the bar as usual, and she waited patiently for him to finish his work.

"The captain told me to take you shopping."

"I know." Delight sounded glum.

Ollie smiled, thinking her attitude typical of a young boy, "Don't like to mess with clothes, eh?"

She was surprised at Ollie's train of thought and was glad to have that as an excuse to protest the shopping trip. "It seems silly to me, but the captain said if I was going to work for him I had to look good."

"That's true enough. He's a strict one about appearances, he is," Ollie agreed. "But don't worry. This will be painless. In fact, the captain told me that the Line will pay for this set of clothes."

Delight looked at him, surprised. She had been worried about how she was going to pay for everything.

"I can't let him do that."

"And why not?"

"Well it's—it's charity."

"No. It's business," Ollie argued, glad to see that the youngster had some pride.

"Business?"

"Yes. The captain wants you to look the part of his cabin boy, so he'll pay for your first set of clothes. After that, you're on your own."

Delight nodded. "That's very generous of him. I know what clothes cost."

Ollie smiled, glad that his assessment of Murphy had been correct. And if he hadn't been reading Jim wrong, Jim was growing fond of the boy, too.

"Well, I'm done here. Shall we go?"

Grinning, and enormously relieved at not having to pay for

the clothes out of her meager paychecks, Delight followed Ollie from the ship.

It was late afternoon when she returned. Ollie had decided
to stop at a bar for a drink, so Delight had come on back on
her own. Loaded down with parcels, she hurried to her cabin
eager to get cleaned up and change clothes.

Jim was not around, and for that Delight was truly grateful.
Shutting herself up in her own room, she stripped down for
the first time in two days. Pouring water into the bowl on her
small washstand, she scrubbed herself thoroughly. It was cold,
but refreshing, and she felt much better when she finished.
Unwrapping her packages, she took out the long underwear
Ollie had insisted upon and put them on. Stifling a giggle, she
was pleased that the top fit snugly, for it successfully camou-
flaged her breasts. Slipping into the heavy flannel shirt that
she had deliberately picked out a size too big, she buttoned it
securely and then tugged on the dark blue woolen pants Ollie
had suggested.

She had just finished buttoning the pants when she heard
the outer door to Jim's cabin open.

"Murphy! Are you in there?"

"Yes, sir. I'll be right out," she called, and after pulling on
her new socks and boots she went out to face him.

Jim gave her a cursory glance. "That's better." He turned
from her to get an envelope. "I need you to run this over to
my brother's law office."

"Yes, sir," she responded respectfully, silently wondering
how she was going to come face-to-face with Marshall Westlake and not be recognized.

"The office is on Fourth Street. Are you familiar with the
area?"

"Yes, I know where it is."

"Good. See that my brother Marshall gets the papers personally. It's important that he sees them right away."

Groaning to herself, she took the proffered envelope and

went back to her cabin to get her new coat and the stocking cap Ollie had advised her to buy.

As she started to leave she turned to Jim who was once again working at his desk. "Thanks for the clothes. I appreciate it."

Jim gave her a brief, distracted smile and then motioned for her to be on her way. "There was no doubt you needed them. Now hurry, he needs to review those contracts tonight."

"Right." And Delight left the boat, anxious to prove her worth to her demanding boss.

Her trip to Marshall's office was fruitless, for he had already gone for the day. Remembering that Jim had been adamant about his brother's seeing the papers right away, she headed for Lucas Place and Marshall Westlake's house.

Keeping her head down and clutching the important envelope, Delight made her way quickly down Lucas Place. She was glad for the snow now for there were few people out walking. She could just imagine running into Sue or Martin or one of her neighbors . . . it was going to be bad enough handing the contracts over to Marshall without being recognized. Delight hoped that Renee wasn't around, for although the secret of her real identity would be absolutely assured if ever her friend did recognize her, still she didn't want to take that chance.

The impressive three-story brick home that belonged to Marshall and Renee loomed over her as she paused to ready herself on the freshly shoveled front walk. Finally, feeling in control and reasonably certain that no one would recognize Delight de Vries, the society belle, in the guise of a young errand boy, she mounted the steps and knocked at the front door.

It was answered almost immediately by Renee's maid, and she was ushered inside.

"I have some contracts here for Mr. Westlake. They're from the captain."

"Of course. Wait here. I'll go get him."

As the servant disappeared upstairs, young Roger Westlake peeked out of the front parlor.

"Hi," he greeted.

"Hi," she returned.

"I'm Roger. Who are you? Do you work for my Uncle Jimmy?"

"If you mean the captain, yes. My name's Del—Del Murphy."

Roger ventured bravely out into the hall, smiling warmly at this person who worked for his adored uncle.

"I bet it's fun working on the boat with Uncle Jimmy."

"I wouldn't say it's fun exactly, but it is interesting."

"What do you do? I haven't seen you before and Papa takes me on the boat all the time."

"I'm new. Your uncle just hired me yesterday. I'm his new cabin boy."

Roger seemed really impressed and Delight stifled a smile. While she hadn't thought of it before, to a young child her position would seem really adventuresome and exciting. At the sound of footsteps in the upstairs hall, Delight looked up to see Marshall coming down the staircase.

"Ah, good. You've brought the contracts. Thank you." He greeted her cordially.

"Yes, sir." She handed him the papers, trying to keep her face averted without being too conspicuous. "The captain said I was to give them to you personally."

"And I appreciate it—uh—I don't believe we've met before, have we?" Marshall was looking at her curiously.

"No, sir, Mr. Westlake. I'm the captain's new cabin boy, Del Murphy."

"Well, Murphy, you've done a good job."

"Thank you, sir. I'd better be going now," she told him as she heard the sound of feminine chatter coming toward them from the back of the house and recognized Renee's voice.

"Of course." Marshall walked her to the door.

"Good-bye."

As Marshall closed the door behind Delight, his wife spoke. "Who was that, darling?"

"Jim's new boy, Murphy."

"Oh." Renee looked puzzled for a moment. "Well, no matter, but he sounded so familiar. Have I ever met him?"

"No. He's new."

"I suppose it's not important." She smiled at him and they went into the parlor with their son.

Delight was so nervous that she ran all the way back to the riverfront. Thank God that she'd gotten out the door before Renee came in. She wouldn't have thought that she'd be thinking of the steamer as home so soon, but she did. And she didn't feel really safe and protected until she was up the gangplank and heading for Jim's cabin.

Chapter Eight

Delight was so glad to be back on board that she entered Jim's cabin without knocking. The sight that greeted her left her momentarily frozen in place in the open doorway.

"Murphy! Damn it! Close the door, it's freezing out there!" Jim bellowed as he stood at his washstand, stripped to the waist.

Delight quickly shut the door and, keeping her eyes carefully averted from the broad expanse of Jim's bare, furred chest and broad shoulders, headed for her own room.

"Well?" he questioned.

"Well, what, sir?" she asked, stopping abruptly.

"Did you give the papers to my brother?"

"Oh," she almost sighed. "Yes, sir."

"What the hell took you so long?"

"He wasn't at the office, and, since you'd told me to make sure that he got them personally, I took them by his house."

Jim regarded her with open approval. "Good. And now that you have finally gotten back, you can start getting my clothes ready."

"Ready for what?"

"I'm going out tonight. I'll need my dress clothes."

"Yes, sir." She was jittery as she shed her new coat and set about getting out his evening wear.

Delight had never been around a naked man before and, although the most intimate parts of him were still covered, she felt overpowered by his very maleness. She tried not to stare, but her gaze continually returned to visually explore the powerful corded muscles of his back.

Suddenly, it again occurred to Delight that she found Jim Westlake very attractive. Disgusted with herself for even having such a thought, she forced her attention back to what she was doing. This was not the time for romance, for heaven's sake! He thought she was a boy! Delight was saddened by the realization that had they met under other circumstances they might have had a relationship, but there was no chance of that now. Her life was in a shambles, and she doubted that she would ever have any real happiness in her future.

No, she would have to make the best of her situation and pray that she could save some money. For when the truth finally did come out about her identity, Delight knew she'd be looking for other employment. Jim Westlake would be furious at her deception, and she wouldn't blame him.

"Your clothes are all laid out."

"Thank you. I won't be too late, but there's no need for you to wait up."

"Yes, sir." Delight started to go to her room, but Jim was talkative and seemed to want her company.

"How do you like working on the ship?" he questioned earnestly as he stripped off his trousers.

Delight cringed inwardly at the sight of Jim in only the bottom half of his long underwear and when he started to peel them off, too, she hastily looked around for something to occupy her hands and her eyes. Turning her back to him, she straightened a few odd things on his desktop.

"I like it just fine. You've been very generous, and I hope I can repay the trust you have in me."

"You're doing very well for only your first day on the job," he commented.

"Thank you. I want to do my best. You really helped me out last night and I appreciate it . . . more than I can tell you."

Delight glanced quickly over at him to find that he had already put on his dress pants and was pulling on a clean white shirt.

"Keep on top of things around here and there'll be no problems." He moved to stand before the small mirror over his washstand to tie his cravat.

"I will," she pledged, more than seriously. She would have to stay at least one step ahead of everyone, including him, if she was to maintain her secrecy.

Delight knew she should beat a safe retreat to her room, but she wanted to be with him. For some reason, she was beginning to feel very secure in his company, which, when she considered it, was totally ridiculous. For if Jim Westlake ever found out about her, no doubt he would take her back to her home with no questions asked. . . .

"Get my coat," he instructed. "I'm late enough."

Coat in hand, Delight went to him, and he turned away from her so she could help him slip it on with more ease. She watched with avid interest as the fine material stretched in a perfect fit across his wide shoulders. Delight wondered what it would feel like to run her hands across his back and to know the strength of his embrace. As soon as the thought came she berated herself mentally for losing her perspective. There could be no time for that. And who was to say that he would even have noticed her if he had met her as Delight de Vries.

"I'm ready," he informed her. "Take the night off."

"Yes, sir."

"You might remind Ollie that I'll be at the Morgans'."

"I will."

"Good. I'll see you in the morning, then." He turned to face her, and he looked so handsome in his evening dress that Delight felt as if her breath had been stolen away.

"Yes, sir," she managed.

"Are you all right, Murphy?" He noticed a change in her expression and wondered what was wrong.

"I'm fine, Captain," she protested, quickly masking her feelings.

"Well, good night."

Delight didn't relax until the door was shut firmly behind him. Her shoulders drooping, she shuffled into her own little room and sat down wearily on her bed. Oh, how she wished she was the woman he was going to visit. . . .

Jim stopped by Marshall's house first. After being admitted by the servant, he was swept into a warm embrace by Renee, who happened to be in the hallway as he came in.

"I didn't know you were coming by. What a wonderful surprise!"

"It's good to see you, too," he told her.

"Here, let me take your coat. Come on in; Marshall's in the study."

"All right." He shed his heavy coat and then followed her down the hall.

Marshall looked up questioningly as the door opened.

"Jim," he greeted his brother, coming around the desk. "I'm glad you stopped by."

"I'm on my way to Annabelle's, and I thought I'd pick up those contracts. Are you through with them?"

"I was just finishing up. Get yourself a drink and sit down for a minute while I go over the final details."

"Fine."

"I'll leave you two to business," Renee told them before disappearing out into the hall and closing the door behind her.

"Where is everybody tonight?" Jim wondered at the absence of his parents and his sister Dorrie, who lived with Marshall and Renee whenever they were in town.

"They were all invited to the Taylors' for dinner tonight."

Jim nodded and fell silent again as Marshall continued to work. When at last Marshall looked up, Jim was waiting expectantly.

"Well?"

"They're all in order."

"Good. I'll sign them tonight. Mark said they were the same as the last ones we signed." Jim took the papers his brother held out to him and put them safely in the inside pocket of his coat.

"They are," Marshall agreed. "Do you have time to visit for a while?"

"No. I'm expected at the Morgans'."

"Have a good evening." Marshall's eyes twinkled knowingly, but Jim looked uninspired.

"I think I'm too tired," Jim remarked. "I'm going on forty-eight hours with no sleep.

"Well, once you're married, I'm sure you'll be spending a lot more time in bed," Marshall chuckled.

"I may be in bed, but I doubt that I'll get much more rest," Jim countered.

"When are you leaving again?"

"Mark said sometime after midnight tonight. You know how he likes to keep the exact time quiet. I think he's worried."

"I was wondering if the rumors I've been hearing had any truth to them."

"What rumors?"

"Just the usual, really. That Rebel spies and informers are everywhere. Not that there have been any new developments. There haven't. But with the situation for the South becoming so desperate . . . I guess the sympathizers are getting more desperate, too."

"No doubt," Jim agreed. "I'm always cautious, but I've had

no reason to be afraid yet. When that day comes, I may tell Mark to find me an ironclad." He laughed, trying to ease any fears his brother might have. While they were equal partners in the steamship line, Jim had the more dangerous work.

"Tell Mother and Father that I was sorry I missed them . . . Dorrie, too."

"I will. You'll take care?"

"I always do." Their eyes met in understanding.

Shaking off a strained feeling of déjà vu, they smiled and walked to the study door. Just as they were about to turn the knob, the door flew open, seemingly of its own accord, and a miniature Westlake dressed in warm winter-weight pajamas ran full steam into the room.

"Uncle Jimmy!" Roger Fontaine Westlake launched himself into his favorite uncle's arms. "I didn't know you were coming to visit!"

Jim returned the child's hug enthusiastically. "I had to talk to your father for a while, but we're all finished. I thought you were asleep. What are you doing up so late?"

Roger grinned mischievously, a grin that in later years would steal many a heart. "Don't tell Papa," he whispered. "But Mama came and got me up just so I could see you."

"Don't worry," Jim confided. "Your secret is safe with me."

Marshall hid a smile as he watched the two. Roger and Jim had always been close, and the love between them was almost a tangible thing as they stood together, deep in their own private conversation.

"When do I get to meet your wife, Uncle Jimmy?"

Jim chuckled at the boy's excitement. "Miss Morgan's not my wife, yet, Roger, but she will be soon. And if you weren't already in your nightclothes, I would take you with me now to meet her."

"You're going to see her now?"

"Yes, if my estimate of the time is correct, she's waiting for me right this minute."

"I could change real quick and . . ."

"Roger," Marshall said in mock sternness from behind them, "you know it's well past your bedtime. I'm sure there will be another time when you can meet her."

"Promise?"

"Of course, we do," Jim reassured him. "After all, Annabelle is going to be your aunt, once I marry her."

"All right. As long as you promise." He pouted a little as Renee appeared in the doorway.

"Time for bed, Roger." She held out her arms for her son.

"First, I get to give Uncle Jimmy a big hug."

"Make it a good one, Roger. I'll be gone for the next couple weeks and it'll have to last."

Roger's chubby arms clung tightly to Jim's neck and Jim closed his eyes, enjoying the love so freely given. This child was so special to him.

"I'll see you when I get back," Jim told him as he handed him over to Renee.

"I'll be waiting for you and I won't have my 'jamas on then, either."

"Good night," Jim called as he watched Renee take her six-year-old back upstairs to bed.

"'Night, Uncle Jimmy. Hurry home."

When they had disappeared into Roger's bedroom, Jim and Marshall continued on to the foyer.

"How soon will you be back?"

"Probably about two weeks. But it really depends on the weather and how far south we can go this trip."

"Last I heard," Jim said, frowning, "with any luck at all, the river should be open by summer . . . but who knows. The war has dragged on far too long already."

Marshall nodded sadly. "I know. Renee is so anxious for news of home, but there is little we can do."

"I know it was difficult for her, coming North when the war started."

"It was, but I'm glad we did it. Union supporters aren't exactly appreciated in Louisiana right now."

"Have you heard anything from Elise or Alain?"

"Not in months."

"Well, if I can figure out a way to get word to them, I'll let you know."

"Thanks." Marshall handed Jim his coat and then opened the front door for him. "Have a good time with Annabelle. And be careful this trip."

"I will. I'll see you when I get back." Jim climbed into the waiting carriage.

Annabelle had been anticipating Jim's visit and she had taken special care with her toilet for this evening. Though she was considered a natural beauty, she had learned how to accentuate her best features, and she had no qualms about helping nature along if she could. The dress she was wearing was a high-necked, long-sleeved gown of royal blue, trimmed in white lace. On any other woman it would have seemed very prim, but on Annabelle's petite figure it was stunning.

Waiting now with her father for his arrival, she felt a bit nervous.

"Would you like a sherry?"

"That sounds wonderful." She sat down on the sofa and took the fine crystal glass of sherry he handed her. "Thank you."

"You seem tense. Are you worried about Westlake?"

"Not worried exactly . . . it's just that I've never had to play the fiancée before."

Nathan smiled. "That's true enough. And never for a better cause."

Annabelle toasted her father. "I can't believe things have gone so smoothly. And maybe, just maybe, we'll be able to learn something useful from him tonight."

As she spoke, she heard a carriage pull up outside. Giving her father a confident smile, she went out into the hall to meet him.

"Good evening, Jim." She was smiling as she met him in the foyer.

"Annabelle." He greeted her warmly, impressed once again by her blond loveliness. "You look ravishing this evening."

"Thank you." She handed his coat to a servant and led him into the parlor where her father awaited them.

"Good evening, Jim." Nathan was more than pleased at his presence.

"Nathan. It's good to see you again," Jim responded as they shook hands.

"Please, sit down." Nathan waved him to the plush sofa facing the fireplace. "What can I get you to drink?"

"A scotch will be fine, Nathan. Thank you."

"Annabelle, would you like another sherry?"

"Please, Father."

Sitting down beside Jim, Annabelle gave him a provocative look and was pleased to see a flame of desire flicker to life in his eyes. She knew that he found her attractive, and she intended to exploit that weakness whenever she could. She wondered idly what it would be like to have Jim as her lover, but quickly dismissed the idea. Though Jim Westlake was handsome, Annabelle didn't want to get too involved with him. She only wanted to use him to get the information she needed. That was all.

"Here's your drink." Nathan handed Jim a tumbler filled with scotch and Annabelle a small crystal glass of sherry.

"To your engagement," his future father-in-law toasted.

Jim's eyes met Annabelle's, and their gazes locked. They raised their glasses and sipped slowly.

Nathan was thrilled that things were progressing so well. Anxious to leave them by themselves, he pleaded unfinished business and excused himself.

Jim was only slightly surprised at being left alone with Annabelle, but he wasn't about to complain. The quick embrace they had shared the previous afternoon had hardly been satisfying, and he wanted to spend as much time as possible with her.

"Would you like another drink?" Annabelle offered as soon as her father had gone from the room.

"Yes, please. It's been a long day and I do need to unwind a little."

Taking his glass, Annabelle moved gracefully to the liquor cabinet, making sure that her skirts were swaying seductively. Jim was open in his admiration as he watched her cross the room, and he felt quite content with the decision he'd made. Rejoining him, Annabelle held out his drink, but Jim grasped her wrist instead, pulling her down close beside him.

"I've been wanting to do this since yesterday." He spoke his intent softly, setting their glasses aside and sweeping her into his arms.

Annabelle had no time to protest as his mouth covered hers in a passionate kiss. Startled by his ardor, she offered no encouragement as she lay passively in his embrace. Jim felt her reserve, but knew that such female defenses could easily be broken down. They were to be married soon; so surely, she could not object to his touch. It was only when his lips left hers to caress the sweetness of her throat that Annabelle struggled to be free from him.

"Darling, what is it?" Jim asked with true concern. No woman had ever denied him before, and he certainly hadn't expected it from his fiancée.

"We have to be careful," she lied. "Father may come back, and I don't want us to embarrass ourselves."

Jim accepted Annabelle's excuse with dignity and moved a respectable distance away, but he could not hide his irritation. While it would be embarrassing to be caught in a heated embrace by your future father-in-law, surely she could have been more responsive. Her reaction to his kiss had been nothing short of nonexistent, and that puzzled him. If Annabelle loved him as she said she did, wouldn't she be eager to be with him?

If Jim had known Annabelle's thoughts, he would have been less concerned. She had been stunned by her own reaction to his kiss. Something in his touch had set her blood racing, and when he'd tried to deepen their intimacy, she'd known she'd better escape his embrace or she would be lost completely in her sensual arousal.

Looking at Jim now from beneath lowered lashes, she regarded him with a new respect. She wanted him . . . and the thought surprised and frustrated her. There was no time for dalliances . . . she had to get the information, and fast.

Annabelle's thoughts were interrupted by Nathan's return, and the rest of the evening passed in a comfortable fashion. It was after ten when Jim finally rose to leave.

"Thank you for a wonderful evening," he told them.

"Must you go so soon?" Annabelle sounded disappointed and, in truth, she was. She knew her lack of response had troubled him, and she had hoped they'd have another chance to be alone so she could lay those fears to rest.

"Yes, I'm afraid so. In fact, I meant to tell you earlier . . . we're pulling out tonight."

"Tonight?" Annabelle was upset for more reasons than one.

"I've got to make a run. We'll be leaving sometime after midnight."

"But when will you return?"

"It will be every bit of ten days, possibly longer, but go ahead with your plans for the party. I'm sure I'll be back in town by then."

"All right, but I'm going to miss you. I was hoping that you'd be here to help me with all the details." She pouted prettily.

"I'm sorry, Annabelle. But you know my job has to come first."

"I know," she admitted. "And I do understand. It's just that on such short notice . . ."

"From now on, I'll try to let you know a little further in advance," he promised, glad that she was going to miss him. "If you do need any help with your planning, I'm sure my mother and sister would be glad to help."

"Well, be careful. I've been hearing rumors," Nathan put in.

"Haven't we all," Jim agreed as they moved into the hall to

get his coat. "But there's no need to worry. I'll be fine. And I'll see you as soon as possible."

"Good night," Annabelle called as he left the house, and then, after watching his carriage drive away, she slammed the door in a fury. "Damn!"

"I know. If only we could have found out a few hours sooner . . ."

"There has to be a way."

"We'll figure it out. I have every confidence in our plan. But if we are unsuccessful, there's always Wade's idea. He can be most persuasive."

Annabelle nodded in agreement. "He certainly can be, and from what I've seen of Dorrie Westlake, she'll be no match for Wade's practiced charm."

"Good."

"You know, Father, I'm not going to rest easy until we've delivered the gold."

Nathan looked at his daughter, his pride in her determination quite evident. "Neither will I, Annabelle. Neither will I."

Chapter Nine

Jim banged loudly on the connecting door, bringing Delight straight out of her bed.

"Get up, Murphy! It's after four!" Jim's voice thundered as he pounded on the portal. "Get my breakfast up here."

Having slept in her clothes. Delight took only the time necessary to pull on her boots before grabbing her coat and running from her little sanctuary.

"Yes, sir. I'm on my way."

Jim only growled at Murphy's retreating back, and Delight

picked up her pace, not wanting to risk his displeasure. She needed this job, of that there was no doubt.

She was back in a few short minutes with his meal, for the cook was well aware of the captain's schedule and had the food ready. Struggling to close the cabin door, she almost dropped the tray, and Jim glared at her for her clumsiness.

"Are you always like this, Murphy?" he asked sarcastically. Morning was not his best time of day, especially when he'd gotten little sleep the past three nights.

"No, sir."

"Good. I'll be looking forward to seeing an improvement." When he noticed her disconcerted look, he instructed, "I eat at my desk."

"Yes, sir." Quickly placing the breakfast on his neatly cleaned-off desktop, she hastily withdrew to what she hoped was a safe distance. "Do you need anything else now?"

"No," came his curt answer.

Delight had a great desire to stick her tongue out at him, but she fought back the thought. As she busied herself picking up his cabin the way Ollie had instructed her to the day before, Delight studied him covertly. Even early in the morning he was impressive. And, though his mood could hardly be called jovial, his presence was, as always, commanding.

Though Delight knew very little about him as a man, she felt an instinctive wariness that she credited to female intuition. There was no doubt in her mind that Jim Westlake was in charge of every part of his life and that he would brook no foolishness from those around him.

"Murphy."

He startled her and she almost jumped as she was straightening his bunk.

"Yes, sir?" she gulped.

"That can wait. Go on down to the galley and get your breakfast."

"I don't mind, Captain," she protested dutifully. "I'd just as soon get this done now."

"Murphy—" his tone was threatening as he turned to look at her. "The cook only serves breakfast until five thirty. Now get the hell down there unless you intend to go without eating until noon."

She didn't even bother to answer but bolted from the room.

Jim watched her go and half-smiled to himself. Murphy had possibilities—he was eager to please and, according to Ollie, a fast learner. If he made it through the week, Jim was certain he would have a future with the ship. He made a mental note to get to know the boy better during these next days on the river and then turned his attention to his meal.

Delight entered the galley a bit timidly, but Ollie was already there waiting for her.

"How did your night go with the captain?" he inquired.

"Fine. I was asleep when he finally came in last night. What time did we leave St. Louis? I was so tired I slept through the whole thing."

"It must have been two thirty or so before we actually shoved off. The captain was up all night again."

Delight nodded in understanding. "Then that explains it."

"Explains what?"

"He woke me at four to get his breakfast for him. But you told me yesterday that he usually eats at five thirty."

"That's on a normal day. When we're leaving port it's hard to tell when we'll get time to eat. So always remember to grab whatever food you can, whenever you can, 'cause you just might have to miss a meal here and there."

Delight nodded as she ate the hearty breakfast set before her.

"It'll be hard to keep up with the captain for a while, but you'll learn. And once you get the hang of it, you'll know what he wants before he asks for it."

"I'm looking forward to that day," she grinned, forcing herself to eat like a half-starved, still-growing young boy.

"Just relax and try to stay out of his way."

"I'll do my best," she promised.

They finished their meal in quiet and then returned to their respective duties.

It was still dark as Delight made her way back up to the texas deck. There was no moon, only a morning star shining palely in the distant heavens. A chill of fear swept through her as the realization came over her that she really had severed ties with her home and that she was truly all alone. She felt lonely and bereft and wished that there was someone she could talk to . . . someone who cared. Rose did, but she would be defenseless against Martin's brutality. Delight knew then that there was no one left she could turn to. She had to rely only upon herself.

Her thoughts turned to her mother, and she said a quick prayer that her health was improving. Then, after adding a plea for guidance and protection, she squared her shoulders and prepared to return to Jim's cabin.

Delight was hoping against hope that the captain would be gone when she got back. His presence made her jittery and unsure of herself, and she found it difficult to concentrate when he was nearby. She was not to be given a reprieve, though, for when she reentered the stateroom Jim was at his desk busily going over some papers.

"Did you get breakfast?" he asked, not looking up.

"Yes, sir."

Jim nodded. "Get whatever work you've got to do in here done, because I'm going to bed in about five minutes," he ordered, fatigue evident in his voice.

Without another word, Delight hurried to turn down his bed. With a groan of exhaustion, Jim pushed away from his desk and stood up.

"Don't wake me unless it's a major disaster. Is that understood?"

"Oh, yes, sir," she answered hastily, anxious for him to go to sleep so that she wouldn't have to worry about him.

"Good," he stripped off his shirt and unbuttoned his pants.

"Is there anything in particular you want me to do this morning?"

"No," he told her as he shed his pants and went to the washstand to wash. "There's nothing pressing. Find Ollie; he should have some jobs for you to do."

"Yes, sir," she responded, her gaze straying to his powerful back. He seemed so lean . . . so strong. She felt a strange stirring deep within her and reluctantly forced her eyes away. "Well, I'll be going. Do you need to be up at any certain time?"

He turned to face her.

"Why don't you plan on getting me up about noon?" he yawned, toweling himself off and heading for the bunk.

Delight almost scurried out of his way, but though Jim looked at her oddly for a minute, he was too exhausted to give her behavior a second thought.

"Yes, sir. I'll do that, sir," she told him, making her way to the door. "Good night, sir." Her hand was on the doorknob as she heard the bunk creak under Jim's weight.

"Murphy?" The sound of his voice stopped her dead in her tracks.

"Sir?" she answered meekly.

"It's not night . . . it's morning," he chuckled, pulling the covers up over him.

"Right. Well, uh, good morning then, Captain." And with one last glance in his direction, she fled the cabin.

It was nearly noon when Delight returned to Jim's stateroom with a pot of freshly brewed coffee in hand. She entered quietly. She had experienced his irritation once at her ineptitude, and she intended never to give him another opportunity to criticize her.

Why his opinion of her should matter so much she didn't know, but for some reason she wanted to please him. Delight didn't have time to analyze her feelings, and the way things were right now, she didn't want to. She would do the job Jim had hired her for and hope to avoid trouble until she could find a way to straighten out her life. How she was going to do that, she didn't know. But somehow, some way, in time, she would.

Her long hours working with Ollie that morning had helped to restore some of her self-confidence, and she felt more able to deal with the captain now. Glancing at Jim where he lay on his bed, she let her gaze roam thoughtfully over him. She would never tire of watching him . . . of being with him. He was the most interesting, confusing man she had ever met. Her thoughts flew to that morning and the image of Jim standing so tall and so proudly male before her. He was a magnificent-looking man, and Delight felt the inexplicable urge to touch him.

"Sir," she called, not too loudly, as she poured a cup of the steaming brew "It's noon."

When her word didn't wake him, she approached the bunk. Lying on his stomach with his face turned away from her, the blankets covering his lower half, Jim was still asleep. Delight took the moment to really look at him. He was so handsome . . . her heart skipped a beat as she stood breathlessly by his side.

Delight hadn't really given much thought to men's bodies before today, for she had had no experience with them at all. But the feelings Jim Westlake had awakened in her were totally different from the stark terror Martin's overtures had aroused. The sight of Jim last night dressed for his evening out had created a glowing warmth within her and aroused a bit of jealousy, too, she admitted to herself. And today, watching him sleep, she felt protective . . . the word that flitted through her mind startled her and she frowned at the thought . . . loving? Did she love him? How could she? He thought of her as a boy . . . he hadn't even guessed she was a woman . . . and, after listening to bits of his conversation yesterday with Mark Clayton, she knew that Jim liked his women beautiful. Delight had never met Annabelle Morgan, but she'd heard of her. Her beauty was almost legendary on the St. Louis social scene, and if Jim had won her hand . . . well, what chance did she have with her hair bobbed and dressed in boy's clothes?

Forcing that depressing thought from her mind, she reached out and touched his shoulder. The contact was shocking, as the warmth of his flesh seemed to brand her, and she moved a safe distance away, not wanting him to see her confusion.

"Captain," she said loudly, and, had he been fully awake, he surely would have noticed the tremor in her voice.

"What!" he almost snarled, coming awake suddenly.

"It's after noon, sir. I've brought you some coffee." Delight sounded more self-assured than she felt.

"Oh." Jim rolled to his back. Still tired, he threw a forearm over his eyes and lay still. "Is anything happening?"

"No, sir. But there are an awful lot of Union soldiers on board."

Jim grunted, but didn't move. "You might as well get used to them. We work for the Department of the Army, and we'll have them on board every trip."

"We work for the government?" She was surprised.

Jim heard the curious note in her voice and lifted his arm to peer at her for a moment. Delight was worried, but evidently he was satisfied with what he saw, for he lay back down again. "Just about everybody does now. There wouldn't be much business without them. At least not until the river's finally open again."

"Oh." She let the subject drop, feeling that she had somehow trespassed on a topic that was none of her business. Delight vaguely remembered Mark Clayton's saying something the day before about doubling the guard, but she wasn't sure what it was they were guarding.

"Where are you from, Murphy?"

"I lived out in the country for a while." She wasn't lying, she reassured herself. She had spent some summers with her Uncle Joe and Aunt Faith.

"Then what were you doing down on the riverfront?" Jim rolled to his side and sat up on the edge of the bed.

Delight debated how much of the truth to tell. She wanted to confide in him . . . to share her burden . . . to have him reassure her and tell her that everything would be all right. But she couldn't tell him. Not now.

"I had a run-in with my stepfather and he threw me out." She tried to sound casual.

"But you're just a kid," Jim argued.

"It didn't matter to him. I was just another mouth to feed." She shrugged in what she hoped looked like boyish indifference.

"How long had you been out on your own?"

His question caught her by surprise and she looked up quickly. "Not long," she answered carefully.

Jim stood up to stretch and the covers dropped away. "Hand me my pants, Murphy."

Delight handed him the wanted garment.

"Thank you," he told her sleepily, pulling them on. "Have you had lunch yet?"

"Not yet."

"Why don't you go get something to eat and bring back my lunch when you finish. We've got a lot to do this afternoon and I'm going to need your help."

"Yes, sir."

Delight was glad to get away from Jim and the intimacy of the room, for she was uncertain whether the feelings of closeness and trust he inspired were real or something she'd invented in her own mind. Hurrying down the deck, she tried to dwell on other things, but, as it had been all morning, the vision of Jim, so strong and virile, was burned into her consciousness and she knew she would think of only him for the rest of the day.

"Murphy."

The sound of the opening door and Jim's voice so near

barely penetrated Delight's exhausted slumber. Curled on her side, she slept on, unaware that her boss stood in the connecting doorway of their two cabins, watching her.

"Is he awake?" Mark asked from his seat in Jim's stateroom.

"No," Jim answered, still staring at the boy.

He frowned to himself. Murphy looked like a child as he lay there sound asleep. How could his stepfather have thrown him out? He was so young . . . Jim felt an unfamiliar sense of protectiveness arise within him. He had always made it a point not to get personally involved with his crew, but looking at Murphy now he knew it was hopeless. He would watch over him and try to guide him.

"Is something wrong?" Mark's voice came again, stirring Jim from his thoughts.

"No," Jim answered over his shoulder. "Murphy! Get up."

Delight came awake suddenly, startled by the sound of the man's demanding voice. Her sleep-clouded mind refused to acknowledge where she was and she stared at Jim in open confusion.

"What?" she croaked, an element of terror evident in her speech.

"Murphy, wake up." Jim hid a smile as he snapped out orders to his cabin boy. "I need you to run down to the bar and bring a bottle of scotch back to the cabin."

Shaking her head, she continued to stare at him for a moment until reality cut through her dreamlike state. Why just before she'd awakened, Jim had asked her to dance and they were waltzing and . . . "Oh, yes, sir. Right away, sir."

As Jim started to turn away she practically threw herself from the bed. Hopping on one foot, Delight tried to pull on a boot and in the process fell flat on her rump with a resounding thud. Looking back over his shoulder, Jim quirked an eyebrow as his mouth twisted into a mocking grin.

"I'm not in *that* big a hurry, Murphy."

His words echoed cuttingly through her and Delight was glad when he closed the door behind him. Leaning back forlornly against the side of her small bed, she fought the tears that threatened. Wouldn't she ever be able to please the man?

Angry at Jim for his sarcastic comments, angry at herself for being so clumsy in his presence, and angry at life in general for the cruel twists of fate of these past days, she yanked on her boots and struggled into her coat. Stomping out of her room in a small display of bruised pride, she glared over in the direction of Jim's desk, only to be jolted by the unexpected presence of Mark Clayton.

"I'll be right back, Captain," she muttered. Quickly looking away to hide her fright, she left the cabin.

"I would say your cabin boy doesn't like to get up in the middle of the night," Mark laughed after she had disappeared out the door.

"I'm inclined to agree with you," Jim chuckled. "But he's a good worker."

"Kind of young, isn't he?"

"Yes, he is. But Ollie and I found him wandering the docks getting into all kinds of trouble."

"He's lucky you were the one who found him."

Jim nodded, "I wonder where he'd be now if we hadn't brought him back. . . ."

"Probably dead," Mark said seriously. "Young boys don't last long down on the riverfront. It was bad before the war, but it's worse now."

"I'm sure he didn't realize what really could have happened to him." Jim finished off his drink and looked pointedly at the empty bottle sitting on his desk. With a grin, he added, "And he has no conception of what will happen to him now if he doesn't get back here with that fresh bottle, and soon."

Just as he spoke the door flew open and Delight rushed into the room, slamming the door behind her. She had pulled on her stocking cap to cover her hair and she hoped that the cold had reddened her cheeks and nose enough to help with her camouflage.

"Here you are, Captain." She thrust the bottle at Jim, carefully keeping her face averted from Mark.

"Thank you, Murphy. You can go back to bed now."

"Yes, sir." She headed for the door to her room, tugging off her coat.

Jim watched her progress for a minute and a thought struck him. "Murphy?"

Delight halted, wondered what he could possibly want now. "Yes?"

"You look atrocious. Do you sleep in your clothes every night?"

She turned slowly to face him, anger and embarrassment warring within her. "Yes, sir. It's cold." Delight wanted to add "in case you didn't notice," but she held her tongue.

"You didn't get a nightshirt while you were out."

"No, sir."

"Well, why not?" Jim sounded aggravated.

Delight had the urge to tell him why not in no uncertain terms, but again she held herself in restraint. Sounding like the humble servant boy she was supposed to be, she said calmly, "You said only to buy a change of clothes and a coat, sir, and I didn't have any money of my own."

Jim felt inexplicably irritated at Ollie's lack of foresight. "Wait a minute." Rising from his seat, he went to his trunk and pulled out one of his own nightshirts. "Here, wear this. It's bound to be way too big, but at least you won't look like you just climbed out of bed all day long." He tossed the long flannel sleeping garment to her.

Delight deftly caught it, and, clutching it with two hands, thanked him solemnly. "Good night, sir."

"Good night, Murphy."

When the door between the rooms closed behind her, Mark looked at Jim and smiled. "I think Murphy has a bad case of hero worship."

Jim looked startled. "Why?"

"Didn't you see the look in his eyes?"

"No, I didn't pay any attention."

"He's obviously very impressed with you, and, if I read him right, he'll be devoted to you for the rest of your life."

Jim gave Mark a strange look. "I like the boy. He's honest and industrious, and I'm proud of the way he's handling himself. I don't think most youngsters would be able to handle everything that Murphy's had to deal with."

"Well, whatever," Mark went on, changing the subject. "Tell me more about your engagement. We didn't get a lot of time to talk the other day."

As their voices droned on into the night, Delight climbed back into bed wrapped in the voluminous folds of Jim's nightshirt. The soft, well-worn flannel felt like a caress against her bare skin, and she luxuriated in the faint manly scent that clung to the garment and reminded her of him. She felt safe . . . protected. And, hugging the material close to her, she closed her eyes and fell asleep, lulled into forgetfulness by the indistinct, mellow tone of his voice.

Her mind played tricks on her the rest of the night as it conjured up images of Jim. Jim as he had been that morning—Jim dressed in his evening clothes—Jim as she had seen him that afternoon when he'd helped to move some merchandise on the main deck, his coat discarded, his muscles straining against the fine material of his shirt. An unfamiliar ache grew within her as her body responded to him, and, as he bent to kiss her in her dream, she came awake, at once both startled and disappointed.

With a groan of total frustration, she sat up. Drawing her knees to her chest, Delight hugged them to her and shook her head in mute denial. The feelings she had for Jim were strong and growing more powerful all the time. How long could she keep them hidden from him? Tears fell as she realized the hopelessness of her situation. She would never have the opportunity to be with him as a woman . . . to know the joy of being in his arms.

Trying to shake off the depression that threatened, Delight

climbed out of bed and stripped off the nightshirt. Folding it with loving care, she laid the makeshift gown upon her pillow and then hurried to dress in her own nondescript clothes.

It was still dark as she left her cabin and threaded her way carefully through Jim's. Delight paused only long enough to make certain that she hadn't disturbed him before leaving the stateroom.

Crossing the deck, Delight inhaled deeply of the cool, humid air. Though they had only been on the river for a little over a day, the temperature had risen steadily, and it was now almost mild as she stood at the rail and tried to relax. She had no idea of the time, but she knew instinctively that it would soon be dawn.

Sighing, she turned her back to the passing blackness of the river-night and stared at the cabin door. She felt almost as if she was in a maze with no way out. She loved Jim Westlake, of that she had no doubt. And, even though he teased her in his own gruffly good-natured way, she felt secure in his presence. True, she was still nervous around him, but she recognized now that it was her own reaction to his vibrant maleness that disturbed her, not Jim himself.

With that knowledge came a certain peace of mind. Though she couldn't reveal herself to him, she could enjoy the relationship they did have and only hope that some way, some day, she would be able to tell him the truth.

Chapter Ten

Jim stood in the pilothouse watching attentively as St. Louis came into view. Usually he was glad to see his hometown, for it meant an end to another successful run, but today his feelings were mixed. He was tense. He had been ever since leaving Memphis, and it was not because of business.

Leaving the room abruptly, he sought a secluded place to sort out his feelings. He knew Ollie would be in the bar, but he had no desire to talk to him. It had been Ollie's earlier remarks about his engagement coupled with his memory of Annabelle's reluctant embrace that created the disquiet he was now experiencing.

Jim caught sight of Murphy heading into the Grand Salon, so he went back up to his cabin and locked the door. Hanging up his coat, he pulled his bottle of scotch out of the bottom desk drawer and poured himself a good-sized drink. Sitting down at the desk, he turned the chair to face the bunk and rested his feet upon his bed.

Doubts assailed him. Was he doing the right thing, or was Ollie right? Should he wait for love or marry Annabelle because he thought it was the sensible thing to do? He had no answers. He knew he didn't care for her in the same way he had cared for Renee. But wasn't that feeling something that only happened once in a lifetime?

Jim drained his glass and poured one more, glad that he finally had this time to himself. They had been so busy for the entire trip that he had had little time to think about anything but business. Between dealing with Mark and the gold on the way downstream and working closely with Murphy on the way back home, he had been constantly with people. It felt good to disappear for a while and let the rest of the crew handle things.

Leaning back wearily, he sought the answers to his questions once more. Ollie was his good friend, and he had been right to press him on the question of whether he loved Annabelle or not. But love was not the only reason people married. They married for companionship, to have children, for money . . . but whatever the reasons, most married people seemed reasonably happy, and Jim had no cause to think that his marriage to Annabelle would be any different.

Feeling that the issue was decided, he breathed a little easier.

Not that he wouldn't miss his bachelor days, but he felt that there was something missing in his life. He had accomplished all the other major goals he'd set for himself, and having a family was the only thing left that he hadn't done. He had made a complete success of his business and had become so proficient at his job that even the enjoyment he got out of that had faded in recent years. And, while carrying the Union's bullion was a challenge, His homecomings had become something of an anticlimax.

He felt acertain dissatisfaction with the way he'd been living, and he was sure that a warm and willing wife would make the difference. And Annabelle was the perfect choice. After all, she was the most beautiful woman he could find. What better criteria for picking the future mother of his children?

Telling himself that he had done the right thing, and putting aside the negative feelings he had about Annabelle's reaction to his touch, Jim left the cabin and went back out on deck. The boat had docked and the roustabouts were busy tying the thick ropes to the heavy metal rings buried deep in the wharf.

"Captain!" Murphy's voice reached Jim as he stood staring out into the busy throng of people on the riverfront.

"What is it, Murphy?" He turned to face the youth, who was hurrying to his side.

"I've been looking all over for you. Ollie said he needed to see you right away."

"Where is he?"

"Still in the saloon, sir."

"Fine, tell him I'll . . ." Jim was interrupted by a woman's call.

"Jim!"

He looked up to see Annabelle sitting in an open carriage, waving to him.

"Ollie will have to wait," Jim said abruptly as he walked off toward the woman. Striding down the deck, he quickly left the boat and made his way across the cobblestones to her conveyance.

Delight stood alone on board, watching him. She bit her lip to stem the tide of tears that threatened. So that was the fair Annabelle Morgan. . . . Swallowing with great difficulty, she followed his progress until he reached the carriage and took her hand. It was too hard for Delight to watch any further and she fled the scene, wishing that she had never seen them together. It would have been easier then to imagine that Annabelle didn't truly exist.

Jim lifted Annabelle's hand to his lips and smiled at her. "This is an unexpected pleasure."

"I was hoping you'd be back today. Our party is tomorrow, and I was worried that you'd been detained," Annabelle told him. She didn't mention that she had used his return as an excuse to haunt the riverfront for the last few days in hopes of finding out some other valuable bits of information.

"We picked up a little more business than I had expected," he explained briefly.

"No matter. Things have worked out very well."

"I'm glad. What time shall I come by?"

"The party begins at eight, so anytime before that will be fine. Can you stop by tonight?"

"It looks doubtful at this point. We've just docked and there's a lot of last-minute things I have to take care of personally. Let's just plan on tomorrow."

Annabelle pouted prettily. "Well, all right, but it would be good to spend some time with you before the party."

"I'll see if I can make it over for a little while tonight," he said, pleased.

"Good," she smiled. "Until tonight, then?"

"Until tonight."

He leaned forward to kiss her, but Annabelle quickly offered him her cheek. And, with a wave of her hand, she directed the driver to head home, leaving Jim standing alone on the wharf. He watched her vehicle disappear behind the stacks of merchandise and then turned back to his ship, wondering at the odd, empty feeling inside him.

Chapter Eleven

He was gone. . . .

Delight stood looking at the door that had just closed behind Jim, her expression one of distraught frustration. Now what? The question was riveted in her mind, leaving her with no answers . . . no solutions. After tonight, he would be officially engaged to another woman.

Delight wanted to scream that it wasn't fair. She had given up her home . . . her mother . . . but did she have to give up the man she now knew she loved without a fight? Didn't she deserve some happiness in her life?

She searched her memories of their time on the boat. The hours under his tutelage had been exquisite torture for her . . . being constantly close to him . . . listening to every word and trying to impress him with her intelligence. For, after all, as a boy there was nothing else she could do.

Was it possible that she could have done anything differently during their long days together? And if she had, would it have changed what was happening tonight? In all honesty, she had to admit that there had been nothing else she could do. She was caught in a role from which there was no escape. To Jim she would always be Murphy, the cabin boy.

Moving to the bed, she picked up his hastily discarded clothes and mechanically began to hang them up. He had looked so attractive in his evening attire. What woman wouldn't want him? And Annabelle Morgan . . . Delight wondered if the woman really appreciated the man she was going to marry. Jealousy flared as Delight thought of Jim in a heated embrace with his fiancée.

She finished straightening up his cabin without conscious thought and then stood looking helplessly around for something more to do. Jim had told her to take the night off, but there was nowhere else she wanted to be . . . nothing else she wanted to do than to be near him. The knock at the cabin door made her jump, and she turned guiltily as it opened.

"Jim?" Ollie stuck his head inside. "Oh, Murphy, is he gone already?"

"He just left about five minutes ago." Her tone was less than enthusiastic.

"Damn." Ollie frowned and came into the room, closing the door behind him.

"What's wrong?"

"Nothing . . ." He shrugged. "Listen, why don't you come on up to my cabin and we can talk for a while?"

She brightened at the thought of Ollie's company. "I'd like that." Being with him might just keep her mind off of Jim.

"Well, get your coat. I'll wait for you."

Delight hurried into her own room to grab her jacket and soon was following Ollie down the cold, windswept deck to his room. Once inside, they shed their coats and sat down in relaxed comfort. Delight had come to admire and respect this older man who was her friend, and she gave him a friendly grin as he produced a bottle of bourbon from his trunk of belongings.

"Ever had a drink, Murphy?" he asked with a twinkle in his eye.

"No . . ." Her eyes widened at the thought.

"Well, it's time you did. How old are you now?"

"I'll be fifteen in July," she told the half truth easily.

"That sounds old enough to me. Want to try?"

She looked startled for a minute and then smiled broadly. "Why not?"

Chuckling, he poured them both a liberal amount into two tumblers that he produced as if by magic, and then, handing her one, said, "Here you go. Drink up." Ollie tilted his head back and downed his whiskey in one swallow. Then, leveling Murphy with a serious look, he encouraged him, saying, "Your turn."

Delight looked from the glass to her friend and then aped his method of drinking. She was rewarded by a violent coughing spasm, followed by tears and choking.

"You should have warned me!" she protested when she could finally speak.

"Every man has to learn his own way. If I had told you it'd burn all the way to the pit of your stomach, you probably wouldn't have wanted to try. Right?"

"I sure would have given it a second thought," she grinned, holding out her glass for more. The burning had turned to a comforting warmth and she felt no fear of trying again. This new boldness she was discovering about herself pleased her, and she watched with interest as Ollie filled her glass another time with the golden liquid.

"You're sure about this refill?"

"Why not? The worst is over, right?"

"I like your style, boy. You're not afraid of anything," Ollie complimented.

"Not anymore," she bragged, the mellow effects of the whiskey making her feel confident.

Forgetting herself for a moment, she sipped at the drink, her thoughts miles away with Jim and his soon-to-be fiancée.

"Murphy, sometimes you're too damned pretty to be a boy," Ollie remarked sagely.

His statement jerked her back to the present and she gave him a vicious frown.

"Don't worry. There's nothing girlish about you." Ollie laughed heartily at the youth's reaction.

"Thanks," she growled in her best imitation of youthful embarrassment, not knowing whether to be upset or glad at his assessment. "Nothing girlish—really!"

Ollie drained another drink and poured himself some more. "You know, I think our captain is making a big mistake."

The mention of Jim drew her immediate attention and she looked at him questioningly. Ollie had never talked much of Jim to her before, and she was ready to hang on his every word.

"I didn't think the captain made any mistakes," she responded lightly, trying to cover the depth of her interest.

"Not usually, but this time . . ."

"What do you mean?"

Ollie settled back on his bunk and fixed Murphy with a serious look. "This engagement of his . . . I just don't feel good about it."

"Why?"

"I wish I knew why. If I did, then maybe I could explain it to Jimmy," Ollie said, confused by his own thoughts on the matter.

"Don't you like Annabelle Morgan?"

"Never met her," he replied shortly. "But I don't think she's the woman for Jimmy."

"How come? I saw him on the levee with her when we tied up and they looked plenty happy to me. . . ." Her voice was tinged with a bitterness she couldn't hide.

"But did you notice how tense he got these last few days before we docked?"

"He did seem extra grouchy, but I thought he was just tired."

"No, the captain doesn't snap like that when he's tired. I know him pretty well, and the only time he gets in that kind of mood is when there's something bothering him."

"Well, he certainly was feeling no pain when he got back from seeing her last night," Delight said, finding it hard not to show her feelings.

"You thought he was with her all last night?" Ollie looked at Murphy in surprise as the cabin boy nodded in response. "He met me at Harry's Bar about eleven o'clock. He only spent about an hour with her."

Now it was Delight's turn to be surprised. "Why didn't he spend the whole evening with her?"

"He wanted to, from what I can figure out, but she told him she had to get to bed early so she could be fresh and well rested for the party tonight." Ollie obviously thought the excuse sounded flimsy.

"That doesn't sound right. It seems to me if you love somebody, you'd want to be with them all you could. Especially if they've been gone for almost two weeks," Delight said.

Ollie gave her a helpless look. "I thought the same thing, but there he was at Harry's. We drank together for a couple of hours, but, you know, he never said a word."

"He didn't even talk to you? You're his closest friend, aren't you?"

"Jimmy hasn't been much of a talker for quite a while now. There was a time when he told me just about everything, but ever since he fell in love with Renee all those years ago . . ."

"Renee?" Delight blurted out in shock.

"You know Renee?"

"His brother's wife, right?" she added, covering her mistake. "I met her that day I had to deliver the papers to Marshall for him."

"Oh, that's right. Anyway, a long time ago, when Renee first came to town, Jimmy fell in love with her. She only had eyes for Marshall, though. It was kind of rough for him, because he'd never had any woman trouble before that. Why, that boy used to have women all up and down the river just waiting for him. . . ."

"And he doesn't anymore?"

"Nope. Not since Renee. That's why I just don't feel good about this Annabelle. I'd almost swear on a stack of Bibles that he doesn't love her."

"Why would he get engaged, then?"

"His family's been after him for years to settle down, and I think it just dawned on him that it's about that time. He's successful at what he does, he doesn't have a worry in the world where money is concerned. . . ."

"But to marry without love . . . it seems so cold."

"That it is. And that's why I'm worried."

"Did you try to talk to him about it?"

"Oh, sure. Right after he first told me of his plans."

"And did he say he loved her?"

"He said he did, but I've seen Jimmy in love, and I know how he acts when he is. He doesn't love Annabelle Morgan . . . not in the way he should," Ollie concluded.

Delight thought on that for a long, silent moment before murmuring. "He'll ruin his whole life if he marries without love."

"He obviously doesn't think so." Ollie refilled both their glasses and Delight drank the whiskey straight down without a flinch. Ollie smiled to himself as he thought of the head the boy was going to have on him in the morning. . . .

Delight sank deep into thought. "I don't want to see the captain unhappy, but if this is what he really wants to do, I guess there's nothing we can do or say."

"That's the problem. He deserves better. But he thinks because she's beautiful he'll be happy with her."

"I have heard it said that she's lovely," Delight remarked, and Ollie caught her on it.

"Where did you hear that?" he asked sharply.

"Oh, just one of the hands . . ." she covered her second lapse. She took a nervous drink from her glass and wondered idly why she hadn't noticed before what a smooth drink it was.

"Maybe that will be enough. I know he doesn't believe that he'll ever care for another woman the way he did for Renee, so maybe he is settling for second best."

Delight pondered Ollie's conclusions. If that was true, it was so sad . . . Jim should have every good thing life had to offer. He was a kind and generous man. He needed someone who would care for him deeply . . . someone who would love him for the man he was . . . like she did.

"Do you think she loves him?" Her final question was important. If Annabelle did love Jim, then maybe she could be the woman for him. If her love was strong, maybe she could make him fall in love with her in time.

"Murphy, I just don't know. But I hope so."

Delight nodded slightly. She hoped so, too. She wanted "her captain" to be happy . . . even, she thought sadly, if it took another woman. But she couldn't help but believe that she loved him more. . . .

They let the subject drop, for there was nothing else they could say. They both knew that they cared about Jim and they only wanted what was best for him.

The Morgan house was ablaze with lights and the festivities were in full swing. Annabelle stood with Jim, greeting their late-arriving guests and flashing the diamond and ruby engagement ring he had given her. When the last of the people had disappeared into the ballroom, she turned to Jim and smiled seductively at him.

"Thank you for my ring. It's lovely." She felt very bold and daring tonight as she ran a hand up the lapel of his jacket. Jim Westlake was such an attractive man . . . she was beginning to enjoy being his fiancée.

"I'm glad you like it. It suits your beauty."

Her lashes fluttered and she leaned against him. "I missed you dreadfully while you were gone on your trip."

Jim would have liked to believe it, but her behavior last

night had given him pause. Having finished his work earlier than he'd anticipated, he had dropped by the Morgan house. Annabelle had seemed a little put off by his appearance, and they had had no opportunity to be alone together, for Nathan had stayed with them the entire time.

What Jim didn't know was that Wade MacIntosh had been there, too, hiding behind closed doors until Jim left. Annabelle had been furious, but there had been little she could do except to get rid of Jim as quickly as possible.

"I missed you, too," he told her, sliding his hand down her back to her waist and pulling her toward him.

Just as he was bending to kiss her lips, her father came into the hallway and she was forced to move away from him. Annabelle had been anticipating his kiss and she was more than a little disappointed at her father's untimely arrival.

"There you two are," Nathan said jovially. "Come on in. The music is about to begin and we'd like you to lead off the first waltz."

"After you, my dear." Jim gave her a little bow and she swept ahead of him, throwing him a tantalizing, promising look as she went. She was looking forward to resuming their embrace.

They walked to the center of the dance floor, and, as the first chords of music lilted through the air, he took her in his arms and held her tightly against him. Annabelle was a bit startled by his ardor, but decided to relax and enjoy it. It was her engagement party, and Jim was her fiancé.

Moving with him about the floor in easy rhythm, she appreciated Jim's finesse as a dancer. He was strong yet graceful for a man his size, and she felt as if she was floating on air as he squired her about the room. Maybe this engagement wasn't going to be such a sacrifice for the Cause, after all.

Annabelle looked up at him and her eyes met his in a heated exchange. Wanting only to encourage his devotion, she let her hand slide up his shoulder until she could caress the back of his neck in a seemingly innocent way. Annabelle felt his immediate response and her lips lifted in a confident smile. She was going to succeed in her quest. Of that she had no doubt.

Delight made her blurry way back to Jim's cabin. Not bothering to lock the door, she weaved through the room and threw herself on his bed. The scent of him filled her head and she allowed herself the luxury of a good cry.

Things seemed so unfair . . . and after tonight what was she going to do? Could she go on indefinitely playing the boy, while loving him as a woman? Her mind demanded that she do just that, but her heart cried out, "No!"

Logic would have told her, had she been logical, that she should stay with him as long as she could. She was safe here and protected. But her emotions, given free rein by the copious amount of whiskey she'd consumed, demanded that she do something . . . to let him go without ever having loved him now seemed unthinkable. And once he was married, he would be lost to her forever. . . .

Raising her head, she looked around the cabin with heartrending sadness. This was his home . . . the ship . . . the river. If she gave in to the impulse to love him she would no longer be a part of his life. But if she held back, the day was going to come when she would have to be gone from him anyway. She was well aware that her disguise couldn't last forever.

There was no real choice for her to make. Her liquor-laden mind had already chosen the path she would take . . . the path that would give her a night of love to remember, no matter what the rest of her life held in store. . . .

Chapter Twelve

Jim walked slowly up the gangplank. He had forsaken his usual scotch tonight, and the champagne he'd consumed in unending celebration of his upcoming nuptials had wreaked havoc on his senses. He grinned to himself as he recognized the symptoms . . . he was drunk.

Instead of continuing directly on to his cabin, he wandered across the deserted main deck, absorbing the feel of the vessel he loved so much. Staring out over the cold, rushing black waters, he leaned heavily against an upright and closed his eyes. Where was his feeling of peace? Where was his inner contentment? It had been so long since he'd felt good about life. . . .

Trying to shake off the malaise that threatened, he realized that he was a very lucky man. He was rich. He was successful. And he was engaged to a beautiful woman.

Jim frowned. Annabelle was a paradox. One moment she would be openly seductive, then, when he followed through on her encouragements, she would back off. He'd understood such tactics before he'd proposed, but why now? The wedding date was set for March, and she was secure in his life . . . so why deny themselves the opportunity to know each other more intimately?

Drawing a deep, cutting breath of the frigid night air, he turned away from the fast-flowing river and the shadowed outline of the dark landscape and headed up the companionway to his cabin. He had spent too much time thinking tonight. It was time to relax.

Jim fumbled noisily with the lock on his cabin door, and was amazed to find that the door hadn't been secured. Damn Murphy, anyway . . . he'd have to remember to get on him in the morning. Just because they were home didn't mean you could let things go. But at least the youth had left a lamp burning.

Moving noisily into the room, he shut and locked the door behind him and then began throwing off his clothes. The greatcoat, his jacket, and his cravat all landed in a wrinkled heap on the floor. With one purpose in mind, he sat down at his desk and pulled out his bottle of scotch. Not bothering with a glass, he tilted it to his lips and drank deeply of the fiery liquid.

Kicking off his shoes, he leaned back in the chair. Comfortable at last, he had the urge to talk . . . to try to understand what it was he was feeling, but there was no one around he felt he could confide in. Murphy was too young, and Ollie . . . well, Ollie knew too much already; although, he would never admit it to him. It would have felt good to talk to Marshall, but by now he was home, in bed with Renee. Jim remembered all the times they'd confided in one another during their youth, and he missed that camaraderie. He had allowed himself to become too much of a solitary man, and he vowed this night not to shut himself off from his family anymore.

Taking another swig from the bottle, he set it on the desk and made his unsteady way to his bed. Shrugging out of the rest of his clothes, he stretched out on the bunk and was soon fast asleep.

Delight sat huddled nervously on her bed, waiting. Jim had returned earlier than she'd expected, and she wasn't ready yet. Listening quietly, she traced his movements about the cabin. It wasn't until she heard the creak of his bed that she relaxed again. She had been afraid that Jim might come into her room and find her so open and so vulnerable. . . .

Minutes dragged by as she sat in limbo, pondering the decisions of her heart. She loved him . . . she wanted him . . . and soon he would be married to another woman. Her situation was hopeless. There could be no happy ending for her. There could only be this one night of bliss.

Delight had no intention of being there in the morning, though. She knew that after she had shared her love with Jim she would have to flee into the darkness. Even befuddled by drink, she'd realized that much. But it was worth any sacrifice to her to know him as a man just this one time. And regardless of what the future held in store for her, she knew she would never regret it.

Slipping from her bed, she silently opened their adjoining door and peeked out. Her gaze was drawn magnetically to the bunk where he lay. Delight knew by the sound of his regular, steady breathing that Jim was sound asleep. Emboldened by that knowledge, she ventured forth, the long flannel nightshirt she wore trailing the floor behind her.

The burning lamp cast a weak, flickering light in the room as she came to stand by his bed. His features seemed hardened by the shadowy lamplight and Delight almost panicked when he stirred, afraid for a moment that he wouldn't want her . . . that he would reject her. She knew then that her only hope was darkness. She had to come to him under the cover of the night, to love him anonymously, to give her greatest gift in secret devotion before fleeing his life forever.

A serenity enveloped Delight as she turned out the lamp. It seemed so right. She needed to be with him, to be held in his strong arms, to be a part of him. Swept up in her desire to love him, she stepped free of Jim's nightshirt and approached him.

Delight wasn't aware that she appeared as a wraithlike vision as she moved about the cabin. And Jim thought he was dreaming when he opened his eyes and saw the ivory-bodied goddess of the night coming toward him. Held captive by his intoxicated state, he lay still, letting his gaze roam over the silent, graceful woman who seemed to be floating as she drew nearer. Her face and hair were hidden in the shadowy darkness of the room, but her alabaster flesh gleamed with a purity that stole his breath.

"Who are you?" he managed to croak, the thrill of this midnight illusion making coherent thought impossible.

Delight was scared . . . she hadn't expected him to waken . . . not yet. Her lack of experience frightened her, but she decided to brazen it out. She wanted to be with him . . . she had to be with him. Driven on by a need as old as time, she drew no closer, but played on the fringes of his mind.

"I've come to love you, my captain," she whispered, her voice as soft and feminine as a gentle breeze.

Jim didn't move for he was afraid that his beauty would vanish if he tried to touch her. Sure that the combination of champagne and scotch had conjured up this heavenly dream of a woman, he made a note to drink them together more often. A crooked smile touched his lips.

Delight saw the smile and fear clutched at her heart. Had he recognized her?

"Then love me, my beauty." He spoke to her gently, slowly extending a hand in her direction.

Delight needed no further encouragement. He wanted her . . . he wasn't rejecting her. She put her hand in his big warm one and felt herself pulled gently but with steady strength toward him. Glad she had extinguished the lamp, she surrendered herself to Jim's embrace.

"Are you real?" he murmured in profound confusion as he drew his dream lover down upon the bed with the utmost care.

How could this be happening to him? Had he been sober he would have bolted from the bed and demanded an explanation from this beautiful young woman who was giving herself to him. But the liquor had dulled his rationality; he was caught up in the sensuousness of the moment and he wanted only to enjoy every second of his dream.

The blackness of the night surrounded them as their bodies touched intimately for the first time, and her hands clutched at him, holding him tightly, never wanting to let him go.

"Relax, beauty," he told his illusion. "I'm here, and we have all night."

A sob caught in her throat. Just this one night . . . that was all they had . . . and it was more perfect than she'd ever thought possible.

His mouth descended to hers slowly, sensuously opening her lips to him and drawing her life from her in a devastating kiss unlike anything she'd ever dreamed. The boldness of his tongue as he tasted hers sent a thrill of desire through her that eclipsed all of her previous imaginings. It was perfect, this blending of male and female, and she reveled in the discovery.

"What pleases you, beauty?" he asked between short, breathless kisses. Never before had a kiss stirred him so deeply . . . so sensuously. He felt moved from the depths of his soul, and he longed for the ultimate union with her slim, cool body.

"Your touch pleases me, my captain," Delight responded without thought. "As I hope the gift of my love pleases you."

Jim groaned as his mouth possessed hers again. Delight felt that she was losing herself in him as a heated yearning pulsed to life deep within her. She couldn't control the urge to move against the hardness of his muscled body, and Jim was thrilled at her uninhibited response.

"Not so fast, little one." He slowed her with gentle hands. "Let's go slowly . . . together."

"I'm yours, my captain, to do with as you will." Her tone was softly feminine yet serious in intent, and Jim looked down into her night-shrouded features.

"I wish I could see you. . . ." he muttered. "All of you . . ."

But Delight distracted him, pulling him down to her for a kiss.

Jim gave himself up to the artless wiles of this tender woman who was gracing his bed. With practiced, learned strokes he caressed her.

Twisting restlessly under his tantalizing touch, Delight longed for more. Why was he doing this to her? Didn't he know how she felt? Didn't he know that she was burning with desire for him? Couldn't he tell that she needed him to possess her fully . . . to take her and brand her body with his so they would always belong to each other?

"I love you, Jim Westlake. I love you," she whispered.

Jim was torn between the need to take her quickly and the desire to savor each moment in her enthralling embrace. She was like a wildfire, burning out of control, possessing him body and soul. His dream lover was entrancing him, bewitching him, mesmerizing him in a vortex of emotion unlike anything he'd ever known before. Ignited by her passion, Jim could hold back no longer. He made her his own.

The shock of their joining amazed him as a powerful current of emotion surged through him. Theirs was a mating of souls . . . a longing of the flesh that transcended time and place . . . and Jim was lost in his need to love her.

As ecstasy claimed them, they collapsed together, wrapped in each other's arms.

"Did I please you?" she whispered in his ear.

A tremor of excitement shook Jim as he lay still, trying to grasp the reality of what had just happened.

"Oh, you pleased me, all right," he growled, rolling over quickly and taking her with him. "You pleased me too damn much."

"Too much?" She was worried, he sounded so fierce. "I didn't mean to upset you. . . ."

"No, no, my love. You haven't upset me." His feelings were so new and so powerful that he was at a loss to explain himself to her.

"I would never want to hurt you," she vowed. "You mean everything to me."

"Rest with me for a while and then we'll talk," he invited, hugging her close.

"You only want to rest?"

Her innocent words aroused him in a way no other ever had before.

"You're right. I could never rest with you in my arms," he said fiercely, kissing her. "You are my dream."

He made love to her again, hungrily, passionately.

"I love you, Captain," she sighed as they rested in the aftermath of their spent desire.

"You're perfect, my love," he whispered. "I'll never stop wanting you. . . ."

Delight closed her eyes and breathed deeply of the manly scent of him. This was heaven. She lay languidly as Jim moved his weight off of her and pulled her to his side. A sense of real peace, the first she'd felt in weeks, overcame her, and she curled against her love, resting her head on his shoulder. She knew that she would have to leave him soon, but she wanted to wait until he was asleep and then slip noiselessly into the night.

Jim felt her nestle beside him and he leaned over her to frame her face with his hands for another kiss. He had never experienced such an overwhelming passion before, or such a willing partner. She was wonderful, his beauty. And, he decided in his intoxicated state, he wanted to keep her with him forever.

Delight lay against him, exhausted, yet excited, by his stimulating lovemaking. She listened carefully to his breathing, waiting for him to fall asleep so she could make her escape. She hoped it wouldn't be long, for the sky was beginning to lighten to the east. Closing her eyes, she decided to rest for just a moment, knowing that she would feel better if she could just sleep for a little while. . . .

Chapter Thirteen

It was not early. Jim could sense that just by the sounds he could hear. He wondered if the sun was out, but he dreaded opening his eyes. His head was already pounding, and he knew that in a direct confrontation with that bright, shining orb he would come out the loser. His mind was foggy but relaxed, as though he had just experienced a wonderful dream whose essence had momentarily escaped him. He didn't want to move. In fact, if he had his own way, he probably would stay in bed for the entire day. That had been some celebration last night . . . all that champagne and . . .

He stretched. The touch of a warm body nestling softly near his own nearly sent him scrambling from the bed. My God! He sat up in a jerky motion, rubbing a hand over his eyes. What had he been thinking of? Had the champagne ruined his good judgment that badly? He never brought women to his cabin . . . never. What had Murphy thought this morning when he'd passed through on his way out?

His movements seemed almost in slow motion as he turned to look at the woman curled by his side. The woman, who could have been Murphy's twin, lay sound asleep with a look of blissful contentment on her face. Jim shook his head groggily, trying to remember, and it was then that he noticed her short hair.

In a panicked move that jarred the entire bed, he threw back the covers and stared in mind-boggling confusion as Murphy came awake slowly. Snatches of the night just past came back to him with a vengeance. A night of passionate love . . . a night of unknown beauty and seduction. . . .

"Murphy?! What the hell is going on around here?!" he thundered.

"Captain?" she asked sleepily, trying to understand why he was shouting and why her head hurt her so badly.

"I think you'd better start talking and fast!" he demanded in a cold voice, one that was deadly with murderous intent. The truth be known, Jim was so confused he wasn't sure what to say, and he wanted Murphy to do all the explaining.

Delight was horrified. Oh, God! She had actually fallen asleep . . . she hadn't meant to. She had only wanted to rest for a while . . . she had felt so good in his arms . . . so loved . . . so protected. . . .

"I'm sorry," she squeaked, and the sound of her own voice sent a vicious pounding of pain through her slowly recovering senses.

"You're sorry?!" Jim was incredulous. He stared at Murphy for a long moment before realizing that he was nude. Climbing over her, he searched fruitlessly for his pants. "Where the hell are they!?" he bellowed, before finally locating the pair he'd worn the night before wadded up in the corner. Hopping on one foot, he struggled into them while keeping one eye on the female lying on his bed.

"Captain," she said earnestly. "I'll go. I'm sorry if I've embarrassed you. I hadn't meant to fall asleep." Delight gave him a small, helpless grin, and, with a sedateness she didn't feel, she climbed down from his bunk and started to her room, leaving Jim totally disconcerted, staring after her.

Jim watched the door close behind her and stood stock-still, unable to move. His brain certainly wasn't working at peak efficiency this morning. He rubbed his eyes again. Murphy—a girl? No, definitely not a girl—a woman. Murphy—his dream lover? His beauty?

Barefoot, Jim marched to the closed portal, and, with barely restrained violence, he threw it open. The hinges screeched their protest as the door banged viciously against the wall.

Delight looked up from pulling on her work pants. Standing, facing him bare-breasted, her hair in a riot of short curls about her face, she looked like an adorable pixie-woman, and Jim had the unbidden desire to clasp her to him. They had just loved all night, hadn't they? His mind was searching frantically for answers.

"You're a woman?" He stared at her breasts, remembering their silken softness and the way she'd moaned when he'd touched them.

Again, she gave him a lopsided grin. "I think that's obvious at this point, Captain." She gestured in resignation to her bare state.

"But . . ."

"I know. Believe me, I understand your anger and I'm going, just as soon as I get dressed."

Delight was amazed at the calm way she was dealing with the situation, and, turning from him, she pulled on her shirt, quickly buttoning the material over her bosom. She felt just a little shy this morning, and she was totally unsure of Jim. When she had planned to love him, she had also planned not to face him the day after.

"Going? I've got news for you, Murphy. You're not going anywhere!" Jim snarled. He needed time to think. It came as no little surprise to him that his cabin boy was in reality a woman full-grown. "What kind of a game are you playing, Murphy? What do you want from me?"

She stared at him aghast, and tears blurred her vision. What a nasty accusation! Did he really think that there was some evil plot behind her desire for him? She hurriedly turned away from him, but not before he'd caught sight of her upset.

Jim stood helplessly watching as she presented him with her back.

"I don't want anything from you, Captain," she hissed, too hurt to say more. "Please, let me go."

"Murphy—" he began again, his tone belligerent.

Jim didn't know if he was angry with her or with himself, but he *was* angry. Furious, in fact. He'd been made a fool of. How could he have been so stupid?

"Murphy," he began again when she didn't respond.

A loud banging on his deck door thwarted his attempt to force her to speak.

"Damn!" he swore, growing more frustrated by the minute. "Who is it?" he shouted, moving out of the room.

"It's Ollie, Jim. Mark Clayton is down in the saloon and he says he needs to talk to you right away. It's important."

Jim cursed heatedly under his breath, "All right, all right. Tell him I'll be down shortly."

"Right," Ollie answered, and Jim could hear his footsteps retreating down the deck.

"Murphy?" his tone was stiff, but more civil than before, and she came to stand in the connecting doorway.

"Yes, Captain."

For some reason, Jim didn't like her calling him "captain" anymore, but he had no time to tell her so now.

"I've got to go meet Captain Clayton. I'll be back. I want you to stay here until I return. Is that clear?"

She nodded, her eyes wide with the knowledge that this would be the last time she would see him, possibly forever. "Yes, sir."

Jim glanced at her quickly and shook his head, wondering how he'd ever been fooled by her pitiful disguise. She was gorgeous.

Delight started to turn away, but he called her back.

"Murphy?" His tone was less demanding, and she looked at him speculatively.

"Yes?"

"Would you please find me a pair of clean pants?" Jim ran a hand nervously through his hair. He seemed unable to do anything right at the moment.

Hurrying, she laid out his clothes and went back into her cabin while he dressed. She had sensed his discomfort with her in the room, and she thought it wiser to leave him to his own devices.

Sitting nervously on the edge of the bed, she waited until she heard his door close before venturing out. Relaxing a bit now that he was gone, Delight made her plans. She had to leave, now. There would be no time for recriminations. She didn't want to do that to what they had shared last night. His love had been perfect, and she wanted the memory to stay that way.

Bundling up her few personal possessions, she donned her coat and started out of the cabin. Pausing, she quickly scribbled him a short note. Leaving it on his desk, she looked once more about Jim's stateroom, staring at the bed where she'd learned so much about giving and loving unconditionally. She closed her eyes, savoring the sweetness of the night, and then hurried from the boat. Her absence would prove to him that she hadn't wanted to take anything from him. She had only wanted to give.

Jim sat in the saloon, listening halfheartedly to the news that Mark was imparting. His attention span was almost nil and he had to force himself to heed what his friend was saying.

"Jim, the river is frozen solid from here to New Orleans, and the army just walked across at Vicksburg and took the city. What do you think about that?" Mark said sarcastically, as he realized that Jim was not with him. "Jim?"

"I'm sorry, Mark." Jim snapped back to the present. He had been lost in thoughts of Murphy's embrace. "You were saying?"

"Is there something wrong, Jim?"

"No," he denied quickly. "What makes you say that?"

"You're acting strange this morning."

"It was all that champagne last night. I'm afraid I overdid it."

Mark looked at him speculatively, but didn't push for a further explanation. He had been at the engagement party last night, but Jim hadn't seemed all that drunk to him.

"Would you like to get together later today? Most of what I have to tell you is important, but it can wait."

"Whatever you say, Mark," Jim replied vaguely, and Mark knew it would be better to put it off. Jim was definitely not himself this morning.

"Why don't I meet you for dinner?"

"Sure."

"Planter's House?"

"All right."

Mark gave him a puzzled look, but Jim took no notice of his confusion. He was too concerned with his own thoughts. They shook hands and agreed on a time to meet to eat and then walked out on deck together.

"Try to get some rest today. You look pretty tired," Mark suggested.

"I'll do that."

"See you tonight."

Jim was glad when Mark disappeared down the gangplank, and he hurried quickly back to his cabin. He wanted to sit Murphy down and find out exactly what was going on. Jim realized now that he had been hasty in his accusation that morning, but at the time nothing had made sense. Calmer now, and more in control of his emotions, he was ready to talk it out with her. What they had shared last night went beyond words. Something elemental had happened between them . . . something that he didn't want to lose.

He had a sudden fleeting thought of Annabelle, but he pushed it aside. There would be time to consider her later. Right now, Murphy was more important.

Bolstered by his feeling of rationality, Jim entered the cabin easily, ready to talk and ready to listen.

He knew immediately that Murphy wasn't there. There was a silence hanging in the air . . . a painful one. With long, purposeful strides, he crossed the room, throwing wide her door once more and staring at her deserted quarters. She was gone.

Jim was stunned by the sense of loss he felt, and he cursed Mark and Ollie for their untimely interruption. Important, indeed! A light of hope entered his mind . . . maybe she had gone on to work. He was ready to rush from the cabin in search of her when he spied the note lying on the desktop. His hand shook as he reached for it. Eager, yet afraid of what the missive might say, Jim gently unfolded it.

My captain—

I'm sorry. I know it's impossible between us, so please don't look for me. You have your life and I have mine.

I wish you every happiness. I hope you will remember all we shared with fondness.

I love you—

Murphy

Jim stared at the piece of paper in awestruck silence. She really had gone. Just like that. He didn't know whether to be angry or sad. Jim felt an unfamiliar burning in his eyes, and, in a fit of uncontrollable rage, he wadded up the paper and threw it viciously across the room. Damn her!

Slumping down in his chair, he stared blindly at the rumpled bed, noticing for the first time the virgin's blood that stained his sheets. It was only then that he began to understand the enormity of what Murphy had done. Jim groaned to himself as he realized the damage he had caused by accusing her of having some ulterior motive. He had been so selfish and so stupid. . . .

He wanted to make it up to her, to tell her that he was sorry, to tell her that last night had meant everything to him. He wanted her to know that he had never experienced anything like it before in his life and that he never would again in his future. Thoughts of Murphy assailed him. Her quickness at learning, her good-natured acceptance of his teasing, the time they had spent working closely together. How could he have been so blind? She was a lovely woman, not a boy. . . .

Jim looked up, determination written on his features. He would find her if he had to tear the city apart. She couldn't have gone too far; he'd only been gone from the cabin for a half an hour.

Standing, he started for the door. It was then that he saw it . . . his rumpled nightshirt . . . the one he had given her. With careful hands he picked it up and lay it gently on the bed. Then, retrieving the note, he smoothed out the wrinkles and folded it neatly, storing it in his vest pocket . . . the pocket nearest his heart.

Chapter Fourteen

It was late afternoon, cloudy and cold. A vicious wind whipped down the deserted streets and alleys, discouraging all but the most hardy of souls from venturing out.

Delight slowly made her way down the treacherous, icy side street. The frigid wind stung her face, chilling the tears that clouded her vision as she struggled on, heading in the direction of Rose's house. Although Delight didn't want to go back there, knowing that her presence might cause trouble for Rose with Martin, she also knew that she had no real alternative. Necessity was forcing her decision, for she would freeze to death if she tried to stay on the streets.

Delight thought of Jim and wondered if he'd discovered that she'd gone yet. A small, troubled sigh escaped her as she realized that all ties with him had been severed. There could be no going back.

But knowing that she'd made the right decision in leaving didn't ease the painful loneliness that engulfed her when she thought of him. And, while it hurt that he'd accused her of using him, she still loved him with all of her heart. A lone, forlorn tear trickled down her cheek and she wiped at it sadly. It was going to be difficult, of that she had no doubt, but somehow, in time, she would manage to put Jim and her love for him behind her and go on with her life.

Sitting under the light of the single lamp in her living room, Rose was diligently working on her mending when she was startled by a knock at the door. Fearful of who it might be, she peeked cautiously out a window. Seeing Delight, she rushed to open the door to her friend.

"Delight! Oh, thank God you're back! I've been so worried!"

Embracing her with loving affection, Rose pulled her into the warmth of the small room, closing and locking the door behind them.

"Are you all right?"

"I'm fine, Rose," Delight reassured her as she took off her coat and went to stand before the stove.

"Good. You look half-frozen, though. Make yourself comfortable while I get you some hot tea." Rose quickly poured the warming brew and brought it to her. Sitting down with Delight on the sofa, she asked, "Where did you go? I looked everywhere for you."

"You went looking for me?"

"I felt so guilty just letting you leave like that . . . I wanted to do something more to help you."

"But you did help me," Delight insisted, relaxing as the steaming tea warmed her. "If it hadn't been for you, Martin surely would have caught up with me that first night."

"Thank God he didn't." Rose spoke solemnly, fear evident in her voice.

"He did come here, then?"

"Yes, he came and he was so furious."

"Did he hurt you?"

"No . . ." Rose paused, remembering his bruising grip and his hate-filled words. "No, he didn't hurt me. But he would have hurt you if he'd found you that night."

"I don't doubt it. Have you heard anything since? How's my mother?"

"Your mother is much better."

"Good. But what about Martin?" Delight was ready for whatever news there was. "I need to know what's going on at home."

"Martin must have panicked when he couldn't find you, because he had to explain your disappearance to everybody."

"What did he say?" Fear struck at her again.

"Don't get upset," Rose calmed her. "For once the man did a good job. His lie was very logical, really. He told your mother and anyone else who asked that you had gone to help your aunt. He said that your uncle had been injured and that your aunt wanted to go to him, so you went to stay with the children."

Delight nodded. "It certainly is believable. I have helped them on more than one occasion. Maybe his lie will work to my benefit."

"I hope so. But where were you all this time?"

"I've been doing odd jobs on the riverfront." She shrugged and changed the topic. "My mother really is better?"

"Much," Rose confirmed again, knowing how anxious Delight must have been, worrying about her mother's health and not being in a position to find out anything.

"Good. That means Martin wouldn't dare come near me" Delight pondered what action to take.

"You're not considering going home, are you?"

"I have to go back, Rose. If not today, then next week or next month. There's nothing else I can do. The longer I stay away, the harder it will be for me to explain my absence. Martin's story will only hold up until Mother hears from Uncle Joe or Aunt Faith."

"That's true enough, but do you really want to?"

"No." Her answer came flatly, with little emotion. "I hate the thought of living in the same house with Martin again."

"I can imagine; that's why I left. But you don't have to accept that behavior from him."

"I know." Delight's expression hardened. "He caught me off guard. I was naive. But I'm not anymore."

"So, what are you going to do?"

"I know it's going to be hard, but I'm going to face him down."

"How?"

"I'm going to tell him that if he ever comes near me again, I'm going to my mother and let her know just exactly why I left so abruptly."

"Why don't you tell her now?"

Delight was thoughtful. "She loves Martin, Rose. She really does. And with her just recovering from such a serious illness, I'd worry about the effect of such news on her."

"So you're going to give him another chance?"

"I have to, for Mother's sake. But I won't hesitate to tell her if he ever tries anything again."

"But he might hurt you."

"I doubt it. Not now that Mother's better. Martin may not be one to forgive and forget, but he's certainly not stupid." Delight looked Rose straight in the eye. "And neither am I."

Rose shivered at the intensity of feeling Delight exuded. "You've grown up."

"Before I wanted to, that's for sure. It was nice being safe and cosseted. But I doubt that my life will ever be that 'nice' again."

"Surely you'll be happy," Rose hurried to cheer her. "Why, you'll meet a nice young man and get married . . ."

A pain grew within Delight's breast at Rose's predictions. No, she could never marry, not after what she'd shared with Jim . . . not after last night.

"Well, that remains to be seen," she returned, her voice cold and clipped.

"Do you want to go home tonight?"

"No. Tomorrow will be soon enough. We've some shopping to do before I can go anywhere." Delight grinned as she thought of going home in her boy's pants.

"You'll need some kind of a hairpiece, too."

"I hadn't even thought about my hair." She ran her hand through her short curls.

"It's going to need something, unless you want to try to start a new rage?"

"I don't think so."

"How are you planning to handle Martin tomorrow?"

"First, I want you to get a letter to him for me. Do you have some paper and a pen?"

"Right here." Rose brought her the necessary instruments.

"Thanks." Delight quickly set to work.

A short time later, she looked up at her friend and smiled. "This should do it."

"I'll take it over right away."

"No, not yet. If you deliver it now, he'll spend the whole night looking for me. We'll get it to him first thing in the morning. That way he won't have time to plan anything."

"You're right. He'd come straight here if he thought you were back."

"It's still light outside; do you want to go shopping now? If I'm supposed to be returning from a trip, I'd better have some baggage with me."

"Do you need money? I've got a little you can have."

"No, I can charge everything. Do you still have my old clothes?"

"Right here." Rose retrieved the dress and underthings she had left behind the fateful night, and Delight began her transformation from cabin boy back into Delight de Vries.

Ollie looked at Jim skeptically. "I don't believe it."

"Believe it, Ollie."

Their expressions were grim. "But where would he have gone."

"I don't know." Jim sounded as worried as he felt. "I wish I did."

"He's too young to be out there all alone. Didn't he say

anything? Did you two have a fight? He seemed fine last night."

"Last night?"

"Murphy came up to my cabin and we had a few drinks." Ollie smiled as he remembered the youth's first slug of whiskey.

"Murphy was drinking last night?" Jim stared at his friend. "Had he ever done it before?"

"No," Ollie chuckled. "I kinda thought that that was why he was so late coming down this morning. I was sure he was going to be quite hung over . . ."

Jim could have groaned . . . she had been drinking. She probably would never have done what she had, except for the liquor. Damn her! How could she just up and leave? Didn't she realize that he'd worry about her? That he cared?

On second reflection, Jim realized that she didn't know how he felt. All she had known was that he had been furious with her this morning for her deception, and that he was now engaged to another woman. Seeing things from her viewpoint, he understood how hopeless her situation must have seemed to her.

"We have to go look for him, Ollie." Jim was too embarrassed to tell his friend the truth.

"Let's go. There had to have been a good reason for him to take off like that without saying good-bye, and I intend to find out what it is," Ollie declared heatedly, and they left the boat anxious to locate Murphy as quickly as possible.

For four hours they searched the entire riverfront, combing all the possible places Murphy could have gone with no money and few clothes, but no one had seen a boy matching his description.

"Now what, Jimmy?" Ollie's concern was written all over his tired features.

"I wish I knew," Jim said slowly, trying to figure out where she could be.

He wanted to tell Ollie the whole truth, but he held back.

Jim had all the trouble he could handle right now without invoking Ollie's ire, for once the older man discovered what had really happened, he was afraid there would be no peace between them.

"Let's walk uptown. He was probably running away from us." Jim tried to sound like he was guessing.

"But why?" Ollie argued.

Jim was silent, and the question went unanswered as they walked in the direction of Marshall's office, hoping to catch a glimpse of the slender, defenseless youth.

Delight climbed into the hired carriage beside Rose and pulled the door shut behind them.

"Delight, do you really want me to move back home with you?" Rose asked, stunned by her offer.

"Absolutely. I don't know why I didn't think of it before." Delight smiled at her. "Don't you want to do it?"

"Of course. I loved working for you and your mother."

"Well, good. Then it's settled. And between the two of us, I think we can manage to stay a step or two ahead of Mr. Martin Montgomery!"

"I hope so." Rose grimaced.

"I *know*." She grew serious. "We still have to make some plans before I meet with Martin tomorrow. We . . ."

Delight let her gaze drift out the carriage window as she started to speak and the words caught in her throat. There, strolling past as if they didn't have a care in the world, were Jim and Ollie.

"Let's head down to Harry's and get us a drink. What do you say, Jimmy?"

"Sounds goods to me," came Jim's seemingly lighthearted response.

Delight quickly sat back in her seat, her color paling.

"Delight? What's wrong?"

She didn't answer right away as her mind went over the bit of conversation she'd just heard. Jim wasn't looking for her . . .

he was going drinking with Ollie. Last night had meant nothing to him . . .

It occurred to her then that she had been secretly hoping he would somehow track her down, declare his love, and steal her away in a romantic elopement that would stun all of society.

Delight gave a harsh, brittle laugh that echoed hollowly in the carriage. Such childish dreams! Such foolishness! No longer could she sit back and believe that her dreams would come true. She was a woman now . . . a woman who had to face the cruel harshness of life as it really was and act upon it. Jim Westlake was no hero . . . no knight in shining armor. He was just a man who had taken what had been so eagerly offered. That was all. Disillusionment mingled with great sadness settled in her heart, yet she turned to Rose and gave her a tight smile.

"Nothing's wrong. Everything is going to be just fine. You'll see."

Chapter Fifteen

Jim took only a small drink of his scotch as he sat with Ollie at a table in Harry's saloon. He had never before felt so completely frustrated. She was gone, and all he had left of her was the note. His hand strayed to check his pocket and he was relieved to find that it was still there. It was his only connection with what had been the most beautiful experience of his life.

He frowned, remembering that morning and his bewilderment upon finding out that Murphy was a female. What a god-awful shock it had been to him to wake up with Murphy sleeping there beside him . . . Jim would have smiled if it hadn't been so tragic. She had given him so much, so freely, and then, in his embarrassed confusion, he had turned on her, accusing her of wanting something from him. How could he have been so stupid? His later discovery that she had been a virgin had only served to compound the guilt he was experiencing. Her loving had been a gift . . . a gift that he had tried at first to reject but one that he knew he would carry in his heart forever. . . .

"What now, Jimmy?" Ollie's question dragged him back to the present.

"I don't know if there's anything else we can do, Ollie. We've searched everywhere and we asked people to keep a lookout for him. Do you have any other ideas?"

"No," Ollie sighed. "But if we knew why he'd gone, we might be able to figure out where he's gone."

Jim fixed his friend with a serious gaze. "I'll tell you why, Ollie."

The sound of Jim's voice, so deadly earnest, startled Ollie, and he turned to face him directly.

"You know why?"

"Yes. But you're not going to like it." Jim prepared to tell him the whole story.

"What happened? What did you do?" Ollie charged.

Jim was momentarily shocked. "Why do you think I did something?"

"Because we'd talked about you last night. The boy nearly worshipped you. He wouldn't have left. He liked his life on the boat."

"You were as blind as I was, old man!" Jim snarled, bristling under Ollie's criticism.

"What the hell are you talking about?" Ollie returned heatedly.

"Murphy wasn't a boy . . . Murphy was a girl!" There, he had said it. Glaring across the small table at Ollie, Jim downed the rest of his drink and quickly poured another.

Ollie stared at Jim, unmoving, and then extended his glass to be refilled, too.

"Murphy? A girl?"

"Yes." Jim's words were final, and a heavy silence fell between them as they both reviewed their own private memories of Murphy.

And, while Jim was almost distraught with worry, Ollie suddenly burst into laughter.

"That's terrific! A girl!"

"Shut up," Jim said threateningly, but Ollie only looked at him over the rim of his glass and laughed harder.

"You slept in close quarters with her for almost two weeks and you never knew?" Ollie retorted between chuckles.

"Not until this morning," Jim affirmed.

"What happened this morning?" Ollie suddenly turned serious. "How did you find out?"

Jim tensed, not wanting to reveal more. He wanted to protect her. He didn't want to sully Murphy's reputation, even though he knew Ollie would never think any less of her. In fact, if Ollie was going to think less of anybody, it would be him.

Jim fixed him with a piercing look. "Suffice it to say that I made a few mistakes this morning. Mistakes that I will rectify as soon as I find her."

"Jimmy—" Ollie grasped the situation without anything further being said. "How are we going to find her? I'm really worried about her now. As a boy she had a chance, but a girl? Alone?"

"I know, Ollie. I know." Jim's answer was almost a groan, and their eyes met in silent communication. "I'll find her," he pledged. "Somehow, some way."

It was late. Night had enveloped the city, enshrouding it in darkness, and the cutting northwesterly wind howling through the streets proclaimed the threat of another winter storm.

The houses on Lucas Place were shuttered and deserted-looking this night, and they added to the sense of desolation that was overpowering Jim as he made his way down the walk. Moving on, Jim ignored the dropping temperatures and the first falling snowflakes. Head down, he strode purposefully toward Marshall's home, his mind set on finding answers. Jim wasn't sure how his brother could help, but he hoped that he might have some idea of what to do next. The Lord knew he'd tried everything he could think of. . . .

A lamp was burning invitingly in the parlor window as Jim mounted the front steps, and he was glad when the maid quickly admitted him.

"Good evening, Captain," she greeted him. "They're in the parlor. Go on in."

"Thanks." After shedding his coat, he headed quickly in the direction of the welcoming light.

Marshall looked up from where he sat in front of the fireplace reading the newspaper. "Jim? This is a surprise. Come on in." He rose to greet his brother. "Have you recovered from last night?"

"Jim," Renee came to him, too, and gave him a hug. "Sit down. Would you like a drink?"

"Coffee would be great." He kissed her cheek and shook hands with Marshall before sitting down in a wing chair.

"To what do we owe this honor?" Marshall asked after Renee had gone to get Jim's drink.

"I need to talk with you."

Marshall was immediately struck by the seriousness of Jim's tone.

"Do you want to go into the study?"

"I think we'd better," Jim said flatly.

Renee returned just then with the tray of coffee. "Here you are."

"Thanks, that's great." Jim poured himself a cup.

"We'll be in the study for a while," Marshall told her as they left the room.

"Business, again?" she moaned in mock protest.

"Again," Marshall grinned as he led Jim down the hall.

When the door was firmly closed behind them, he turned to face his brother.

"What's the matter? Is there bad news? Has something happened to one of the boats?"

"No, no," Jim hurried to reassure him as they both sat down before the roaring fire in the fireplace. "In fact, I've just come from dinner with Mark. Everything is on schedule and there have been no further reports on the spies."

"Then what's bothering you?" Marshall was puzzled.

"It's personal," Jim said tersely, setting his untouched cup of coffee aside.

Marshall gave him a sidelong glance trying to read his expression.

"I'll do whatever I can to help. Is there a problem with Annabelle?"

"No, this has nothing to do with her." Jim was vague.

"Why don't you just tell me what's happened?" he encouraged.

Jim sighed and got up to pace nervously about the room. He ran a hand through his hair in an agitated gesture as he turned to him.

"Do you remember Murphy?"

"Murphy?" Marshall frowned. "Oh, yes, your cabin boy, right?"

"Right."

"Well? Did he steal something? Is that your problem?"

"No." Jim hesitated again, not quite knowing where to begin. Finally, in a fit of desperation, he blurted it out. "Murphy was a girl."

"Murphy was a girl?" Marshall's tone reflected his disbelief.

Jim nodded.

"Did you know this all along?"

"No. I just found out this morning."

Marshall gave a curt nod, trying to understand what it was Jim was trying to say. "I don't quite know what you want me to do."

"I don't know what I want you to do, either. All I know is that she ran away this morning and I can't find her."

"You're trying to find her?"

"Yes."

"Why?"

Marshall's question cut straight to the core of Jim's dilemma.

"Why?" Jim repeated.

"Yes, why?" he demanded of his brother.

Jim gave him a quixotic look that turned to a lopsided half smile. "Because I love her." It was as big a revelation to him as it was to his brother.

Marshall stared at Jim in profound confusion. "You love Murphy? I'm confused."

"If you think you're confused, how do you suppose I feel?"

"What happened between you two? This is all so sudden . . . what about your engagement to Annabelle?"

"I haven't gotten that far yet." Jim tried to explain. "What happened last night was so special. . . ."

"What did happen last night?"

"Murphy and I made love."

"But you were at your engagement party. . . ."

"It was later . . . when I came back to the boat. Here, read this." He thrust Murphy's note at Marshall.

Marshall read it quickly and looked up at Jim.

"I would say you obviously don't love Annabelle."

Jim had the grace to look guilty. "No, I don't. But what can I do about Murphy? I've searched everywhere for her. Ollie and I combed the riverfront all day."

"What would you do with her if you did find her?" Marshall asked sagely.

"I—" Jim had never thought past finding her. "I don't know."

"Well, I think you'd better find the answer to that question before you think about anything else. Are you prepared to break off with Annabelle?"

Jim let his thoughts drift over last night, comparing Annabelle with Murphy . . . socialite versus cabin boy . . .

"Yes." He answered firmly. "But I have to find Murphy first"

"From the sound of this letter, Murphy doesn't want to be found."

"I know."

"Why?"

"I accused her of using me. . . ."

"You what?"

"I was so astounded when I woke up with her in my bed that . . ."

Marshall erupted into laughter. "That would have been a revelation!"

"It wasn't funny then!"

"It most certainly is now." Marshall continued to laugh, drawing Jim's anger.

"Oh, just shut up and help me!"

"What is it that you want me to do?"

"Help me find her."

Marshall sobered. "Is Murphy her real name?"

"I don't know."

"Then we really don't have anything to go on." He paused to think for a moment. "Did she ever make mention of her past? Any names, dates, places?"

"All she ever said to me was that her stepfather threw her out and that she'd lived in the country."

"Do you think she would have gone back home?"

"I don't know how she could have . . . if he'd thrown her out once, wouldn't he do it again?"

"It's hard to say." Marshall paused thoughtfully. "There are a few people I can talk to, and I'll put the word out to watch for her. Although, for the time being, I'll tell them that Murphy is a boy."

"Good idea. She didn't have any other clothes, so I'm sure she's still dressed that way." Jim thought of all the times when they'd worked so closely together and he'd never known she was a woman. "I feel so stupid . . . I lived with her for almost two weeks and never had a clue. . . ."

"She must be a good little actress. You know, I met her, too, and she had me fooled."

Jim nodded. "She had everybody fooled. I just hope nothing happens to her. . . ."

"If she's still in town, we'll find her." Marshall sounded so positive that Jim's spirits lifted. "But what about Annabelle?"

That question was still haunting him as he strode back toward the riverfront later that night. What was he going to do about Annabelle?

With her red velvet robe wrapped tightly about her slim body to ward off the chill, Annabelle Morgan stood at her front bedroom window in her family's elegant home watching the deserted, snow-crusted street beyond. Where was he?

The loud chiming of the mantel clock shattered the pre-dawn silence as it marked the passing of yet another hour. Startled by the realization that it was almost four in the morning, Annabelle turned in frustration from her vigil. The endless hours of waiting had worn on her nerves, and she felt tense and on edge.

Moving to the hearth, she threw a small log on the dying fire and stirred new flames to life. Savoring its flaring warmth, she sat in the closest chair, mulling over the happenings of the last few days.

Annabelle was a woman of action, and the part of the helpless female that she was being forced into just didn't sit well with her. While it was true she could play it to perfection, her petite blond beauty helping her to carry it off, she chafed under the restrictions it placed on her. Annabelle knew that as Jim Westlake's fiancée she must never appear directly to challenge men's authority and that she must always be submissive. And, while the role itself was boring, she was finding Jim to be more and more intriguing.

Now, waiting for Wade to return from a meeting with the sympathizers, she found it a bit disturbing that her thoughts were of Jim. Tall, handsome, confident, successful—had she been interested in picking a real husband, she couldn't have done a better job. Jim Westlake was devastatingly attractive, and Annabelle could not deny that she found him desirable. She shivered as she remembered the way Jim had held her in his arms whenever they had danced. . . .

The sound of a horse in the street brought her to her feet, and she rushed to the window, pleased to find that Wade had finally arrived. With no thought to her attire, she hurried downstairs to admit him.

"I was beginning to think you weren't going to come," she complained. "What went on at the meeting?"

"Nothing important, that's for sure. All they could talk about was the gold, and they wanted to know why we didn't have the information yet."

"Really?" she sneered. "I suppose they think they could do a better job?"

She started to turn away from him, but he reached out and pulled her to him. "Frankly, darling, I don't care about those old fools. All I care about is how I felt watching you dance with Westlake last night."

"Oh?" Annabelle asked coyly. "And how was that?"

"I was burning for you, and you damn well know it!" he said almost viciously as his mouth sought hers in a searing brand.

"Let's go upstairs," she encouraged, breaking away from him.

"Your father?"

"He left for St. Charles this afternoon and he won't be back until late tomorrow."

There were no further words between them as they mounted the staircase together and disappeared into her bedroom, closing the door behind them.

Later, when the heat of their first coupling had cooled and they lay spent together on her rumpled bed, they spoke of other things.

"Did you get to meet Dorrie Westlake at my party?"

"Yes, I did, and she seemed very receptive. I've been invited to the Taylors' ball next weekend, and she's supposed to be there, too."

"It's a shame that Jim will be gone. I'd like to watch you in action," she said throatily, running a hand down his chest.

"Why don't you attend with your father?" Wade asked, responding to her touch immediately, and he forgot all thought of Dorrie Westlake.

"Maybe I will," she said huskily as she kissed him again.

Chapter Sixteen

The sun's reflected glare off the crystal and snow-encrusted city was blinding as the morning dawned bright and clear. Knee-deep drifts of the frosty white powder, a legacy of last night's bitter wind, made travel even more difficult on all the streets and sidewalks. Groaning and stiff from the weather's abuse, St. Louis came awake slowly, shivering in protest as it struggled to break free of winter's hoary hold.

Jim sat in his cabin at his desk, staring blankly at the papers spread before him. Sleep had eluded him all night, and now he found himself tired yet unable to rest. Every time he'd stretched out on his bunk, memories of Murphy had assailed him.

Glancing around the deserted room, he was amazed at how lonely it seemed without her companionable presence. Even before their explosive night of love, Jim had come to enjoy her quick wit and easy manner; and now . . . he pushed away from the desk and stalked across the room to the connecting door. Throwing it wide, he stormed into her small chamber, hoping to find some clue that would lead him to her . . . something she might have forgotten in her haste to be gone. But the room was empty, totally devoid of any trace of Murphy. It was almost as if she'd never been there at all. Saddened and frustrated, Jim wandered back out into his own cabin and was surprised to come face-to-face with Ollie.

"There you are, Jimmy—I knocked but you didn't answer."

"Sorry." Jim's answer was preoccupied.

"Did you find anything?" When Jim looked at him questioningly, Ollie indicated the room. "Did she leave anything behind? Something we can use to find her?"

"No. Nothing."

"Damn." Ollie was as upset as Jim. "I hope she turns up. I miss her already."

"I do, too."

They looked at each other in resignation as they realized they had done all they could. All that was left to do was wait.

Following Sue into the parlor, Martin Montgomery asked her impatiently, "What is so important that you had to interrupt my breakfast with my wife?"

"A young boy just delivered this note and said that I should give it to you personally, in private, right away." She handed him an envelope.

"Who did you say delivered this?"

"I didn't recognize him, sir. He was just a boy. He said to make sure that you got the letter when you were alone."

Martin looked down at the envelope and immediately recognized the handwriting. His heart lurched, but he maintained his composure in front of Sue. "You may go."

"Yes, sir."

Once she had left the room, Martin ripped open the envelope with shaking hands. It was from Delight; he knew it.

Martin—

I understand that my mother's health has improved.

I am ready to return home, but it is important that we talk first, in private. Meet me at the Barnum Hotel on Second Street at 11 A.M.

—Delight

Martin broke out in a cold sweat. She was coming back. The moment he had been waiting for was here, yet he wasn't sure whether to be excited or worried. Not wanting to raise Clara's suspicions, he hurried back to her side.

"Was it important, darling?" she asked, her eyes shining with her love for her husband.

"Just business, but I will have to go out for a while this morning. Will you be all right alone?" he asked, coming to kiss her cheek.

"Of course. Sue will be here with me."

"Good. I'll be back as soon as possible."

With that he was gone, and Clara sat back, pondering her luck at having so young and handsome a man in love with her. Martin had been so very attentive during her recent illness, and, now, he had taken charge of most of her business affairs, too. Totally satisfied with her life, she went into the parlor to await his return.

Delight sat in the hired carriage outside the Barnum Hotel watching for Martin's arrival. Here, away from the intimacy of the house, she could tell him exactly what she was going to do without mincing any words, for she wanted to set things straight between them before returning.

When Delight saw Martin enter the hotel, she signaled her driver to go in after him. A moment later, they came back out and Martin boldly approached her vehicle. As he drew near, a shudder of revulsion shook her. She hadn't considered what her physical reaction to him was going to be, but, regardless, she was going to see this through. She was going home.

"Delight." he breathed her name softly. Martin couldn't believe his luck. She had come back! Maybe things weren't as bad as he'd originally thought.

"Get in, Martin," she said, keeping her voice cold and un-emotional.

Martin opened the door and climbed in. Sitting opposite her, he let his gaze run over her assessingly. She looked lovely as she sat wrapped warmly in a hooded, fur-lined cape, and his desire for her returned full-force. "You look well," he managed.

"No thanks to you." Her remarks left no doubt as to her feelings about him. The memory of his touch still made her flesh crawl and confirmed her determination never to have to suffer his attentions again.

"I can make it all up to you," he told her smoothly.

"I'm sure you'd like to try, but you're not going to get the chance."

"Really?" Settling back, Martin crossed his arms across his chest and tried to figure out what she was up to.

"We need to talk, Martin, and we're going to do it right here in full public view."

"Fine. Was there something in particular you wanted to talk about?" He spoke arrogantly, covering the nervousness he was feeling.

Delight stared at him. It was going to be difficult keeping herself under such strict control, but she knew it had to be done, for if Martin sensed any weakness in her he would use it to his advantage.

"I think we have a few things to settle between us."

"Such as?" His tone was mocking.

Delight looked up at him with determination. "Such as—if you ever come near me again, I will tell my mother in no uncertain terms exactly what happened between us."

Martin gazed at her steadily, almost unnerving her. "And do you really think she'll believe you?"

She faced him squarely. "Of course, for I have no reason to lie . . . whereas you have everything to lose and nothing to gain by such a story." When he said nothing, Delight continued. "I know that my mother loves you, Martin, and I don't want her to suffer any more than she already has."

"Yes," he replied with a certain smugness. "She does love me. Even more so now that I've nursed her back to health. She knows what a devoted husband I am."

Delight gave him a scathing look. "I hardly think devoted is the word, but I'm not going to discuss semantics with you. My mother's happiness is very important to me, and that's the only reason why I am not going to tell her the truth."

"How kind of you," he sneered. "Since you're the one who so blatantly encouraged me."

Delight had thought that he might try to switch the blame, and she was prepared for this tactic.

"Truly? I think it's highly improbable that I drugged myself. But at any rate, I'm not going to discuss that night with you—*ever*. As far as I'm concerned, it never happened. Do you understand?"

"Perfectly, Delight," he answered calmly, picking nonchalantly at a piece of lint on his jacket sleeve. "Is there anything else?"

"Yes. Rose is coming home with me. She will be my personal maid and companion. You're not to go near her, either."

"Believe me, my dear, Rose is the last woman I would want to warm me on a cold night." Then, looking at her slyly, his eyes filled with sexual suggestion, "You know I do enjoy your mother's complete affections now that she's recovered."

Delight didn't respond, wondering how her mother could suffer the man's possession.

"Shall we head home now? I'm sure Clara will be overjoyed by your unexpected return. Do you know the story I concocted to cover your unexplained absence?"

"Rose told me."

"Ah, Rose," he murmured, regretting that he hadn't been a little more forcefully persuasive in his dealings with her. "Are you prepared to embroider my tale to make it more palatable to your mother?"

"I'll do whatever is necessary to ensure my mother's happiness.

That includes tolerating you." She cut him to the quick, and he glanced at her sharply.

"You've sharpened your wit."

"Necessity breeds many things, Martin."

Delight gave the driver instructions. As the carriage jolted forward, Martin reviewed silently all that had been said. He was pleased by Delight's return and quite relieved by her decisions. At least, he wouldn't be losing his comfortable lifestyle.

Grateful for small favors, he immediately turned his attention to other things. Living under the same roof with Delight again was going to be pure torture for him, for he was now torn between his need for revenge and his still powerful desire for her. Martin wasn't sure what he was going to do, but he knew he would make her pay for his frustration and embarrassment, one way or another. Glancing across at her, he smiled to himself. Yes, he was really going to enjoy evening the score with Miss Delight de Vries.

Clara was thrilled by her daughter's return, and they spent the entire day in warm reunion. Delight glossed over the time she'd supposedly spent with her aunt and uncle and immediately set about caring for her mother, who, though she had improved, was still not in perfect health. Clara relished Delight's tender attentions, for she had always cherished her only child and had missed her greatly.

Martin, however, roamed the house like a cat on the prowl. He made a conscious effort to stay out of Delight's way, for he found her presence very disturbing. Haunted by his memories of the night in her room, he struggled to control the passion she aroused in him.

"Sir? Is there anything wrong?" Noting how upset Martin looked, Sue stood in the doorway of the study uncertain whether to enter or not.

"What?" He looked up quickly, confused for a moment. "No. No, nothing's wrong."

"I needed to dust in here, sir; that is if I won't be disturbing you."

"Come in, Sue," he invited, lecherous thoughts occurring to him as he looked at her as a woman for the first time. He needed a woman right now . . . one who could ease his lust and take his mind off Delight. "And close the door."

Sue gave him a curious look, but did as he instructed and then went straight to work. Busy with her dusting, she didn't notice Martin's heated gaze upon her.

Martin shifted uneasily in his chair as he imagined bedding Sue. Though his tastes usually ran to slimmer, less full-figured women, right now the thought of burying his face in her lush breasts stirred him greatly. Rising, he approached her, his footsteps muffled by the thick carpet.

"Sue?" His voice was thick with desire, but the maid did not recognize his passion.

"Oh!" she jumped, startled by his quiet approach. "Yes, sir. Do you need something?"

Martin gave her a warm smile as he thought of his "need." He reached out hesitantly and ran a hand down her arm. He kept his touch impersonal just in case she might protest, for the last thing he needed today was a reluctant wench.

"Do you enjoy your job here, Sue?"

"Oh, yes, sir," she told him eagerly. Sue admired Clara very much and she thought Martin to be the most handsome man she'd ever seen. "Your wife is wonderful and . . ."

"I'm not talking about my wife, Sue. Are you happy working for me?"

"Of course." Her eyes widened at the implication of his words. She had always found him attractive. "Sir." She added belatedly, with a certain intimate quality, "I love taking care of you."

"I had hoped you'd say that, Sue." His hand paused on her arm and drew her easily toward him. "You know, I'm sure I could find some more intimate duties for you to perform. Something that you might not find quite so taxing as ordinary household chores. And, since Rose is returning to our employ, it will be easy for me to arrange for you to have more free time to relax and enjoy yourself."

Sue was thrilled by his approach. She knew Martin wielded much power in the household and that by pleasing him she could easily better her lot in life.

"I'd like that, sir."

"Good, good." Martin was relieved. He pulled her against his chest and let his hands roam suggestively over her lush figure.

"Oh, sir," Sue moaned, her knees weakening at his bold touch.

Martin was pleased that he could arouse her so easily. "We'll do well together, Sue."

"Yes, sir."

"Finish your work here. We'll take care of our other 'business' later," he instructed.

Sue scurried to finish her dusting as Martin moved back to sit behind the desk.

He watched her progress about the room. At last he'd found a woman who wanted what he could give her, and he intended to take full advantage of the situation.

Delight undressed slowly that night. It had been a long, tiring day, and she was glad the worst was over. Her mother had been receptive to the idea of Rose's coming to stay with them again, and Delight was looking forward to her friend's moving in the next day. Martin had played his role perfectly, and, although she had sensed his eyes upon her often during the course of the day, she could find no actual fault with his behavior.

It felt wonderful to Delight to take a warm, scented bath again, but when she slipped into one of her own gowns, she suddenly missed Jim's nightshirt and wished that she'd brought it with her. Climbing into her own bed, she paused, and then hurried back to make sure she'd locked her door securely. Certain that she was safe, Delight went back to bed and curled up beneath her heavy blankets.

The winter night was clear and cold. The brightness of the full moon cast shadows as it reflected off the white brilliance of the snow. An unexpected feeling of loneliness swept over her as she huddled there beneath the warmth of her quilts, and, try as she might, she couldn't keep Jim from her thoughts.

In her sleepy mind, she saw him as he had been during their night of endless passion, powerful and potent, eager and tender. How she longed to hold him close and tell him of her love . . . sighing, she closed her eyes, but a vision of him stayed with her, and when she finally drifted off to sleep her dreams were of her captain . . . loving her . . . needing her . . . wanting her, forever.

It was late as Jim paced restlessly in his cabin. The walls seemed to be closing in on him, and he found the experience very irritating. He had never been uncomfortable in his own stateroom before, yet now all he wanted to do was escape from the memories it held for him. Memories of a moment in time so rare and beautiful that it could never be equaled again.

Angry at his inability to get his mind off Murphy, he sat down at the desk and once more tried to find solace in work. But, as he stared at the papers spread out before him, Jim knew that he was too tired even to make the attempt. Shuffling them aside, he pulled out his faithful bottle of scotch and poured himself a drink. He looked at the bottle sightlessly for a moment as he remembered the night Murphy had gotten it for him, and he couldn't stop the chuckle that came when he recalled her struggle to pull on her boots. How he wished he'd known of her feminnity before that last fateful night. . . .

He sighed and stood up, making his way into her small room. Leaning against the door frame, he took a deep drink from his glass and stared at her bed. All the nights they had shared—and yet he had only one to treasure. His heart felt heavy, and he quickly turned away. Draining the scotch, he placed the glass back on the desk and pulled on his coat. He would find no solace here tonight. With no further thought, he left the stateroom and headed for the pilothouse, hoping to find some interesting, mind-diverting companionship there.

Chapter Seventeen

Jim sat at the bar in the *Enterprise*'s saloon with Mark Clayton late the following afternoon. He was exhausted, and he looked it.

"Have you been sleeping all right?" Mark inquired, wondering at his friend's haggard looks.

"No, I haven't." Jim offered no explanation.

"Sick?"

"No, just a lot on my mind," Jim replied curtly.

"Anything I should know about?"

Jim gave him a quick look. "It'll pass."

"Good, because you're scheduled to leave tonight."

"Tonight?" Jim was taken by surprise. He hadn't expected this. He'd thought he had some extra time to continue his search for Murphy. "What's so important?"

"We've just heard that there's a group operating in the area who has pinpointed your line as the one carrying the payroll. It's important that we keep your schedule irregular from now on, so they don't know exactly when we're moving the bullion."

"How did they find out?"

"We're not sure, but I have the feeling it's someone on the inside leaking the information."

Jim nodded, understanding their predicament but irritated by it. "Do you have any idea who it might be?"

"No, so we can't take any chances. You haven't hired any more new help, have you?"

"Not since we talked last," Jim told him, his thoughts automatically going to Murphy and her disappearance. Surely, Murphy couldn't be a spy . . .

"And your new cabin boy?"

"He quit already. Couldn't handle the work, I guess. We don't have to worry about him." Jim automatically covered for her and then quickly wondered why.

"Good. We'll start making these diverting runs just to keep things unsettled."

"Will we still carry the guards?"

"I think it's best if we do."

"I hope your plan works."

"It should. But we'll have to be even more vigilant in our efforts to keep silent."

Jim nodded. "I guess I'd better get over to see Annabelle. I had told her that I wouldn't be leaving until the end of the week."

"I'm glad you have an understanding fiancée," Mark grinned.

"She has been so far, but if I keep pulling out on short notice she might not stay so patient." Jim forced a lighthearted smile.

"I'm sure you can find a way to make it up to her," Mark laughed, knowing of his friend's remarkable luck with women.

Jim just grunted, and they both stood to leave the bar. "What time tonight?"

"It'll be around eleven, but I'll see you again before you go."

"Fine. We'll be ready."

Annabelle was happy to see Jim and ushered him quickly inside before kissing him daringly.

"I'm so glad you came by," she told him as she took his coat. "Father's gone out for a while and we're all alone."

Her smile was suggestive as she led him into the privacy of the parlor.

"Can I get you anything?"

"No, not right now."

"Would you like to stay for dinner?"

"I won't be able to tonight, Annabelle." Jim sat down on the sofa and she joined him there, pressing close to his side.

"Oh?" She frowned her displeasure.

"I'm leaving again at midnight."

Annabelle pouted prettily. "But you promised you'd tell me ahead of time! You told me you'd be here all week."

Jim found her calculating feminine ways suddenly irritating. "I know and I'm sorry, but there's nothing I can do about it."

"But I thought you were your own boss."

"Most of the time I am, but we all have to answer to somebody." His answer was cryptic, and he left it that way.

"Well, I suppose we'll just have to enjoy what time we do have together," she murmured, as her mind raced in search of ways to get the news to Wade and the others.

Jim was relieved by Annabelle's reluctant acceptance, but he still felt uncomfortable in her presence and wished himself gone. How had his life gotten so complicated?

"You look tired, darling," Annabelle said soothingly as she moved nearer, pressing against him. "You've just been working too hard. What you need is a little relaxation. . . ."

Gently pulling Jim's head down, she kissed him eagerly. She had been wanting to know his passion since the night of the engagement party, and even long hours of loving in Wade's arms hadn't erased her desire for Jim.

But Jim, having played her little teasing games many times previously, was in no mood for it tonight. With a tight rein of control, he loosened her arms from about his neck and moved slightly away.

"But . . ." Annabelle was shocked. She had never been refused before! What was he doing? He had pursued her for weeks, and now that she was ready to give him what he wanted he was rejecting her.

"Not tonight, Annabelle."

"Don't you want me?" She was genuinely confused.

Jim stared at her for long moments, sensing the truth, yet not ready to speak it.

"Of course, I want you. You're very beautiful. But I must leave. I have a lot to get done before we shove off." He stood abruptly.

She nodded silently and followed his rapid exit from the parlor. "You'll be back soon?"

"Hopefully within ten days. I'll be in touch as soon as we get in."

"Well, all right," she said sullenly. "But you know I'll miss you," Annabelle added seriously. She had been anxiously waiting for a time when they could be together, and now he had to leave.

Jim managed to smile at her, and when she moved into his arms he kissed her. Annabelle put her whole body and soul into that kiss, but to Jim she was a clinging woman and he felt as if he were suffocating in her possessive embrace.

Releasing her, he pulled on his coat and was gone, leaving a frustrated and confused fiancée behind.

Marshall was always glad to see his brother, and this evening was no exception. He had been wondering how Jim's search for Murphy was going and waited eagerly now to hear whatever news Jim had.

"I've been thinking about you and also making inquiries. Have you had any luck?" Marshall asked as Jim joined him in the privacy of the study.

"No, what about you?"

"I haven't learned a thing. She didn't come back on her own?"

"No."

"I was hoping she would."

"So was I . . . Listen, there's something I'd like to discuss with you, if you've got a minute."

"Sure. What is it?"

"Mark came by the boat to see me this afternoon and he wants us to leave again, tonight."

"But there's no payroll, is there?"

"No, but Mark has heard that the word is out that we're carrying it, and he wants to start diversionary trips to confuse the issue."

Marshall nodded his agreement. "You're going to be gone a lot more, then."

"Right. In fact, I'll be back on the river by midnight."

"It makes sense. But what I want to know is, how did the information get out?"

"That's what I'm worried about. Do you think that Murphy—?" Jim let his voice drift off, not wanting to believe it.

"Murphy? A spy?" Marshall was incredulous for a moment and then paused to consider it seriously. "How did you meet her?"

"We just ran into her on the streets one night. Two drunks were about to beat her, and Ollie and I showed up just in time."

"Was there any way that the sympathizers could have known where you and Ollie were going to be in order to set it up?"

Jim thought back over that night, not wanting to believe it was possible. "I don't think so. We only decided at the last minute to go to Harry's. There was no way anyone else could have known. And besides," he rationalized, "why send a woman to do a man's job? Surely if they wanted to get a spy on board, they could have picked a more likely subject than Murphy."

Marshall had to agree with Jim's assessment. "That's true enough. She could hardly have defended herself against you. But what about those contracts she brought here to me?"

Jim almost flinched as he remembered. "She was slow getting back with them, but she said it was because you weren't at the office and she had to bring them here."

"She did show up with them, but did she read them or copy them on her way?"

Their eyes met in a concerned exchange.

"It is possible." Jim had to force the words out. "But why would she just up and leave like that?"

"That's simple enough. She probably felt that she'd gotten all the information she could."

"But she didn't have to make love to me that last night. She didn't learn anything from me in the 'heat of my passion.'" Jim wanted to believe that Murphy was innocent.

Marshall shrugged, turning away from his brother's confusion. "Maybe she really did fall in love with you. But the opportunity was there for her to get the information, and it does seem strange that she was able to disappear so quickly and so completely."

Jim didn't respond.

"We'll have to just wait and see what happens. There were no exact dates in those contracts either, so they can't really know too much. All they can be sure of is that we are the ones who are carrying the gold."

When Jim looked up at his brother, his face was an expressionless mask. "If you find her, I want her."

Marshall nodded and watched in silence as Jim left the room and the house.

Delight stood patiently in the middle of her room as Rose buttoned the back of the gown she was wearing for dinner.

"You know, neither Martin nor Mother noticed my hair."

"I told you that switch we bought matched perfectly. As long as we keep your hair done up on top of your head, we'll be all right. I just hope nobody asks you to wear it down." Rose smiled.

"Me, too." Delight grinned. "Did I tell you that we're going to the Taylors' ball Saturday night?"

"Things are finally getting back to normal for you, aren't they?"

"I hope so," Delight murmured, wondering if she would ever feel normal again. "Mother is feeling better, and it will be good to see my friends."

"Well, I'm just glad you're going. It will do you good." Rose finished the last button. "There, you're all buttoned up."

"Thank you."

"Is there a particular gown you'd like to wear Saturday night?"

"I haven't really given it much thought. Why don't you pick one for me?"

"You trust my judgment?"

"Of course. The last suit of clothes you picked out for me fit very well," Delight teased.

"You know, you did look cute," Rose returned. "Do you still have them? Maybe you could wear them to the ball . . . you'd certainly get all the attention."

Delight paled and replied almost vehemently. "I don't think I ever want to wear them again."

"I'm sorry, honey. I didn't know you were still so upset . . . you never have talked about the time you were gone, you know." Rose looked at the younger girl questioningly.

"There's nothing to talk about," Delight said, too quickly.

"You didn't get into any trouble while you were gone, did you?" Rose sensed that there was more to Delight's story than she was telling.

"No." Delight dismissed the subject curtly. "Now, why don't we take a look at those gowns before I go down to dinner?"

Thwarted in her attempt to get Delight talking about the two weeks she'd been missing, Rose let the matter drop. She knew that something had happened to her, but Delight evidently wanted to forget that those two weeks had ever happened. Rose respected her wishes, but she also knew that she would always be there for her if she ever needed to talk about it.

Nathan sat closeted with Wade and Annabelle in the shuttered study, his manner nervous and unsure.

"You say he's leaving tonight?"

"Yes, Father. He stopped by just a little while ago to tell me. He said that they were pulling out around midnight."

Nathan and Wade exchanged surprised looks. "Do you think this is it?"

"I don't know."

"Did he say anything else?" Nathan pushed. "Or give any reason for his abrupt change in plans?"

"No, nothing."

Wade frowned. "We have no proof that he's moving gold this time."

"I know. What if we were to go after him and then discover that he didn't have the bullion? It would be a wasted effort, and our cover would be blown. No, we've got to be careful. I'll get in touch with the other men and see if they can help keep the boat under surveillance. Maybe we can pick up some more information that way," Nathan said.

"I agree," Wade concurred. "I'll go down to the riverfront and see what I can find out. If I hear anything important, I'll report back."

"If we don't get word from you before midnight, we'll assume that there was no gold on board this trip."

"Right."

With that Wade was gone, anxious to discover what Mark Clayton and Jim Westlake were up to.

It was near two in the morning when Wade finally returned to the Morgan house, and he took extra care not to be seen by any neighbors who might wonder at his late-night activities. Nathan and Annabelle were both awake, waiting for him.

"Well?" Annabelle was as anxious as her father. "What did you find out?"

Wade helped himself to a glass of bourbon before telling them what he'd learned.

"They weren't carrying any gold that I could see, but I wasn't able to get close enough to really find out what was going on. There was a full armed guard on board, though."

"Could they be trying to divert our attention? Do you think they're on to us?"

"I don't know. I haven't heard any new rumors, but I'll keep checking. Nathan, you'd better get in touch with Gordon Tyndale and make sure that they're all keeping their mouths shut. The one thing we don't need is for Clayton and Westlake to find out about us."

"I'll pay Gordon a visit first thing in the morning."

"Good." Wade seemed to relax a bit. "Will I be seeing you both at the Taylors' Saturday night?"

"I've talked Father into taking me." Annabelle gave him a knowing look.

"I hope I'll have some luck with Westlake's sister Saturday."

"Keep us posted," Nathan encouraged.

"Yes, please do," Annabelle drawled, and Wade smiled at her, aware of her thoughts.

"I'll do that," he agreed, downing his drink. "Now, if you'll excuse me, I'd better be getting back. Nathan, let me know what Tyndale has to say for his little group. I'd be interested in knowing. I'll also keep you informed of any rumors I hear concerning the gold shipments and the changing of Westlake's schedule."

"Until the weekend, then." Nathan walked Wade to the door.

"Until then."

Chapter Eighteen

The Taylor mansion, so elegant in its Greek Revival style, was ablaze with lights on this cold winter's night, giving it a welcoming, festive appearance. The soft, muted strains of a waltz drifted across the moon-caressed, icy landscape as the carriages of the late-arriving guests lined up under the portico to discharge their passengers.

Indoors, Wade MacIntosh stood at the refreshment table surveying the myriad of couples swirling about the dance floor. He usually found this type of social event dull, but tonight he was of a different frame of mind. Tonight, the chase was on.

Wade had made it a point to arrive extra early just in case Dorrie Westlake did, too, but, so far, his planning had gone unrewarded. Making a definite effort not to overimbibe, he sipped casually from his glass of bourbon while keeping his attention directed to the entry hall and the guests who were just now coming in.

Wade had noted Annabelle and Nathan's arrival shortly after his own. Now they were making their way around the room, busily greeting all their friends and acquaintances. It amazed him that no one ever suspected Nathan Morgan of still being an ardent secessionist, for in the beginning he had been quite vocal about his feelings, even to the point of participating in a riot against a Union officer, Captain Nathaniel Lyon, who had arrested some Confederate troops. But that had been a few years ago, and somehow during the intervening years Nathan had managed to portray his position to his best advantage and now enjoyed not only the company of the most ardent of Union supporters, but also their trust.

Annabelle, Wade knew, was determined to play her part as the lonely fiancée tonight. They all knew that some of the Westlakes were going to be in attendance, and she wanted to impress them with her devotion. She wore a full-skirted off-the-shoulder gown of deep emerald green satin, and her beauty was flawless. Wade was one of many men who envied the absent Jim Westlake.

With knowing eyes, Wade observed her progress about the room, and when she finally reached his side he gallantly bent over her hand.

"Your beauty is unsurpassed here this evening, Miss Morgan." He kissed her hand, his tongue boldly caressing the soft flesh.

Annabelle stifled a gasp at the brazenness of his move and managed to smile at him serenely. "And your audacity is surpassed only by your passion!" Her tone was scolding, but her eyes sparkled with unfeigned delight.

"Thank you, my dear," Wade answered in deep, even tones, the undercurrents strong between them as they both remembered the last night of passion they had shared.

Annabelle wanted to say more, but her father's arrival at her side prevented the exchange. Wade shot her a smug look, pleased with himself that he'd gotten the last word with her, and then turned to greet Nathan.

"Nathan, so good to see you this evening."

"It's good to see you, too, Wade. How did your week go?"

"I'm afraid it was quite uneventful. And yours?"

"The same." Though they were mouthing small talk, both were aware of the underlying substance of their discussion.

"Wade," Annabelle broke in, nodding in the direction of the front entry hall, "I do believe my future in-laws have arrived. If you gentlemen will excuse me?"

"Of course, my dear." They both were gracious as she headed across the room.

Annabelle moved with grace and poise in the direction of the Westlakes, who were just now entering the ballroom. She noted with interest that Dorrie seemed somehow more attractive this evening, and she wondered if it was just her sudden awareness of her as a "rival" for Wade's attention or because she had never taken the time to really look at her before.

Tall and willowy, Dorrie Westlake was the female counterpart of her good-looking brothers. Her cloud of dark hair, which she preferred to wear loose, was now neatly arranged into a mass of looping curls. Her dark eyes were warm and reflected her intuitive intelligence, which she no longer tried to disguise with what she called "silly feminine airs." Dorrie had experienced much during the recent past, and she had matured far beyond her twenty-two years. Observing Annabelle's approach with barely concealed disgust, she spoke in an undertone to Renee.

"I told you she'd show up, even if Jimmy was out of town."

"Dorrie, be nice!" Renee corrected her opinionated sister-in-law. "Jim has chosen her, and that's enough for me."

"It may be enough for you now, but you weren't so happy about it when he first told you."

"I know, and that was a mistake. I should have been happy for him." Renee regretted now that she had not been totally supportive when Jim had announced his engagement to the family. "I didn't notice you raising any protest at the time."

Dorrie shrugged, "There wasn't any point then. But now that I've had a chance to see them together . . . and apart . . ." She let it drop as Annabelle joined them.

"Annabelle, what a pleasant surprise. I didn't know you were going to be here this evening." Renee greeted her quickly, giving her a small hug.

"Father wanted to come, and I thought it would be good to get out and socialize for a night. It's so lonely with Jim gone all the time."

"I'm sure it is." Renee spoke with sympathetic understanding, determined to treat her as family.

Dorrie was of a different frame of mind, and she cringed inwardly at Annabelle's sugary sweetness. She had known her for several years and did not like her. Dorrie considered herself a good judge of character, and, in her opinion, Annabelle didn't have one. Having watched her in action, Dorrie knew her future sister-in-law to be a totally selfish person who never gave a serious thought to anything but her own desires. She had not spoken her mind to Jim for fear of alienating him, but Annabelle definitely would not have been the girl she would have picked for him to marry. Shrugging mentally, Dorrie realized that her opinion didn't matter anyway. Jim was a grown man and she supposed he knew what he wanted. Or, at least, she hoped he did.

"Hello, Annabelle. You look stunning, as usual."

Dorrie's attention returned to the present at Marshall's comment.

"Thank you." Annabelle preened under Marshall's manly regard. He was a handsome devil, and had he been unattached Annabelle was sure that she would have had a hard time trying to choose between the two brothers. "Dorrie, it's good to see you again. Your dress is very becoming."

"Thanks." Dorrie's reply was short and to the point, and she was relieved when she looked up and saw Mark Clayton coming toward her. "If you'll excuse me?" She begged off, anxious to be away from Annabelle's phoniness.

"Dorrie, darling." Mark took her hand and smiled at her, his affection for her quite obvious. "I'm so glad you came."

For years, Mark had loved Dorrie from afar, and her betrothal at the beginning of the war to Paul Elliot, a lieutenant attached to Captain Nathaniel Lyon's command, had seemed to dash all his hopes of ever winning her hand. Then, when Paul met his untimely death in a military confrontation with Confederate sympathizers, Dorrie had been devastated. It had been over two years now, and, though she was not in mourning, she seemed to him to hold herself aloof from any close involvements with men . . . especially soldiers.

Looking at her, Mark knew he would never love any other woman, and that if it took the rest of his life to convince her of his devotion, he would do it.

"I'm glad you're here. I wasn't sure if you were in town or not. . . ." Dorrie had always enjoyed Mark's company and to-night was no exception.

"I didn't have to travel with Jim this trip."

"Good." She met his gaze for a moment and was startled by the intensity of longing she saw there.

"Will you dance with me?"

"I'd love to," she agreed, and he led her out onto the floor just as a waltz began.

They blended in with the other dancers as they swayed and twirled about the ballroom, Mark totally absorbed in the wonderful sensation of at last holding her in his arms and Dorrie relieved to have been saved from a boring conversa-tion with Annabelle.

Renee looked up at Marshall, her eyes aglow. "I certainly hope Mark wins her over soon. He loves her so."

Marshall grinned at his wife. "You're an incurable ro-mantic."

"You're complaining?"

"Never." He hugged her to his side. "But not everyone is as lucky as we were."

"You don't think they'll ever get together?" Renee was sad-dened by the possibility. She thought a lot of Mark Clayton and she knew instinctively that Dorrie would be happy with him.

"I can't predict what Dorrie will do anymore. She's become so independent that it's hard to say."

"I know."

Renee was reluctant to agree with her husband's assess-ment, but she had to. Since Paul Elliot's death, Dorrie had changed. Once her period of mourning for him had ended, she had seemed encased in ice. She had refused to let any men court her and had remained deliberately distant with those few she did consider friends. Renee knew that Dorrie was only trying to protect herself against further heartache, but in the process she was missing out on all the joys that life truly had to offer. Though Paul was dead, Dorrie's life had gone on, and Renee was sure that Dorrie had not fully accepted that yet.

"Do you want some punch or would you like to dance?" Marshall invited, his hand resting possessively at her waist.

"I'd love to waltz," she told him eagerly before turning to Annabelle. "Annabelle, do you mind if we desert you for a few minutes?"

"Not at all, providing I can claim your handsome husband for a dance later?"

"It will be my pleasure," Marshall told her graciously before leading Renee out onto the dance floor.

Annabelle watched them go, her eyes narrowing in thought. So, Mark Clayton was in love with Dorrie. That could complicate things. Knowing that she should tell Wade the news, she casually let her gaze sweep the crowd, trying to locate them.

Though Wade stood in a far corner watching Dorrie Westlake dance with Mark Clayton, his thoughts were of Annabelle. He wanted to sweep her into his arms and waltz her about the room, but he knew that such a rash action would soon set tongues to wagging.

Forcing his attention to Dorrie, he was well aware that he should make his move. Setting his mind on a course of action, Wade waited until the music had ended and then made his way, unobtrusively, to her side.

"Good evening, Miss Westlake," he greeted her warmly.

"Good evening, Captain MacIntosh. Do you and Captain Clayton know each other?" Dorrie asked as he joined them.

"Yes, we've met before. Captain Clayton, how are you?"

"I'm fine, MacIntosh, and you?"

"Just fine. I'd like to ask Miss Westlake for a dance, if you don't mind?"

"Dorrie?" Mark stepped back to let her make the decision, hoping futilely that she would refuse and stay with him.

"Captain MacIntosh, I'd be delighted." She took his arm. "I'll see you later, Mark."

Mark watched them leave, his expression guarded, his heart once again disappointed. Would he ever be able to break through the defenses she'd erected against becoming involved with a man again and win her heart? Frustrated but not defeated, Mark moved silently to the refreshment table.

Annabelle observed Wade's luck with Dorrie and decided that her warning was immaterial. After all, what woman could resist Wade MacIntosh when he was his most charming? Confident that Wade would win Dorrie over, she went in search of her father.

Martin sat next to Clara in the Montgomery carriage, but his eyes were on Delight. As usual, he was fighting his desire for her. Even an illicit rendezvous with Sue a little earlier had not relieved the pulsing passion Delight aroused in him. The one thought that kept Martin from total frustration was the fact that he would be able to manuever her into dancing with him tonight. He knew it would be tricky. He would have to catch her in front of a group of her friends so she couldn't refuse him, but he didn't care. All he wanted was to touch her and hold her as closely as possible, even if it was in front of a hundred people.

Delight was glad when the carriage finally drew to a halt in front of the Taylors' home. She had felt the intensity of Martin's gaze upon her during the whole ride and she was eager to get away from his heated scrutiny. Though he had been totally compliant with her demand that he never come near her or Rose again, Delight still felt threatened by him and she wished that there was some way she could escape from his subtle domination.

"Here we are." Martin spoke jovially as he climbed down from their vehicle.

Turning to aid Clara in her descent, he handed her down and then reached for Delight. She knew that she could do nothing to avoid his handling of her, but the feel of his hands on her waist, even through the thickness of her coat, was repulsive, and she couldn't suppress a shiver of disgust.

"Cold, my dear?" He asked.

"A little," Delight murmured in response, hurrying away toward the welcoming warmth of the brightly lighted house.

Martin chuckled to himself as he followed after her with Clara on his arm.

"It feels so good to be going out again," Clara told him as they started up the front stairs.

"I missed socializing, too, but your health is always foremost in my mind."

"You're so sweet, Martin." Clara pressed his hand in appreciation of his sentiment. "I'm so lucky to have you."

Delight was far enough ahead of them that they couldn't see her expression, and she was glad. His declarations left her nauseous and aching to tell her mother what Martin was really like. . . .

With a gaiety she little felt, Delight went into the Taylors' followed closely by her mother and stepfather. After shedding their coats, they entered the ballroom and were immediately surrounded by friends who were eager to welcome Clara back after her extended illness.

As soon as it was possible, Delight eased herself away from Martin's side and went in search of a glass of punch. In truth, she wished that she could drink a quick bourbon, for she well remembered the false bravado it had instilled in her the night she'd had her first taste of it with Ollie. But young ladies did not imbibe straight whiskey, so she settled for a mildly spiked punch that did little to settle her taut nerves.

"Delight!" Renee's friendly call drew her attention and she smiled in relief as she saw her approaching. "I didn't know you were back home! When did you return?"

"The first of the week," Delight confirmed as they embraced with affection.

"Is your uncle well?"

"He'll be fine, I'm sure." Delight told the half truth easily, but she had to stifle the urge to jump nervously at the sound of Marshall's voice coming up behind her. She had never realized that Jim and Marshall sounded so much alike. "Marshall, it's good to see you again."

"Delight, you look as lovely as ever."

"Thank you, kind sir," she grinned up at him, marveling suddenly at how much he resembled Jim.

Marshall sensed something odd about the way Delight was looking at him and he gave her a curious half smile. "Is something wrong?"

Delight blinked, confused by the deviousness of her own subconscious. "No, not at all. I was just thinking of how handsome you are, but I didn't want to say anything because I know how jealous your wife gets." She was proud of herself for her quick comeback and laughed in good humor with Renee.

"I suppose he could be considered good-looking if you go for older men," Renee teased, looking up at him in a mocking, critical way.

"Have I aged well?" he quipped.

"I did a good job when I picked you. You're holding up beyond all expectations," she retorted, and he laughed loudly.

Delight listened to their loving banter silently, knowing how deep their feelings for each other really went. Renee had told her of their tempestuous courtship and of the tragedy that had struck right after their marriage, when Marshall had been kidnapped and presumed dead. Only the strength of Renee's love had seen her through those terrible months when she'd been so alone and pregnant with Roger. Delight envied their deep devotion to each other and couldn't help but wonder what it would have been like if she and Jim had fallen in love.

She had tried not to think of Jim all week, but he had constantly haunted her thoughts. She had tried to hate him, too, but she couldn't. The love she felt for him ran too deep; instead, she felt a deep disappointment that he hadn't believed in her. His accusations had been so cruel. . . .

"So much has happened while you were gone . . . I just don't know where to begin," Renee was saying, and Delight smiled politely.

"Like what?"

"Well, you know how I'd been wanting you to meet Marshall's brother, Jim?"

"Yes." Delight kept her face frozen, knowing what news was coming next.

"He went and announced his engagement to Annabelle Morgan without any forewarning at all."

"Really? Annabelle Morgan . . . I don't believe I know her."

"She's here tonight," Renee confided. "I'll introduce you as soon as I see her again."

Wonderful—Delight thought. It was bad enough that she had to keep away from Martin all night, but suffering through Jim's fiancée was going to definitely take all the fun out of the evening.

"I guess it wasn't meant to be," she managed to respond lightly, looking absently around the room.

"I suppose," Renee said simply. "But I did so think that you two would have liked each other." She shook her head in confusion.

"I'm sure my Prince Charming is out there somewhere. I just haven't met him yet," Delight told her confidently.

As they were talking, Annabelle joined them.

"May I have this dance, Mr. Westlake?" she approached Marshall, smiling at him coyly.

"Of course," he responded gallantly before introducing her to Delight. "Annabelle Morgan, this is Delight de Vries, a dear friend."

"It's a pleasure, um, Delight, is it? What an unusual name," Annabelle said with little real interest.

"My father chose it."

"I'm sure." Annabelle dismissed the conversation, feeling she had little in common with this young woman. "Marshall, shall we?"

Marshall was stunned at Annabelle's crude attitude toward

Delight, but could do nothing more than quickly sweep her out onto the dance floor. Renee looked at Delight helplessly.

"I'm sorry."

"For what?" Delight hurried to mask her hurt. "I'm used to people wondering about my name. I think I'll go see how my mother's doing, if you don't mind?"

"Of course." Renee felt that something was terribly wrong, but Delight seemed unwilling to discuss it. She watched quietly as Delight disappeared into the hall and then turned back to watch her husband dance with Annabelle.

Delight stood with a few acquaintances, listening halfheartedly to their gossip. What had seemed interesting to her before no longer held her attention. She found this girl-talk extremely boring and wished idly that Ollie was here so they could have a good "man-to-man."

Smiling wryly to herself, she was about to turn away when Martin's voice assailed her.

"Here you are, Delight. I was hoping to find you. Would you care to dance?"

The boldness of his invitation astounded her, but she also knew there was no way she could refuse him.

"Of course, Martin."

Without hesitation, he led her out onto the ballroom floor just as a waltz was beginning. To those watching them, his embrace seemed friendly, but Delight felt like a butterfly caught and held, pinned to a mat. The heat of his hand on her back dredged up memories she had tried to put from her mind, and she had to force herself not to cringe.

"You dance divinely, my dear. Has anyone ever told you that?"

"No."

"Well, you do. Are you having a good time?" Martin tried to get her into a conversation, but Delight would have none of it.

"Marvelous."

"I would like us to at least appear to be friends, Delight," he finally remarked with a certain threat in his voice.

"Or?"

"Or I can make life uncomfortable for you."

"Really?"

"I do control the purse strings now, you know."

"But I have a trust fund."

"Which will not become yours until you're twenty-one."

"So?"

"So, for the sake of your mother, look like you enjoy dancing with me. Not as a lover but as a friend."

"Naturally," she sneered, giving him a forced smile. "Is this good enough?"

Martin glared at her for a moment but let it pass. "For a start . . . for a start." He had plans for her. . . .

They finished the dance in silence, Delight longing to be away from him and Martin relishing every second that her body was touching his.

Dorrie smiled easily at some remark Wade made as they walked to the refreshment table together.

"Are you enjoying yourself?" he inquired, sensing her aloofness and wanting to break through it.

"Yes," she answered blandly, not wanting to encourage him too much.

Wade nodded in response to her simple reply. He was frustrated and getting angry. What was wrong with this woman? Was there no getting through to her? Though he had managed to get them onto a first-name basis, she seemed totally uninterested in him as a man and that was a reaction Wade was not accustomed to.

"Can I get you something to drink?"

"Punch will be fine," she told him easily as she greeted some of her other friends, and Wade went after her drink, leaving her alone momentarily.

Returning with a cup of punch, he handed it to her and then escorted her to two vacant seats nearby.

"Shall we rest for a while?"

"That sounds good." Dorrie agreed and then, knowing the best way to keep a man happy, she asked him about herself. "Where are you from, Wade? Have you been in St. Louis long?"

"Yes, I was with Captain Lyon back in sixty-one and now I'm with . . ."

Dorrie's interruption stopped him. "You were with Nathaniel Lyon's troops?"

"Yes," Wade answered seriously, glad that his ploy had worked. He had not been with Lyon, but he knew that her fiancé, Paul Elliot, had been. Elliot had been killed in an early skirmish between Union forces and Confederate sympathizers, and Wade was not above using his death to get to Dorrie.

"Then you might have known my fiancé, Paul Elliot?"

"Elliot?" Wade managed to look pensive. "He was killed, wasn't he?"

Dorrie looked away quickly, revealing just how deeply she was still affected by the thought of her lost love.

"Yes," she murmured softly.

Immediately pressing his advantage, Wade took her hand, "Dorrie, I'm sorry if I've upset you. . . ." And he almost grinned at his success when she pressed his hand intimately.

"No, I'm all right . . . really."

"Would you like to walk out into the hall for a few minutes?" Wade was anxious to get her away from the prying eyes that surrounded them.

"Yes, please." Dorrie set her glass aside and allowed Wade to escort her from the room.

Once out of the ballroom, Dorrie looked up at Wade with hopeful eyes. "Did you know him?"

Wade managed a pensive look. "Was he blond? Not too tall?"

Dorrie nodded, and, stifling a small sob, she turned quickly away. She was furious with herself for her weakness, but Paul had meant so very much to her.

"Dorrie . . ." Wade slipped an arm gently about her waist after making sure they were alone. Drawing her nearer, he caressed her back in a soothing motion.

"Marshall, what do you think about . . . ?" Mark's conversation came to an abrupt end as he and Marshall stepped into the hall to find Dorrie and Wade MacIntosh in a seemingly heated embrace.

Mark drew himself up stiffly as his face paled. Dorrie? MacIntosh? "Marshall, if you'll excuse me?" Holding himself rigid, he turned and left the house.

Marshall watched Mark leave and then faced his sister. "Dorrie? I believe Renee wanted to talk with you about something important."

Wade had observed the entire scenario with barely disguised delight. In one bold move, he had eliminated Mark Clayton as a possible rival and broken through Dorrie's icy reserve. Pleased with himself, he reluctantly let her go.

"I'll speak with you later," he told her intimately.

"Thank you." Giving her brother a cold look, she followed him into the ballroom.

"Dorrie," Marshall intoned under his breath as they were crossing the dance floor to join Renee, "I usually don't interfere in your affairs, but . . ."

"That's right, you usually don't, so don't start now!" she hissed at him, startling herself and him by her vehemence. With her head held high, she hurried ahead of him, leaving him at a loss for words.

Mark rode quickly away from the Taylor house. The cold night air helped to clear his head, but it did little to control the angry jealousy that burned inside of him. How could she? After all the time he'd spent trying to win her over, she let

Wade MacIntosh step in and take her in his arms in one night.

Furious with Dorrie and furious with himself for being so patient with her, Mark galloped back to his quarters. No longer would he play the nice guy, content with just a few kind words and an occasional smile from her. He was fed up with her cool, distant manner. He loved her, damn it! He had loved her for years, and it was time she realized that he was not her lap dog! He was a man with the same needs as any other man.

Determination set in as Mark undressed and lay down. He was going to show Dorrie just how much she meant to him. He had been bending to her wishes for too long now. But before he changed his tactics with her, he was going to do some serious checking on Captain Wade MacIntosh. There had been something he didn't like about the man even before he'd made his move on Dorrie, and Mark was determined to find out everything he possibly could about his background.

Delight undressed slowly, glad that Rose had gone on to bed. What a horrible night! Between Annabelle Morgan's smugness and Martin's "friendly" overtures, she was exhausted— mentally and physically.

It had never occurred to Delight that she would run into Annabelle tonight, for they had always seemed to travel in different social circles. But there she'd been, in all of her blond beauty, flashing Jim's engagement ring and bemoaning the fact that he had been called away on business.

Tears stung her eyes as she thought of Annabelle and Jim together. What a handsome couple they would make. Delight sighed wearily. She was so tired. Nothing seemed to be right in her life. While it was true that she was back home and her mother was well, all she could think about was the night she'd spent in Jim's arms and how perfect it had been.

Climbing into bed, she curled on her side and hugged her pillow to her. Somehow Delight knew she would have to find a way to get over Jim. She couldn't go on like this forever . . . remembering only his love and not his rejection. He had been so furious that morning. . . .

And the thought that she might come face-to-face with him at some future social gathering made her shiver. No, she didn't need that kind of confusion in her life. She would make certain that she steered clear of Jim and Annabelle.

Closing her eyes, she let sleep overtake her, sweeping her away into the soft clouds of her dreams where a loving Jim eagerly awaited her return.

Chapter Nineteen

Jim strode wearily down the texas deck, his broad shoulders hunched against the vicious assault of the bitter winter wind. Exhaustion showed plainly on his handsome features as he let himself into his office. Quickly shutting the door behind him, he shed his greatcoat and turned up the lamp.

Home . . . at last they were heading home. His relief was overwhelming. This trip had already dragged on much too long, as far as he was concerned. Opening his bottom desk drawer, he extracted a half-full bottle of scotch and a semi-clean tumbler. Sloshing a liberal amount into the glass, he drank it eagerly in hopes that its fiery warmth would ease the tight knot of tension deep within him.

Sitting down at his desk, Jim leaned back in his chair. Though he was tired, for the first time in days he felt good about himself. He had taken this time on the river to analyze his situation, and he knew now what he was going to do.

The knock at the door brought a "come in," from him, and Ollie wasted no time getting in out of the cold.

"Problems, Ollie?"

"No. I'm fine. What about you?" he asked, taking off his coat and accepting the drink Jim was offering.

"As of right now, I'm fine, too."

Ollie looked at him questioningly. "Oh? I know you've had a lot on your mind lately . . . have you finally worked things out?"

"Lord, I hope so." Jim finished his scotch and put his glass away. He had had enough of drinking for a while. He needed a clear head from now on in.

"So, what have you decided?"

He shrugged. "I've done everything I can do where Murphy is concerned." His tone was almost bitter as he continued. "She obviously doesn't want to be found."

As the long days had passed on this trip, Marshall's suggestion that Murphy might have been a spy had instilled doubts in his mind . . . doubts that had eroded Jim's idealized, romantic view of what had taken place between them that night.

Ollie nodded. "So what are you going to do now?"

"Nothing. I've wasted enough time looking for her."

Jim had now managed to convince himself that his time with Murphy had been a momentary aberration . . . a moment in time magnified beyond all reality by his overactive imagination. Surely no woman could have been as wonderful as he had imagined Murphy to be. Why should he ruin the rest of his life chasing after a dream that in all probability had existed only in his mind?

"Then you're going to let her go?"

"I have to." He looked at Ollie grimly. "I have my own life to live. I can't spend the rest of my days searching for a woman who doesn't exist."

"Murphy was no figment of your imagination, Jimmy." Ollie defended her in her absence.

"Maybe not." Then Jim blurted out, his manner hostile, "But she damn well could have been a spy!"

"Murphy?" Ollie was incredulous.

"You're damn right! Right after she disappeared, the word was out that we were the ones carrying the gold."

"And you think Murphy had something to do with it?"

"She hand-carried the contracts to Marshall. She had ample opportunity to read them." The possibility of her involvement still made Jim miserable, but he knew Ollie should know the truth.

"Murphy wasn't a spy," Ollie stated bluntly. "I know it, and so do you."

Jim scowled at his friend. "How can you be so sure? It would certainly explain her disappearance."

"Maybe so, but there could have been other reasons for her leaving like that." Ollie wanted to go on, but he sensed Jim's agitation and let the subject drop. If it was easier for him to believe the worst about Murphy, so be it. The long hours of searching for her had certainly taken their toll on him, and he understood Jim's need to get on with his life.

"We'll never know, will we?" His tone was sarcastic.

"I don't suppose we will."

Having finally spoken out loud the thoughts that had been haunting him ever since he'd left St. Louis, Jim felt as if a great weight had been lifted off his shoulders. His conclusions were logical; his decision to go ahead with his marriage to Annabelle was sound.

"You're staying with Annabelle, then?"

"Yes."

It was only a short time later that Ollie left Jim's cabin. He couldn't help but feel that Jim was making a big mistake by continuing his betrothal to Annabelle Morgan, but with Murphy gone there was no argument he could use to deter him.

After Ollie had gone, Jim walked slowly over to his bunk and lay down. Thoughts of that night with Murphy assailed him, but he staunchly pushed them from his mind. What had happened between them had been a mistake, and it was in the past. He had his own future to think about, and his future was with Annabelle.

Annabelle crossed the room to join Wade on the sofa. "How are you doing with Dorrie?"

Wade chuckled cynically. "It's amazing what dredging up a dead fiancé can do for you."

"What do you mean?"

"I was having a hard time breaking through that reserve of hers, so I brought up Paul Elliot."

"And?" She eagerly anticipated his next ploy.

"I told her that I'd been serving under Lyon the same time he was. I even convinced her that I'd known him."

Annabelle laughed delightedly. "She believed you?"

"Totally. You would have been amazed by the transformation that took place. She went from an ice maiden to a forlorn, vulnerable woman in a matter of just a few sentences." Wade was smug.

"How do you do it?"

"I haven't accomplished anything yet, my love," he warned her.

"I'm sure it's just a matter of time. When are you planning on seeing her again?"

"I didn't have the opportunity to set anything up with her. Mark Clayton and Marshall caught us in the hallway."

"Caught you? Doing what?"

"Nothing spectacular. I was just comforting her, but to them it must have looked quite scandalous. Clayton stormed out of the house and Westlake told her his wife was looking for her."

"Oh, how charming. You almost compromised her." Annabelle couldn't help but smile. She had known that Wade would succeed. "I'm so proud of you, but what are you going to do now?"

"Wait."

"Wait?"

"If I read Miss Dorrie Westlake right, she'll be contacting me, and soon."

"Do you really think so?"

"I'd bet on it," Wade answered confidently.

Dorrie stared at the note she had just written and hesitated. Should she send it? Never before had she done anything so brazen . . . unattached females just did not write notes requesting meetings with single men. But surely the chance to hear more about Paul was worth it. . . . Without further debate, she sent the note.

Clara and Delight wandered happily through the shops on Veranda Row. It was their first shopping spree together since Clara had been ill, and they were enjoying every minute of it. Delight was overjoyed that her mother was at last fully recovered, and they had spent the entire afternoon just relaxing and being happy in each other's company.

"I have a wonderful idea, darling," Clara told her daughter affectionately as they paused outside of a dressmaker's shop.

"What, Mother?"

"I think we should have a party. It's been so long since we've done any real entertaining."

"You're right. But are you sure you're up to it?" Delight asked.

"I'm fine now, so don't worry about me. It will be great fun, don't you think? And, of course, we'll need new gowns." Clara loved to be extravagant when it came to clothes.

"It's not necessary," Delight hastened to reassure her.

"It may not be necessary, but it does sound exciting." Taking Delight by the arm, she led her into the shop. "Come on, we're going to buy the most beautiful gowns in St. Louis. And if we can't find what we want, we'll order them made."

An hour and a half later, they were on their way home, exhausted but pleased with the success of their trip.

"Will two weeks give us enough time?" Clara was growing more excited by the minute as she planned the upcoming party.

"It should. I'll check with Rose and Sue to make sure they can get everything done in time. But I don't think it'll be a problem."

"Good. I'll tell Martin when we get home. I'm sure he'll enjoy entertaining once again. We haven't done it in so long." Clara paused, looking at Delight thoughtfully. "You did like the pattern we picked for your gown, didn't you?"

"Oh, yes. It's going to be beautiful. And I love the matte taffeta. But you don't think that the color is too bold for me, do you?"

"Nonsense. You'll look stunning in it. The deep cranberry color suits you; it will set your hair off perfectly."

"I've never worn that shade before, but, I must admit, I did like it."

Clara patted her hand. "You'll be the most gorgeous woman there. Wait and see. Now, what shall we serve?"

Their conversation turned to the mundane as their carriage arrived back at their home.

Dorrie was pacing the study restlessly, and Renee looked up at her from the sofa where she sat busily working on her needlepoint.

"What on earth is bothering you today? You're nervous as a cat."

Feeling a bit guilty for not having told Renee what she'd done, Dorrie faced her and prepared to explain. "I've invited a friend over this afternoon."

"That's nice, dear, but why are you so jumpy? All you've done all morning is wander through the house. . . ."

"I've invited Wade MacIntosh." She said it in an almost defiant tone of voice, and Renee had enough sense not to show her displeasure at the news.

"Oh?" she responded as nonchalantly as she could.

Dorrie relaxed visibly. "I thought you'd be upset."

"Whatever for? This is your home, just as it is ours, and you're free to invite over whomever you choose. What time are you expecting him?"

"Around two."

"I'll try to make myself inconspicuous."

"Thanks," Dorrie grinned at Renee.

"You're welcome." She smiled back in understanding.

When Wade knocked at the door a little while later, Dorrie answered it herself and graciously ushered him inside.

"Good afternoon, Dorrie. You're looking lovely, as always."

"Thank you, Wade." She took his coat and then led him into the parlor. "You know my sister-in-law, Renee, don't you?"

"Of course. Mrs. Westlake, nice to see you again."

"You, too, Wade," Renee greeted him cordially. "How have you been?"

"Just fine."

Renee watched Wade covertly. "Good. Well, if you two will excuse me, I'll leave you to your own devices."

Wade stood as she left the room and then sat back down as Dorrie called the maid and ordered that refreshments be brought in to them.

"Is tea all right with you, Wade?"

"That will be fine."

Returning to join Wade on the sofa, Dorrie was relieved that everything had gone well. Knowing how Marshall felt about her involvement with Wade, she had not expected Renee to be so cooperative.

When the maid returned with the tray, Dorrie took it from her and poured them each a cup of the steaming brew. "Here you are."

Wade took the cup and set it gingerly aside, for it was too hot to drink just yet. "You've been well?"

"Yes. And you?"

"I've missed you, Dorrie," Wade told her with a sincerity that would have fooled even the most perceptive miss.

Dorrie blushed, confused by his sudden confession. She hadn't expected such an ardent declaration from him. She liked him as a friend, but her real interest in inviting him here was to find out more about Paul.

"I didn't mean to embarrass you."

"You didn't really embarrass me, Wade. You just surprised me."

"Why? Surely you realize that I care for you?" When she didn't respond, Wade knew he was moving too fast. "I'm sorry; here I've gone and upset you again, when all I really wanted to do was have the chance to visit with you."

Dorrie smiled at him as her nervousness left her. "I did, too . . . want to visit, that is."

"You want to talk about Paul, don't you?" He looked at her questioningly.

"If you don't mind," she said hopefully. "It's not often that I meet someone who knew him."

"We weren't well acquainted, mind you, but I do recall meeting him on several occasions. And I was there that last fateful day. . . ."

"Oh."

"He died a senseless death, but I'm sure you know that already. It was so futile . . . the crowd was unruly and the shots were fired at random. No one ever knew who fired first, but it didn't matter after it was over. The damage had already been done."

Dorrie sighed. "I know. We tried to find out more at the time, but everything was all so confused. . . ."

"Dorrie?" Wade drew her thoughts back to the present.

"What?"

"I don't want us to dwell on the past." He took her hand gently. "I like you, and I want us to be . . . friends."

"Why, we are friends," she remarked.

"Good. I'm glad."

Dorrie smiled at him warmly. "So am I."

Wade returned her smile, pleased that she was opening up

to him. With very little effort on his part, he had won her confidence. Now, with a little serious courting, he would have her right where he wanted her.

They passed long minutes in polite social conversation before Wade finished his tea and decided it was time to go.

"I'd better be going."

"So soon?" Dorrie had been enjoying his company, and her expression reflected her disappointment.

"Duty calls," he told her regretfully, and in truth he did regret having to leave. But he didn't want to push his luck with her too far just yet. Standing, he headed for the hall. "May I see you again?"

"I'd like that," she told him.

"I'll be in touch." He bent over her hand in courtly fashion.

The unexpected sensation of his lips on her flesh tingled through her, and she watched with some confusion as he left the house.

It was four days later that the *Enterprise* finally docked at her home port, and the travel-weary riverboatmen were definitely ready to celebrate their homecoming. Jim and Ollie stood in the pilothouse watching the unloading taking place below.

"I'm really afraid that we're never going to recover all the business we've lost since the beginning of the war, with the river's being closed to the gulf, Ollie." Jim was prophetic in his statement.

"I know. I've been talking to the men on the Missouri run, and, from what I can find out, everything's being shipped North now, through Chicago."

"It only makes sense for them to do it, but it doesn't make it any easier for me to accept."

Ollie nodded. "Things always have a way of changing, even when you don't want them to."

"I know," Jim agreed and then asked, "Can you handle things here? I've got a few important calls to make."

"Sure. We're almost done. You go on ahead. Do you want to meet me at Harry's later?"

"I don't know. I've got to pay Annabelle a visit, and then I want to stop by and see Marsh for a while."

"You'll be late, then."

"Probably. But if I can make it, I'll be there by midnight. All right?"

"Sure." Ollie watched as Jim left the pilothouse on his way to the Morgans', and he wondered what would happen if Murphy would show up. The possibility made him smile, and he turned back to his duties, his mood considerably lighter.

Chapter Twenty

"Mr. Westlake is here to see you, ma'am," The maid announced to Annabelle as she lay upon her bed resting.

Her eyes sparkled at the news and she got up quickly. "Tell him I'll be right down, and then come back and help me dress."

"Yes, ma'am."

Thrilled that he'd returned, Annabelle hurriedly selected her most becoming day gown from her wardrobe and spread it out on the bed to await the maid's help in putting it on. Checking her hair, she smoothed a loose curl back into place and dabbed a bit of her favorite perfume behind each ear. Satisfied with the way she looked, she sat at her vanity table and waited impatiently for the maid's return.

Thank heaven he was back! It had only been ten days, but to Annabelle it had seemed an eternity. She hoped he was as anxious to see her as she was to see him. They hadn't parted on the best of terms, and she was determined to make it up to him. Realizing now that he did not respond to pouting feminine tactics, she would take care never to make that mistake with him again.

Annabelle was going to do everything she could to prove her "love" to Jim while he was home this time. Somehow she would make sure that they had no more interruptions. She wanted him and she was going to have him, even if it was just for a little while.

When the maid returned, Annabelle dressed with care and then prepared to leave her room.

"He's waiting for you in the parlor, Miss Annabelle."

"Thank you."

Sweeping gracefully from the room, Annabelle descended the stairs in search of her fiancé.

Jim was standing, staring out the window when she entered the room. "Darling." She smiled as she went to him and kissed him passionately. "It's so good to have you back."

Jim gazed down at her, his eyes warm with admiration for the perfection of her beauty. "It's good to be back."

"Did you miss me?" she asked coyly.

"Of course." He grinned, and, pulling her into his arms, he bent to kiss her. His mouth moved over hers in a sensual exploration that stirred Annabelle's desire but left him feeling oddly bereft.

When they broke apart, Annabelle breathed, "I missed you, too. More than you'll ever know." Taking his arm, she led him to the sofa. "Will you be staying in town longer this time?"

"After that welcome, I certainly hope so." He sat down next to her and drew her close beside him.

Annabelle was thrilled by his responsiveness and pressed willingly against him. "Good. I don't ever want us to part again like we did the last time." She drew his head down to her for another passionate exchange. "I worried about it the whole time you were gone." She murmured in between short breathless kisses, "I'm sorry if I seem too possessive . . . It's just that I love you so much."

"I understand." He told her, claiming her mouth in a flaming kiss. "I thought of you, too, while I was gone."

"And you're not angry with me?"

"No," he confirmed, and Annabelle felt much relieved.

"Good." She smiled and sat back for a moment, plotting what to do next to get him into her bed. "Will you join me for dinner tonight?"

"I'd love to. Will your father be joining us?"

"No. I'm afraid Father's been called out of town on business, but I'm sure we can have a good time by ourselves." Her statement was suggestive, and Jim was surprised at her brazenness.

"I'd like that." As he looked down at her, Jim was struck by the sudden memory of a darker, more innocent beauty, whose short-cropped curly locks had helped to disguise her sensuous femininity. Shaking himself mentally, he directed his thoughts to Annabelle, silently cursing himself for the momentary lapse. Restless, now that Murphy had intruded on his thoughts at a most private moment, he stood. "But I do have to run by Marshall's first. There's some business we have to discuss."

"Why don't you plan on being back here about six thirty?"

"That sounds fine."

"I'll be waiting for you . . ." Her tone was sultry as they walked to the door, and Jim knew that the evening could have a very different ending from their previous ones together.

Annabelle was soaking in a scented bath when her maid knocked at her bedroom door.

"I'm sorry to interrupt you, ma'am, but Captain MacIntosh is here and he'd like to speak with you."

"Wade?" She paused thoughtfully. "Send him up in five minutes."

When the maid had gone, Annabelle arose from the tub in a splash of shimmering splendor. Toweling herself, she let her thoughts drift to the night to come, and the friction of the soft cotton cloth on her sensitive silken flesh only served to increase her awareness of her need for Jim's body. Slipping into a fashionable dressing gown of pale blue satin and ecru lace, she wrapped another towel around her damp hair and seated herself at her dressing table. Glancing up at the mirror and feeling inordinately pleased by what she saw reflected there, she took the time to admire her own classic beauty, and it was in this narcissistic position that Wade found her when he walked unannounced into her boudoir.

"Darling, I have some fantastic news!" Wade stopped just inside the doorway, his hand resting on the knob of the still open portal. "My God, you're gorgeous . . ." His breath caught in his throat as he took in the scene before him . . . Annabelle barely clad in a silken wrapper, the dampness of her skin encouraging the clinging material to reveal far more than it was ever intended to.

"Hello, Wade." She turned to smile at him with practiced seduction. "You have news?" She arched a delicate eyebrow at Wade, very aware of the effect she was having on him.

"News?" He blinked and then remembered what it was he'd come to tell her. "Yes . . . my news, I've been promoted."

"How wonderful for you," she replied with little real interest and she turned away from him to look in the mirror once again, her mind racing ahead to the hours she would have alone with Jim.

"I am now Major MacIntosh assigned to the regimental paymaster."

"Are you serious?" Annabelle's eyes widened at the possibilities, and she turned to regard him seriously, her dressing gown gapping widely in front to reveal the fullness of her breasts as she faced him.

"Absolutely," he answered confidently as his gaze dropped to the pale-hued flesh so tantalizingly displayed by the loose-fitting wrapper.

"Oh, Wade, that's wonderful," she told him as he slowly closed the door and came to stand in front of her.

"Yes. It is," he agreed, reaching out with a tentative hand to caress the soft curves still hidden by the seductive material.

Annabelle allowed herself to enjoy his touch for a moment and then stepped away. "We won't have any trouble now getting the information we need, will we?"

"I should be able to find out everything we need to know with a minimum of difficulty."

"Good. The sooner we get done with this, the better." Annabelle made a production of tying her robe tightly about her, and Wade took the hint with some difficulty.

"Shall I come back later tonight?" he asked softly, his intent obvious.

"No . . . Not tonight."

"But isn't your father out of town?"

"Yes, he is, but Jim's back, and he's coming to dinner tonight."

Wade stopped cold in his tracks. "What time is he coming?"

"Soon. So I'd appreciate it if you'd leave now." Annabelle faced him squarely.

"Of course," he responded; his jaw clenched in anger and frustration. She had never refused him before, and it didn't sit well with him.

"I'll let you know if I find out anything."

"You be sure to do that." His tone was smooth, but his words had a cutting edge.

"Wade . . ." She spoke softly and he stopped his progress from the room.

"What?"

"This is business. I don't interfere with what you have to do . . ."

"You realize, of course, that there is no need for you to remain engaged to Westlake now, don't you?" he asked curtly.

Annabelle glanced at him quickly. "We can never have too many sources."

Wade wondered at her reluctance to end her involvement

with Jim, but he knew better than to challenge her. "You're right." He crossed the room and took her in his arms. "As usual."

Annabelle did not protest as Wade kissed her ardently, but her thoughts were on Jim and how exciting it would be to know him fully as a man.

Satisfied that she would one day be only his, Wade released her and strode from the room, intent on ending this masquerade as quickly as possible.

After she heard the front door close, Annabelle returned to her dressing table and began her toilet, anxious to look her best for the night to come . . . with Jim.

"Here's the coffee you wanted," Renee told Jim as she came bustling into the room with a heavily laden tray. "And a few goodies to tide you over."

"Thanks." Jim leaned forward to accept a cup from her.

"Marshall should be right back. He had to run back to the office to pick up something, but that was almost an hour ago. You don't mind waiting for him, do you? I know he wanted to talk with you."

"No. I don't mind at all. You know I enjoy your company as much, if not more, than I do his." He grinned.

Renee graced him with a loving smile. "You still know just the right thing to say to make me feel good."

"I'm glad. I've always wanted you to be happy." Their eyes met in mutual understanding.

"I know," she told him and then quickly changed the subject. "Would you like to stay and eat with us?"

"I'd love to, but I'm dining with Annabelle this evening." He took a deep warming drink of the hot coffee and sat back again.

"That's nice. How is Annabelle? I haven't seen her since the Taylors' ball."

"She's just fine," Jim replied almost indifferently and then changed the subject. "Did Mother and Father go back out to Cedarhill?"

"Yes, they left a couple of days ago. They wanted to make the trip while the roads were clear. Dorrie went, too."

"No wonder it's so quiet around here. Where's Roger?"

"Playing next door. He should be coming home soon."

"Good. I haven't seen him in a while."

"He was just asking about you last week. I know he's going to be glad you're here." Renee settled in the chair opposite him. "So, what's new? How did your trip go?" she asked, her concern real.

"The trip was successful."

His uninformative answers always irritated Renee, but she knew he was limited in what he could say about their shipping arrangements. "Will you be in town long?"

"I'm not sure. I hope, at least a week."

"Well, good. If you're still in town, you and Annabelle can join us Friday night.

"What's Friday night?"

"The Montgomerys are having a party."

"Are you sure we'll be welcome?"

"I don't see why not. You know your mother and Clara are good friends, and the invitation was addressed to 'the West-lakes.'"

"All right. I'll tell Annabelle tonight to plan on going if I'm still in port."

"Good. The rest of the family will be back by then, too, so we'll all make a night of it."

"Sounds fine."

"What sounds fine?" Marshall questioned as he came into the room.

"Hello, darling. I didn't hear you come in." Renee lifted her face to accept Marshall's kiss. "I was just inviting Jim and Annabelle to go with us Friday night to the Montgomerys'."

"Can you join us?"

"I'd like to, if Mark doesn't send me on another wild-goose chase."

Renee excused herself. "Well I'll leave you two alone for a while. I'm sure you have plenty of business to discuss . . . as always."

When Renee had gone from the room, Marshall closed the door to ensure their privacy.

"Have you found out anything?" Jim asked with restrained urgency.

"No. I'm sorry. I've checked everywhere I could think of, and there's no record of a Del Murphy in the city of St. Louis."

Jim sighed heavily, "Damn . . . I was hoping you'd have some news for me."

"I was, too."

"I've been giving a lot of thought to what we discussed before the last trip, and I think you're right."

"You mean about Murphy being a spy?"

"It's the only thing that makes sense."

"If that is the case, then I doubt that we'll ever locate her. She's probably long gone by now."

"I know." Jim nodded a little sadly.

"Then you're content to stay engaged to Annabelle?"

"The woman I thought was Murphy doesn't exist," he said, a certain coldness returning to his voice.

"I see." Marshall hesitated. "Are you going to be in town long this time?"

"I won't know for sure until I meet with Mark, but the men need a few days off, and so do I."

"I agree. You've had a lot on your mind lately, and it'll do you good to take it easy for a while."

"That's exactly what I intend to do, beginning right now." Jim stood up and started for the front door.

"Jim . . ." Marshall started to say more about Murphy, but he didn't know how to begin.

Jim turned to face him. "What?"

"Have a good time." Marshall offered lamely, sensing that his brother did not want to discuss his elusive "cabin boy" any further.

"Right." Jim frowned at Marshall's confusing remarks as he left the house and started on his way back to the steamer.

It was exactly six thirty when Jim arrived back at the Morgans' for dinner. The maid let him in and directed him into the front parlor where Annabelle was waiting for him.

"Good evening." Her voice was throaty as she came to him. "I've taken the liberty of pouring you a scotch." She handed him a crystal tumbler filled with a generous portion of the amber liquid.

"Thank you." He kissed her lightly as he took the glass from her. "You look lovely tonight."

Though demurely styled, the royal blue gown Annabelle had donned for this evening fit her in such a way that it emphasized her tiny waist and the fullness of her breasts. "Thank you." She had chosen this dress purposefully for her seduction of Jim, knowing how it enhanced her air of elegant innocence. "Are you ready to eat?"

"If you are." He sipped from his drink as they moved off toward the dining room.

The meal was delicious and afterward they settled in the parlor to enjoy their time alone. Annabelle kept talking of the wonderful life they were going to have once they were married, but for some reason Jim couldn't explain, her words left him on edge.

He stayed on a while longer, sharing several passionate kisses with her, before he realized he needed to leave.

Annabelle was surprised that he didn't want to stay later. She'd hoped to work her wiles on him tonight.

"Are you sure you have to go?" she pouted.

"I need to get back on board. You know business comes first."

Annabelle's smile was slow and sensuous as she regarded

Jim in the soft light, his striking good looks stirring her and making her eager to be in his arms. "When the war is over and our lives get back to normal, we could dine like this every night."

Damn! He thought viciously, *Where was she?* Unless he found her and convinced himself completely that she was guilty, he knew the memory of her so freely given love would haunt him forever. She had become an obsession to him, and he had to locate her, so he could put his mind at rest. Until then, he knew there would be no real peace in his life. And certainly not in Annabelle's arms.

His determination to find Murphy having returned, Jim felt inordinately better. And though the change in his mood puzzled him, he did not attribute it to the reborn hope of possibly seeing her again. Instead, he merely suspected that he felt better because he knew the cause of his problem and he knew now how to solve it. Once he had seen her again, he was sure he would be able to dismiss her from his thoughts and go on with his life with Annabelle.

It was late and the Westlake house was quiet. Lying together, wrapped in the warmth of their love, Renee and Marshall courted sleep.

"Darling?" she said softly, nestling against his side. "What's really bothering Jim?"

Marshall was jarred by her perceptiveness. "What do you mean?"

"He looks . . . I don't know . . . unhappy, maybe. Anyway, I think there's something going on that I don't know about." She raised up on an elbow to stare down at him.

He grimaced. "You're too smart."

"Don't flatter me in hopes of distracting me. And I have a feeling you know what it is."

"I do," he confessed uneasily. "But I don't know if Jim would appreciate my talking about it yet."

"Why? Is it that bad?"

"It's not bad at all, really . . ." Marshall hesitated.

"Well?" Whatever was going on sounded most intriguing, and Renee plumped her pillow and sat back up against the headboard in expectation of her husband's story.

"Do you remember Murphy? Jim's cabin boy?"

"Yes, although I never really met him. I just heard him out in the hall that night . . ."

"Well, it turns out that Murphy was a girl in disguise."

"A girl?" Renee couldn't hide her surprise.

"Maybe I should say a woman. At any rate, from what I can figure out, she fell in love with Jim while she was working for him. And on the night of his engagement party, she made love with him."

"She what?"

"Evidently Jim was well in his cups and didn't think it too odd that a woman climbed into his bed. At least not until the next morning."

"Oh, no."

"He was furious and before he had time to calm down and talk with her about it, she had disappeared."

"Poor Jim. And he's been looking for her ever since?"

"Yes. I've even been looking, but there's no record of a Del Murphy anywhere. It's a dead end."

"Surely, she couldn't have just disappeared completely?"

"That's what we thought. But the more things fall into place, the more suspicious her behavior becomes."

"Suspicious? What are you talking about?"

"She may have been a spy. Right after she disappeared, Mark told Jim that the word was out that we were carrying the gold. Murphy had access to those contracts the night that she came by our house."

"Then you have to find her. If not for Jim, then to help Mark."

"We've been trying, but so far we haven't had any luck."

"But where could she have gone?"

"I wish we knew, love. I wish we knew." He pulled her down

beside him then and kissed her deeply. "Now are you satisfied?"

"After one kiss?" she teased, catching him off guard. "Never!"

And with that, Marshall proceeded to satisfy her completely.

Renee lay in a half sleep, her mind still subtly active. As she rested between consciousness and forgetfulness, the name was haunting her—Del Murphy, Del Murphy . . . but she could put no face to that voice that had seemed so familiar. Finally drifting off, Renee dreamed of parties and dancing and of Jim and his elusive cabin boy.

Chapter Twenty-one

Delight stood before her full-length mirror, critically surveying her own reflection. "Well, Rose, what do you think?"

"I have never seen you look lovelier."

Her answer was reassuring, and Delight smiled in relief. Turning to her friend, she hugged her. "Thanks."

"You don't have to thank me. It's the truth."

Swirling, Delight enjoyed the feel of the full skirt as it swayed gracefully with her movements. "Well, I guess I'd better be getting downstairs."

"Your mother and Martin went down about twenty minutes ago," Rose told her as she parted the drapes and looked down as a carriage halted below. "And your first guests have just arrived."

Delight hurried toward the door.

"Delight?" Rose's voice held a note of warning, and Delight

looked back at her questioningly. "Stay away from Martin tonight."

"I fully intend to. I just hope he doesn't press me in front of
everybody like he did at the Taylors'."

"He'll probably try."

"I know." Delight was not anxious to fight off Martin's
subtle advances again. "I'll just have to be ready for him." And
with that she was gone, unaware that the events of the next
few hours would change her entire life.

Martin was standing in the front hall with Clara, greeting
guests, when Delight started down the stairs.

"Delight, darling." Clara smiled her approval. "You look
marvelous."

Pivoting slowly, lest he seem too anxious, Martin let his
gaze wander up the circular staircase to his stepdaughter. A
wave of heated longing shook him at the first sight of her.
God! How could he be with Delight all night and keep the
desire he had for her under control?

"Delight, my dear." He met her at the bottom of the steps
and extended his hand to her. "Come and greet our guests."

Taking his hand, she allowed him to escort her to her
mother's side.

Jim sat with Marshall and Renee in companionable silence as
their carriage made the short trip to the Morgan home to pick
up Annabelle. The entire week had been an exercise in frustration for him. Originally, Mark had scheduled them to leave
port on Wednesday, but the gold shipment had been delayed
and they had been forced to remain for an extra week. Not
that Jim had minded, for it had given him the time he needed
to continue his search for Murphy, but each new avenue he'd
explored in his quest to locate her had been a dead end.

Thwarted at every turn and almost ready to admit defeat,
he had found new energy once again when Marshall had suggested bringing in the authorities. Despite the fact that she

very well might be a Confederate agent, the memory of her vibrant loving held him captive, and he knew that he had to be the one to find her. And when he did . . .

Jim realized then that he had been so caught up in the search that he hadn't decided what to do if he ever really did locate her. The possibility of her involvement with the spies was very real. But surely, Murphy would have been more effective in that capacity if she'd remained and fed information about the actual shipments to them, rather than leaving as abruptly as she had. Confused, yet more resolved than ever, Jim continued on in his single-minded pursuit of his elusive cabin boy.

To Annabelle, he had said not a word, for he felt there was absolutely no reason for her to know his business. And, while he had spent every night in her company dining and attending various social functions, he had spent every day tracking down leads and investigating all possible Southern connections, in hopes of turning up some new information about Murphy.

Jim was dragged back to the present by the sound of his brother's voice. "Did you say something, Marshall?"

"I was wondering how your meeting with Mark went this afternoon. That is why you were late, isn't it?"

"Yes. I'm sorry I held you up, but by the time we finished with business, it was almost seven."

"No problem," Renee told him. "Dorrie and your parents went on ahead to let Clara know that we'd been detained."

"Good."

"So what did Mark have to say today?" Marshall asked.

"He did have some news that I found rather interesting."

"Such as?"

"Wade MacIntosh has been promoted."

"MacIntosh?"

Jim nodded, "He's now Major MacIntosh and he's been assigned to the paymaster . . ."

"Does Mark have to report to him?" Marshall could sense trouble brewing.

"Not directly, but Wade does outrank him now, and Mark's more than a little upset about that."

"I can certainly understand why . . . especially since they're both courting Dorrie."

"I guess we'd better keep an eye on them tonight," Marshall suggested.

"You two just mind your own business," Renee told them pointedly. "Dorrie's a big girl now, and I'm sure she can handle Mark and Wade just fine without your brotherly interference."

Marshall and Jim looked at her, a little surprised, and then let the subject drop.

When the carriage came to a halt in front of the Morgan home, Jim climbed out and went to get Annabelle. Within short moments they were back and on their way to the party.

Marshall was the first to climb down when they finally arrived at the festively lighted Montgomery home, and he turned to help Renee and then Annabelle to descend.

Delight was standing near a front parlor window visiting with friends when the sound of a carriage drew her attention and she glanced out to see who was so late in arriving. Though it was dark, she recognized the Westlake conveyance and excused herself to go and meet Renee.

It was on the way down the front hall that Martin accosted her.

"My dear, I haven't had the opportunity to tell you how absolutely lovely you look tonight," he said smoothly, stepping in front of her and successfully blocking her path.

"Thank you." She tried to move past him. "If you'll excuse me—"

"No. I'm afraid not. It's time that we danced together."

"Martin. You know how I feel about . . ."

"It's perfectly natural for you and me to dance. In fact, it's expected. Now, won't you please reconsider? Or do you plan to make a scene?" He tried to take her elbow but she shook off his hand.

"Don't touch me!" she hissed. "We have guests arriving . . ." Nodding toward the door where her mother was welcoming the Westlakes, she managed to distract him for a moment and she started forward to greet Renee and Marshall.

"Clara, thank you so much for having us. Delight!" Renee called out a greeting as she saw her friend coming toward her.

Delight was relieved to have gotten away from Martin and she smiled widely at the sight of her friend. "I'm so glad you finally got here."

Renee gave her a quick hug and then continued easily, "I hope you don't mind that we brought Marshall's brother, Jim, with us." Renee turned her to face Jim. "Captain Jim Westlake, I'd like you to meet my friend Delight de Vries." She beamed as she introduced them. "And I believe you already know Annabelle, his fiancée."

Suddenly, without any advance warning, she was looking at Captain James Westlake. Though it was only a matter of a few seconds, to Delight it seemed that an eternity had passed as she stared at him in mute surprise. Her eyes feasted upon him, lovingly tracing the broad width of his shoulders and his handsome features, until their gazes met and locked. Forcing herself not to run from him, she met his regard steadily and waited.

It took Jim a long minute to realize that this was actually Murphy standing so brazenly before him. A bolt of white-hot joy seared his soul, and he tensed.

Annabelle, who was clinging to his arm, felt his muscles bunch beneath her hand and looked up at him questioningly.

Jim quickly recovered his composure and schooled his expression, his eyes shuttering the unanticipated excitement that had shaken him. So, Jim thought in vicious victory, Murphy was none other than Delight de Vries. And the whole time he'd been out combing the city for her like a wild man, she'd been right here.

His eyes narrowed as he studied her. Was a spy ring being

operated out of this house? Why had she done it? Could there possibly have been another reason for her disguise? As Delight de Vries she had everything—money and an assured position in society. And there had never been any doubts about the loyalty of the Montgomery/de Vries family . . . at least, not until now.

Jim's thoughts were chaotic as he tried to figure out the best way to handle the situation. Finally, in a flash of momentary brilliance, he decided to do absolutely nothing. Let her sweat for a while and wonder what he was going to do. Grim in his determination to get to the bottom of her scheme, Jim knew that before this night was over he was going to have answers to all of his questions. Controlling himself admirably, he slipped a possessive arm around Annabelle's waist and spoke first.

"Miss de Vries." His tone was bland as he took her hand. "How nice to finally meet you. Renee's spoken so highly of you."

"Thank you, Captain," she murmured as a thrill shot through her at the touch of his hand. She glanced up at him quickly to see if he'd felt the same thing, but his features reflected nothing. He appeared very remote, almost cold, and slightly mocking, and she was forced to look away.

"Please, call me Jim," he offered, and then added outrageously, "I feel as if we've known each other for a long time. And may I call you Delight?"

"Of course." She felt trapped and wondered at his game. Obviously, he'd recognized her, so why was he carrying on this charade?

"And you know my fiancée, Annabelle."

"Annabelle." She acknowledged the other woman's presence, although it sent a shaft of burning pain through her heart to do so. They did make a handsome couple . . . Jim so tall and debonair and Annabelle so tiny and fair, clinging to him so adorably.

Delight suddenly thought she was going to be sick. How had

she gotten herself into such a mess? Her first instinct was to hide for the rest of the night, but she fought that down. She had done far more difficult things in her life than watch the man she loved with another woman. Lifting her chin as her pride surged forth to steady her, Delight knew that she would make it through the coming hours, torturous though they might be.

Her heart constricted as Jim turned easily away from her to greet her mother and stepfather, and tears burned her eyes as she longed to be the woman at his side. Drawing on her innermost resources, Delight smiled brightly and continued to make small talk with Renee.

Jim observed Martin Montgomery with subdued interest, wondering if there was any truth at all to the story she'd told him about her stepfather's being the reason she'd run away. The possibility bore looking into, and he decided to make discreet inquiries as the night progressed.

It amazed him that he suddenly felt almost lighthearted now that he had found her, and he frowned. The little witch! He'd spent long, miserable weeks searching for her and, he hated to admit, worrying about her. Quickly forcing himself to think about the spy charge, his expression grew thunderous. If there was some covert operation going on here, he was going to uncover it tonight.

Delight had been watching Jim from beneath lowered lashes, and a shiver shook her as he turned back to her. His eyes snared hers, his look relating all the frustration and anger that was built up inside of him. But Delight mistook his look for one of contempt, and she felt in that moment that he was lost to her forever. Turning away, still chatting gaily with Renee, she moved ahead of them down the hall.

Jim watched her progress, admiring her trim figure. As Murphy she had been a pretty woman, but as Delight de Vries she was gorgeous. He followed her progress until a petulant remark from Annabelle drew him back to the present.

Delight walked down the hall toward the ballroom, totally confused. What was he doing here? And why, since she was sure he had recognized her, had he not revealed all that had passed between them? On edge, she paused in the open doorway to watch the other couples dancing.

"Darling, I can't wait to dance with you again," Annabelle told Jim.

Delight stiffened at her words.

Jim chuckled as they swept past Delight's tense figure to enter the ballroom. "We have the whole evening, and I intend to have you in my arms as often as possible."

She watched as Jim swept his fiancée into his arms and guided her expertly about the dance floor.

"Delight?"

She almost jumped at the sound of Marshall's voice so close behind her. "Yes?" Delight kept her smile firmly in place.

"Let's dance."

"I'd love to," she replied eagerly, and she was more grateful than he would ever know when he squired her out among the swirling couples.

"What happened to Renee?"

"She was waylaid by a pair of dowagers in the hall, and I had no intention of being dragged into that conversation for any length of time. Thank you for saving me . . ." He grinned down at her.

"My pleasure, believe me." She laughed lightly just as Jim and Annabelle danced past them.

The sight of Delight obviously enjoying a dance in Marshall's arms sent a wave of cold anger through Jim. What the hell was his brother doing dancing with her? Unused to being assailed by such strong emotions, he shook himself mentally. When he realized how ridiculous his reaction was, he scowled.

"Jim? Is something wrong?" Annabelle sensed a change in him and wondered at the cause.

"No. Nothing." He smiled at her distractedly and was glad when the music ended. "Shall we get some punch?"

"I'd love some."

As they headed for the refreshment table, Renee joined them. "I thought Mrs. Peterson would never stop talking . . ." She was relieved to be away from the older women. "Have you seen my husband?"

"He was dancing with Delight a minute ago." Jim's tone was cold and Renee looked at him quickly, wondering at his mood.

"Good. She is such a sweet girl." Renee saw them approaching from across the crowded dance floor. "Here they come now."

Jim had almost snorted in disbelief at Renee's remark. Murphy/Delight, sweet? He would never have chosen that adjective to describe her. She was either incredibly shrewd or terribly naive. His mind told him that she was the first; his heart protested the decision. It was an unending conflict within him that could only be resolved by discovering the truth. Anxious not to appear interested in her, Jim bent attentively to Annabelle and engaged her in conversation.

Delight saw Jim standing with Annabelle, and she knew she couldn't join them. Excusing herself from Marshall, she went out into the hallway, searching for a quiet place where she could get control of her emotions once again. She wouldn't have believed that anything could hurt this badly. She felt as if her whole world had just come crashing down around her. All her fantasies of Jim's wanting her and needing her were just that . . . fantasies. He was engaged to Annabelle Morgan and he would marry Annabelle Morgan, and there was nothing she could do about it. She had been right to flee that morning after they'd made love. He didn't really care about her. He never had, and no doubt he never would. That was why he hadn't looked for her. That was why he was ignoring her now.

Hurrying down the hallway, she rushed into the deserted study and shut the door.

A drunken Martin Montgomery had seen Delight's nervous flight from the ballroom, and, after waiting a short length of time, he followed her out into the hall, unaware that Jim's eyes were upon him. He didn't know why she was upset, but it offered him the perfect opportunity to corner her, alone. As he left the ballroom, he saw her enter the study and close the door, and he hurried down the hall in pursuit. Quietly, he turned the knob and let himself in, shutting it silently behind him.

Delight was standing at one of the full-length casement windows staring out into the darkness of the night.

"Were you waiting for me?" Martin asked snidely.

Her startled gasp was his answer.

"Well, no matter. I'm here now, and we are very much alone."

"Hardly," she replied haughtily. "We have a house full of company. Any of whom might decide to come through that door at any moment."

Martin stalked toward her, and Delight tensed. In her desperation to get away from Jim, she had not even considered Martin.

Stopping in front of her, he let his lascivious gaze devour the smoothness of the tops of her breasts. "Your breasts really are lovely," he murmured and reached out to touch her.

Delight quickly slapped his hand away. "You've had too much to drink. Leave me alone or I'll let the whole world know what kind of a lecher you are!"

"One kiss, my dear, and I'll leave," he bargained, wanting to feel her pressed against him one more time.

"There is no way you'll ever get that close to me again!" she hissed, backing away from him. But Martin didn't even seem to hear her as he advanced toward her, intent only on his own pleasures.

Grabbing her by the shoulders, he pulled her fiercely toward him.

"No!" Her scream was cut off by his painful, silencing kiss.

When he saw Martin Montgomery leave the room so soon after Delight, Jim excused himself from Annabelle for a moment and followed. Pausing in the ballroom doorway, he watched as Martin almost furtively entered the study. Walking slowly in that direction, Jim hesitated outside the closed portal. He could hear the sound of voices, male and female, but the words were indistinct. He was about ready to move away when he finally recognized Delight's voice and then heard her quickly muffled cry.

With a casualness he little felt, Jim opened the door and stepped into the study. The sight that greeted him sent a wave of fury through him, and it was only thanks to his own rigid, iron-willed self-control that he didn't throttle Martin to within an inch of his life right then.

"Oh . . ." he said in a loud voice. "Excuse me."

Martin froze and then twisted to see who had entered the room. "Mr. Westlake." He nodded stiffly. "Is there something I can help you with?"

Delight took advantage of his momentary discomfort to edge away from him.

"I was looking for Delight," Jim replied smoothly. "I believe this was to be our dance. Your mother told me I might find you here." Jim lied easily. "But, if you're busy . . ."

"No!" she answered, eagerly moving to Jim's side. "I'm not busy. In fact, you're right about this being our waltz. If you'll excuse us, Martin?"

Martin watched them leave the room, alternately torn between frustrated anger at being caught and worry that Clara would find out.

"Thank you," she whispered as Jim guided her out of the study. But, when he took her elbow and directed her, not toward the ballroom but into the quiet of the music room at the end of the hall, she panicked.

"I thought we were going to dance . . ." Close to the breaking point, she glared up at him, jerking her arm free of his strong, yet oddly gentle, grip.

Jim cocked an amused eyebrow at her, his tone mocking. "Murphy . . . or should I call you Delight? There are many things I'd like to do with you right now, but dancing is not one of them." With a certain finality, he shut the door behind them.

Delight swallowed nervously, her eyes wide, reflecting her inner tension. "I really have to get back to my guests . . ." She tried to turn and leave the room, but Jim's hand snaked out and grasped her wrist, pulling her back tight against his chest.

"Not so fast. I think we have a few things to settle between us." The feel of her pressed full-length against him set his heart to thundering, and he gazed down at her, suddenly a captive of her startled, fawnlike gaze.

"Jim." Her voice was breathless. "There's nothing to settle . . . it's over . . . it never really was . . ."

Her heart was dying as she denied her innermost feelings. He was here . . . in her own home . . . holding her as she'd always dreamed he would. But that was where the fantasy ended. He wasn't here to declare his love and claim her for his own. He was here with his fiancée to attend a party. Their meeting tonight had been a chance thing. He hadn't looked for her. He didn't care. She closed her eyes as the painful realization seared her.

"Murphy." The word was spoken softly, and she couldn't prevent the shiver of anticipation that shook her as Jim released her wrist and brought his hands up to frame her pale face. "Ah . . . Murphy." Her name came from him in a strangled, soul-wrenching sound as he bent to claim her lips in a tender, sweet-soft kiss.

Delight trembled as his mouth met hers. Though fragile and dreamlike, the effect of his embrace was electrifying, and she fought against it. He was going to marry Annabelle! And Annabelle was right in the next room! With all the strength she could muster, she tore herself from his arms.

"No!" Her chest was heaving as she faced him, terrified of the power he had over her. "Do you think I got away from Martin just to come in here with you? Go back to your fiancée, Jim Westlake, and leave me alone!"

Turning on her heel, she fled the room, leaving Jim standing in the middle of the room aching with his need for her.

The next few hours passed slowly and almost painfully for Delight. She danced with all who asked, drank glass after glass of the potent punch, and kept her smile bright and her laugh light, but inside she felt cold . . . lifeless. And Jim's presence only made matters worse. Every time she looked up he was there. And he was always with Annabelle . . . dancing with her . . . talking with her. . . .

As the music ended, Delight's current partner accompanied her from the floor and went to get her a cup of punch. Standing momentarily alone, she was unprepared for Jim's sudden unexpected appearance at her side as the orchestra began another waltz.

"I believe this is our dance." His tone brooked no comment as she looked up at him, startled.

"No . . . I mean . . . I'm tired and I thought I'd rest for a while."

"Murphy . . ." he threatened, and she glared at him.

"Don't call me that!"

"Then dance with me. You owe me that much."

"I owe you nothing!" she hissed, schooling her features into a mask of politeness.

"You owe me plenty, little girl!" Jim was as close to losing his temper as he'd ever been in his life. It was bad enough that she'd walked off and left him earlier with his body aching for the touch of hers. And then he'd had to suffer through watching her dance with all the available young men there tonight. He'd had enough. With a grip that was none too gentle, he took her into his arms and swept her out onto the dance floor.

Delight was furious and more than a little shaken by the emotion she'd just witnessed in him. What did he mean, she "owed" him?

"Jim . . ." She began.

But he cut her off. "Shut up. If you value your reputation, just shut up."

Sensing a barely restrained violence in him, she fell silent, paling at the thought of what he could do to her if he so chose.

Jim's movements around the dance floor were smooth and deceptively easy, as he held her as close as he could without causing a scandal. He could hardly believe that she was finally in his arms. She fit as if she belonged there, and they danced in a strained, silent wonder, moving as one in time with the lilting strains of the waltz.

Although she was very nervous, Delight closed her eyes for a minute and let herself believe that her dream really had come true . . . that he *had* been searching for her . . . that he had come to take her away with him . . . that he did love her as she loved him. The thought made her smile.

Jim glanced down at her as he felt some of the tension leave her body. But when he noted what he assumed was an expression of sublime contentment on her face, his expression hardened. How dare she look so content after the chase she'd led him on!

Jim's voice was almost too sharp when he spoke, and she looked up at him quickly. "We have to talk."

She trembled as the harshness of his voice grated on her nerves. "I don't see the need . . . it'll only make matters worse."

"I want some answers from you," he demanded.

"I don't want to talk about it," she stated flatly. What more was there to say? He had Annabelle and his life, and she—well, she was doing just fine.

"I've got news for you, lady. We're going to talk, and right now."

"But why? There's nothing more we can say to each other. What happened was an accident."

Jim was seething. Did she mean that she didn't really love him? "So, you *did* use me," he concluded scathingly.

"Use you?" Delight looked up at him, tears threatening.

Wanting to hurt her as she was hurting him, he dragged up the spy charge. "The contracts . . . you did have ample opportunity to read them . . ."

"Contracts? What are you talking about?"

"I think we'd better get out of here. Is there somewhere we can go to talk? Someplace private?" He refused to look at her again, for the pain he'd seen in her eyes had seared his soul, and he needed to set things straight between them. Now. The dance ended, but Jim didn't release her. "Well?" he demanded.

"Maybe the study . . ." she said brokenly.

"Let's go."

They were starting out the door when Annabelle's call stopped them. "Jim, darling . . . could you join us for a moment?"

He turned, forcing himself into a semblance of civility. "Of course. I'll be right with you, Annabelle." Turning back to Delight, he spoke in earnest. "What I have to say will take a while, and this is not the time or place. After the ball . . . I'll be back. Be waiting for me outside, or I'll wake up the whole damned house."

Delight blanched.

"Do you understand me, Murphy?" He emphasized her "name."

"I understand," she managed as Annabelle came to Jim's side and took his arm.

"Thank you for the dance, Delight," he said courteously, bowing slightly before walking away with Annabelle.

And Delight sighed in defeat as she watched them go.

Chapter Twenty-two

Although he was anxious for the evening to draw to a close, Jim was trying carefully to disguise his emotions. Rejoining the party, he tried to pay court to Annabelle; but, though he danced each dance with her and listened attentively to her every utterance, his thoughts were only for Murphy/Delight.

He had learned much this night, and most of it was quite disturbing. He knew now that Martin Montgomery very well could have been the reason for Delight's flight into anonymity. As an innocent young woman, what recourse would she have had if her stepfather abused her, except to run away? Jim could understand her predicament, if indeed Martin was the cause. All that was left in doubt now was her possible connection with the Southern spies.

Wanting to discuss the situation with Marshall, Jim finally managed to draw him aside.

"I need to speak with you alone," he said urgently.

"Why?" Marshall was surprised by his unusual request.

Jim gave him an impatient look. "Trust me. It's important."

"All right. Let's step out into the hall; maybe there's somewhere we can speak in privacy."

Leaving the room together, they sought a quiet niche at the end of the long hallway.

"What's the matter?"

"Nothing's the matter, actually. I've just located Murphy."

"Murphy? Here?"

"My darling cabin boy, Murphy, is none other than Miss Delight de Vries," Jim told him triumphantly.

"Murphy is Delight?!" Marshall was stunned. "What did

she say? Did she explain why she ran away and disguised herself as a boy?"

"I don't know all the answers yet. I really haven't had a chance to speak with her at any length, but I'm going to."

"You're not going to do anything foolish, are you?"

"No. Of course not. I just have to set a few things straight between us."

After a thoughtful silence, Marshall spoke again. "Well, that certainly eliminates Murphy as the possible spy."

"Are you sure? Isn't there a chance that a spy ring may be operating out of this house, or that she might have contact with them somehow?" Jim pushed, wanting her to be completely vindicated in his mind.

"None. Renee has known Delight for years. There's no way she could have been the one passing the information about our gold shipments," he concluded.

Jim nodded, his expression one of vast relief. "Good. That's what I wanted to know."

Putting a companionable arm about his brother's shoulders, Jim headed them back into the ballroom—feeling considerably lighter of spirit now that his mysterious beauty had been found, as well as proven innocent of spying. Marshall was greatly amused by his brother's predicament and wondered what in the world Jim was going to do about Annabelle.

Moving from his vantage point in the shadows at the end of the hall, Martin smiled evilly to himself. He had been livid when he'd overheard Marshall and Jim discussing Delight, but now he was glad that he'd eavesdropped. So, the little vixen had spent those two weeks away practically living with Jim Westlake as his cabin boy?

The conclusion he reached was inevitable. It hadn't been an accident that Westlake had walked in on them in the study. Why Delight had probably been waiting for Jim to join her. . . . Fury and jealousy shook him as he realized that she could no longer be the sweet innocent. Somehow, he would find a way to pay them both back—Delight for refusing him, and Jim for stealing what Martin irrationally considered his.

With the information he had just learned concerning the Westlakes and the gold shipments, Martin knew now that he was in a powerful bargaining position. Perhaps, if he made the right contacts with Confederate sympathizers in the area, he might be able to make an arrangement that would be satisfactory to both sides.

Dorrie Westlake was standing near the refreshment table when Mark Clayton joined her.

"Good evening, Mark." Her smile was tentative, for he had seemed distant and preoccupied all evening. "It's a lovely party, don't you think?"

"Yes, it is." His answer was almost curt.

"Is something bothering you tonight, Mark?" she asked, hoping to draw him out a little.

"No," he replied, finishing off his bourbon and then setting the glass aside. "Nothing's wrong, but I would like to dance with you."

"I'd love to dance, Mark." Dorrie liked Mark and had always found him to be a good friend.

Mark had been drinking all night, and now, emboldened by the liquor he'd consumed, he was ready to change his tactics in pursuit of Dorrie. No longer would he be satisfied with only being her friend. He needed more than that. He needed her love.

Leading her out onto the dance floor, he took her into his arms and joined the other couples as they circled gracefully about to the sensuous rhythm of the music.

Mark had been tremendously relieved when Wade MacIntosh had drawn duty tonight. He had known that Wade had been invited to the party, and he had dreaded the possibility of a confrontation with him over Dorrie. Tonight he wanted her all to himself, so he could convince her of his intentions. Studying her dark beauty as they danced together, Mark knew that he would never be satisfied with any other woman. For him it was Dorrie or no one.

"Dorrie?" When she looked up at him questioningly, he continued, "I have to leave with Jim later this week, but I will be off duty Monday, and I was wondering if you'd like to go on an outing?"

She was surprised at his unexpected invitation. "Why, I'd like that Mark, very much."

He smiled widely at her acceptance. "Good. I'll plan on picking you up about two o'clock, and we can take in one of the expositions downtown."

"It sounds lovely. Thank you."

As the dance ended, he led her out into the now-deserted hall. "I'd like to speak with you privately for a moment, if you don't mind?"

"Of course not, Mark."

Opening the door to the deserted music room, he ushered Dorrie inside. When he closed the door behind them, she turned to him, puzzled.

"Mark?"

Without wasting time, his resolve strengthened by drink, he strode to her purposefully and kissed her.

Dorrie was at first a bit surprised by his actions, but, as she relaxed, she found Mark's embrace to be quite pleasant. Slipping her arms about his neck, she returned his kiss, and she was surprised at the ardor he displayed at her small encouragement. She had never thought of Mark in romantic terms before, but now, wrapped in his arms and held tightly to his chest, she found the possibility wildly exciting.

Not since Paul had she allowed herself the luxury of a man's caress, but tonight, with Mark, it suddenly seemed so right . . . all thoughts of Paul fled her mind as Mark's lips explored hers with a fervor that lit fires deep within her. Fires that she'd thought she'd never experience again.

Mark was burning with desire for her. And, when she'd responded to his overtures, he had been ready to profess his love. But a little common sense remained, and he released her reluctantly, knowing that he was moving too fast for her.

"Until Sunday . . ." he said abruptly, and then turned and quit the room, leaving Dorrie standing there, staring after him.

As the final few guests departed the house, Clara closed the door and turned to hug Delight. "It was a wonderful party, don't you think?"

"Yes, Mother. It was." Delight tried to sound enthusiastic, but her upcoming confrontation with Jim was weighing heavily on her mind.

"What's wrong, dear?" Clara noticed her daughter's less than excited manner.

"I think I'm exhausted." Delight sighed heavily, hoping Clara would not look beyond the obvious. "We've had one busy, long day."

"That we have, darling, but it was worth it. You were stunning. Why, I don't think you sat out a dance all evening." Clara beamed, proud of her beautiful daughter's social success.

"I don't think I did, either."

"Well, you go on up to bed. We can talk more in the morning."

"Good night, Mother." Delight kissed her cheek. "Martin . . ."

Martin had been watching the two of them, his expression enigmatic. "Good night, Delight."

Delight started up the staircase, very aware of her stepfather's piercing, stripping gaze upon her. Hurrying down the upstairs hall, she entered her room and shut the door behind her. There wasn't much time . . . Jim had left the party almost an hour before, and she was sure that he would be back at any moment. . . .

Delight paced her room in anxious despair, alternating between the fear of seeing Jim again and the exciting thought that before the night was over she would once again be in his arms. Listening and hoping that her mother and Martin would soon retire for the evening, she waited.

* * *

"Would you like me to refill your drink?" Annabelle offered, gazing up at Jim adoringly.

"No. I'm fine," he told her. "In fact, I must be leaving shortly. It's getting late."

"Must you go so soon? Father's already gone on to bed," she offered, pressing more closely to him.

"I'm afraid so. Tomorrow's going to be a very busy day." He knew he wasn't lying about that."

"Will you have time to stop by?"

"I'll try," he promised, setting his glass aside. Standing up, he drew her up with him. "Walk me to the door?"

"Of course." Her lips curved into an inviting kissable pout, but, when Jim didn't take her up on the offer, she wondered at his thoughts. He had been most attentive at the party, but since they'd come back to the house he'd seemed introspective . . . as if there was something important on his mind.

When they paused before the door, Jim drew her to him and kissed her lightly. "Good night." His words were soft as he let himself out, and Annabelle stood alone in the foyer, staring at the closed door.

Chapter Twenty-three

Her eyes downcast, her hands clenched nervously in her lap, Delight sat silently across from Jim in the swaying carriage as it rumbled down the cobblestone street.

"Where are you taking me?" Marveling at how calm she sounded, Delight waited for his answer. She looked up and tried in vain to make out the expression on his handsome features in the gloom of the darkened conveyance.

"Someplace you're quite familiar with, my dear." His voice

was smooth as silk, and Delight saw the flash of his smile in the deep shadows.

"Oh?"

"My cabin. It's the one place we're guaranteed privacy."

"I don't know why we can't say what needs to be said right here," she stated with a firmness she little felt.

"Don't you?" he asked sardonically.

Swallowing nervously, she didn't respond, but waited, much like a fly caught in a web, for what was to come next.

Jim sat back, intent on watching her every move. He knew she was upset, but there was no help for it. He had to see her . . . touch her . . . hold her . . . one more time. They had to talk about what had passed between them, and there was no better place to do that than back in his cabin where it had all happened. He didn't want this to be difficult for her, but damn, when he'd tried to help her into the carriage she had shaken off his helping hand and sat as far away from him as possible. The thought that she might not feel the same way he did unnerved him, and he was anxious to be alone with her so he could discover the truth.

When the carriage drew to a halt on the levee near the *Enterprise*, Delight grew tense. The sight of the big white steamer brought back all the memories of her days with Jim, and she didn't want to think about that . . . not now. She had to keep her wits about her. He was going to marry Annabelle. What was he doing taking her back to his cabin? Did his betrothal mean so little to him?

But Annabelle was the furthest thing from Jim's mind as he helped Delight down from the carriage and escorted her up the gangplank. They spoke not a word as they made the companionway to the texas deck.

"Jimmy? Is that you?" Ollie's call drew their attention, and Jim cursed under his breath as they came face-to-face with him. "Murphy?" His tone was incredulous as he stared at her feminine beauty in the dim light of the boat's lanterns.

"Oh, Ollie!" she cried, throwing herself into the gentle man's arms.

Ollie stood bemused for a moment and then patted her back reassuringly. "Where have you been? The captain and I've been so worried. My, you look like some fine lady . . . are you all right?" His words soothed her, and, sniffing loudly, she moved slightly away.

"You were worried?" She looked at them both.

"We were frantic. Why Jimmy's been searching the town for weeks now."

"That's enough, Ollie." Jim cut him off, furious at Ollie's revealing words.

Ollie waited only a second before continuing. "So, he finally found you, did he?"

She nodded, looking nervously at Jim. Had he really been looking for her? Hope flared within her breast, but she quickly denied it to herself.

"Yes. I found her all right. Her name is Delight de Vries, and she's a close friend of Renee's."

"You're the Delight Renee wanted Jim to meet all those weeks ago?"

"The same," Jim replied dryly, and Ollie couldn't help but chuckle. "Now, if you'll excuse us?" Taking her by the arm again, Jim steered her toward his cabin. "We have a few things to discuss."

"Yes, sir, I'll just bet you do. Delight, it's nice to finally know who you really are." Ollie was still smiling as he went on down to the saloon, thinking that his captain certainly had his hands full tonight.

The sound of the cabin door being closed and locked completely unnerved Delight, and she turned to Jim quickly as he stalked across the room.

Standing before her, his emotions masked behind a cool expression, Jim paused momentarily to study her, his eyes capturing and holding hers with an intensity that left her breathless. Then, in a simple motion, he reached out and unfastened the clasp at the throat of her cloak. The warm garment fell to the floor in a soft heap, but neither moved to pick it up.

"You look beautiful tonight," Jim murmured, his eyes caressing every inch of her.

He wanted her . . . God, how he wanted her! His body ached with the sweet need to be joined with hers, but there were things he had to settle between them first. He knew he could take her now, but he didn't want that kind of relationship with her. When they came together, he wanted what they'd had that first, magical time. Shaking himself mentally, he turned away.

"Why did you do it? Why the disguise?" he asked bluntly.

Delight felt a moment's panic. She didn't want to talk about Martin, but she knew that on that subject Jim deserved the complete truth. "It was Martin. You saw what he tried to do tonight . . ."

"Yes, I did." His manner softened, and he wanted desperately to hold her and let her know that he would always be there to protect her, but he held back, sensing her agitation.

"He's wanted me ever since I returned from school to live with my mother, but I was too naive to understand what that meant. At least, I was until that night you and Ollie found me wandering the streets . . ."

"Go on." Jim understood the difficulty she was having in retelling what must have been a traumatic event in her life.

"My mother had been ill, and I'd been caring for her." She wrung her hands in an unconscious nervous gesture. "I was so tired, and Martin said he would sit up with Mother that night . . . when I woke up he was in bed with me and . . ."

"What did he do to you?" Jim demanded as a powerful killer instinct previously unknown to him surged to life. The man would pay for whatever he had done, and he would pay dearly.

"Nothing—I got away, thank God. If it hadn't been for Rose—" she said plaintively.

He started forward, wanting to take her into the shelter of his embrace, but Delight would have none of it, and she moved quickly away from him.

"Who's Rose, darling?" he asked quietly.

"Rose is my companion. She used to work for my mother, but that was before Martin came. She quit when he approached her . . ."

"I get the picture." He stopped her explanation. "Remind me to thank Rose, will you?"

Delight glanced back at him, reading his very real concern for her. The emotion she witnessed on his face gave her pause, but she dismissed it quickly. He was to be married! He had no business approaching her this way and forcing her into an impossible situation. Determined to settle things between them quickly, she continued.

"What did you mean when you said that I'd used you?"

"It's not important anymore." Jim didn't want to explain his doubts about her loyalty, but Delight pursued it.

"It *is* important," she insisted. "I want to know what you meant!" He took a few steps in her direction, but she held up a hand to stop his progress. "Don't you come any nearer to me, Jim Westlake. We can talk just fine the way we are."

Frustrated, but anxious to have this whole unsavory scene over with, he retreated to his desk and sat down.

"Well?" she demanded.

"There has been a serious breach of security concerning our gold shipments, and 'Murphy' was the most likely suspect to have done the dirty work."

"Me?" She was totally shocked. "You suspected me?"

Jim nodded, more than pleased by her very real surprise and knowing then, without a doubt, that she was innocent. He gazed across the desk at her, seeing her for the first time for what she really was . . . A beautiful young woman, victimized by a lecherous stepfather, pursued by an engaged man, desperate for some peace and contentment in her life. He smiled to himself. From now on he would personally see to it that she had everything she deserved in life. "Yes. But after tonight . . . well, there no longer is any doubt of your guilt or innocence. Marshall has assured me that you are in no way connected with the Southern spies."

"Marshall assured you?!" For some unknown reason it infuriated her that he had to ask Marshall for a character reference. "You believed that I was capable of spying?"

"Delight . . ." He spoke her name softly, liking the way it sounded now that he was getting used to it. "How could I trust my own instincts where you're concerned? After all that's happened, I find that I can't be quite as objective as I should be about you . . ." Jim stood and came around the desk to stand before her.

When she didn't move away from him, he took it as encouragement and pulled her into his embrace. He bent to kiss her, but Delight pushed away, moving from the haven of his arms.

"Delight?" Jim questioned, wondering at her sudden withdrawal . . . one minute she seemed willing, and the next . . . "What's wrong?"

"Nothing's wrong." She managed to sound cold and almost indifferent. "I've told you what you wanted to know; now take me home." Delight had felt too safe and too comfortable when he'd held her, and she wanted to get away from his overpowering presence before it was too late. She loved him, but in despair, she knew he would never be hers.

Jim could wait no longer to have her. In one quick move, he pulled her to him and kissed her. His mouth seared hers in a fiery brand that was breathtaking in its intensity while his hands moved over her in an intimate rediscovery of her softness.

Overpowered by his ardor, Delight was lost momentarily, drowning in the ecstasy of his desire. This was Jim, and he knew who she was and he still wanted her . . . There was no darkness disguising them . . . no liquor to cloud their senses. She looped her arms around his neck and moved closer, enjoying the feel of his hard male form against her softer, more supple one.

Jim rejoiced as he felt her surrender. She was his! Eagerly, he slipped a hand within the bodice of her gown to stroke the tempting silken flesh of her breast.

It was the shock of his bold touch that forced Delight to face reality. He wanted her all right, but he was engaged to marry another. She couldn't allow this to happen, no matter how much she desired him, no matter how much her body ached with the need to meld with him.

"No, Jim . . . please, stop . . ." She fought to free herself from his ardent caresses.

"What's wrong now?" He released her, stunned by her sudden refusal. Would he ever understand her?

"This attraction we have for each other is wrong, Jim," she told him, struggling with the agony of the decision she had to make.

He stared at her in confusion, "I don't understand. How can anything this beautiful . . . this perfect . . . be wrong?"

Delight was scandalized by his attitude. "Does your engagement to Annabelle mean so little to you?"

"My engagement?" As he finally understood her reason for denying him, his love for her swelled deep within him.

"Yes, your engagement." She turned away from him, afraid that at any moment she might throw herself into his arms, regardless of Annabelle.

"Delight." His voice was like velvet over her frayed senses, and he went to her, taking her once more into his arms. He drew her rigid form to his chest. "Darling, what we have is so special . . . I knew that I had to find you . . . to make you mine. Love me, Delight," he told her, as he kissed her softly and with infinite tenderness.

"Oh, Jim . . . I love you, too! So much! But . . ." Before she could protest, his mouth descended to claim hers.

As their lips met, their fate was sealed. Joined in spirit as one, they blended together, tasting and touching each other until their passion for completion drove all thoughts from their minds, except the need for that ultimate union.

Shedding their clothes with a desperate urgency, they moved together to his bunk. Jim threw the blankets aside carelessly and then lifted her into his arms and laid her down on the welcoming softness. Lying on his side, he stretched out with her, drawing her full to him. He shuddered at the touch of her smooth body against his.

Gone were all thoughts of right and wrong. All that existed was Jim and her undying need for him. Delight clung to Jim then, drawing his head down to her so she could kiss him, expressing her full need for him in that flaming caress.

Knowing that he couldn't hold himself in check any longer, Jim moved up over her.

"My beauty . . ." His voice was husky with emotion as he looked down at her. "You're no longer just a dream."

With infinite care, he claimed her as his own.

Giving and taking, they melded into one as his steady rhythm stoked to life the flames of their need. Her hands were never still as she held him and caressed him, her touch fueling the fire that was already burning out of control within him. Delight was consumed by the heat of his desire. Straining against him, her body crying out for the release only Jim could give her, she joined him in a spiraling climax. She called out his name in reverent love as his mouth found hers in a gentle kiss that soothed the painful beauty of their fervid mating.

Clasped in each other's arms, they floated back to reality, and it was only then that Delight realized with a heavy heart that Jim had never declared his love.

"You feel so wonderful to me," he told her as he held her. "I could keep you like this forever."

"How would you explain that to your fiancée?" The words were out before she could stop them, and Delight was mortified that she'd revealed so much of what she was feeling.

"Annabelle has nothing to do with us," Jim began, but the moment of exquisite loving was gone, shattered by Annabelle's unspoken presence. He wanted to tell her that by tomorrow she would never have to worry about Annabelle again, but before he could explain Delight left the bed and began pulling on her clothes.

"Please . . . take me home now." She kept her back to him, afraid that he would see the pain she was feeling clearly etched on her strained features.

"Delight . . ."

But she refused to listen to anything he had to say. "I'm leaving here, with or without your help, Jim Westlake."

Reluctantly he got up and began to dress, hoping that by tomorrow everything would be straightened out.

Martin had observed Delight's secretive departure from the house, and he was livid. He had seen her get into the carriage with Jim Westlake, and he knew what she was up to now . . . why she was nothing more than a slut!

The mental image of Delight naked in Jim's arms drove Martin nearly insane with jealousy. He was outraged by what was happening, and he threw caution to the wind as he stalked up the servants' stairs to Sue's bedroom. Without knocking, he entered her room and woke her abruptly.

"Martin? Is something wrong?" Even though she was still half asleep, Sue could sense the violence in Martin.

"Come with me." He spoke curtly.

If he couldn't have Delight tonight, at least he could have the next-best thing . . . Sue in Delight's bed. Grabbing Sue by the forearm, he practically dragged her down the staircase to the second-floor hall.

"Where are you taking me?" she whispered as they headed down the hallway past the master bedroom.

"Where I want to be," he replied mysteriously as he pulled her into Delight's room and locked the door.

The ride from the levee seemed interminable to Jim, for he could not coax Delight into a conversation. To his every ventured question, her expression remained impassive—almost stony—and Jim wondered at her mood. He didn't understand how she could have been so responsive in his bed only moments before and now wouldn't even look at him. It was as if she wanted to forget the entire night . . .

As the hired carriage pulled to a stop a block away from Delight's house, he finally gave up the struggle to understand her. Deciding that he would see her tomorrow after he'd broken off with Annabelle, he opened the carriage door and climbed out.

"I'll walk you the rest of the way," he offered, not wanting to part from her so quickly.

"There's no need," Delight responded with frigid indifference. She had to get away from him as soon as possible. She couldn't break down in front of him. He didn't love her . . . he had used her . . . forced her own body to betray her, and now he was taking her home as casually as if nothing had passed between them.

"There is every need!" He was growing angry.

She shrugged. "Suit yourself." And she started off at a brisk pace down the sidewalk.

Jim stood in total frustration for a minute and then went after her, accompanying her in silence all the way to her back door.

"Delight," he murmured as she started to open the door and go in.

"Good night, Captain." And then she was gone, leaving him staring in thoughtful surprise at the closed and now locked kitchen door.

Saddened and feeling somehow cheapened by the night that had just passed, Delight headed slowly upstairs to her room. The hour was just before dawn, and she was more than startled to find Rose bustling about her bedroom when she opened the door.

"Rose? What are you doing?"

"I thought I heard a commotion up here, so I came up to check on you and discovered that you were gone. I was worried."

Delight went to her and hugged her tightly. "Thank you for caring . . . but why are you straightening up the room? It was clean when I left."

Rose debated whether or not to tell her what she'd discovered when she'd come in to check on her. Deciding that Delight should know what was going on, she braced herself to explain.

"When I came in I found this." She held up the remnants of the once lovely negligee.

"My God . . . do you suppose Martin did it?"

"I know he did, and also what he did right here in your bed!" Rose said vehemently, pointing to the pile of dirty sheets she'd just pulled off Delight's bed.

"He's sick, Rose. He must have seen me leave," she murmured thoughtfully.

"Where did you go tonight?"

"It's a long story, Rose . . ."

"One that I'm sure you should have told me long ago."

Desperately needing to unburden herself, Delight blurted out the whole story. Telling her dearest friend of her time disguised as Jim's cabin boy and of how she'd fallen in love with him, she left out only the truth about their lovemaking, but Rose was sensitive enough to know what had already taken place.

"So, you do love him?" Rose asked gently.

A sigh shuddered through Delight as she faced her. "Yes. I love Jim, but he doesn't love me. He's engaged to Annabelle, and I know there's no hope." Tears stung her eyes, and when Rose opened her arms to hug her, Delight was grateful for the comfort.

"Let's just wait and see what tomorrow brings," Rose consoled her. "Things may not be as bad as they seem."

Delight forced a teary smile. "Thanks, Rose."

"Now, let's figure out what we're going to do about Martin."
Rose looked at the gown in disgust.

"I'll just have to make sure to lock my door every night."

"And I'll start sleeping in here with you, beginning tonight."

"That's a good idea, Rose." And Delight wondered if maybe
it wasn't time to tell her mother the truth about Martin . . .

Chapter Twenty-four

Martin stood in the darkened hall outside Delight's bedroom listening to Delight and Rose's conversation. So, she
was in love with Jim Westlake, was she? It didn't matter to
Martin that she declared that Jim had no love for her. He was
determined to have no obstacle in his way to having Delight . . . especially now that he knew she was no longer the
sweet young innocent. She was going to be his, and if it
meant getting rid of Westlake, well, that's what he would do.

As soon as possible, Martin decided, he was going to do a
little investigating. From what he'd heard tonight, Jim would
be leaving very shortly on a trip downriver, and more than
likely he would be carrying gold. Martin knew that certain
Southern sympathizers in town would pay handsomely for information about the gold shipment, and they might also elim-
inate the problem of Jim Westlake for him in their quest for
that gold. His thoughts were black as he plotted Jim's demise.
No one would ever have Delight except him . . . no one!

Set on a definite course of action, he went on to bed, anxious to put his plan into motion.

Startled to wakefulness by the soft knock at her bedroom
door, Annabelle called out in irritation, "What is it?"

The maid opened the door and told her in hushed tones, "It's Mr. Wade, Miss Annabelle. He's downstairs and he wants to see you. He says it's urgent."

"Wade? Here? Now?" Annabelle looked groggily around her dark room. "What time is it?"

"It's about five o'clock, ma'am."

"Oh." Realizing that it must be very important or Wade would never have come at this hour, Annabelle rose and threw on her dressing gown. "Tell him I'll be right down."

"Yes, ma'am." The maid disappeared down the hall while Annabelle took a few quick moments to pull herself together.

He was waiting in her father's study when she finally came downstairs.

"Wade? What is it?" Her question was urgent as she entered the room and closed the door to ensure their privacy.

"I have some news that I thought you'd be interested in."

"About the gold?"

"No. I'm afraid it's more personal than that."

"Tell me." Annabelle could not imagine what it was that he knew.

"After I got off duty, I decided to ride down to the river-front to see if anything was going on."

"And . . . ?"

"And I saw your precious fiancé going on board his boat with a woman. . . ."

"Jim? With another woman?" She was shocked and hurt. While admittedly he had seemed a bit distracted when he'd left her tonight, she'd never suspected that he'd had a rendez-vous with anyone else. "Who was it?" Her voice was hard and dangerously quiet.

"I waited, because I knew you'd want to know. They went to his cabin and it was a good hour before they came back out. I couldn't make out who she was, so I followed them. It was Delight de Vries, Annabelle."

"Delight de Vries . . . that slut! With my fiancé?!" She was livid. How dare Jim Westlake play her for a fool!

"I'm afraid so." Wade knew that he'd upset Annabelle, but secretly he was delighted. He loved her, and he didn't like this engagement of hers to Westlake. It seemed to him that lately it had come to mean more to her than just an arrangement to get information for the Cause.

Annabelle paced the study in a controlled rage. Had Jim no honor? How could he see another woman while he was betrothed to her? It didn't occur to her that she had slept with Wade since her engagement. It only mattered that Jim obviously was not totally under her power. She had failed, and failure didn't sit well with Annabelle.

"I'm sure there must be a valid explanation for his behavior. I'll just have to ask him," she rationalized.

"Of course," Wade responded dryly. "He just happened to pick her up at three in the morning and take her back to his boat for a friendly visit. It happens all the time. . . ."

"Shut up!" She turned viciously on Wade. His snide comments rankled her, and she refused to listen to him.

"What are you going to do?"

"I'm going to ask Jim about it first thing tomorrow."

"You are?" Wade was indeed surprised.

"I'm sure he'll be able to reassure me that it was a very innocent happening. Jim Westlake loves me. He wouldn't do anything so foolish as to risk what we have together."

"You're a fool, Annabelle," Wade declared harshly as he swiftly crossed the room and took her forcefully into his arms. With cruel fingers, he gripped her chin and tilted her face up to his. "But, God help me, I love you . . . more than life itself." And he kissed her, savagely.

Annabelle was too stunned by Wade's revelation about Jim to respond one way or another to his embrace. She remained passive, and Wade thrust her away from him in disgust.

"I'll come back later. Maybe after you've heard his wonderful reason for spending an hour unchaperoned with Miss Delight de Vries, you'll be more receptive to my advances."

And with that he was gone, leaving Annabelle alone to

ponder her situation. While it was true that her engagement to Jim had started out to be just a ruse to get information for the South, she knew now that it meant everything to her. Whether she got news of the gold or not, she wanted to marry Jim Westlake.

"Well, did you get a chance to speak with Delight last night?" Marshall asked as he sat with Jim in the study early the next morning.

Jim had not slept at all after he'd returned from taking Delight home. Instead, he had spent the last hours before dawn pacing his cabin and trying to decide on the best way to handle the very delicate situation he was in. He had wanted to propose to Delight last night, but he felt that he owed it to Annabelle to wait until after he'd broken off with her. Once he was free, he would not hesitate to claim Delight for his own. His mind finally made up, he had waited until daylight and then gone to Marshall's, knowing that they would be up early.

"Yes. I did," Jim told him.

"And?"

"And I'm on my way to Annabelle's right now."

"For what?"

"I have to break the engagement. There's no way I can even think of marrying Annabelle, feeling as I do about Delight," Jim stated firmly.

Marshall drew a sharp breath. "I'm pleased that you and Delight have worked things out, but I don't envy you your visit with Annabelle."

"I know. This is going to be difficult, but it's something I have to do." He sipped at the cup of coffee Renee had served him earlier. "What time is it?"

"A little after nine, now. You do realize that that's the fourth time you've asked me in the last hour?"

Jim shrugged as he realized that the time had come to face Annabelle.

"What are you going to tell her?"

"I don't know . . . the truth, maybe?"

"I wish you luck."

"Why are you wishing Jim luck?" Renee asked as she rejoined them.

Marshall and Jim exchanged quixotic glances before Jim answered, "He's wishing me luck because I'm on my way to Annabelle's to break off our engagement."

"You're what?" She was taken completely by surprise, for Marshall had not yet told her the news about Delight.

"He's found 'Murphy,'" Marshall clarified.

"You have?"

"You know about Murphy?" Jim frowned.

"I told her in the beginning."

"Oh."

"Is she the spy?" Renee was immediately concerned.

"Hardly," Jim replied, smiling ruefully.

"Who is she? Where is she? What are you planning to do?"

"First, she's none other than Delight de Vries."

"Delight is Murphy?" She couldn't believe it. Why would Delight have done such a thing? But, then, it all fit together . . . her supposed visit to her uncle's . . . Del Murphy. . . .

"As to your second question, I hope she's at home, because that's where I'm going as soon as I'm finished talking to Annabelle. I intend to ask her to marry me as soon as I'm free to do so."

"Jimmy, that's wonderful!" Renee was rapturous.

"I know." He grinned boyishly. "I thought I'd never see her again . . . and when I discovered who she really was last night, I couldn't decide if I was angry or excited."

"My guess is excited," she teased. "But Marshall's right . . . it's going to be hard for you to break off with Annabelle."

"I guess I'd better not put it off any longer." He stood up reluctantly. "I'll let you know how it goes."

"We'll be waiting to hear," Marshall said as he walked with Jim to the door and saw him off. When Jim had gone, he returned to the study to Renee.

"Why do you suppose Delight did it?" Renee was truly puzzled.

"I don't know. Jim didn't say, and I don't suppose it really matters now that they've found each other again."

"I guess you're right, but I am curious . . . Maybe someday she'll tell me why."

"Maybe she will, but until then, do you think we can go ahead and have breakfast?" he asked innocently, and, laughing, they went into the dining room for their delayed meal.

Jim paused on the Morgans' doorstep to take a deep breath before lifting the knocker. The maid answered almost immediately and ushered him into the parlor to await Annabelle's coming.

Annabelle, who was in her room, was very surprised by Jim's early arrival. She hadn't expected to hear from him until later in the day, and she was glad now that she could confront him with Wade's damning evidence and get it over with. She had convinced herself that there was nothing to Jim's nocturnal visit with Delight, but she had to let him know that he could not treat her in such a casual manner. He was, after all, her betrothed.

Knowing that she looked her best, Annabelle swept gracefully into the parlor, ready to accept his abject apologies and get on with their life together.

Jim was standing and staring out the window.

"Jim." She greeted him, making sure to keep her tone a bit cool.

"Good morning, Annabelle." He turned to face her.

"Is it?" she challenged as she shut the door to ensure their privacy.

He frowned. It had never occurred to him that she might have heard of his activities last night. "What do you mean?"

"I understand that you were with Delight de Vries last night after you left me, and I was hoping you would explain. . . ."

She looked at him expectantly, totally unaware of Jim's real reason for being there.

"There are times in our lives when mistakes in judgment are made," he began, and Annabelle was thrilled when she thought that he was about to apologize for causing her any embarrassment.

"I understand." She nodded in agreement, but still held herself a bit aloof.

"I'm afraid this has been one of those times . . ." He paused to gather his thoughts. "Our engagement was a mistake, Annabelle. I'm sorry, but I can't marry you."

"What!? How can you say that? I love you. . . ."

"But I don't love you, and it would be a grave injustice to both of us if we were to continue with our plans to be married."

"What did that little slut do last night to change your mind?" she demanded furiously.

"Delight didn't do anything to change my mind." Jim drew himself up stiffly at Annabelle's slurs on Delight's character. "I'm sorry if I've hurt you, but it's over."

Stunned by the finality of his statement, she completely lost her temper and slapped him as hard as she could. "You are a cad, sir! You have abused my tender affections! You have used me! I despise you!"

Without another word, Jim abruptly turned on his heel and left the house, leaving Annabelle in a frustrated rate. Up until when she'd hit him, he'd felt badly about ending their engagement, knowing how difficult the situation would be for her. But all his feelings of guilt had died when she'd struck out at him. Without looking back, he headed for Marshall's again, feeling the need for a stiff drink before going to see Delight.

Rubbing his cheek in remembrance of Annabelle's fury, Jim leaned back in the wing chair and closed his eyes. Thank God that was over. . . .

"Here's the scotch you wanted." Marshall handed Jim a tumbler filled with a liberal amount of scotch.

"Thank you." He took a deep swallow of the potent liquor and then sighed loudly. "I needed that."

"How did it go?"

"I think it was the hardest thing I've ever had to do in my life. I hope I never have to go through anything like that again."

"What did she say?"

"Not much, actually. Annabelle distinguished herself more as a woman of action." Jim could grin now as he thought about it. "She slapped me."

"Ouch."

"I'll say. She was one angry woman."

"Do you think she really loves you?"

"I don't know. She told me often enough that she did, but I never sensed that depth of feeling in her. I felt more like I was a trophy for her."

"Annabelle is big on appearances, and you were, pardon me—are—the most eligible bachelor in town."

"Not for long. Believe me, as soon as I talk to Delight, that dubious title will rapidly be awarded to someone far more worthy." Jim grew suddenly solemn as he thought of the possibility that Delight might not accept his proposal. Did she love him? She had said she did in her passion. . . . God, he hoped so, for she meant everything to him. But her mood had been so strange last night when he'd left her. . . .

Chapter Twenty-five

Though the early morning hours passed quietly, Delight had been unable to sleep. Tossing and turning in the softness of her own bed, she found herself haunted by the memory of Jim's kisses and the touch of his warm, knowing hands upon her all too willing body. It angered her that she had given in to him so easily after vowing not to, but how could she resist him? She knew she should have, but she loved him. Those few brief moments of paradise in his arms last night had proven that to her.

Rose's tentative knock on the bedroom door drew her back to the present. "Yes?"

"Breakfast is ready, if you feel like getting up," Rose told her as she entered the room. "And," she added reassuringly. "Martin is nowhere to be found, so there won't be any embarrassing scenes if you come down and eat now."

"All right." Delight agreed halfheartedly. Thank you."

Rose helped her to dress and in a few short minutes she was on her way down to eat. But as she started down the stairway, Sue opened the front door and Jim walked in.

"I'd like to see Miss de Vries, please." The sound of his voice so rich and full, and the sight of him so tall and devastatingly handsome froze her in place.

"Just a minute, sir. I'll see if she's up," Sue told him courteously, glancing upstairs. "Oh . . . Here she is now . . ."

Jim turned slowly and looked up. She was a vision to him as she stood, seemingly with great poise, on the staircase. He didn't notice that she had suddenly paled at the sight of him or that she was trembling slightly. He only saw the woman he loved, and he had to fight down the urge to rush up the steps two at a time and sweep her into a dramatic embrace.

"Good morning, Delight." His lopsided smile was from the heart as he leaned a forearm on the newel post. "You certainly look lovely this morning."

"Thank you, Mr. Westlake. You wanted to see me?" To Delight, who was fearful of being near him lest she reveal her true emotions, his smile looked more like a leer, and his casual stance seemed to reflect a cocky attitude.

"Yes. It's most important that I speak with you right away."

Putting a hand on the railing to steady her shaking knees, Delight descended with a grace she little felt. "Will the front parlor do?"

"Will we be alone?" he whispered for her ears only, and she blushed, much to his pleasure.

Delight didn't respond verbally to his baiting, though, and she led him into the sitting room, and bade him to sit down. Where he went straight to the sofa in hopes that she would join him there, she took a seat in a high-backed wing chair directly across from him.

"What was it that you wanted to see me about?" Delight asked politely, refusing to meet his eyes.

"Delight. I need to talk with you this morning," he began, but the sight of her sitting so tense and nervous brought a curse to his lips. Rising from the sofa, he stalked across the room, and, before she had time to flee, he pulled her to her feet and into his arms. "Don't put me off, darling. I had to see you . . . to hold you." His mouth sought hers in a fiercely loving kiss.

But Delight was infuriated at his high-handed ways. Did he think that she was so easy that he could just walk into her house at any time of day or night and snap his fingers and she would give herself to him? If so, she thought dazedly, fighting against the wonderful feelings his teasing lips were arousing in her, he was sadly mistaken. With a burst of pride, she freed herself from his embrace.

"I want you to leave, right now!" She hissed at him, her eyes filling with angry tears. She didn't want Jim to see how much her refusal of his advances was hurting her.

Jim saw her misery, and he wanted to draw her to him once more. He felt that somehow the situation had gotten out of hand, and he wanted to set things straight between them right now. No longer was he encumbered by Annabelle and his mistaken betrothal. He was a free man, and he wanted to declare himself to Delight.

"Delight . . ." he began impatiently. "You're not making this easy for me."

"Why should I?" she asked heatedly as she glared at him. Her mind wished he would leave, yet her tortured heart was hoping that he would stay.

"Because, darling . . ." he changed his tone, wanting to soothe her and calm her so that they could talk about their future.

"Don't you 'darling' me!"

"Delight!" He was getting frustrated. She refused to listen to him! What an obstinate woman! He hoped she didn't prove so difficult to deal with in the future after they were married. The thought made him smile. "Damn it, Delight! I love you, and I want you to marry me!"

A stunned silence fell upon them. Jim hadn't meant to shout, but he had. And Delight gaped at him in mute surprise.

"You what?" she asked, wide-eyed.

"Murphy . . ." he began, his voice softer, more seductive, now. "I love you."

With a soft cry, she went to him. But just as she was about to surrender to his kiss, she stiffened in his arms. "But what about Annabelle?"

"I broke off the engagement this morning. There's no way I could marry her after loving you . . . no way in the world." And his lips met hers in a caress that transcended time and place.

Clasped in each other's arms, they were oblivious of Clara standing in the parlor doorway. She had been breakfasting in the dining room when she'd heard Jim's romantic declaration, and she rushed into the hallway to see what all the commotion was about.

"Delight?" The sound of her voice brought them both back to reality rather abruptly.

"Oh! Mother . . ." Delight was embarrassed but ecstatic. "You know Jim . . ."

"Yes, I know Jim. Good morning, Jim." Clara couldn't stop the smile that threatened. "What was all that shouting about?"

"I have just asked your daughter to marry me, and I believe she's accepted." Jim gazed down at Delight, his eyes reflecting the depth of emotion he felt for her.

"Oh, yes. I'll marry you!"

"And Annabelle?" Clara asked wisely.

"I've broken off the engagement. Delight's the woman I love."

Looking from one to the other and remembering well how powerful first love can be, Clara smiled. "That's wonderful. You have my blessing.

"Who has your blessing?" Martin asked, suddenly appearing from the back of the house.

"Why, Delight and Jim, dear. Jim has just proposed, and Delight has accepted him."

"What?" He stared at her in disbelief. "Isn't he engaged to Annabelle Morgan?"

"He was, but he broke it off so he could marry Delight. Isn't that romantic?" Clara sighed, watching her husband's reaction.

"Yes. Very." He spoke curtly. "Congratulations, Westlake."

"Thank you." Jim met Martin's hate-filled gaze knowingly. Then, looking down at Delight, he asked. "How soon do you want to be married?"

"Just as soon as possible." she murmured, feeling safe and protected in Jim's strong embrace.

"I'll be leaving Wednesday or Thursday of this week. Would you like to plan on having the ceremony as soon as I get back?"

"Sounds marvelous," she breathed, still caught up in the wonder of the moment.

"Good."

"We have lots of plans to make . . . let's go into the dining room and get started," Clara invited, and they moved off, chatting gaily.

Martin lingered sulkingly behind, glaring malevolently at Jim's back as they disappeared into the other room. Somehow, he would see the end of Jim Westlake before that wedding took place. Delight was his!

After the tentative plans for the wedding were completed, Jim and Delight left the Morgans' and went to tell his family their happy news. Renee and Marshall were pleased, as Jim had known they'd be, and the rest of his family, though a bit surprised by the suddenness of it all, wished them the best, too. Jim and Delight spent a long afternoon enjoying their well-wishes and talking about the future before heading back to have dinner with Clara and Martin.

Exhausted by all the excitement and resulting confusion, Jim and Delight relaxed in the quiet confines of their carriage, savoring their first moment of real privacy that day.

"I didn't know getting married could be so tiring."

"I didn't either." He grinned. "But it's tiring in a good way."

"Um." Delight pressed closer to him, loving his nearness.

"You're positive you don't want to wait and have a big wedding?" he asked, suddenly concerned.

"It would take too long," she explained.

"We could always elope." he suggested hopefully. "Marshall and Renee did."

"We could . . ." Delight kissed him hungrily.

"Why don't you come with me on this trip as my cabin boy?

Or better yet, I'm a ship's captain," he growled, trying to control the urge to take her there in the swaying carriage. "Maybe I can marry us right now . . ."

Delight laughed gently at the thought. "It might be legal, but I don't know how many people would believe it."

"I give up," he said in mock frustration. "I guess we'll just have to wait until I get back, but the next few weeks are really going to drag by."

"Well . . . you don't leave until midweek . . . surely we can find some time to be alone," she teased suggestively.

"We'd better," he declared, kissing her deeply. When he pulled away, though, he was frowning.

"What's wrong?"

"You will be safe while I'm gone, won't you?"

Delight understood his concern over Martin, and she hastened to reassure him. "I'll be fine. But you'll hurry home to me, won't you?"

He kissed her to answer her question. "Never doubt it."

When the conveyance drew to a halt back at the Morgan house, they climbed down and went inside. Their happiness was all encompassing as they shed their wraps and stole quick kisses on their way in to joining Clara and Martin.

Delight stood with Jim in the abandoned front hall later that evening. Martin and Clara had just retired for the night, and at last they were alone.

"Well, my captain," she said huskily, moving into his embrace. "Will I see you tomorrow?"

"I'll be here as soon as I can get away."

"Good. It's going to be a long night."

"I know," he murmured, bending to kiss her. As their mouths met in a soul-stirring caress, Jim held her close to his heart. "God, woman. I don't want to leave you."

"And I don't want you to, either," she told him breathlessly. How she longed to stay with him the entire night, making love and talking of their future.

With a reserve of strength that Jim didn't know he had, he stepped away from her. "I'd better go now, while I can."

Delight couldn't help but grin, "There's always tomorrow . . ."

Jim growled, "But there'll be people everywhere . . ."

"Maybe I can arrange a shopping trip with Rose and we can stop by the boat for a visit."

"I think that sounds like a marvelous idea," he grinned, knowing that if he remained a moment longer they would be in the parlor making mad, passionate love. "I've got to go . . ."

"I know." She walked with him to the door and opened it for him.

With deep regret reflected in his eyes, he walked briskly outside. "I'll see you tomorrow." He started down the steps toward his waiting carriage when he heard Delight's desperate call.

"Jim!"

He turned back to her and she flew into his arms, kissing him with all the love she felt. "I love you so much . . ."

"And I love you . . ." he managed, returning her ardor equally. His smile was bittersweet as they looked at each other. "Now, get back inside before I change my mind about being a gentleman."

Reluctantly, Delight went inside and closed the door. Hurrying to the front parlor window, she watched until his carriage had disappeared down the street in the direction of the riverfront.

Sad at being away from him, yet excited about their future together, she headed upstairs to her bedroom.

Rose was waiting for her when she entered the room. "Well? Is it really true?" She had overheard conversations during the course of the day, but she wanted to hear the whole story from Delight.

"Yes!" Delight's joy was obvious. "Jim proposed this morning and we're going to be married as soon as he gets back from his next trip."

"I'm so happy for you."

"Thank God Jim rescued me that night, or none of this would ever have happened."

"So he did break off with Annabelle Morgan?"

"First thing this morning," Delight assured her. "He's all mine, Rose. And he always will be . . ."

Annabelle sat with Wade in the dimly lit parlor of her home. The day had been a long, painful one for her, and she had been glad when Wade had stopped by late to see her.

"I can't believe he actually did it," she remarked, taking another deep drink from her snifter of brandy. She had been drinking steadily all evening.

"You really shouldn't worry about Westlake too much. I have access to most of the information we'll need in my new job."

"I know that," she replied coldly. "It's just that I've never failed before. It's a bitter pill to swallow."

"Who says you've failed? His ending your farce of an engagement doesn't really change things that much," he said, and then added slyly, wanting to give her an out, "Besides, you were going to break it off sooner or later anyway."

"Right," she agreed. "We'll still get the gold."

"Absolutely. I have every confidence."

Annabelle felt less defeated listening to Wade, and she smiled at him, her expression cold and calculating. "We'll show them, Wade. Just wait . . ."

Chapter Twenty-six

The sun's ascent went uncontested as it rose bright and shining in the clear blue of the late winter sky. There was no howling, chilling wind this day; instead, there was a hint of something promising in the air . . . a damp, wet warmth that evoked a feeling of rightness with the world. Spring was coming.

Delight and Rose had slept little that night. Excitement over her betrothal, coupled with the ever-silent menace of Martin, had made rest virtually impossible. Now, as the morning finally matured, they were ready to venture out on their "shopping spree."

There had been no sign of Martin so far, and both women wanted it to stay that way. They had no desire for a confrontation with him, hoping just to avoid him as much as possible during the next few weeks.

After telling Clara where they were going, Delight and Rose climbed into their waiting carriage, and Delight gave the driver his instructions. "To the levee, please. We want to go to the Westlake steamer, the *Enterprise*."

"Yes, ma'am," he replied, and, without hesitation, they were off.

"Is he expecting you?"

"I told him that we would try to get away on the pretense of a shopping trip."

"So, you had this all planned ahead of time, did you?"

Delight smiled. "Now that I've got him, Rose, I don't ever want to be apart from him."

Rose smiled, understanding the emotion, though she had never experienced it. Her life had been one of survival, and there had been no time for romantic love.

As her thoughts turned to men, Rose frowned. Judging by what Martin had done the other night, she realized they had very little real protection from him. Even if Delight did go through with her threat to tell her mother the truth, there was no guarantee that that would keep Martin away from them. It might, in fact, bring out the viciousness in him and only serve to make their situation more difficult. The safest path, Rose decided, was to get Delight married to Captain Westlake as quickly as possible, so that she would be removed from harm's way.

Forcing her thoughts away from Martin's wickedness, Rose gazed out the carriage window at the passing riverfront scene. The levee was bustling with passengers, arriving and departing, and brawny roustabouts, who were busy loading cartons of merchandise onto the steamers that were preparing to leave.

Not yet threatened by the northern spring thaw, the Mississippi flowed south, its rhythm steady and smooth. Within a few weeks, though, Rose knew all that would change. For, when the Missouri and Illinois rivers emptied their winter runoffs into the now peaceful valley, the seemingly mild-mannered river would be transformed into a swirling, death-dealing, overpowering flood of icy water and fast-flowing debris.

Rose shivered at the thought and turned back to Delight as she was pointing out the *Enterprise* tied up nearby.

"There's Jim's boat," she said proudly as their vehicle drew to a stop near the gangplank. When the driver opened the door for them, they climbed out eagerly. "We won't need you anymore today," Delight informed him as they headed up the steamer's walk.

"Yes, ma'am," he told her and he left to return to the Montgomery house.

"Come on, Rose." Delight led the way across the main deck to the companionway. When they finally reached the texas deck, she went straight to Jim's cabin. "I don't know if he's in his stateroom or not, but we'll check here first."

Knocking once, she opened the door and went on in. Jim was not there now, but he had been, for his clothes from the night before were strewn all over the cabin.

A small smile curved her lips as she remembered the passion they'd shared in that bed . . .

"Where shall we look for him now?" Rose asked.

"We'll try the saloon. If he's not there, at least Ollie will know where we can find him."

She led Rose back downstairs, and they entered the Grand Salon and strode its length, admiring the beauty of its pristine white fixtures and stained glass skylights.

"This is lovely," Rose said in hushed tones. "The only time I ever traveled on a steamboat, it was summertime, and I went as a deck passenger."

"That sounds horrible!"

"It was." Rose made a face. "The boat was carrying a full load of livestock, and the smell was awful."

"Well, the next time you take a trip, I'll make sure you go first class." Delight walked casually into the saloon, drawing curious glances from a few of the men gathered there.

"Delight!" Ollie saw her immediately and beckoned her on into the room.

"Good morning, Ollie." She smiled warmly at him and then turned to introduce Rose. "Ollie, this is my friend and companion, Rose O'Brien. Rose, this is Ollie Fitzgerald."

Ollie came around the bar to greet them, his eyes wandering appreciatively over Rose. "Miss O'Brien, it's a pleasure."

"Please, call me Rose."

"I'd be delighted to, if you'll call me Ollie."

"With pleasure."

"Where's my captain this morning?" Delight interrupted their exchange, too excited at the prospect of seeing Jim to notice the immediate attraction between Rose and Ollie.

"The last I saw of him, he was heading down to the mudclerk's office on the main deck, but he should be back any . . ."

Before Ollie could finish his sentence, Jim entered the room. "Delight!" Surprised and pleased to find that she'd managed to get away so early, he hugged her tightly, and, ignoring the stares of the others in the room, kissed her.

"Good morning," he murmured, releasing her reluctantly when he realized that all eyes were upon them.

"Good morning," she smiled back, sorry that the real world had interrupted their greeting. "How are you this morning?"

"Fine . . . and you?" His eyes drank in the sight of her.

"Wonderful. I hope you don't mind that I came so soon . . ."

"I wish we'd never had to part." His tone was earnest and he had to restrain himself from taking her in his arms again.

"There's someone here I'd like you to meet," Delight began, knowing she had to break the spell between them, but not really wanting to.

"Are you Rose?" Jim turned to the older woman.

"Yes, I am. And you must be Delight's captain?"

"I'm Jim Westlake. It's nice to meet you. I appreciate all you've done for her." He slipped a possessive arm about Delight's waist and drew her to his side.

"I love her too, Captain," Rose told him, glad to see that Jim was a man capable of protecting Delight.

"Please, call me Jim, and I'll call you Rose."

"I will."

"Well, darling, what are your plans for today?" He looked down at her, his eyes sparkling at the thought of being alone with her for a few minutes.

"I hadn't thought beyond coming on board and spending the day with you."

"I like the sound of that, but I do still have some paperwork to do. I've got to finish the work in the ledgers this morning and then get them over to Marshall this afternoon."

"You have to work?" Delight pouted, not wanting to share him with anything or anybody.

"I'll finish as fast as I can."

"All right," she finally agreed, knowing how important the books were.

"Ollie?" Jim turned to him. "Would you like to show Rose around the boat?"

"I'd enjoy that very much. Rose?"

"Thank you, Ollie." She was pleased at the invitation.

"Then we'll see you later," Jim continued, ushering Delight from the room.

"I can't believe it!" Delight laughed, and Jim looked at her questioningly.

"Believe what?"

"We're actually going to be alone for a while. I was so afraid that I wouldn't get to spend any time with you."

"You'll have time with me all right, but I do have some things to finish." He smiled at her. "Do you want to come back to work as my cabin boy? My cabin certainly misses your touch."

"Only your cabin?" she asked, flirting.

"Vixen," he growled, tightening his arms about her. "As you know, I do have a lock on the cabin door. . . ."

"Then, let's use it." She smiled up at him in eager anticipation of sharing his love once again.

The weather was so pleasant after his clandestine meeting with Elroy Lucas that Martin decided to walk back to the house rather than hire a carriage. It gave him time to sort out his feelings and to go over the plans he was making. He needed to be sure that all angles were covered before he revealed what he knew to the correct sources. Elroy had a reputation as a hotheaded Southerner, and it was through him that Martin hoped to make direct contact with the spies who were operating in the area.

Martin had dropped his clues that morning at their meeting, and now he just had to sit back and wait. Surely someone would be in touch with him before the day was out, for there was no time to waste if they were going to make arrangements to attack Jim Westlake's boat while he was carrying the gold.

Reentering the house, he found his wife having tea in the front parlor.

"Good morning, darling," he greeted her, kissing her cheek.

"Where have you been, Martin? You didn't leave word with anyone where you were going," Clara asked, irritated that he had been so inconsiderate.

"I'm sorry. I had thought to be back before you awakened. You were sleeping so soundly that I didn't want to disturb you when I left," he responded smoothly. Then, producing the small gift he'd purchased on his way home, he handed it to her. "I've brought you a present."

Martin was aggravated by his wife's demands, but he knew that she had to be kept happy. He had originally intended to give Sue the small locket, but he could always pick up another trinket for her later. Right now, he had to please Clara.

Sitting down beside her, he helped her to put on the necklace.

"Oh, thank you, Martin." Clara seemed delighted with the gift and she turned to kiss him for it.

Pulling him to her, she kissed him deeply, hoping to encourage him, but Martin stiffened at her bold ploy.

"My dear, it's broad daylight!" He tried to sound scandalized.

"I know," she murmured throatily. "We're all alone in the house, save for the servants, and they wouldn't dare interrupt us."

The last thing Martin felt like doing was going to bed with his wife. He felt no desire for her at all anymore, but he knew that he had to perform or she would think something was wrong between them.

Pretending a passion he certainly wasn't experiencing, he pulled her to him and kissed her. With his eyes closed, he could imagine she was Delight, and he felt the familiar stirring deep within him.

"Let's go upstairs," Clara said, standing up and drawing him up with her.

Without another word exchanged between them, they headed up the front staircase. Just as they were disappearing around the curve, Martin looked back down to see Sue watching them with knowing eyes. He stifled a groan and continued on to the bedroom, thankful that soon he would be more in control of his life.

After leaving Jim and Ollie, Delight and Rose stopped at one of the small shops on Veranda Row to make a few quick purchases, in order to give their story about going shopping credibility, and then they headed home. Both had been excited about their day with Jim and Ollie on the steamer, but both knew that they couldn't say a word about it in Clara's presence. They had been anticipating a scene with Martin when they returned, and they were greatly relieved to find that he was closeted in the study with some gentlemen on business. Glad for the reprieve, they visited with Clara for a few minutes, Delight informing her of her dinner invitation before going upstairs to get ready.

Martin shook hands with Nathan Morgan and Gordon Tyndale. "I trust you find everything I was able to give you satisfactory?"

"Absolutely," they replied, unwilling to say any more.

"Gentlemen, I understand your reluctance to speak freely, and I applaud you for it. Thank you for this." He indicated the neat pile of Union dollars they had just given him. "And if I can be of any help in the future, just let me know. Especially where Westlake is concerned," he added viciously.

"Good day, Mr. Montgomery." Nathan and Gordon quickly left the study and the house.

Martin recounted the money he'd received after they'd gone and then hid it in the false bottom of his desk drawer. When the time came, he might need that money in a hurry, and he wanted to make sure that it was in a safe place.

Straightening his cuffs, he strode from the room, feeling

very self-assured and confident. In less than forty-eight hours, he had made himself a small fortune and arranged for Jim Westlake to be blown right out of the Mississippi River. Not bad for a couple of days' work. . . .

Nathan sent word for Wade to meet him at home as quickly as possible. Annabelle was curious at her father's agitation and questioned him as he stood nervously in the parlor.

"What did you find out today, Father?"

"Nothing, darling, nothing." His tone was distracted and she knew he was avoiding telling her something.

"What is it? I think I have a right to know. I've been involved in this thing since the beginning. This is no time to start shutting me out."

Nathan looked at her, seriously considering her words. "You're right. I'm sorry. I was only trying to protect you from further hurt.

"There are two things. First, Westlake has announced his engagement to another woman . . ."

"*What?!*" Annabelle was stricken.

"That's right. Yesterday he and Delight de Vries announced their betrothal."

"I don't believe it . . . why, that bastard!" She was livid. It had been bad enough to live with the broken engagement, but to live down his marriage to someone else so soon afterward . . . well, that was another story.

"I knew you'd be upset and I'm sorry."

"No, you did the right thing in telling me, Father. Thank you." She spoke slowly, controlling herself with an effort. "What else?"

"There's a bit of intrigue to this part. Elroy was contacted today by Martin Montgomery. It seems he had some information that he wanted to sell to the right group of individuals. Namely—us."

"What kind of information?"

"Montgomery overheard Marshall Westlake verifying that

they were carrying gold and that Jim's next trip would be sometime later this week."

Annabelle was instantly cautious. "Why would Montgomery want to give that information to us?"

"That's what we were wondering. But from what he said, I think he hates Jim Westlake and wants him dead."

"A man after my own heart . . ." she said coldly. "But why this hatred for Jim? I find that a bit difficult to swallow."

"Do you want my personal opinion?"

"Of course."

"I think the man hates Westlake because he got engaged to Delight."

"You mean . . . you think Delight and Martin have a thing going on?"

"I don't know if it's gone that far, but, as you well know, Martin Montgomery is far younger than Clara and when they married he didn't know too much about Delight. All he knew was that Clara had a daughter."

"Ah . . . so along comes Delight, all sweetness and virginity, and Martin thinks he's in love . . ."

"Something like that. Anyway, for one reason or another, the man wants Jim Westlake out of the picture, and we're going to try to take care of that for him when we go after the gold on his next trip."

"Admirable," she said with calculation.

They were interrupted then as the maid announced Wade's arrival. When they had explained the circumstances of what they'd learned that day, Wade was certain that the time was right.

"I'll do some checking on my end and even pull rank on Clayton if I have to. But, one way or another, I'll have everything he told you verified by Tuesday morning."

"Sounds good."

"First, though, I think I'll start with an unexpected visit to Dorrie Westlake. Maybe I can pick up something useful there tonight."

"We'll be waiting to hear from you," Nathan told him.

"I'll have my information to you no later than Tuesday."

Pausing with Annabelle in the front hall, he drew her close and kissed her fervently. "Don't let Westlake get to you. You are still the most beautiful woman in town."

Annabelle needed his reassurances and kissed him back, "Thank you, Wade. If you get a chance to come by . . ."

"I'll be back," he told her fiercely. "It may be late, but I'll come to you tonight."

And, with that promise, he was gone on his quest for more information on the gold.

Chapter Twenty-seven

"Dinner was wonderful, Renee." Jim leaned back on the sofa next to Delight, a contented man . . . almost. Very shortly, they would be alone, and then he would be completely satisfied. His eyes wandered hungrily over her as she sat demurely next to him.

"Thanks, Jim. I'm glad we had this chance for all of us to get together before you leave again."

"Have you made any wedding plans yet?" Martha Westlake asked Delight.

"Nothing specific. We really haven't had much time to talk about it." She looked up at Jim adoringly.

"Well, if you need anything, Mother and I will be glad to help," Dorrie offered enthusiastically.

Their lighthearted conversation was interrupted by a knock at the front door. Marshall went to answer it and he was more than surprised to find Wade MacIntosh on his doorstep.

"Good evening, Wade."

"Marshall." Wade knew that Marshall did not like him, but

at this point he didn't care. "I was wondering if I could speak to Dorrie for a few minutes?"

"Of course, come in," Marshall replied, with a graciousness he hardly felt. "We're all in the parlor. Would you like to join us for an after-dinner drink?"

"Yes, that's very kind of you." Wade handed his coat to a servant and then followed him from the hall.

"Dorrie, you have a visitor," Marshall told her.

"Wade, it's so nice that you dropped by." Dorrie smiled. "Come in and meet everyone. You know my brothers, and this is my mother and father. Marshall's wife, Renee, and Jim's fiancée, Delight de Vries."

"Hello," Wade said to everyone in the room generally. "Congratulations on your engagement Jim, Miss de Vries," he told them cordially. While his manner was sincere he was, in reality, angry with Jim for causing Annabelle so much embarrassment.

"Thank you."

"You're deserving of congratulations, too," Marshall reminded him. "We heard about your promotion."

"I am pleased by it," Wade told them truthfully, for he now had access to information concerning payroll shipments. "I feel I'll be more greatly challenged where I am now."

"What would you like?" Marshall asked as he moved to the liquor cabinet.

"A bourbon will be fine."

"Sit down and join us."

"Thank you." Wade made himself comfortable on the chair nearest to Dorrie's, knowing that he had to keep up the charade for just a few more days. He listened quietly to their chatter, adding a word now and then when they discussed something he knew about, but mostly Wade was an observer trying to pick up facts about when the shipment was going out.

The rest of the evening passed slowly for him, with little real information being bandied about. Only Delight's obscure reference to how much she was going to miss Jim when he had to leave again came close to telling Wade what he needed to know. Finally, realizing how late it was getting, he rose to go, and Dorrie accompanied him out into the hall.

"It was a lovely evening. I hope I didn't spoil anything by coming by unannounced," he said, courting her solicitously.

"Of course not. It was good to see you again."

"Would you like to spend the day together, tomorrow?"

"I'm afraid I've already made plans with Mark, but thank you for asking," she refused him gently.

"I'll be in touch," he told her easily, making a mental note to arrange extra duty for Mark Clayton tomorrow.

Kissing her gently on the cheek, he left the house, eager to return to Annabelle's waiting arms. He made the ride to the Morgans' house in record time and he was relieved to find that Nathan had already retired for the night and they were alone.

"How did it go?" Annabelle asked him as she brought him a drink. She had changed into a burgundy velvet dressing gown that clung to her figure suggestively, emphasizing the delicacy of her curves.

"I would rather have been here with you. I learned absolutely nothing of value. No reference was made concerning the next shipment or Jim's upcoming trip."

"Damn!" She sat down next to him on the sofa, frowning in concentration. "We'll just have to assume that this next shipment is it, unless you can get us any conflicting reports by Tuesday."

"Right." He drank deeply from the bourbon she'd given him.

"Have you figured out how to get on board yet?"

"Gordon is working on that. We're meeting Tuesday night to review the entire operation."

"I want to go, too."

"I'm sure your father won't object. After all, you were instrumental in getting the information."

Annabelle's eyes gleamed at the thought of her revenge

against Jim. Love and hate are but a wit apart, and Annabelle had crossed over that line.

"I'd like Martin Montgomery to be totally satisfied with the raid," she told him, her tone chilling as she visualized the attack on the *Enterprise* and Jim's death.

"I'll do my best for you, love." Wade set his empty glass aside and pulled her into his arms. "I'd do anything for you . . . anything."

"I know, Wade," she said, before rewarding him with a kiss.

Reluctantly, they moved apart. "I have to go. I have duty first thing in the morning."

"I wish you could stay," she said with an honesty that had been lacking in her previous declarations to him.

"Annabelle. You know how I feel about you. Say the word and I'll marry you tomorrow."

"I know, Wade." Annabelle paused. "When all this confusion is over and you're back safely, I want you to ask me again."

Wade embraced her and then kissed her tenderly. "I will."

Jim closed the cabin door and turned slowly to face Delight.

"Alone, at last!" he grinned. "I thought the night would never end."

Delight moved straight into his arms to kiss him.

When the kiss ended, she unbuttoned his shirt and slipped her hands under it to caress the hard muscles of his chest. Resting her cheek against him, she listened to the pounding of his heart. "I've been wanting to do this all night. . . ."

"You're not alone. . . ." His fingers found the fastening at the back of her dinner dress and he worked to free her from the bothersome garment.

He bent to kiss her, his lips taunting hers with gentle, sweet caresses as his hands pushed the dress from her shoulders. "You're going to have to help me with this thing," he finally complained when he couldn't free her from it.

Delight smiled, finding joy in his frustration. It felt wonderful to know that he loved her so deeply and that his passion equaled hers. With slow, easy movements, she shed her dress and underthings, all the while keeping her eyes on Jim's face.

Jim held himself back with an effort as he watched her approach him.

"Now, it's your turn," she said, her voice husky with desire.

"For what?" Jim couldn't take his eyes from the glorious sight of her in the soft lamplight. He wanted to throw her on his bed and have his way with her, but he waited, excited at the prospect of what she might do next.

"You are beautiful, you know." Her tone was serious, surprising him.

"Men aren't beautiful—" he started to protest, but her hands were suddenly on him, distracting him from all thoughts, save one.

Standing before him, she was caressing his chest, eagerly pushing his shirt and jacket off in the same movement. Jim, unable to deny himself any longer, lifted her in his arms and carried her to the bed.

Shedding the rest of his clothes, he joined her there. Their lips met in an ardent kiss as they moved together as one.

It was after midnight when they finally made their way back to the Montgomery house. Neither had wanted to leave the haven they had found on board the steamer, but they knew it was necessary. In just a few more weeks, they wouldn't have to part at all. . . .

Jim didn't trust himself to say a quick good night to her inside, so he kissed her in the shadows on the front steps and watched until she had disappeared indoors. Once he was certain that she was safe, he left, eagerly anticipating their time together the following day.

Delight was halfway up the stairs when Martin came out of his dimly lighted study.

"So, you finally got home," he sneered.

She wanted to go on up to bed but his next words stopped her.

"You bitch! All the while I thought you were so pure, you were giving it away to Westlake like a common slut!"

"Martin, we have nothing to say to each other. I'm going to bed." Delight was frightened, for she knew Martin wouldn't be so openly bold unless her mother had long since retired for the night.

"I'll wager, from the look of you, that you just got out of bed," he said caustically, and he let his gaze run over her knowingly.

Delight gasped at his crudity and ran on up the steps as the sound of his mocking laughter followed her. She didn't feel protected again until she had bolted the door behind her.

Martin listened to her rapid running footsteps and smiled widely. The little whore . . . soon he would be the one receiving the comforts she could give. A mental image of himself lying between Delight's legs and pounding into her submissive body sent a surge of heat through him, and he extinguished the lamp in the study before making his way quietly up to the third floor and Sue.

Chapter Twenty-eight

"What are your plans for the day?" Clara asked Delight as they relaxed together over breakfast.

"Jim's taking me for a ride in the country."

"You've certainly got the perfect day for it; the weather's warmed up a bit."

"Spring's almost here, and I'm glad. I've had enough of cold weather and snow."

"I think everyone begins to feel that way this time of year," Clara smiled. Then, looking up at the sound of footsteps, she greeted her husband. "Good morning, darling. Did you sleep well?" She had been aware that Martin had come to bed late, so she had not awakened him when she got up.

"Just fine, Clara." Martin came to her side and kissed her cheek before joining them at the table. "Delight, you look lovely this morning."

"Thank you," Delight murmured, wanting to avoid all contact with this hateful man.

"Are you going out again today?" he asked. The undercurrent between them was antagonistic, but Clara seemed not to notice.

"Yes, I have plans with Jim," Delight said shortly.

"I hope you don't find yourself too bored when he leaves later this week." Though his words were spoken conversationally, the expression in his eyes was hard.

"I'm sure I'll be fine." She refused to let herself be drawn into an exchange with him. "If you'll excuse me, it's time I started getting ready."

"Of course, dear. You go right ahead."

Martin watched her go, his gaze lingering on the sway of her hips as she left the room. With an effort, he turned his attention to his wife, who was sitting patiently across the table from him.

"She's become quite a woman, hasn't she?" Clara remarked obliquely.

"Yes, Delight has grown up." Martin did not want to discuss Delight with Clara.

Delight made her way hurriedly up to her room. She was eager to be gone from this house and Martin's obnoxious presence . . .

With Rose's help, she donned a comfortable daygown suitable for a trip in the country. When she heard Jim's buggy pull up, she went down to meet him.

"Good morning." Delight's smile was bright as she looked at the handsome man who would soon be her husband.

"Good morning, love." His voice was deep with affection as he kissed her cheek. "Are you ready?"

"Yes, just let me get my cloak . . ." Putting on the wrap, she said good-bye to her mother and Martin.

"Have a good time," Clara called as they disappeared out the door. Turning back to Martin, she was surprised to find him staring out the front window. "Is something wrong, Martin?"

"No," he denied quickly, hiding the rage he was experiencing behind the facade of easy grace he'd perfected. "I was just watching them drive away."

"Would you like to go for an outing in the country today?" she suggested, hoping that they could spend some time alone together and just enjoy each other's company. It seemed as if they'd had little time to themselves since her illness.

"No, not today," he answered curtly. "I have some work I need to catch up on . . ." Without another word, he strode from the room, leaving Clara to stare thoughtfully after him.

Wade handed the missive to the young lieutenant. "See that this is delivered to Captain Clayton right away."

"Yes, sir."

"Report back to me."

He smiled as he watched the soldier rush to do his bidding. Rank did have its privileges. Then, frowning in thought, he leaned back in his desk chair. As soon as he had word that Mark had reported for his unexpected duty, he would head for the Westlakes to see Dorrie.

Wade didn't have to wait long, for the lieutenant was prompt in returning with the news that the message had been delivered, and it was only a few minutes later that an outraged Mark Clayton showed up.

"What is the meaning of this, MacIntosh?" he stormed.

"I'm sure I don't know what you mean," Wade answered coolly.

"These sudden orders for me to report for duty. I'm scheduled to be off all day today."

"Sorry about that, Captain, but your services are needed here," Wade informed him coldly.

"MacIntosh . . ."

"That's Major MacIntosh to you, Captain, and don't ever forget it again. Now, if you'll excuse me. I have a social call to make . . ." Smiling wolfishly at Mark, Wade got his hat and left.

Feeling totally frustrated, Mark stalked to the window to watch Wade ride away.

"We have to make one more stop before we go for our ride," Jim told Delight as they rode away from her home.

"Oh? Where's that?"

"To pick up our chaperone," he grinned.

"Our chaperone?" She was taken by surprise. She had hoped to spend the entire day in some country hideaway making love to Jim; so the news of someone's joining them did not sit well with her.

"I think you'll like him."

"Him?" Now she was intrigued.

"I stopped by to see Marshall for a few minutes this morning, and Renee gave me a very stern lecture on your reputation and how I needed to protect you from unsavory gossip. So, we put our heads together and came up with the idea of a chaperone."

"Wonderful," she grimaced. "I was looking forward to being alone with you."

"So was I, but Renee's right. A day in the woods with me, and your reputation would be in shreds."

Delight looked thoroughly crestfallen, and Jim couldn't help but laugh. "Don't look so forlorn. We'll be married in a little over two weeks."

"Right," she sighed. "Keep reminding me of that, all day. All right?"

"I most certainly will," he agreed, pulling her closer to his side.

"So, who's the mysterious protector of my virtue?"

"Roger," Jim grinned.

"Roger?"

"Absolutely. He loves going to the country," he said as he

reined in the horse in front of Marshall and Renee's. "Do you want to wait here while I go get him? It shouldn't take a minute."

"Fine." Delight was amused.

It wasn't long before the sturdy little boy came running from the house to climb easily up beside her. "Hi!"

"Hi, yourself."

"I'm glad I get to go with you. We're going to have a lot of fun, aren't we, Uncle Jimmy?"

"We sure are." Jim joined them in the small carriage he had rented for the day and they were off. "Where do you want to go?"

"Cedarhill!" Roger exclaimed. "I haven't been there since last summer."

"It's a long drive . . ." Jim tried to suggest something else.

"Please?"

"Delight? Did you have anything in mind?"

"No, Cedarhill sounds fine to me. I've never seen your family's country home. I think I'd like that."

"All right, but it'll take a while to get there."

"That's fine. You drive and Roger and I will sit back and enjoy the scenery."

"Cedarhill it is, then." And Jim turned the carriage in the direction of the country estate.

The trip to Cedarhill went smoothly as they chatted and generally enjoyed being together. Listening to Jim and Roger, Delight couldn't help but wonder what it would be like to have Jim's son. The thought made her smile.

"That's a bewitching smile, darling," he said, for her ears only. "I just wonder what's on your mind?"

"You'd be surprised. . . ."

"That's what I'm afraid of," he grinned, and then was distracted by Roger's shout that he'd finally spotted the house in the distance.

Turning up the drive, they tied up the horse and buggy out front and went inside.

Louise, the maid who lived at Cedarhill all year round, was delighted to see them. "This is wonderful!" She greeted them excitedly hugging Jim and Roger. "I never get much company this time of the year."

"Louise, I'd like you to meet Delight de Vries. Delight, this is Louise. She rules Cedarhill with an iron hand."

"I do not," Louise argued with Jim affectionately. "I just like to keep things running smoothly."

"It's nice to meet you. I hope we haven't disturbed you by stopping by like this."

"Nonsense!" She ushered them toward the kitchen. "Come in and get comfortable. I'll make you some lunch."

"That sounds great!" Roger followed her enthusiastically.

"We'll be along shortly. I'm going to show Delight the rest of the house."

"You know where Roger and I will be," Louise called.

"I think I'd like to show you the upstairs first. . . ." Jim said thoughtfully as he took Delight's cloak and hung it up with his coat. Then, directing her up the steps, he led her down the long, wide hall with its highly polished floor and brilliantly colored throw rugs to the last bedroom on the left.

"Is this yours, by any chance?" Delight asked, her tone sultry.

"I do believe it is." He opened the door for her.

She entered ahead of him slowly, taking the time to admire the pure masculinity of the bedroom. Delight's gaze was drawn to the heavy, four-poster oak bed that dominated the entire room.

"It's beautiful," she murmured, going to run her hands over the intricate carvings on the massive headboard.

"I would love to see you lying on it right now . . . naked." Jim vocalized his deepest yearnings, and Delight felt the heat well up inside of her.

"I'd love to be lying on it . . . waiting for you to come to me."

The temptation to lose themselves in a stolen moment of passion gripped them as Jim took her in his arms and kissed her fiercely, his hands possessively caressing her soft curves. But the reality of their situation kept them from letting things go too far. Smiling ruefully, he stepped away from her and headed back out into the hallway.

"I think we've seen enough bedrooms for now. . . ."

"I suppose you're right." Her voice reflected her disappointment and frustration. "Did Louise say something about lunch? Maybe food will take our minds off our other cravings."

"Maybe, but I doubt it. I think I could live on your love." Jim stopped in the hall to pull her to him and then pressed tender, quick kisses on her neck. A shiver went through her at the touch of his lips, and he sighed, reluctantly letting her go.

"Lunch?" Delight managed, trying to get control of the wild emotions Jim always aroused in her even with his lightest touch.

"Lunch," he nodded, turning with her to start back downstairs.

It was midafternoon when they thanked Louise for her hospitality and climbed back into the carriage to begin their return trip home. Roger's stimulating presence hadn't left them a quiet moment all day, and Delight was surprised to find that the time had passed so quickly.

Settling back in the buggy, she prepared herself for the bumpy ride back. Roger, who was exhausted from the day's busy activities, curled up beside her, and Delight put her arm around him so he could rest more easily. Within a few moments, the child was sound asleep. Jim glanced at them and smiled tenderly.

"Madonna and child," he said softly, and she smiled serenely back at him.

"He's a sweet little boy. I hope we have a son just like him someday," she murmured.

"So do I, love. So do I."

Dorrie had been more than a little disappointed when she received the hasty message that Mark had sent her informing her that he'd been called back to duty and that he had to cancel their date for the afternoon. She had been looking forward to being with him again . . . especially after their explosive embrace Friday night.

Dorrie's thoughts had been confused all weekend as she had tried to sort out her feelings for Mark. What had happened between them had been so unexpected that, initially, she had found herself denying it. But the memory of his fiery kiss had haunted her continually, finally forcing her to admit the truth to herself. She loved Mark Clayton. The revelation astounded her.

After all the years of self-imposed isolation from emotional involvement, Dorrie found that she could hardly wait to see Mark again so she could tell him of her love. He had been so patient with her . . . and so kind. She knew now that he had been waiting for her to come to him. What a fool she'd been. . . .

Dorrie was musing on these thoughts when Wade MacIntosh arrived, reissuing his invitation for her to attend a display with him downtown. She didn't want to go, but his persistence won out. Finally she agreed, but only after he promised to have her home early. She was hoping that Mark might stop by when he got off duty, and she didn't want to chance missing him.

Wade was being his usual solicitous self, catering to her continually, but today Dorrie found him boring. Her thoughts were all of Mark.

Accompanying her through the exhibition at the St. Louis Museum, Wade was growing angry. Dorrie had been distant and quiet all afternoon. Their conversation had been stilted and mostly one-sided as he had attempted to draw her into the intimacy that they had once shared. Even a subtle mention of Paul had no effect on her, and he was getting more frustrated with each passing minute. Glad when they came to the end of the displays, he helped her with her coat and then took her arm to escort her outside.

"Would you like to go somewhere else? It's still early," he offered.

"No. If you don't mind, I'd just like to go home now."

Wade almost snarled that he did mind, but he held himself back. "Shall we walk back? The weather is pleasant today."

"That sounds fine," Dorrie smiled, trying not to be too difficult. Wade was a nice man, but she wanted to be home waiting for Mark.

Wade searched for a way to bring their conversation around to Jim and the gold. "So, how are Jim and Delight's plans coming along for their wedding? Is it going to be soon?"

"As soon as Jim gets back from this next trip. He leaves later this week and it'll probably take him about two weeks. Although, with Delight as his inspiration, he might set a new speed record from here to Tennessee." She smiled, knowing how deeply in love her brother was.

Dorrie wondered idly how Annabelle was taking the news. She knew that she would find Jim's sudden engagement to Delight a bitter pill to swallow so soon after their breakup. Dorrie almost wished that she could have been there to see her face when she'd gotten the word.

Then, realizing that Wade was speaking to her, she dragged herself back to the present and made an attempt to seem interested in what he had to say. She thought they would never get back home, and she was greatly relieved when they finally started up the front steps. Knowing that she couldn't send Wade away so callously, she invited him in for refreshments. Just as she opened the door, he made a clever remark that drew a laugh from her, and, turning to enter the house, she came face-to-face with Mark and Marshall.

"Hello, Dorrie." Mark's voice was cool as he surveyed her quickly, noting her easy manner and apparent lightheartedness.

"Mark," she gulped, hating herself for ever having agreed to go out with Wade.

"If you'll excuse us," Marshall interrupted their tense exchange. "Mark and I have some business we need to take care of."

Leading the way into the study, Marshall closed the door behind Mark, leaving a stunned Dorrie and a gloating Wade alone in the hall. Dorrie tried to recover her equilibrium as she showed him into the parlor. Calling for the maid to bring them a light snack, she sat down nervously in a chair opposite him.

"You seem upset, Dorrie. Is there something wrong?" Wade asked with smooth innocence.

"No. Nothing's wrong," she answered, listening for the sound of Mark's voice in the hall.

Dorrie wanted to run to Mark and tell him of her newly discovered feelings, but instead she was stuck in here with Wade MacIntosh. She was angry with herself for having given in to his prodding to join him in the first place. She hadn't wanted to go and now she was paying the price for not doing what she really had wanted to do. Stifling a groan, she managed to make pleasant small talk with Wade until the refreshments arrived and she could busy herself with them.

Mark paced the study like a caged animal. "I don't believe it! The man is a snake!"

"Calm down, Mark," Marshall said, pouring them both a drink. "It's probably not what you think."

"Let's face it. MacIntosh deliberately had me called back on duty so he could spend the day with Dorrie."

"So?" Marshall was trying to be logical. "You've known Dorrie for years. One afternoon is not going to matter in your relationship."

Mark glared at him, "Would you have liked it if Renee had gone out with another man before you were married?"

"She *was* seeing another man."

"And did you like it?"

"Hell, no, I didn't like it!" Marshall replied. "But there's a difference here. I happened to overhear Dorrie's conversation with Wade before she went out with him this afternoon. She was not anxious to go, but he was so persistent that she finally gave in."

Mark looked at Marshall skeptically. "She hardly looked

like she was having a bad time when she came through that door."

"And she looked a little upset when she came face-to-face with you. Why do you suppose that was?" Marshall challenged. "She certainly had nothing to feel guilty about. You had broken your date and she was free to do whatever she wanted to."

Mark was quiet for a minute. "You're right."

"My advice to you is to stay for dinner. I'll manage somehow to make sure that MacIntosh is out of here before then. All right?"

Mark nodded and finished off his drink.

"Good. Now, what's the news on the next shipment?"

It was over an hour later that they heard Dorrie bid Wade good-bye. Mark was tempted to step out into the hall, just in case Wade was trying to kiss her, but he managed to control himself.

Marshall, leaning back in his desk chair, motioned toward the door. "What are you waiting for? Go get her."

A curious mixture of fear and confidence assaulted him. What if she really did care for MacIntosh . . . what if the response he'd felt in her on Friday night had been nothing more than a physical reaction . . . what if . . . ?

"Mark!" Marshall's sharp tone forced his attention. "I heard the front door close. Wade is gone. You'd better catch up with Dorrie before she goes upstairs."

"Right." Taking a deep breath, Mark placed his glass back on the liquor cabinet and went out to find her.

Dorrie stood at the front parlor window, staring out at the passing vehicles.

"Dorrie?" The sound of Mark's voice caused her to jump, and she turned to him quickly.

"I'm glad you're still here." She began tentatively.

"So am I," he said, approaching her slowly.

They stood apart, their expressions wary as they looked at each other.

"I'm sorry about having to cancel our plans for today." His tone turned bitter as he continued. "Someone pulled rank on me and had me rescheduled for duty."

"I'm sorry, too. I was looking forward to our date. Are you free tonight? Could you stay for dinner?" she invited, hoping he'd stay.

Mark relaxed a little and smiled gently at her. "I'd love to. Thank you."

Dorrie smiled widely at his acceptance, and it was all the encouragement Mark needed. Taking the last step, he took her in his arms. With all the tenderness he could muster, his lips brushed hers softly. While his body demanded he do more, he was careful to restrain himself. He didn't want to frighten her with his ardor.

But Dorrie didn't want the sweet, innocent kisses he was giving her. She wanted another taste of the wildly erotic embrace they'd shared at the Montgomerys'. Slipping her arms about his waist, she moved closer to him, pressing against his hard male form.

Her unexpected response brought a low growl from Mark as he deepened their kiss. Lost in a sea of sensuous bliss, they clung together, discovering the joy of their as yet undeclared love. When they broke apart, they were both breathless, stunned by what had just occurred.

Mark's voice was harsh with emotion as he held her at arm's length. "Dorrie. I've been wanting to tell you this for a long time, but until today I wasn't sure you'd want to hear it."

"What?" She frowned at his confusing words.

"I love you, Dorrie, and I just can't go on this way any longer," he began, his expression serious.

Dorrie gazed up at him, tracing his features, so dear to her, yet, so new; for she was looking at him now for the first time through the eyes of love. Mark, not understanding her silence, rushed on.

"I know how you feel about Paul, but that's been years ago. . . ."

"Felt," she interrupted him, firmly.

"I don't understand . . . ?" Mark looked at her questioningly.

"How I felt about Paul, Mark. He's dead," Dorrie explained, pausing to draw a shaky breath. Then, her lips curving tremulously into a timid smile, she went on, "I will always miss him. He was a wonderful man, and I did care deeply for him. But Mark—I've found that I love you now."

His face reflected his joy. "You do?"

Dorrie nodded. "Very much."

Hugging her to him, he kissed her again, showing her by his actions how much she meant to him.

"I take it you two have worked everything out between you?" Marshall's inquiring, humorous words interrupted their reverie.

"Everything," Dorrie told her brother, not taking her eyes from her beloved.

"Good. I'll tell Renee that Mark will be staying for dinner."

When he had gone, Mark looked down at her. "But what about MacIntosh?"

"I don't care about Wade. The only reason I talked to him in the first place was because he knew Paul. They served together under Lyon . . ."

"What?" Mark asked sharply. He had done a little investigating into Wade's background, and he knew for a fact that Wade had not been anywhere near St. Louis in 1861. But what reason would he have to lie to Dorrie? There seemed to be more to Major MacIntosh than met the eye. . . .

"Wade was there when Paul was shot. . . ."

"I hope his dragging all that up again didn't disturb you," Mark said protectively.

"Just for a moment, and that was when you saw him holding me in the hallway at the Taylors'."

"And then I immediately assumed that you'd fallen in love with him."

"So, that's why you left so quickly. . . ."

"Yes, my love, that's why I left so quickly. I couldn't bear to see you in another man's embrace."

Dorrie hugged him tightly to her. "You'll never have to worry about that again!"

"Lord, I hope not." His lips met hers tentatively, then again, with more passion. "I love you Dorrie. I always have and I always will."

"Jim, I need to talk with you," Mark told him privately as the evening was drawing to a close. "It's important."

"Sure. We'll leave together." Jim, after taking Delight home, had arrived with Roger just in time to finagle an invitation to dinner.

Surrounded by the entire Westlake family, Mark and Dorrie's good night was less than heated, and, in a very few minutes, Jim and Mark were on their way to the riverfront. Mark waited until they were in Jim's cabin on board the *Enterprise* before broaching the subject.

"I think I'm on to something. . . ."

"What?"

"I just found out tonight that MacIntosh has been lying to Dorrie. He told her that he'd served with Paul back in sixty-one. I guess, to win her trust and encourage her to confide in him. But, Jim, Wade MacIntosh was nowhere near St. Louis then."

"How do you know?"

"I'd done some checking up on him previously and . . ."

"You did? Why?" Jim urged.

Mark looked a bit shamefaced, "In the beginning, it was because I was jealous, I guess. But now it's paid off."

"So you think he might have been trying to use her?"

"Surely, if Wade really wanted to court Dorrie, he wouldn't begin their relationship by talking about her long-dead fiancé. And what about today, when he deliberately had me rescheduled? He must have known that Dorrie and I had plans, so he figured the easiest way to get rid of me was to put me on duty."

"He did stop by last night. . . ."

"Everything fits . . . you know Dorrie would be a logical choice if someone wanted to get inside information about your steamers."

The two men considered the possibility in silence.

"How long has Wade been actively courting her?"

"Since the Taylors' ball."

Jim paused. "We had word that they'd pinpointed us before that night, though. So it couldn't have been him, not with Dorrie's unsuspecting help, anyway."

Mark considered his words. "I'm going to keep a close watch on him. Our next shipment is critical."

"Be careful," Jim agreed. "If he is part of a conspiracy, he probably has friends."

"I'll let you know if I find out anything."

"Good. I'll be waiting to hear from you."

Chapter Twenty-nine

"Gentlemen, the gold arrives in town tomorrow night late. It will be taken on board the Westlake steamer *Enterprise* at approximately midnight. There will be at least a double guard staying with this shipment at all times until it reaches its final destination," Nathan concluded. "Now that Wade and Annabelle have provided us with this very delicate information, it's up to us to follow through. Gordon? Are you prepared to act?"

Gordon Tyndale was ready. Spreading out a map, he indicated a place on the Mississippi near the Arkansas-Missouri border.

"This is it." He glanced around the room to make sure that he had everyone's attention. "At the fueling station, near New Madrid . . ."

"You've made the necessary contacts?" Nathan pressed.

"Everything is set. Our people have been informed. Now all they're waiting for is the final word."

"You have it," Wade confirmed, his eyes alive with the thrill of an imminent victory.

A furtive noise from outside the window silenced everyone in the room.

"Wade," Nathan said in a deadly tone. "Find out who or what made that sound. There can be no mistakes made now."

Wade quietly left the back room of Nathan's home. Circling the house, he drew his sidearm in anticipation of a confrontation. He didn't want to use his gun, but he knew he would if it was necessary to ensure the success of their venture. They had worked too long and too hard for it to fall through now.

The young man hiding in the bushes beneath the window where the meeting was taking place didn't realize that he'd been discovered until it was too late. Wade hit him as hard as he could at the base of the skull with the butt end of his gun, and he slumped forward, unconscious.

Glad for the concealing darkness, Wade dragged the limp man around to the back of the house. Knocking softly, he was grateful when Nathan opened the door right away. With a violent curse, he dumped the spy inside on the floor and quickly locked the door.

"Damn! Someone must be on to us!" he swore as the other men crowded around.

"What are we going to do with him?" Gordon asked nervously.

"We have to get rid of him. He knows who we are and what we're doing. Nathan—we'll need some rope and something to gag him with. Blindfold him, too. We don't want him to see any more than he already has . . ."

Nathan rushed to get the needed materials as Wade unceremoniously rolled the injured man over. Searching the pockets of his jacket and pants, he found nothing important but decided to keep all of his possessions to make what happened to him next look like a robbery.

Thrusting the various articles at the other men, he said, "Here, get rid of these. We don't want him to be too easy to identify when they find him."

"You're going to kill him?" Elroy Lucas squeaked in terror.

"What the hell did you think I was going to do with him? Invite him in for a drink? Of course I'm gonna kill him. This is a war, Elroy," Wade sneered. "Or have you been so safe and protected here in the city that you've forgotten what's really happening out in the field?"

"But it's murder." Elroy quaked.

"No. It's called saving our necks. Do you know what they'd do to us if they found out about our plans?" When the room fell silent, Wade smiled grimly. "We would be either hung or shot, probably before the week was out . . . Annabelle, too." He glanced in her direction.

Standing proud and unafraid, she reflected his determination. "Kill him."

Nathan came back with the rope and cloths just as the man started to stir. Wade made a quick job of blindfolding and gagging him, and then he bound his hands behind him and tied his feet together.

"Get a carriage around back," Wade ordered tersely. "Annabelle, I'll need a blanket or two."

By now the man was fully awake, struggling in vain at the bonds that were cutting off the circulation in his hands and feet. Wade kicked him viciously in the side, knocking the wind from him and forcing him to lie still.

"I'll be back," he said, glancing in disgust at the stricken faces of the men surrounding him.

Throwing the blankets over the prone man, he hoisted him over his shoulder and carried him out to the waiting carriage. Shoving him inside on the floor, he made sure the blankets were covering him completely and then shut the door. Borrowing a nondescript black coat and hat from

Nathan, Wade disguised himself as a driver and then drove off at a slow speed, careful not to draw attention.

Wade made his way to a deserted place near the river a little north of town. It was a dark night and the wind had died, leaving everything ominously silent. Opening the carriage door, Wade pulled the covers off his cargo and dragged the man from the vehicle. Levering him over his shoulder once more, he struggled through the overgrowth to a small clearing where he let him down.

The man was conscious and completely helpless, and Wade grinned to himself. It gave him an extraordinary feeling of power to know that he had total control over the situation.

"I want some answers, and I want them now. Do you understand?" Wade asked, his voice sinister.

The man nodded.

"I'll take off your gag so you can answer. If you so much as say one word out of turn, I'll put a bullet through your head. Do you understand?"

Again he nodded.

Wade slipped the tight gag from him. "What's your name?"

"Sam," he managed to croak. "Sam Wallace."

"Sam, I'm only going to ask this next question once. Who hired you?"

Sam swallowed nervously, knowing that he'd failed in his job and that this man would do anything to get the answers he wanted.

"Sam—I'm not a patient man." Wade drew his revolver and cocked it.

Familiar with the sound of a gun's being readied, Sam broke out in a cold sweat. "Captain Clayton hired me . . ."

"Clayton . . . for what? What were you looking for tonight?"

Sam was openly sobbing now as Wade pressed the cold metal of the gun barrel against his temple. "I was supposed to follow Major MacIntosh and let Captain Clayton know everything he did."

"That was all?"

"Yes, sir."

"And what have you reported to Captain Clayton so far?"

"Nothing . . ." His voice broke.

"Good," Wade said smugly, holstering his gun. "Now, don't move."

Sam breathed a deep sigh of relief as he heard the gun being slid back into the holster. Thinking himself saved, he sat perfectly still as Wade untied his feet.

"Stand up. I'll lead you out."

Sam was tempted to run, to try to get away, but he had no idea where he was, and his captor had a gun. Struggling to his feet, he followed the sound of Wade's voice across the uneven ground, stumbling as his numb feet refused to support him.

"Stop right there," Wade commanded.

Sam stood anxiously awaiting the next order. But there was not to be a next order. With swift, silent deadliness, Wade struck him again from behind, and Sam collapsed heavily without making a sound.

Hauling him by his armpits, Wade dragged him the last few feet to the drop-off at the river's edge. Untying his hands and removing the cloth around his eyes, Wade felt no emotion as he pushed him over the small bluff into the icy blackness of the Mississippi.

Wade smiled ferally when he heard the ensuing splash and then turned to make his way back to the carriage. It would be days before Sam's body would be found, and by then the gold would be theirs.

Pleased that he'd thought of an alternative to using his pistol, for a gunshot might have drawn unwanted attention, he calmly took up the reins. Wade hoped that the meeting was over so he could avoid the other men. He found their sniveling presence revolting, and he could hardly wait until this operation had been completed so he wouldn't have to deal with them anymore. Concentrating on his driving, he headed back toward Nathan's.

* * *

Standing near the warmth of the fireplace, leaning negligently against the mantel, Martin sipped slowly at his after-dinner brandy. His eyes hooded to disguise his feelings, he observed Delight and Jim as they sat together on the sofa. It had been Clara's idea to invite Jim to dinner tonight, and Martin was finding it difficult to control the emotions that were raging within him as he watched them.

Delight, wearing a modest but seductive dinner gown, looked beautiful, as usual. The dress seemed to cling to the curves of her breasts, and Martin was hard put not to stare in open fascination at her. Forcing his thoughts away from her delectable body, he glanced at Westlake, who was sitting at her side.

Jim had his arm resting on the back of the sofa, and his hand was idly caressing the nape of Delight's neck. Martin wanted to tell him in no uncertain terms to get his hands off her, but he knew that Clara approved of such loving displays and that he would get no support from her. Westlake looked too confident, as far as Martin was concerned, and he wished he could be there to watch when the Rebs caught up with him on this next trip.

Yes, after this week, Delight would be his for the taking. A half-sneering smile curved his lips as he recalled her struggle to get away from him the last time he'd had her in his arms. Never again would he have to worry about her refusing him . . . not once she realized how powerful he'd become . . . Once more he had to force himself to think of other things.

"So, you'll be leaving us soon, won't you, Jim?" he asked cordially, already knowing the answer.

"Yes. Much to my regret." Jim looked down at Delight with open adoration.

"He won't be gone long." She reaffirmed the fact that he'd be away probably less than two weeks.

"I'm planning on making this a rush trip." Jim grinned at Clara.

"Good. I'm looking forward to your wedding," Clara told

them cheerfully. "It will be a wonderful day for all of us. Don't you think so, Martin?"

"Absolutely, my dear," he answered suavely, giving her what he hoped passed for a tender look.

Clara seemed satisfied with his response and fell silent, comfortable in the glow of Jim and Delight's newfound happiness.

"I hate to do this, darling." Jim looked at Delight regretfully. "But I have to go. I have a nine o'clock meeting with Mark."

"Can't it wait until tomorrow?" Delight protested. She hadn't been alone with Jim since yesterday in the bedroom at Cedarhill, and she was longing for his embrace.

"I'm afraid not, sweetheart. It's business."

"But you worked all day . . . don't you need a little relaxation?"

"I do, but I'm not going to get it." He grinned, knowing her ploy. "I should have more time for you tomorrow. I promise."

"All right. I understand, but that doesn't mean I have to like it." She smiled at her next thought. "I think I will travel with you once we're married."

"Delight!" Clara exclaimed in surprise.

"Don't you think that's a wonderful idea? We'd never have to be apart."

"It just isn't done," Clara began and then had second thoughts. "Is it, Jim?"

"We could always be the first . . ." He chuckled at Clara's shocked expression. "Don't worry Clara. I won't let her do anything outrageous. I love her too much."

"Thank heaven." Clara laughed. Then, realizing that Jim had to leave, she stood. "We'll give you two a few minutes of privacy, since you have to go. Martin?" Clara turned to her husband expectantly.

"A good idea, my love." He took her arm and they left the room together.

Jim traced the delicate line of her jaw with his thumb before tilting her face up to him. "I love you," he whispered before his mouth descended to hers, pledging her all of his love.

Delight slipped her arms around his neck and returned his kiss full measure. They only had one more day together before he had to leave! She wanted to absorb Jim within her . . . to keep him with her all the time . . . to never let him go . . .

With great regret, Jim moved slightly away from her. "I do have to meet Mark . . ."

"I know," she sighed, leaning forward to brush her lips tantalizingly against his. "Just one more?" she asked, not giving Jim time to really decide before she kissed him deeply.

He was more than willing to spend the rest of his life making love to her, but tonight he had pressing business that couldn't wait. With more control than he believed himself capable of, he gently loosened her arms from about him and stood up, drawing her up with him.

"Walk me to the door?"

She grinned at him mischievously. "I almost convinced you to stay, didn't I?"

"Were I a man of less fortitude, I don't think I could ever leave you. . . ."

"Good," Delight grinned as they started out into the hall. "Tomorrow?"

"Of course. It will be during the afternoon, but I'm not sure of a time yet."

"I'll be waiting to hear from you."

With one last passionate embrace, he left her, eager now to have the trip over and done with so they would never have to go through these senseless good-byes again.

"So, you did what had to be done?" Nathan Morgan asked Wade as he handed him a double bourbon.

"Yes," came his answer.

"Should I know anything more about it?"

"There's no need for you to involve yourself. Suffice it to say that he won't be telling Captain Clayton anything about our activities."

"Did Clayton suspect us?"

"No. He was only after me, and I think it was because of our mutual interest in Dorrie Westlake."

Nathan nodded his understanding.

"How is dear Dorrie?" Annabelle asked snidely.

"I spent practically the whole day with her yesterday and learned very little. Either she doesn't concern herself with her brothers' business or she just doesn't care."

"It must have been boring for you."

"It was. Although I did find out that Jim and Delight are going to be married very soon. Supposedly after this next trip."

"How wonderful for them . . ." Annabelle seethed, her emotions a combination of anger and forbidden jealousy.

"Don't worry, darling," Wade said easily. "That is one wedding that will never take place. Aren't you glad that Delight is going to be the one in mourning for him and not you?"

"When you put it that way, it does sound better." She managed to smile convincingly, although Jim's rejection was still a painful memory for her.

"Just a few more days and it will all be over." Nathan sighed in relief. "I can't tell you how glad I am that there's another group involved in the actual raid on the boat. I don't think Gordon has any ability in that area at all."

"I don't know about Gordon, but the rest of the men are useless. Can you imagine what would happen if they were the ones handling the raid?"

"Bungling the raid would be more like it," Annabelle added.

"Who did they contact?"

"One of the guerrilla bands that's operating in the southeastern part of the state."

"Good. Now all we have to do is sit back and wait." Wade smiled confidently, convinced that they'd done everything possible to ensure the success of this mission.

"What if something goes wrong?" Annabelle suddenly worried.

"Nothing can go wrong. We've all covered our tracks. There is no possible way that a raid near New Madrid by a band of Southern guerrillas could be traced back to us," Nathan assured her.

"Then let's drink to it."

And, raising their glasses in a toast, they drank to the Cause and to the success of their plan.

Jim sat with Mark in the deserted saloon on board the *Enterprise*.

"Have you heard anything?"

"Not a word." Mark frowned. "Sam's been tailing him all day, and he was supposed to report back to me by eight o'clock."

"Do you think he's on to something?"

"I don't know. But it is unusual for him to be late. He's always been reliable in the past."

"Should we go looking for him?"

"No. If he has discovered something, we might ruin everything. We'll sit tight. Sam will show up. He always does."

Jim looked worried. "All right. But if we haven't heard from him by morning, we'd better check up on him."

"Fine. Now, we'll be pulling out of here in the early morning hours Thursday, and there will be a double guard."

"Who else knows all this?"

"Just a few people in the payroll command. All of whom, I believe, are trustworthy."

"Then, ideally, there should be no problems."

"None. What about your deckhands? Did you hire on a new cabin boy?"

"No."

They both sat silently for a few minutes, trying to think of angles they might have missed in their efforts to ensure the safety of their next trip.

"I guess we've covered everything. But until we hear from Sam we won't know for sure. Are you worried about anything in particular?"

"No . . . not really. I just have a feeling that something's not right . . ." Jim shrugged. "It'll pass. It's probably just nerves. But you have to admit that this is the most serious threat to our security we've ever had."

"I know," Mark agreed. "And I won't rest easy, either, until we've delivered the gold and we're heading back home."

Jim nodded and said no more on the subject as they started out to the deck. Tomorrow it would all come together, as it always did, and, once they were on the river, he felt certain that things would go smoothly.

"Stop by in the morning and let me know what you hear from Sam."

"I will," Mark told him, following him out on deck.

"Are you going to see Dorrie tomorrow?"

"I promised her I'd stop by in the afternoon for a while, but I won't have much time."

"I know the feeling. It'll probably be late before I can get over to the Montgomerys'."

Mark grinned as they parted. "It will be easier once you're married."

"I hope so. I'm not looking forward to this separation from her at all," Jim smiled. "But after the next two weeks, we'll never have to go through this again."

"I wish I could say that."

"When are you two getting married?"

"We haven't talked about it yet. Maybe I'll try to pin her down before we leave."

"Let me know. We could always make it a double ceremony." And they laughed in friendly companionship as Mark left the boat.

Jim was tired as he made his way slowly back to his cabin. It had been a long day, and tomorrow promised to be another one. Throwing off his coat, he didn't even bother to undress as he stretched out on his bunk.

Chapter Thirty

Mark strode up the gangplank, his expression grim.

"What's wrong, Mark?" Jim had seen him ride up to the levee and he'd gone down to meet him.

"I'm not sure. Sam never reported back last night, and I haven't heard from him this morning."

"Did you check where he lives?"

"Yes. The woman who owns the boardinghouse hasn't seen or heard from him since yesterday afternoon."

"What about Macintosh?"

"He reported for duty on time this morning."

"I don't like any of this."

"Neither do I. Maybe if we had more time we could search for Sam, but it's too late now . . . the gold's already arrived."

"Damn!" Jim cursed under his breath. "Are you going to load it ahead of schedule?"

"No. We'll leave things the way they are for now. If there are any changes, I'll let you know."

"Fine."

"In the meantime, I've put out the word that I need Sam right away. Hopefully, he'll turn up before we sail."

"And if he doesn't?"

Mark shook his head. "We'll just have to be extra careful tonight."

Delight almost ran down the hall when she heard the sound of Jim's voice later that afternoon.

"Darling!" She was in his arms then, hugging him tightly. "I was so afraid that you'd be too busy to get away." Her arm around his waist, she led him into the parlor.

"I don't have much time, but I knew I couldn't leave without seeing you one more time." As soon as they were within the privacy of the room, he embraced her heatedly, his mouth searing hers in a fiery kiss.

Finally, when neither of them could stand the exquisite torture any longer, they broke apart, breathless in their excitement.

Jim smiled at her tenderly and reached out to caress her flushed cheek with gentle fingers. "You're so beautiful . . ."

Delight turned to press a kiss into his palm. "I don't like this."

"What?" he murmured, mesmerized by the provocative look she was giving him.

"Parting."

"Neither do I, sweetheart." He slid his hand down to her throat where he could feel the wild throbbing of her pulse. "Do you want me?" His voice was soft.

"Very much," she answered, with no hesitation.

"And I want you," he told her earnestly. "That will never change." With an easy pressure, he drew her forward and sought her lips in an agonizingly sweet kiss of pure devotion. "Never."

"I know," she managed as she rested her head on his broad shoulder. "You'll miss me?"

"Every minute I'm gone. Can you doubt that?"

"No. And I'll miss you, too." She confessed what he already knew. "You'll hurry?"

"If it were possible for man to fly, I would."

They moved slowly to sit together on the sofa, touching, yet not embracing, for their passion was still white-hot, and they needed to stay in control of the flames that threatened to consume them.

"How long can you stay?"

"I should go now, but I don't want to leave you yet . . ."

She smiled painfully. "I don't want you to go. You know that. But I understand how important your business is."

Jim knew what she was feeling, for the same emotions were tearing at him. He'd never felt this way before, and he was having trouble dealing with it. In all of his thirty some-odd years, not once had he regretted leaving anyone behind. And, now, all he wanted to do was carry Delight off with him. He didn't want to go alone. He wanted her in his cabin and in his bed, all the time.

"You'll be safe while I'm away?"

Delight glanced nervously toward the hallway door. "I'll be fine. I have Rose with me."

"Rose will be of little help to you if he should decide to use force," he said fiercely, keeping his tone low.

"I'll stay out of his way. In fact, if it will make you happy, I'll stay locked in my room until you come back," she teased, trying to lighten his protective mood.

"That's not a bad idea," he agreed, before smiling as he recognized her ploy. "All right. I give up. But you know I'll be worried . . ."

"I know. But I'll be worried about you, too. You're in more danger than I ever could be."

"And it will all be over soon. Then we can be together as we want to be."

The sound of Clara out in the hallway forced them apart.

"Delight? Is Jim here?"

"Yes, Mother. We're in the parlor."

Jim rose as his future mother-in-law came in to join them. "Jim. It's so good that you came by before you had to leave. Can you stay for dinner?"

"No, I'm sorry, Clara. I have to get right back."

"That's a shame. We would have enjoyed having you. You have a safe trip and hurry back to us." She kissed his cheek.

"I will," he promised her.

"Good." She smiled warmly at the two of them. "I'll leave you alone now. Jim, I'll see you when you return." And she was gone, giving them the last few minutes of privacy they needed.

Jim looked down at Delight. "Darling, I have to go."

She stood up and went into his arms. "Kiss me, Jim. Please. Just once more . . ."

Unable to resist, he kissed her thoroughly, leaving her in no doubt about his feelings, and then he let her go. "I'll be back." Turning from her, he strode quickly from the room, knowing that if he looked back his resolve would weaken.

Delight watched him go, fighting back the tears that burned in her eyes. She loved him so . . . dear God, how she loved him.

Martin was admitted to the Morgan house by Annabelle. "Come in, Mr. Montgomery. My father's in the study; go right on in."

"Thank you, my dear."

Wondering what further business he could have with her father, she watched him disappear into the room and close the door securely behind him.

"Nathan." Martin crossed to the desk and shook hands with him. "I hope you don't mind my dropping by."

"No, not at all. What can I do for you?"

"I just wanted to check and make sure that everything was going according to our plan."

"To the best of my knowledge, it is," Nathan told him confidently. "I can't go into detail for you, but rest assured that by tomorrow night, at the latest, you should have your wish."

"Westlake will be dead?"

"Yes."

"Good." Mentally, Martin rubbed his hands together. "That's what I wanted to know."

"Would you like a drink to celebrate?"

"I most certainly would."

It was growing dark as Mark and Jim stood together in the deserted pilothouse. "There's been no word from Sam Wallace."

Jim nodded. "And you think something's happened to him?"

"I don't know what to think. Macintosh has been on duty all day. I've been keeping an eye on him myself."

"Could Wallace have gone on a drunk? Or taken off for any other reason?"

"No. Not Sam. He prides himself on doing a good job."

"Do we have time to send a man to the hospitals? Maybe he was injured . . ."

"I've already done that. No one's been admitted by that name."

"Well, we've done everything we can for now. We'll just have to hope that he turns up before midnight."

"Sam's a good man. If it's possible, he will."

It was cold . . . so cold . . . and wet. Grasping at the protruding tree roots with numb hands, he hung on. How long had it been now? Where was he? And why was his head pounding so badly that it hurt to think?

The sound of children's voices came to him . . . distantly. They were laughing. . . . He opened his mouth to try to call out, but all he could do was croak. He'd been calling for what seemed like hours but no one had come . . . no one had heard. . . .

"Look!" The boy paused at the top of the muddy riverbank. "Run, Charlie, get Mama! Quick!"

Without another word, Charlie ran full speed back through the brush. Long minutes passed. Sitting down, the boy who'd remained watched the man clinging to a slippery root near the riverbank.

"Mister?" he called out. "Mister? Are you awake?"

There was no answer to his plaintive call, and he shivered in fright. The child was relieved when he heard his mother's approach.

"Mama! There's a man! He's stuck in the river!" He ran to her, taking her hand and dragging her forward. "Look!"

"Thank God you saw him, Danny!" She looked around

desperately, but there was no one anywhere near them. "I'll have to get him out. You children wait here."

Sarah Webb lowered herself slowly down the slippery incline and made her way cautiously to the water's edge.

"Be careful, Mama!"

"I will, darlings," she tried to reassure her two young sons as she stepped out into the cold, dirty water.

Praying that there were no steep drop-offs between herself and the man, she moved forward cautiously as the icy river soaked through her heavy skirts and swirled frigidly about her legs. She lost her footing once and fell sideways, drawing cries of fear from the boys, but she waved to them a second later as she stood up once more and then continued forward to grasp the unconscious man.

"Can you hear me?" she asked, but received no response.

Taking the last fateful step, Sarah wedged herself against the root he was holding and grabbed his arm. With a violent pull, she managed to tug him loose, but she almost lost her grip on him as the current tried to steal his now free-floating weight from her. His head went under, and Sarah was forced to surge forward and grasp his upper arm to keep his head up. Trudging one step at a time, she made her way back toward the bank and collapsed, holding the man's body beside her.

After long minutes, she turned to look at him before calling up to her sons, "Danny—Charlie—go get help."

"We don't want to leave you, Mama!" Danny, the older boy, cried.

"You have to, sweetheart. He's still alive, but I can't get him up the bank by myself. Now, run and bring help. Hurry!"

"We will, Mama." And they were gone.

Annabelle descended from her carriage, aided by the driver, and then bade him to wait for her. "This will only take a few moments, I'm sure."

As she started up the walkway to Delight's house, she felt a surge of feminine power, and she smiled cruelly as she raised the knocker and let it fall. Jim Westlake might think he was done with her, but she was not about to let him take up with Delight so easily.

She had given it a lot of thought since Martin had left their house earlier that afternoon, and she'd decided to make sure Jim and Delight's romance did not run smoothly. Why, the bitch had stolen her fiancé! Certainly a little female revenge was in order. . . .

Rose was stunned when she answered the door and found Annabelle Morgan on the doorstep.

"I'd like to speak with Delight, please." Annabelle didn't wait to be invited in, but brushed right past Rose to enter the foyer.

"Of course." Rose directed her to the parlor. "Have a seat in the parlor while I get her for you."

Without another word, Annabelle swept into the sitting room, while Rose hurried upstairs to get Delight.

"Delight!" She knocked softly on her bedroom door.

"What is it, Rose?"

"It's Annabelle Morgan. She's downstairs and she wants to talk to you!"

"Annabelle?!!" The possibility of a confrontation with Annabelle had never occurred to Delight, and she hurried out into the hall. "What does she want?"

"I don't know. All she said was that she wanted to speak to you. There was no way I could put her off . . . she just walked right into the house."

"It's all right, Rose." Delight patted her hand reassuringly. "I'll go talk to her."

With more bravado than she felt, Delight went downstairs and sought out Annabelle.

"Annabelle?" Delight paused in the doorway of the parlor. "Is there something I can help you with?"

Annabelle looked up at Delight, her expression clearly one

of smug superiority. "No . . . as a matter of fact, I've come to help you. . . ."

"Oh? And just what is it you're going to help me with?"

"I thought you might like to know a few things about your precious fiancé."

"I don't think you can tell me anything about Jim that I'd want to know." Delight remained standing, feeling that it gave her an advantage over Annabelle.

"Ah, but that's where you're wrong. You see, I know what kind of a man Jim Westlake really is. . . ."

"You do?" Delight's eyes widened at the implication.

"I do. And I want to warn you about him."

"Warn me? About Jim?"

"Darling," Annabelle drawled with exaggerated patience. "Surely you aren't that naive, are you? Jim is a man who loves women . . . not just one woman . . . all women . . . why do you think he's stayed single all this time?"

"I'm sure I don't know what you're talking about."

"Let me tell you straight out, then. Just a short time ago, Jim was sharing my bed," she lied, "and now I have no doubt he's making love to you. How long do you suppose you can hold him?"

"Annabelle. I think this conversation has gone on long enough."

"Well, if you won't listen . . ." Annabelle shrugged and stood up. "But remember, I did try to warn you. You'll never be able to hold him. You don't have what it takes!" she sneered.

And with that, she quickly left the house and climbed into her carriage. Annabelle didn't look back as the driver pulled away, she was too busy congratulating herself on a job well done.

Delight stood in her slowly darkening bedroom, staring out the front window. She felt cold and alone and her thoughts were confused. She had to see Jim once more before he left.

She had to! But how could she get down to the levee without her mother or Martin's knowing? She was pondering the situation when Rose came back into the room.

"Rose . . . I need your help . . ."

"What now?" Rose was instantly cautious.

"I need to see Jim again," Delight stated with fierce determination.

"Delight—I don't think that's a good idea . . ."

"I know, but I have to."

"But why? You said your good-byes this afternoon, didn't you?"

"That was before Annabelle came by."

"What did that woman say to you?"

"I don't want to talk about it . . . not until I hear what Jim has to say." Delight refused to discuss it. It hurt too badly to think it might be true. "Will you help me?"

"This is crazy. How will you get down there? You know your mother would never approve of your going out unescorted at this time of night. . . ."

"I know. But this is something I have to do." Delight hurried to her wardrobe and pulled out the boy's clothes she'd worn as Murphy.

"You're not?"

"I most certainly am. I intend to see him one way or the other. Now, are you going to help me or are you going to stand there and stare at me all night?"

"I'll have to help you, I suppose, but don't you think I should go with you?"

"No. I'll be fine. I know my way around the riverfront now, so don't worry. And I promise that I'll be back before midnight."

"If you say so." Rose looked worried. "What shall I tell your mother if she should discover that you've gone?"

"Don't tell her anything! If she comes up here, just tell her that I cried myself to sleep. All right?"

Rose shook her head in frustration. "I'll try. That's the best I can promise. But you be careful!"

"I will. I did this before, and I can do it again."

A short time later, Delight slipped out of the house unnoticed. Striding down the streets, she made her way easily to the riverfront and located the boat with no problem. There were Union soldiers everywhere, and she worried for a moment about getting on board, but finally she just squared her shoulders and walked up the gangplank.

Her progress went uninterrupted as she headed for the texas deck. She hoped Jim would be in his cabin, but she knew the chances of that were slim. The door to his stateroom was unlocked, and she let herself in.

After closing the door behind her, Delight looked around the room in amazement. It was a mess! Not wanting to sit idly and let her worrisome thoughts run away with her, she busied herself picking up his clothes and straightening his bed.

Jim left Ollie in charge and then started back to his cabin. There were still a few hours left before Mark was going to load the gold, and he had hopes that he could get some rest. He was about to reach for the doorknob when he heard the faint sounds of someone moving about inside his room.

Who could be in his cabin? And why? Jim wished for the first time that he carried a firearm. He hesitated only momentarily before throwing the door open and bursting into the room.

"What the hell do you—" He never got any further as he came face-to-face with Delight.

Delight's eyes had widened in fear when the door had flown open, and she cowered nervously at the unexpected intrusion.

Jim was staring at her in total confusion. "Do you realize that if I'd had a gun, you'd probably be dead right now?"

"No," she managed to squeak out.

"I thought you were a spy . . . someone searching my room. Damn it, woman!" Jim was shaking as he thought of what could have happened. Wearily, he closed the door behind him and locked it. "Why are you here?" he asked, a little more angrily than he'd intended.

Thinking from his tone that he didn't want her here, Delight faced him and hurried to tell him her story. "I needed to talk to you. I had an unexpected visitor this afternoon."

"A visitor? Who?" He ran a hand nervously through his hair, not yet recovered from the shock of finding her in his cabin.

"Annabelle Morgan, that's who."

"Annabelle?" He realized how traumatic that must have been for her. Turning to her, he opened his arms. "Let me hold you . . ."

"Not until we've talked," Delight declared.

"Delight? What's wrong? What did she say to upset you so?" Jim was tired, and he was due to leave port in just a few hours. The last thing he wanted was a misunderstanding between them now.

"She told me that you'd made love to her . . ." Her eyes met his unwaveringly. "Is it true?"

Jim looked Delight straight in the eye as he answered, "No. It's a lie."

"Oh, Jim . . ." Delight went to him, clinging to his strength. "It was so horrible . . . she said that you had used her and that you would use me in the same way . . . she said . . ."

"Hush. She was only trying to drive a wedge between us . . . to ruin the perfection of what we've found together . . . she's jealous and full of hate, darling. . . ." His mouth covered hers, blending and giving. "I love you, Delight."

"I was so worried . . . that's why I had to come . . ."

"I'm glad you did . . . I need you badly. Right now." He pulled back to look at her. "Will you let me love you? Will you trust me forever and know that you're the only woman I've ever really loved?"

"What about Renee?" she challenged and wished quickly that she could take back the words.

Jim gave her an endearing lopsided smile. "You know about that, do you?"

"Ollie told me . . ."

"I loved Renee; I still do, but what I feel for her is totally different from what we share. And believe me, what we have is so breathtakingly beautiful. . . ."

"I know," she agreed, pulling his head down for a passionate kiss.

With eager hands they began to undress, and soon they were naked on his freshly made bed, discovering the glory of lying together once again. They didn't speak; they didn't want to waste the time. Each moment was precious as they touched and explored and shared the joys of love's mystery.

Jim was as impatient to have her as Delight was to be possessed by him. And their bodies melded in perfect harmony as the tempest of their union played itself out, leaving them rapturously content in its aftermath.

"You're not sorry I came?" Delight was almost afraid to ask.

"No. Never," Jim told her. "I was wondering how I was going to last through the next fourteen long days and longer nights with only a kiss to tide me over."

Lifting a hand, she touched his cheek, enjoying the sensuously rough feel of his day's growth of whiskers against her palm.

Turning his head, he pressed a heated kiss on her palm. "Let's rest for a while. . . ."

"Do we have much time?"

"An hour, maybe. . . ."

She snuggled closer to him. "I love you."

He kissed her softly. "I know. And you're mine now."

Closing her eyes, Delight lay quietly in the security of his warm embrace.

"Delight?" Jim said her name softly.

"Um," she muttered sleepily, from the comfort of his arms.

"It's time."

"So soon?"

"Yes. It's almost eleven. Mark will be here soon."

"Take me with you?"

"I wish I could." He paused to kiss her. "Next time. All right?"

"All right."

Reluctantly, they got up and began to dress.

"I'm going to arrange for a carriage to take you back."

"But Jim, somebody might see me."

He frowned. "Then tell the driver to drop you off a short distance from your house."

"I can walk."

"No. The only way I'll know that you made it home safely is if I send you home in a carriage. Understand?"

"Yes, sir," she replied respectfully.

"Thank you," he grinned. "That's the tone I like to hear. I must have trained you right."

Delight smiled at him, and he went to her and took her in his arms to kiss her. Reluctantly, he finally put her from him.

"You are much too tempting. It's a good thing you're going ashore, or Mark might not see me for the entire trip."

Her fingers were shaking as she finished pulling on her clothes. "I'm ready now."

"All right. I want you to wait in here until I come for you. I'll go get the carriage right now."

He left the room quickly, pulling on his coat as he went, and he was back in a very few minutes.

"Everything's set."

"Thank you." Delight didn't want to look at him, for she knew he'd be able to read the misery she was feeling in her eyes.

"Darling?" His tone was coaxing.

"Yes?" She raised tear-filled eyes to him.

"Your coming down here was the best going-away present I've ever had." He reached out and wiped gently at the crystal-line teardrop that traced a path down the softness of her cheek.

"I'll miss you," she said softly and then, raising up on tiptoes, she hugged him quickly and kissed his cheek before hurrying from the room.

Jim waited, taking a minute to get himself under control before following her outside. From his vantage point on the texas deck, he watched Delight as she started to get into the hired conveyance. She turned toward him only once and lifted her hand in a mute good-bye before she disappeared within the safety of the carriage.

Chapter Thirty-one

Delight instructed the driver to stop two blocks from her house, and went the rest of the way on foot. The streets were dark, damp, and deserted, and she shivered as she hurried the short distance home. Grateful to discover that Rose had left the back door unbolted, she entered the kitchen quickly, anxious to be out of the chill of the night air. It was as she was turning to start up the backstairs that he spoke from the shadows.

"So. You've been to your lover again, have you?" Martin's voice was cold with menace. "And in such clothes . . . is this how he likes you? Dressed like a boy?"

Delight froze in the middle of the dimly lighted room. "What do you want, Martin?"

"You know what I want. And I intend to have it right now."

"There is no way I'm going to let you touch me ever again," she told him, and she was amazed at how calm she sounded.

"We'll see about that, you little bitch," he seethed, and with lightning speed he grabbed her and pulled her to him.

His hands were rough as they tore her shirt, popping the buttons off, and his mouth covered hers in a punishing kiss that muffled the sound of her scream as his groping fingers sought her exposed breast. Struggling, Delight tried to kick him, but Martin was too fast for her. Tonight, he was ready. His lips bruised hers as he roughly pushed her back against the wall, trapping her effectively.

Delight felt faint. How could this be happening? A few minutes ago she had been safe in Jim's tender care, and now she was being ravaged by this animal. Twisting, she tried to break free. She couldn't let him do this, she couldn't! But Martin was too strong for her, and he held her immobile as he continued his assault, forcing her to submit to his fervent caresses. Her tears fell unheeded as she felt herself weakening. Her knees were barely able to support her, and she slumped heavily against the wall as Martin moved closer and wedged himself against her.

It was the sudden brightening of the room, followed by the cold, deadly words that Clara uttered that brought Martin back to reality.

"Take your hands off my daughter," Clara ordered, cocking the pistol she held and pointing it directly at the center of his back.

Martin froze, unable to move for an instant.

Clara repeated her warning as Rose joined her, carrying a lamp. "I said, get your filthy hands off Delight!"

He paled as he realized that he'd been caught, and he quickly dropped his hands from her and moved away.

"She met me down here . . . she tempted me. . . ." he began, but the look in his wife's eyes was one of open contempt.

"Rose," she said softly, looking at Delight as she stood helplessly sobbing against the wall.

"Yes, ma'am?"

"I want you to take her upstairs, away from this pitiful excuse for a man, and pack a few things for the both of you. I'll have the carriage brought around, and I want you to go to Jim Westlake. Tell him what happened here."

"Yes ma'am."

With tender efficiency, Rose led Delight out of the room

and upstairs to the safety of her bedroom. Locking the door behind them, she helped her to the bed.

"Sit here a minute while I get everything together."

"I need a bath, Rose . . . I have to wash . . . I feel so . . ." Delight was shivering uncontrollably from the shock of Martin's attack.

Rose paused in her work and quickly poured a bowl of water for her at the washstand. "Use this for now. We'll get you a real bath on the boat."

"Yes . . . on the boat . . ." Delight said, slightly reassured. "We have to hurry."

"I know. You wash and I'll pack. Here, wear this." Rose handed her the other boy's shirt that she owned.

In less than five minutes, they were ready to go. Descending the staircase, they heard the sound of voices in the kitchen.

"Delight, you wait here. I'll tell your mother we're going."

Delight nodded, not wanting to face Martin again.

"Clara, we're ready."

Standing in the kitchen with the gun still pointed directly at Martin, Clara answered, "Fine. The carriage is out in front. I want her safely on that boat, Rose."

"I'll take care of her."

Clara nodded, and Rose hurried from the room, anxious to be away from Martin's vicious presence.

Clara focused all of her attention on her husband once she heard the carriage drive away.

"I want to hear what you have to say for yourself," she demanded, never wavering in her purpose.

"I have nothing to say. You've already convicted me in your mind."

She looked at him, smiling thinly. "You're right. I convicted you a long time ago, when I found out that you were sleeping with Sue, but I gave you the benefit of the doubt. Until tonight, that is."

"Sue?" He hadn't known that she'd been aware of his activities.

"Of course. Did you think I was so stupid I wouldn't find out?" When he didn't respond, she continued. "Just one question, Martin. Why?"

He looked up at her, regretting that he'd been discovered. She had been a generous wife, and he wondered quickly if he could salvage any of their relationship. "Sue offered." He shrugged. "Surely I'm not the first master of the house to take advantage of a willing wench?"

"I could care less what you do with her. I'm talking about my daughter."

"She's gone now. Let's forget about her. . . ." He thought he'd made progress, for he saw a softening in her expression, but when he started to stand, she lifted the gun toward him again.

"It would be that simple to you, wouldn't it?"

"Why not? It was a mistake. It won't happen again. You can get rid of Sue, too, if you want. Then it will be just you and me. Like it was before Delight returned."

Clara saw him for what he was, then. An opportunist. "No. I'm afraid that won't happen. If you'd really cared about me, you wouldn't have needed other women. Especially my daughter. What you've done is unforgivable. I want you out of here, now."

"But darling—" he began, as his hopes faded.

"Out, Martin. Or I'll use this gun on a part of your anatomy that you're exceedingly proficient with." She lowered her aim and gave a grim laugh as he headed quickly upstairs.

Taking time only to get the money he'd hidden and his clothes, Martin prepared to leave the house. Clara was standing in the front hall when he came down on his way out, but neither spoke. There was nothing left for them to say. When he closed the door behind him, she stared at it for a long time before heading back up to bed, knowing that she wouldn't sleep that night.

Mark arrived with the gold right on schedule. It was loaded onto the *Enterprise* with no problems, and the guards settled in as the boat made ready to get underway for its long journey south. Mark met Jim in the pilothouse, where they were going over last-minute details when the shout of one of the soldiers drew their attention to the dock area.

"Captain! There's a carriage coming at full speed . . . it might be trouble!"

Mark and Jim raced down the companionway so they could get a better look at what was going on. With their sidearms drawn, two guards left the boat to approach the vehicle that was now stopped at the foot of the gangplank. They exchanged a few words with the driver before taking a cursory look inside. Then one of the soldiers came back on board and headed up to where they stood.

"What is it, Corporal?" Mark asked.

"It's two women, sir. And they said they need to speak with Captain Westlake immediately. Some sort of emergency, sir."

"Delight—" Jim glanced at Mark worriedly before hurrying below. Dodging soldiers and freight, he ran full speed down the gangplank.

Rose saw him coming and opened the carriage door to climb out. "Jim—"

"Is she hurt? What happened?"

"It was Martin. . . ." Rose started to tell him, but the look on his face was so fierce that she thought better of it. There would be time for that later.

"No—" He brushed past her to reach Delight. "Darling?"

Delight sat in the shadows, still tormented by what had nearly taken place. She had been so sure that she'd be able to handle Martin, and he had overpowered her so easily. . . .

"I'm sorry . . . I didn't want to worry you. . . ."

"It's all right, love. You're coming with me." He lifted her lithe form in his arms and carried her quickly on board.

Delight clung to him, secure at last in the haven of his strong embrace. Jim took her directly to his cabin and laid her down on the bed. Helping her with her coat, a cold rage grew within him.

"Montgomery did this to you?" His voice was taut with anger as he saw the bruises Martin had inflicted on her.

"Yes . . . he cornered me in the kitchen when I got back . . . I tried to get away from him. . . ."

Jim sat down next to her and pulled her across his lap as she sobbed out her whole story, telling him of the helplessness she'd felt when Martin had forced her back against the wall. With a gentle touch, Jim smoothed her hair back from her face and pressed a soft kiss on her brow.

"It's all over now. You'll never have to go back," he reassured her calmly as he felt her shivering slowly stop. "Never."

Finally calming down, she looked up at Jim, her eyes luminous with her love for him. "Thank you."

He kissed her then, reminding her of all that they meant to each other, and sat holding her close and cherishing the feel of her against him.

Filled with a primitive fury, Jim wanted to track Martin down and strangle him with his bare hands. The bastard had actually laid his hands on her . . . he'd hurt her . . . Jim tensed as he fought to control himself. The mournful whistle from the pilothouse broke through his thoughts, giving him an element of stability to hang on to.

"I need to speak with Mark; it's time for us to shove off. Will you be all right alone for a few minutes?"

She nodded.

"I'll be right back." Against his better judgment, he left her, knowing that the pilot was awaiting his command to leave port. He found Rose and Mark standing anxiously outside his cabin.

"How is she?" Mark inquired with great concern. He'd seen how pale she'd looked when Jim had carried her on board.

"I think she'll be all right. She just needs a little rest right now. Rose, could you stay with her while I go up to the pilothouse?"

"Of course." Without further words, she entered the cabin and closed the door behind her.

Mark and Jim headed for the pilothouse to supervise their leaving.

"What happened? Can you talk about it?"

Jim hesitated, wondering whether to tell him the whole truth, and then decided that it was time. "Delight's stepfather tried to force himself on her."

"Martin Montgomery?" Mark was stunned.

"That's right, the bastard . . . if we didn't have to pull out right now, I'd track the son of a bitch down and kill him without a second thought." Jim's voice revealed the agony of his position . . . his desire for revenge thwarted by his duty not only to his job but to Delight, as well. He knew that she needed him now, more than ever. There would be a time and place to seek his revenge on Martin, but this was not the night, no matter how badly he wanted to see the man suffer.

"Easy . . ." Mark tried to calm him.

"I know. I'm under control, but just barely . . . the thought of what he almost did to her. . . ."

"But he didn't succeed. She'll be fine, right?"

Jim sighed as some of the tension left his body. "Right. It's just that I feel so responsible."

"You? Why?"

"I knew about Martin and I let her go back there."

"How could you have known?"

Jim looked at Mark quickly, "I might as well tell you everything, so you can understand. Martin tried to take her once before, but she managed to get away. She disguised herself as a boy and . . ."

"Delight?"

"That's right. Remember Del Murphy?"

"You're not serious?" Mark was astonished.

"I am. Do you realize she lived with me for all that time and never once did I guess. . . ."

Mark smiled at the thought. "How did you finally find out?"

"Suffice it to say that on the night of my engagement party to Annabelle, Delight revealed herself to me. And then the next morning she fled. I didn't know her name; all I knew was that she was the most perfect woman in the world, and I wanted her for my own."

"When did you find out who she really was?"

"The night of the Montgomerys' party."

"I wondered why you broke off with Annabelle so quickly."

"I didn't love her. Not like I did Delight. She's the only woman I've ever really needed."

"But why did she go back home? Surely she knew she wouldn't be able to stop Martin. Not if he really wanted her. . . ."

"She threatened to tell her mother everything if he didn't stay away from her. . . ." Jim paused. "God, Mark . . . if I ever find him . . ."

"I know." He clasped Jim on the back sympathetically as they entered the pilothouse.

They fell silent then as the pilot skillfully backed the huge steamboat out into the current and swung her around to head downstream. The lights of St. Louis were fading behind them as they once again went back out on deck.

"Did you ever hear anything from Sam Wallace?" Jim forced himself to think of other things as they walked down the deck to the passageway.

"Not a word."

Jim just nodded. "Well, at least we got away without any trouble."

"I just wish I knew what happened to Sam."

"So do I. I'd rest a lot easier if I knew for sure that MacIntosh was clean."

"You're not the only one." They paused at the railing. "You'd better be getting back to Delight."

"I know. Are you set for the rest of the night?"

"Sure. And if I do need anything, I'll just find Ollie."

"Good. I'll be in my cabin."

Jim moved slowly down the texas deck to his room and went in quietly. Rose had turned the lamp down and was sitting at his desk.

"She's asleep," Rose said softly.

Jim nodded, going to stand beside the bed. Curled on her side, Delight looked very young, and he was touched by the innocence of her beauty. "Are you tired, Rose?"

"A little."

"Why don't you use Delight's bed in the connecting room." He indicated the door.

"Thanks. I will." Rose went on to bed then, leaving Jim alone with Delight.

He stood hesitantly for a moment in the middle of his stateroom as he realized that he'd just set himself up with a chaperone. All he had thought about was lying down with Delight and holding her through the night. He wanted to soothe away her fears, but now, with Rose so close at hand, he had no such freedom.

Cursing under his breath at his own stupidity, he slumped in his desk chair and opened the bottom drawer to pull out his oft-used bottle of scotch. Tilting it to his lips, he took a long drink of the strong whiskey. Leaning back, he propped his feet up on the desktop and tried to relax.

So much had happened so fast. Jim let his gaze roam over Delight as she lay sleeping in his bed. He regretted deeply her abuse at Martin's hands, and he would see that the man paid in full for his attempt. Actually, he was glad that she was here with him. Now he would know for certain that she was safe at all times.

Bracing his shoulders against the back of the hard chair, he shifted himself lower in search of comfort. It was going to be a long, lonely night, and he knew he should try to get some rest while he could.

Delight stirred as vivid memories of the evening just passed haunted her. In her dream, she was running . . . trying to get away from Martin, but he was always close behind her, grabbing at her and trying to pull her down. . . . With a soft, wild cry she came awake, her breathing labored, her eyes wide with the stark terror she'd felt in her dream.

"Jim!"

The sound of her voice woke him, and he moved quickly from his seat to the bedside. "Are you all right?"

Delight held her arms out to him in a silent plea, and Jim, not caring that Rose was in the next room, slid into bed next to her and held her close.

"Rest, love. I'll keep you safe from now on." He felt her sigh as the tenseness left her, and in a few minutes she'd fallen back asleep. Jim sighed, too, but for very different reasons. There he was with the woman of his dreams sleeping peacefully in his arms, and there was nothing he could do. He was fully dressed, fully chaperoned, and fully miserable. Resigning himself to a night of complete frustration, he kissed her brow gently and then closed his eyes.

Chapter Thirty-two

The sun was just streaking the horizon with its golden promises when Martin emerged from the saloon. After leaving Clara, he'd taken a room at the Planter's Hotel and then spent the evening trying to devise a plan that would set him up for the rest of his life. Though he was in no danger of financial embarrassment at the present time, Martin definitely needed more money. He'd become accustomed to the good life, and he wanted to maintain that standard of living.

Taking a deep breath of the crisp morning air to clear his head, Martin headed back toward his hotel. He had made many decisions out of necessity before, so he didn't resent the position he now found himself in. The only thing that bothered him was the fact that he had never made Delight his own. But it was too late to worry about that; Delight had made her choice to go with Westlake, and Martin knew that she would get what she deserved. Right now, his own survival was all that mattered to him, and Martin fully intended to come out of this awkward situation in good financial shape.

As he saw it, he had two opportunities—he could go to Nathan and threaten to expose their involvement in the upcoming robbery unless they paid him more money; or he could go to Marshall Westlake and warn him about the planned attack. Though either plan might pay off handsomely, they were both fraught with risks. Nathan and his group just might turn vicious and try to silence him permanently, while the Westlakes might not believe what he had to say.

The possibility of endangering his own life was enough to convince Martin to go to Marshall with what he knew. Not that he wanted to save Jim's life, but he did need to get the most possible money with the least possible effort.

His decision made, he now had to come up with a believable story of how he had come by the information, and he also had to present himself in such a way that his approach did not sound like blackmail. Convinced that the only thing Marshall would buy was desperation, Martin knew he would have to act the part of a hunted man.

It was after nine when he ventured forth from his hotel room and made his way to Marshall's office.

"Good morning," Marshall greeted him.

"Marshall." Martin was grave and a bit jittery as he came forward. Martin wondered quickly if Jim had told his brother of his involvement with Delight, but his cordial welcome belied those fears.

"What can I do for you?"

"I'd like a minute of your time. It's important that I talk with you," Martin said nervously, glancing about the open reception area.

Marshall, sensing an urgency behind his words, said nothing as he ushered him into the privacy of his office. "Please take a seat. Would you like some coffee?"

"No. I don't have time," Martin replied, looking fearfully around the room.

"What's wrong?" Marshall urged, taking a seat behind his desk and assuming his professional manner.

"I'm in trouble."

"What kind of trouble?"

"I accidentally overheard some plans being made. . . ."

"Plans? For what?"

"They were talking about the gold you ship and . . ."

"What?" Marshall was convinced of his agitation and now understood why he was so upset.

"They know that I heard everything that was said. . . . And if they find out that I came here, to you . . ." He hoped he sounded suitably panic-stricken. "I have to get out of town."

Marshall leaned forward urgently. "What did you hear?"

His tone reflecting his agitation, Martin rushed on. "The Rebs are going to attack the *Enterprise*."

"When? Where?"

"I can't be sure. I only heard them say that by tonight Jim would be dead and everything would be taken care of."

"I have to get word to Jim right away." Marshall stood, knowing that he had to act and act quickly. "Do you need any help getting away?"

"I hate to admit it, but I do."

"How much?"

"Whatever you think . . . I need to go somewhere where they'll never be able to locate me. . . ."

Disappearing into the outer office, Marshall returned with a stack of hundred-dollar bills.

"Here's three thousand." He handed the money to Martin.

"Thanks."

"You'll be all right?"

"I should be, once I can get out of town." Martin stood up, stuffing the money into his coat pocket.

"What about Clara? Is she involved in any of this?"

"No. She doesn't know anything about it."

"Good. She'll be safe, then." Marshall nodded as they left.

"Do you have a back door?" Martin asked, following through with his ruse.

"Right over here."

"I won't forget this, Marshall." Martin turned to shake hands before he left.

"Good luck." And Marshall watched him disappear down the alley before turning back into the room. There was little time to waste. He rushed to get his coat, and, telling his clerks that he was leaving, he headed home.

"What do you mean, Jim's boat is going to be attacked?" George Westlake demanded as Marshall related the whole story to his father.

"Martin Montgomery came by the office. It seems that he overheard the plans being made and the spies were after him. He was terrified, so I gave him some money to get out of town."

"What are we going to do?"

"The only thing possible. Catch the next boat south."

George looked nervously at his pocket watch. "I'll bring the horses around. Martha—pack my things."

He strode from the room, anxious that they should be on their way, and Martha followed after him, leaving Renee alone with Marshall.

He gave her a quick hug as he picked up his saddlebags.

"You'll be careful?" she asked.

"Of course. You know I always come home to you." He reassured her further with a passionate kiss and then started downstairs to meet George. There was no time to waste.

Jim was thankful that he awoke first. Easing himself from the bed, he quickly washed up and left the cabin in search of Mark. The sun was just breaking over the treetops as he strode down the deck and entered the Grand Salon. The sound of voices drew him to the saloon, where he found Ollie, Mark, and several of the other soldiers already eating breakfast.

"Good morning, Captain." Ollie was pleased to see him.

"Is there any more food left around here?" Jim asked good-naturedly as he sat down at their table and was served his breakfast.

"Are the women all right?" Mark was concerned.

Jim nodded. "They're still asleep."

"Delight wasn't injured, was she?" Ollie asked.

"No. Physically she's fine."

"Good. I was worried, after what Mark told me." Ollie wanted to say more, but he knew it was best to hold his tongue. Mark had explained how angry Jim was over the situation and talking about it again wasn't going to help.

"It was a rough experience for her to go through, but things are going to work out better this way," Jim grinned.

"Why?"

"Because, as soon as we can find a preacher, I'm going to marry her."

Mark lifted his cup of coffee in a toast. "May you have a long and happy life together."

Delight was already up when Rose emerged from the connecting cabin.

"Good morning, sleepyhead," she teased.

"How are you this morning?" Rose went to her friend and hugged her.

Delight returned the embrace with deep affection. "I'm fine."

"You're sure?"

"Positive. I haven't felt this good since before . . ."

"I understand." Rose knew it was too soon to talk about all the ugliness that had happened. "Do you want to change into a dress? I packed a few things for you last night."

Delight looked down at the trousers and ripped shirt she still had on. "I think I'd better. I don't want to remind Jim of what happened last night."

After a rather quick toilet, she put on an attractive pale green daygown with tiny pearl buttons that buttoned down the front. It was trimmed with white collar and cuffs. Brushing out her hair, she realized that they hadn't brought the hairpiece.

"Do you suppose I'll start a new fashion in hairstyles?"

"Well," Rose grinned. "Shorter hair was the vogue some years back."

Delight brushed her shining ebony locks into a mass of curls and stepped back. "What do you think?"

"If we pin the sides up it might look a bit longer." Rose set to work and in a few moments had fashioned a style that helped to disguise the uneven layering of Delight's hair. "How's that?"

"It looks great. Thanks." Delight glanced in the mirror once more before going to get her cloak. "Shall we go see if we can find Jim and Ollie?"

"That sounds like a good idea. I'm getting hungry."

As they turned to head out the door, it swung open, and Jim and Ollie entered carrying trays.

"So you're up," Jim said as he set the breakfast trays on his desk. "We were wondering how long you were going to sleep."

Delight smiled. "We were just going to try to find you."

"We thought it might be wiser if you ate up here."

"Thank you."

With Ollie and Rose in the room, Jim had to resist the urge to take Delight in his arms. Lying in bed with her last night had been a test for sainthood, but this morning he found that she was even more irresistible. Restraining himself with great effort, he deliberately kept his manner impersonal as he directed her to the food.

"You'd better eat while it's hot," he urged, and the women sat down without hesitation. "Ollie and I will be back later. It will be safer if you stay in the cabin until one of us comes for you."

Delight frowned, but didn't protest as the men left. She

understood the importance of the mission they were on, and she wanted to do all she could to make Jim's job easier.

"Do you think it's really that dangerous, Delight?" Rose was worried.

"Yes. I do. They're carrying Union gold." Delight let the sentence drop as she said a small prayer for Jim's safety.

It was near noon when Delight sensed a change in the boat's rhythm. Opening the curtains, she was surprised to find that they were pulling into a small town on the Missouri side.

"We're stopping, Rose," Delight remarked as the roustabouts threw out the lines. Remembering Jim's instructions not to leave the cabin, she stayed inside and watched as one of the soldiers hurried off in the direction of town.

"Do you want me to go see if I can find out what's going on?"

"No. He told us to wait here. If it's anything important, I'm sure he'll let us know. . . ." She sounded convincing, but in her heart she was worried. Why had the man gone into town? This obviously wasn't one of the regular fueling stops, so why the interruption of their schedule?

Almost a half an hour later, Ollie came to the cabin.

"You're both to come with me," he informed them mysteriously.

"Both of us?" Rose was genuinely surprised.

"Is something wrong, Ollie?" Delight asked and when he didn't answer, she began to worry.

Hurrying them along, he escorted them down the gangplank and up the small levee toward the town.

"Where are we?"

"Sainte Genevieve."

"But why did we dock here? It's not one of your regular stops, is it?"

"No. It's not," was all the answer he would give.

"Where's Jim?" Delight asked, trying not to sound worried, but in the back of her mind she couldn't help but wonder why they'd been taken off the boat.

"I haven't seen him for a while," Ollie said calmly, refusing to give her a clue as to what was going on.

Delight began to panic. Jim had been gone when she'd awakened that morning, and when he'd brought their breakfast to them he'd been almost distant in his manner. Had the thought of Martin's hands on her so repulsed him that he couldn't bear to have her near him anymore? Was he planning on leaving her here? Tears stung her eyes, but she blinked them rapidly away. Refusing to make a scene, she lifted her chin in proud defiance of whatever life would present her with next and walked on in silence.

Rose, sensing Delight's upset, squeezed her hand in a supportive gesture, but didn't speak. The tension grew as Ollie led them down the main street of the town.

"It's not too much farther," he encouraged them as they rounded a corner. "Here we are."

The tears Delight had tried so valiantly to hold back fell freely from her eyes as she saw Jim standing on the steps of the church. Breaking into a run, she went to him and was immediately enfolded in his warm embrace.

"Delight? Why are you crying?" Jim held her away from him and lifted her face to him with gentle hands.

"I thought—"

"You thought what?" he encouraged, pulling her close.

"I thought you were going to leave me here . . . that you didn't want me with you. . . ."

"Oh, God, darling . . . I want you with me more than anything in the entire world." He kissed her deeply and then whispered affectionately for her ears only, "I just couldn't stand the idea of not sharing my bed with you again tonight. . . ."

Delight threw her arms around his neck and kissed him again. "You're sure you want to do this?"

"I've never been more sure of anything in my life. Let's go. The minister is waiting for us."

With Rose and Ollie following them, they entered the

church and approached the altar where the preacher stood waiting for them.

"Are you ready now, Captain?"

"Yes. We're ready." Jim smiled down at Delight who was glowing with her love for him.

The minister began, his wondrous words blessing them and joining them together as one in the eyes of God and man. "Do you, James Thomas Westlake, take Delight de Vries to be your lawfully wedded wife? To love, honor, and cherish from this day forward, until death do you part?"

"I do." Jim's bold declaration sent a thrill of pleasure through her.

"And do you, Delight de Vries, take James Thomas Westlake to be your lawfully wedded husband? And do you promise to love, honor, and cherish him from this day forward until death do you part?"

"I do," she promised breathlessly.

"The ring?"

Jim slipped a narrow gold band on her finger, his hands trembling with emotion.

"Then, in sight of God and man, I now pronounce you man and wife." He paused, smiling at their obvious happiness. "You may kiss your bride, Captain."

Jim turned to her as if in slow motion and, with the most tender of touches, pulled her to him. Then, with infinite care, his lips sought hers in a devastatingly sweet kiss. His caress spoke not so much of passion as of promise; not so much of desire as of dedication. When they moved apart, they stared at each other in awe for a moment before Ollie and Rose overwhelmed them with hugs and good wishes.

They thanked the minister profusely and then hurried back to the boat. They'd lost a valuable hour of daylight traveling time, and Jim didn't want to delay any longer.

When Mark caught sight of them returning, they made ready to pull out. As soon as everyone was on board, the *Enterprise* backed out to midstream and once again headed south.

Jim escorted Delight to his cabin before regretfully excusing himself to return to work.

"I'm sorry I don't have time right now to . . ." Jim started to apologize, but Delight put a finger to his lips to silence him.

"Don't worry. I'll be right here whenever you can get away." Delight smiled at him tenderly, wanting more than anything to spend the rest of the day with him, but understanding the importance of his work.

Jim had originally intended to leave her then, but when she unlocked the stateroom and gave him an inviting look, he couldn't resist the thought of a private moment in her arms. Following Delight inside, he shut the door behind them. His gaze seared her with the intensity of his emotions, and he almost groaned as he took her in his arms.

"God, how I wish I could get away now, wife." He was burning with desire for her.

"I know." Delight moved within the circle of his arms and rested her head on his chest. The powerful thundering of his heart warmed her, and she tilted her head up to him. "But we have the rest of our lives. . . ."

So encouraged, Jim could no longer deny his need, and his lips plundered hers, drawing her unbridled response. With an obvious effort, he ended the kiss and stepped slightly away.

"Tonight," he promised, bringing himself rigidly under control. Though he wanted to lay her upon the bed and lose himself in her sweet flesh, Jim knew there was no time.

"Tonight," Delight whispered in return, and he turned from her and quickly left the room.

Ollie and Rose stood out on deck together. "Wasn't that a beautiful surprise?" Rose remarked softly. "Delight didn't expect it, you know."

"I know," Ollie grinned. "That's why I didn't tell her."

"Is there somewhere else I can sleep tonight?" Rose asked, not wanting to interfere with the privacy of their wedding night. "I don't think they'll want me in the next room."

"Of course," he offered. "We aren't carrying any passengers this trip; so it will be easy to arrange for you to have one of the staterooms."

"Thank you. I didn't want to chance spoiling their special night," she smiled.

"I just hope he can get away to spend time with her," Ollie said. "We make our first wooding stop right after midnight."

"Jim has to be around for that?"

"Everyone will be on guard. We're taking extra precautions this trip," he explained. "Things are getting more dangerous all the time."

"You mean the Rebs?"

Ollie nodded. "They're everywhere down here—raiding and pillaging. You know how the rumors were flying before we left St. Louis."

"I know."

"So, whenever we tie up, we have to really be careful. We're most vulnerable then. . . ." He was interrupted by Jim coming out of the cabin. "Jim, I'm going to arrange for Rose to have one of the staterooms tonight, if that's all right with you?" Ollie asked as he came to join them.

Jim smiled easily. "I think that's a wonderful idea, Ollie. Give her the nicest one we've got."

"Yes, sir."

"I'll be on the main deck if you need me." Jim strode off toward the companionway, excited at the prospect of the coming night in his wife's arms.

Ollie grinned. "There goes one happy man."

At the top of the sloping Missouri hillside, Colonel Jed Burford, CSA, sat his stallion with the easy grace of a man long accustomed to living in the saddle. "What time tonight?" he asked impatiently.

"Sometime between ten and midnight," Lieutenant Matt Carson answered.

"That's all you know?"

"That's it, sir. There's been no further word from Morgan, so we have to assume that everything's on schedule."

Swinging his gaze down to the wood yard below, he surveyed their objective dispassionately. "We'll wait until dark. There's no point in rushing. Besides," he grinned at his companions, "I'm in no great hurry to load wood on steamers."

"I'm with you on that, Colonel," Corporal Zack Prescott commented.

Jed dismounted, hobbling his horse, and his men followed suit. "Let's rest them while we can. We're going to have one hell of a ride tonight."

"Yes, sir." The men of his command obeyed his every order without question, for they knew him to be a fair and cautious man.

"Colonel?"

"Yes, Lieutenant?"

"Do you want me to move in closer and see how many men there are working at the station?"

"Later. Near dusk when we have better cover. For now, just take it easy and post a lookout. We don't want to be caught off guard at this stage of the game. We're too close to success."

Marshall and George stood at the railing of the steamboat, their nerves stretched taut. Each passing hour seemed longer than the last as they made their way slowly south. They had been lucky enough to book passage on the next boat out of St. Louis, but the *Enterprise* had a good headstart on them, and they knew they would not catch up unless there'd been trouble.

"I could use a drink. How about you, son?" George broke the strained silence.

"That sounds good," Marshall agreed. "I can't stand not knowing. . . ."

"I know what you mean." George led the way into the saloon.

Jed's soldiers moved quietly as they used the darkness to their advantage. The three workers at the wood yard had no chance.

They were quickly overpowered and slain by the Confederates.

"Well done, men," Jed complimented them. "Now all we have to do is hold it until the *Enterprise* shows up."

"Colonel? There are some clothes in here that belonged to those men. Do you think we should change?" the lieutenant asked.

"It can't hurt. Did you get rid of their bodies?"

"Yes, sir. Nobody will find them."

"Good. You're in charge here, Carson."

"Yes, sir."

"Let's go over the plan once more." Jed dismounted.

"Right." The lieutenant went to stand by his commanding officer's side.

"When she docks, load the wood as usual. I'm sure you've been on enough steamboats in your life to know the proper procedure." He gave Matt a critical look.

"Yes, sir," came his confident reply.

"On your last trip on board, I want the box with the explosives left out in plain sight."

"I've got the box right here, sir." Matt indicated the wooden box.

"Good. Then, after you load it, get the hell off the boat and behind some cover."

"Yes, sir."

"I'll be with the sharpshooters. As soon as we see that you're clear, we're going to blow that ship."

"How big of an explosion is it going to be, Colonel?"

"Big enough so we don't have to worry about the damned Yankee guards or the steamboat men. I want them dead or so busy fighting the fire that they don't have time to worry about anything else."

"Yes, sir. We'll take care of our end."

"I'm counting on that, Lieutenant." Jed mounted. "I won't speak with you again until after we attack. Good luck, Lieutenant."

"Thank you, sir," Matt said, but the colonel had already gone, turning his horse without a word and disappearing back through the trees to await the arrival of the *Enterprise*.

Delight smiled warmly as Jim entered the cabin. "Good evening." Her tone was sultry and suggestive as he came to her.

"Good evening, wife." He paused. "I like the sound of that."

"So do I," she agreed slipping her arms around his neck. "Can you stay for a while?"

"Is that a question or an invitation?" he murmured as his lips sought the sweetness of her throat.

"Both." She sighed as his touch stirred to life the flames of her desire for him.

He lifted his head and looked questioningly about the room. "Where's Rose?"

"With Ollie. They're having dinner together."

"Remind me to give that man a raise when we get back," Jim smiled.

"I will." She smiled and then, giving him a seductive look, she added, "And she's already moved her things to a stateroom on the promenade deck . . . Just in case you were wondering."

"So, we won't be interrupted?"

"Hopefully not."

Jim released her for a moment to lock the door and then returned to take her in his arms. "I love you, Mrs. Westlake."

"That sounds so nice." Delight pulled his head down for a flaming kiss. "Mr. Westlake."

Their hands were restless as they embraced, and each pleasing touch encouraged another until the tension between them grew unbearable. With impatient fingers, Jim unbuttoned her dress and helped her to slip it off along with the petticoats and chemise she had on.

"Undress for me," Delight urged him.

Lifting her, Jim carried her to the bed and lay her down before taking the time to shed his own clothes. Coming to her, he stretched out beside her and drew her to him.

"I have waited all my life for this night. I want it to be perfect," he told her as his hands moved slowly over her silken limbs. "I want to love every inch of you."

"And I, you." She arched to him, shivering, as he kissed her shoulder. "Love me. Please . . ."

Jim needed no further encouragement to possess her.

"It feels so right." Delight tried to voice the joy she experienced at this, his ultimate caress. "So perfect . . ."

Caught up in the serene beauty of the moment, Jim kissed her. Jim had hoped to take his time, to commit to memory every touch . . . every look . . . every word . . . but the storm-tide of his passion swept over him. He was lost in their loving.

The sense of peace that came to them as they lay clasped in each other's arms was overwhelming, and unlike anything they'd ever known before. They spoke, but words held little meaning for them now. Their bodies had spoken of love far more eloquently then they could ever hope to. Limbs intertwined, they rested, wanting this time alone together to last forever.

Jed paced restlessly in the small clearing where he waited with his men. Three boats had come and gone, but there had been no sign of the *Enterprise*.

"Time, Hutchins?"

"Eleven thirty, sir."

"Thank you." Jed stared upstream, hoping to catch sight of the steamer. There was no moon tonight, and he was grateful for that, because the darkness would be essential to their getting away safely. But right now, it offered him little comfort. All that mattered was the arrival of the *En-*

terprise, for without the boat there could be no success for his mission.

Delight lay in bed, watching Jim with hungry eyes as he buttoned the last button on his shirt. "You're sure you have to go?"

"Positive," he said, his disappointment at having to leave her most obvious.

"How long will you be?"

"It shouldn't take more than a couple of hours. And, as soon as we're back on the river, we'll have our 'wedding night,'" he vowed, looking over at her as she stretched languidly. "You're lovely."

"Thank you." Her voice was husky as she remembered the perfection of their bodies united in love.

Taking her wrists, he drew her to her knees before him. "Stay just the way you are. I'll be back as soon as humanly possible." He kissed her almost savagely then, and strode quickly from the room.

Delight watched him go, and she felt suddenly alone when the door closed behind him. Slipping back under the covers, she decided to rest until he returned, for she wanted to make this night one he could never forget.

Chapter Thirty-three

Jim stopped by Mark's cabin on his way down to the main deck. "What took you so long?" he complained good-naturedly when Mark finally opened the door.

"I was asleep," Mark responded, yawning. "Come on in."

Jim entered and leaned negligently against the wall while

Mark sat on his bunk and pulled on his boots. "We should be there in the next half hour. Have you given the guards their instructions?"

"Yes. Most of them have made the run before, so they know what to do."

"Good. We should be all right, but I never like to let my defenses down."

Mark got his coat and they left the cabin and headed for the stateroom where the gold was being kept under guard. After checking in with the soldiers now on duty and assigning two men with rifles to stand watch on the promenade deck, Jim and Mark descended to the main deck to supervise the loading of the wood. Without conscious thought, Mark drew his sidearm and checked the chambers before holstering it again.

"Worried?"

"Every minute until it's delivered," Mark answered, his tension increasing as the boat slowed and pulled into the wooding station.

Torches were burning brightly on the shore, and their flickering flames cast eerie shadows over the muddy landing as the wooders and roustabouts quickly began the task of carrying the stacks of wood on board.

Jed Burford stood in the darkness watching the scene being acted out below. Everything was going smoothly. There had been no questions asked when the boat had docked, just the exchange of money and the subsequent loading of the wood. They were almost done now, and he could feel the excitement surging through his blood. Now was the time! They would soon be heading south with the gold that was so desperately needed by their cause.

Moving silently, he checked with his men to make sure they were ready. All rifles were aimed at the boat. Whispering instructions, he directed each man to a different target.

"Sloan—take out the two guards on the promenade deck.

Roger—you hit that box of explosives. Anderson—I want you to try to hit the Union captain and the ship's captain. We can't guarantee that the explosion will kill anybody, so make each shot count."

The men nodded their understanding and refocused their attention on the riverboat below. They smiled in victory as the lieutenant casually stacked the box with the explosives near a pile of logs within their range of fire. As the last of their men left the steamer, the gangplank was taken in and the *Enterprise* reversed her engines to pull neatly away from the bank.

"Now!" Jed's voice roared through the stillness of the night, and their gunfire erupted, spewing forth death and destruction.

The explosion rocked the *Enterprise* from stem to stern, ripping away a portion of her superstructure and causing half of the promenade deck to collapse. Flames spread forth from the boilers, which were damaged by the force of the blast, illuminating the boat in a fiery light that helped the Rebs in their quest.

The sharpshooters were relentless, picking off the Union guards one by one as they raced from the cabin where the gold was being kept. The screams of the wounded and those trapped in the growing fire were drowned out by the continuous fusillade, as the guerrillas reloaded and continued to shoot the men who were trying to escape. Roustabouts and soldiers alike died under the relentless firing. The soldiers' horses, terrified by the growing fire, broke free from their tethers on the main deck and plunged overboard. Scrambling up the bank, they scattered in the surrounding woods as they tried to find their way to safety.

With her boilers useless, the *Enterprise* drifted back toward shore. The men who minutes before had been loading wood on her eagerly awaited the chance to climb back on board and get the gold off before she turned into an inferno. As she came to rest against the bank, the Rebs hauled themselves up on her deck and made for the treasure they were after. The shooting from the hillside paused as the guerrillas worked their way through the fiery rubble to the gold. It took them only minutes to fight off the last surviving guard before they were running from the steamer with the strongbox. Jed and his men mounted quickly, and, leading the others' horses, raced down the hill to meet them. As soon as the men had divided the gold, they were off on their desperate flight south.

Delight was thrown to the floor by the explosion and she lay huddled there, breathless and horrified, as the bullets crashed through the window and splintered the walls. Jim! She had to get to him . . . Scurrying across the floor, Delight stayed low as she pulled on the only clothes she could find—her trousers and flannel shirt. Slipping on her boots, she moved cautiously to the door and opened it slowly.

Smoke and heat were billowing up from the lower decks, and she knew she had to get off fast. The gunfire had ceased and the night was silent, except for the roar of the ever-growing blaze. Racing down the texas deck, she started around the corner only to spot the Rebels leaving the ship with the strongbox of gold. Stepping back into the shadows, Delight looked around helplessly for a weapon, but knew it was useless. Tears spilled forth as she watched them ride away. When she was sure they were gone she tried to get to the companionway, but the lower deck had collapsed on that side, leaving her no alternative but to turn back and work her way down on the opposite side of the steamer.

The bank was slippery as Jim staggered ashore, and he fell heavily to his knees, gasping and choking. The force of the blast had blown him overboard and had evidently saved his life. As awareness returned, he almost panicked—Delight! Turning to his boat, he scanned the decks trying to see if there was anyone moving. Hauling himself to his feet, he knew he had to go back . . . he had to save her or die trying. Wading out to the hull, he managed to pull himself aboard. His shoulder was aching, but he had no time even to think about it. Moving steadily and cautiously, he sifted his way amidships, searching for a way up.

The heat of the fire drove him back twice before he finally climbed on top of some of his freight and pulled himself up to the promenade deck. Two barrels of water still stood at the far end, and, with all the strength he could muster, he dumped them over, hoping that it would contain the inferno just a little longer.

"Captain!" The shout drew his attention to the pilothouse, and Jim looked up to see his pilot, injured but moving.

"Walter! Check on my wife and then get off! There's no saving the boat!"

"Right!" With no ceremony, the pilot raced to Jim's cabin, only to find it deserted.

Jim, meanwhile, made his way to the stateroom where the gold had been. There were six soldiers lying on the deck near the door. All had been shot and killed as they had raced from the room with their guns ready. Gathering up their weapons, Jim checked the cabin and then hurried to the other side of the ship.

"Where's Delight?" he asked as he came face-to-face with Walter.

"She wasn't there, Jim. I checked the cabin. The door was open but there was no sign of her."

"All right. Get off as fast as you can, but check each deck as you go for survivors," Jim directed, handing him the guns and casting a nervous look up toward his cabin. When Walter had disappeared below, he hurried to check on Delight himself, but, as Walter had said, there was no sign of her. Cursing and fearing for her safety, he raced down the companionway and then lowered himself to the main deck.

"Jim! I've found Captain Clayton!"

Jim raced to help Walter free Mark from the wreckage. "How bad is he?"

"I don't know, but he's still alive."

Jim lifted the timber that had pinned Mark to the deck, and Walter pulled him free. After making sure that Mark was breathing, they carried him closer to the side and laid him down.

"He should be safe here for a few minutes while we check to see if there's anybody else . . ."

"Jim!"

The sound of Delight's voice thrilled him, and he turned to see her at the opposite end of the steamer.

"Stay there!" he shouted. "I'll come to you!"

"Ollie's here and he's hurt!"

Jim climbed off the boat and helped Walter lower Mark over the side before rushing to Delight's aid. Skirting the heat and flames, he pulled himself once more on board and took her in his arms.

"Thank God," he groaned, embracing her quickly. He took only enough time to make sure she was really there and well before he went to Ollie.

"He's got a terrible cut on his head . . ."

Jim knelt by his friend and then glanced back over his shoulder at the fire that was threatening. "We have to get him off." He hoisted Ollie over his shoulder.

"What about Rose?"

"You haven't seen her?"

Delight's eyes were wide with terror. "No. I thought she was with Ollie."

"Let's get him ashore, and I'll come back to check."

With no further delays, they climbed off the boat and climbed up the bank to where Walter had taken Mark. As carefully as he could, Jim put Ollie down on the ground.

"Delight, you stay here with Ollie." Jim's tone brooked no argument. "Walter, I need your help. There's a woman still trapped somewhere on board." His eyes ran the length of the burning steamer.

"Let's go."

If they felt fear, they did not show it as they made their way back on board the *Enterprise* and began to look for Rose. When their search of the lower deck turned up nothing, they headed up to the promenade deck. They were just about to give up when they heard a plaintive call. Following the sound, Jim and Walter dug desperately at a huge pile of timbers.

"Rose! If you can hear me, keep yelling!"

"Jim!" Her cry was growing louder as they threw aside the wood and finally found her. "Oh, thank God . . ." She was bruised and shaking when they helped her from beneath the rubble, and Jim carried her down to the main deck.

"Delight? Is she all right?"

"She's fine." He reassured her as he handed her over the side to Walter.

Jim jumped down from the boat and trudged up the muddy bank to where the survivors had gathered. Four of the roustabouts who'd been working on the main deck had found their way to safety and were huddled, wet and miserable, with the others.

"Was there anyone else, Jim?" Walter turned to look back at the ruined steamer after he'd set Rose down by Delight.

"No one I could find." Jim stared at the flames blindly, thankful that they decided not to carry any passengers on this run. "The guards . . ."

"I know," Walter told him. "Whoever did this knew exactly what to expect."

"I intend to find them, Walter, and when I do . . ." Jim let his words die in the roar of the pilothouse crashing through the burned-out deck.

Delight, who'd been intent on her care of Ollie and Mark, looked up at the sound, and she watched in horror as the *Enterprise* self-destructed. When she caught sight of her friend, she ran to her. "Oh, Rose. I'm so glad they found you . . ." The women embraced, needing the comfort of one another's touch to ease the trauma they'd just lived through.

"I was trapped . . . I couldn't get out. If it hadn't been for Jim and the pilot . . ." Rose started to shake again as she remembered the complete helplessness of her situation.

"You're safe now." Delight held her tightly. "We're alive . . ."

Suddenly Rose drew back, "Ollie? How's Ollie?"

"He was injured and he hasn't come around yet." Delight led Rose to him.

Kneeling next to him, Rose examined his wound carefully. "I'll need some fresh water and bandages, if you can find some."

"I know. I'll go look in that cabin, maybe there's something in there we can use." Delight hurried off in the direction of the wooders' small house in hopes of finding the supplies they needed.

The light from the fire was blinding as Mark slowly opened his eyes and stared around him. He groaned as his full consciousness returned and he struggled to sit upright. Rose went to his side to help steady him.

"Rose, where's Jim?" he asked weakly. "Is he all right?"

"He's just fine. Don't move. I'll go get him for you." Rose rushed to get Jim.

"Captain Clayton's awake, Jim," she told him, drawing him from the morbid spectacle of his dying steamer.

At her urging, he turned away from his own angry thoughts and went to check on Mark. "How are you?"

"I don't know yet. What the hell happened? The last thing I remember is standing with you on the main deck as the boat started to back out. Did the boilers blow?"

"No." Jim's tone was flat. "It wasn't the boilers. As near as I can figure, we were blown out of the water."

"How?"

"The wooders. Evidently, they were Rebs."

"But what about my men?" Mark struggled to get to his feet, his gaze never leaving the hideously fascinating scene before him.

"They're dead. All of them."

"How?" Mark was horrified.

"There must have been sharpshooters. They were picked off as they ran out of the cabin."

"Damn them!!" Mark sobbed as he thought of their useless deaths, and he stumbled away from Jim needing time to pull himself together.

Jim let him go, knowing that this was something he had to deal with by himself.

"Jim?" Delight, having witnessed Mark's agony, spoke softly.

"What?" He looked up, his emotions raw as he, too, dealt with all that had happened.

"There are beds in the cabin." She indicated the small house. "I think we should take Ollie up there."

"He's no better?"

"Not yet . . . Rose is doing her best, but he needs a doctor."

"Help will be here soon," he told her with more confidence than he was feeling. "But I'll get Walter and we'll move him for you." Jim went to find the pilot and a few minutes later they carried Ollie to the shelter.

When they had settled the women in the cabin, Walter went to fetch water for them, and Jim went in search of Mark. To his surprise Mark had found two of the horses and had tied them near the landing.

"Where are the guns, Jim?" Mark asked, his voice cold and deadly.

"Down on the bank. Why?"

"Get them," Mark ordered as he headed toward the small barn near the house.

Jim hesitated but finally went to retrieve the weapons.

When he returned, Mark was saddling up the horses with the tack he'd found in the barn. "I'll take those guns."

"Why? What are you planning to do?"

"I'm going after them," Mark stated matter-of-factly.

"You can't. You're in no condition . . ."

"I said I'm going, Jim. Either you can come with me or I'll go alone." He didn't look up as he continued to tighten the cinch. "Well?"

"Mark, you just can't . . ."

"I can't stay here, Jim. Not after my men have been shot down like dogs. I'm the only one left! I have to do something!" The desperation in his voice was real, and Jim knew Mark had no choice.

"All right. I'll go with you. Give me a minute to straighten things out here."

Jim strode away from Mark in the direction of the cabin. Delight saw him approaching and went to him, thinking that the worst was over.

"Darling. I'm so glad you're alive," Delight sighed, slipping her arms around his waist. But as she leaned against his chest she felt the tenseness in him. "What is it?"

Jim smiled gently at her perception and, with a tender caress, smoothed her hair back from her face. "I'm going with Mark."

"Going? Going where?"

"We have to go after the Rebs. They took the gold."

"But it's suicide!" she cried. "Can't you wait for help?"

"There's no time to waste. By the time help gets here, they could already be behind the Southern lines. Our only hope is to catch them unawares. They probably think we're all dead, so they won't be expecting us."

"Jim, don't do this. It's crazy . . ." she protested, but he stopped her angry words with a kiss.

"Delight. It's something I have to do," he told her firmly, easing himself from her arms. "Mark needs me."

"But I need you, too!"

"I know." He was solemn as he gazed down at her.

"Then take me with you," she began quickly, as she sensed him withdrawing from her.

"No. I can't." He glanced at Mark, who was already mounted and waiting for him. "And I don't have the time to argue with you. Kiss me, love. I'll be back. Wait for me in town, at Renee's."

With a small cry, she embraced him, pulling his head down for one last tormented kiss. "Be careful," she breathed as he moved away. "Please, be careful."

"I will," he said firmly and then, after leaving instructions with Walter, he joined Mark. "Let's ride."

Delight's heart was breaking as she stood near the cabin and watched them ride off. She knew the danger he was about to face, and she longed to go with him . . . to be at his side in case he needed her, but it was not to be. As Jim and Mark disappeared into the woods in pursuit of the guerrillas, Delight said a silent prayer for their safety and then went back inside to help Rose.

Chapter Thirty-four

The storm developed quickly as the warm, humid winds from the southwest met and clashed with the cold northern breezes. Lightning erupted across the nighttime sky, streaking the darkness with flashes of brilliance before playing itself out in a thunderous roar of unleashed power. The rains came then, all along the Mississippi from Ste. Gen south to Memphis, drenching the countryside in a torrential downpour.

Huddling together in the protection of the cabin, the survivors stared at the smoldering remains of the *Enterprise*.

The steady, driving cadence of the tempest had smothered the last of the fire on board, and she rested on the shallow bottom now, wedged in at the landing, a blackened, smoking hulk. There was no vestige of her previous beauty left . . . no telltale sign by which she could be identified. The *Enterprise* had died in a blaze of vicious Confederate glory, and few were left to mourn her passing.

The night had been a long one for Marshall and George. They had stayed on deck, anxiously anticipating each turn of the twisting river, until the rains had driven them indoors. Sleep had been hard to come by, and it had been after three in the morning before they'd both fallen into an exhausted, uneasy slumber.

"Mr. Westlake? The captain would like to see you in the pilothouse." The voice of the steward coming through their cabin door alerted both men.

"We'll be right there. Thanks," Marshall answered as he came fully awake.

He was up and dressed in a matter of minutes, and George quickly followed suit. Neither man spoke as they grabbed their coats and rushed from the stateroom on their way up to the pilothouse.

Henry Bell, the captain and pilot of the steamer, was waiting for them. "I think there may be trouble up ahead." He pointed to the smoke that, despite the rain, was hanging heavily over the treetops on the Missouri side farther downstream.

"That's the wooding station, isn't it?" George questioned, as he peered through the gloominess of the early morning in the direction Henry had indicated.

"Could be," Henry said as he carefully maneuvered his boat down the river. "We'll stay out a ways until I can see what we've got."

Slowing to half speed, he approached the station cautiously.

If there was a fire, he didn't want to be anywhere near it, rain or no rain.

George gripped Marshall's arm as the ruins of the *Enterprise* came into view. "My God . . ."

"Henry . . . We've got to get in there. Put in as soon as you think it's safe."

Henry, too, was horrified by the burned-out hull, and he skirted by the heated remains, docking far to the south of it. "Is it the *Enterprise?*"

"I don't know yet. But whoever it is, they'll be needing our help," Marshall told him, his eyes not leaving the wreck.

"Marsh—I don't see anybody . . . You don't suppose they're all . . ."

"No." Marshall cut off his father's words. "It looks like it's been burning most of the night. The survivors must have gone for shelter . . ."

"I'm sure you're right," George agreed, breathing a little easier.

Marshall looked down at him and realized for the first time how old his father was getting. In the muted morning light, tense with worry over the identity of the demolished steamboat, he looked every bit of his sixty some-odd years.

"Come on. Let's get down below so we can get off as soon as we tie up."

They hurried down the companionway to the main deck and waited impatiently for the thick ropes to be securely tethered before they left the ship. As some of the men from the steamer joined them, they rushed in the direction of the station. The brush near the shoreline was thick, slowing their progress as they fought their way onward through the pouring rain.

"Hello!" they called as they finally broke through the bushes into the clearing.

Marshall caught sight of the low light in the cabin just as Walter heard the sound of their call.

"Help's here!" Walter shouted as he ran forth to greet the men who had come to rescue them.

"Walter?" Marshall and George stopped, paralyzed, as they recognized one of their own pilots.

"Mr. Westlake! Thank God you've come!" Walter rushed forward to shake their hands and they moved to stand under the protection of a spreading tree.

"So it is the Enterprise . . ." George looked back at the boat, his expression grave. "Jim . . . is he . . . ?"

Just as Walter was about to answer, Delight came hurrying out of the cabin. "Marshall! George!" she cried.

"Delight?" Marshall was stunned, and he and George exchanged questioning looks. "What are you doing here?" He turned to take her in a comforting embrace. There was no sign of Jim, and he was dreading the news she was about to give them.

"Oh, Marshall . . ." She was crying as he hugged her supportively. "It was so terrible . . . there was the explosion and fire and . . ."

"Delight," George interrupted, needing desperately to hear news of his son. "Jim . . . Where is Jim?"

"He went with Mark . . ." She faced him and started to explain.

"With Mark? Where?" Marshall pressed.

"After the guerrillas. They attacked the boat just as we were pulling away. There must have been explosives on board or something, but there was a tremendous explosion and then the fire started . . ."

"And the Rebs . . . did they get the gold?"

"Yes. That's why Mark and Jim went after them."

"Just the two of them?"

She nodded, "There were at least fifteen of the Rebels . . . I begged him not to go . . ."

George looked worriedly at his son. "How long ago did they leave?"

"It's been hours."

"We'd better track then, before the rain washes out the trail completely," Marshall said. "How bad are the injuries?"

"Ollie's the worst. We've got him in bed in the cabin. He has a bad head injury. Rose and I . . ."

"Rose is here with you, too?"

"Yes, we both made the trip with Jim."

George and Marshall wanted to know the whole story, but right now there was no time. They had to go after Mark and Jim and try to help them.

"How many survivors are there?"

"Eight, not counting Jim and Captain Clayton," Walter answered.

"I want you all on board Captain Bell's ship. Walter, you take charge and see that everyone gets back to St. Louis as quickly as possible," George instructed. "Don't worry about the cost."

"Yes, sir."

"I want to see Ollie before we go," George was saying as he started toward the cabin with Walter, leaving Marshall and Delight alone momentarily.

"Jim was all right?"

"He seemed to be . . ." She looked up at him. "You're going after him?"

"Yes."

"I'm so glad you're here. But why . . . ? How did you know?"

"We have Martin to thank . . ."

"Martin?" She almost panicked. "What has he got to do with this?"

"He came to me this morning. He'd overheard some plans being made, and he related everything he'd heard to me."

"Martin said he'd heard plans about the attack?"

"Yes." Marshall noticed that she'd paled at the mention of her stepfather's name. "Why?"

"Didn't Jim tell you about Martin?"

"What about him?" He suddenly stiffened.

Delight looked up at him nervously. "He's the reason I ran

away in the first place . . . and he's the reason why I'm here right now . . ."

"I don't understand."

"Martin tried to force himself on me. After I threatened to reveal his real nature to my mother, I thought it was safe for me to go back, but Wednesday night he tried again."

"You're saying he attacked you Wednesday night?"

"Yes. In fact, I barely made it to Jim in time."

Marshall was totally disgusted. What an accomplished con man Martin was . . . he actually had had him believing that he was in serious danger. Probably the only danger he was in was from Jim. And here, he'd given him money to get away.

"Then it was all an act. But how would Martin have known about the raid?"

"I don't know, but I think we'd better find out when we get back." She was furious as she realized that Martin probably had helped to arrange the attack as revenge against Jim and herself.

"Well, you go with Rose and Ollie . . ."

Marshall was dismissing her and she would have no part of it. "No." She stated simply.

Marshall glanced at her quickly, noting the determined look in her eye. "No?"

"I'm going with you."

"There's no way . . ." he began.

"There is a way," she insisted. "I've even found a horse." She pointed to the mount she had tied to the hitching post. "I'm going."

"Delight, this chase will be no place for a woman," Marshall argued.

"If you don't take me with you, I'll follow you anyway," she declared.

"But I'm sure Jim would be happier if he knew that you were safe in St. Louis."

"Marshall, I'm going along. Jim may need me."

"No." He was used to having his orders followed, and Delight's stubborn nature was new to him. Renee had never openly defied him.

"Marshall." She glared at him. "Jim and I were married yesterday afternoon in Sainte Genevieve. And I have every intention of helping you find him. Even if I have to follow you on my own."

"You got married?"

"We did." Her chin rose as she became even more determined in her efforts. "He is my husband now."

Marshall hugged her quickly, catching her by surprise. "That's wonderful. But don't you think it would be better if you went home . . . ? Stay with Renee. We'll be back as soon as we can . . ."

"No." She said the word with such intensity that he argued no further.

He studied her for a moment before starting off toward the small house. "Let's see what Father's doing."

George was coming out as they mounted the rickety front steps. "He's still unconscious . . . they're going to take him on board now."

Two of Bell's men carried Ollie as carefully as they could from the shelter, while Rose dogged their every step.

"Delight. I'm going on ahead with Ollie." Rose paused briefly.

"Fine. I'll see you when I get back."

"What? Get back? From where?"

"I'm going with Marshall to find Jim. You go on, Rose. Ollie needs you."

"Be careful." Rose hugged her quickly.

"I will." She managed a small smile. "Go ahead . . ." Delight watched her friend hurry after Ollie and then turned back to her new brother and father-in-law.

"Delight's going with us," Marshall confirmed as George gave him a strained look.

"We don't have time to take any women with us . . ."

"George," Delight's firm tone reflected her mood, "I'm going."

George thought the idea was outrageous and started to say so, when Marshall stopped him. "We don't have the time to debate this. Delight is Jim's wife." He let that statement sink in.

"You really were married?" George looked at the woman who had just lived through hell this past night and a new respect for her grew.

"Yes, sir." She smiled at him. "Yesterday."

"You're sure you're feeling up to this . . . it won't be easy."

"Yes, George. I have to go . . . I can't just sit and wait."

"She's dressed for it," Marshall supported her. "She has her own horse, and she's told me she's going whether we want her to or not. So I suggested we dispense with the arguments and get on the trail."

"All right," George finally agreed. "I'll talk with Bell; you get our horses."

"Fine. Delight, wait here."

The two men disappeared back toward the other steamer and were gone for long minutes, leaving Delight to wonder at the wisdom of her decision. She knew they didn't want her along, but she felt she had no alternative. The thought of going back to St. Louis and waiting in helpless comfort was totally unacceptable. She had to go with them . . . she had to. Without Jim she had nothing. He was her whole life.

Finally, Marshall and George reappeared on horseback. George waited off to one side, while Marshall approached her.

"Here, put this on." He handed her a slicker. "I can't have my new sister-in-law coming down with pneumonia."

She flashed him a grateful smile and put on the oversized garment. Then without any hesitation, she mounted up. "I'm ready. And I promise, I won't cause you any trouble."

"You already have." He grinned at her, understanding full well how his brother could have fallen in love with her. "But we'll manage."

She smiled widely and then reined her horse in line with his. "Let's go."

They headed off then, with George in the lead, following Jim and Mark's trail.

Jed took a swallow from his canteen and walked around the small cave. He was tired of sitting and needed to stretch his legs for a while. They had ridden the entire night and everyone was exhausted. The rains had slowed them, but they had still traveled a goodly distance and were confident that all was well. After posting two men as lookouts, he had told the rest of the men to retire. Now, it was just a matter of keeping the horses rested and in good shape so they could make it to their drop-off point.

Jed paused at the mouth of the cavern and leaned easily against the rocky opening, savoring the peace of the moment. It had been so long since he'd had any real peace. Against his will, his thoughts went over the past three years . . . three years of unending turmoil during which he'd learned how to hate and how to kill. He took a deep breath and let it out slowly as he remembered how simple life had been before the war.

And it had been simple for Jed. He'd been happily married; his wife, Emily, had been pregnant with their first child; and he had just bought his own farm in southwest Missouri. Everything had been perfect, until that day when he'd gone out with the one slave he owned to work the fields and they'd attacked . . . the pro-Union forces had burned his house, and when Emily had tried to fight them off they had killed her, but not before they had used her for their sport. His life had never been the same since that day. He had buried the woman he'd loved and, along with her, his dreams for the future.

He'd had no reason to stay on there for everything he'd cared about was gone. So, he'd sold the land and joined the Confederate army soon after that. Since that time, his days had blended together in a long procession of raids and skirmishes in which he'd been neither the victor nor the vanquished. Until tonight . . . at last he felt he'd accomplished something worthwhile. He knew the gold could make a difference for the South, and he wanted to deliver it to the right people in time for it to do some good.

When the shots rang out, he dropped to his knees and flattened himself against the rocky wall, gun in hand. The men who had been sleeping in the cave were instantly awake and grabbing for their weapons.

"What was it, Colonel?"

"I don't know . . . it might have been one of the guards." He shifted position to try to get a better look up the path that approached the cave. "I don't see anyone yet . . . I'm going out."

As the men hurriedly gathered up their things and got ready to move, Jed disappeared outside, moving slowly through the surrounding bushes and trees, watching and waiting for some indication of what the trouble had been. When he heard the sound of a horse coming full speed in his direction, Jed jumped behind a fallen tree and took aim, ready to shoot if it was anyone besides one of his own men. The sight of Matt Carson heading his way relieved him considerably, and he rose from his hiding place.

"Lieutenant!" He hailed.

Carson reined in, and then picked his way through the underbrush to his commanding officer's side.

"What happened?"

"They were following us, sir."

"Who, for God's sake? I thought we'd killed them all . . ."

"Evidently we didn't, sir."

"How many?"

"Just two. I shot them both."

"Good work, Lieutenant. But we'd better ride anyway, just in case there are more coming behind them."

"Right, sir."

They headed back to the cave where the men had assembled, ready to travel, and then mounted up and headed south.

Jim and Mark had been riding at top speed since they'd left the station. The pelting, chilling rain had soaked them to the skin, but they paid little attention. The downpour was rapidly washing out the Rebs' trail, and they knew they couldn't stop. Any delays in following would probably result in their losing them completely. The hours passed in slow, wet determination as they relentlessly pursued the guerrillas. It was at the first light of day that Mark paused on the bank of an overflowing creek.

"What do you think?" he asked, surveying the muddy trail.

Jim urged his horse up next to Mark's. "I don't know. As bad as the weather is, I doubt that we've gained on them. But then, they can't run forever . . ."

Mark looked around, the silence of the woods grating on his nerves. "I keep thinking that we're missing something . . ."

"I don't think we have. The trail's not all that fresh. Do you want to rest? We just passed that old abandoned farmhouse not far back; we can always go there and dry off for a while."

"No. We can't afford to stop . . . not while it's still raining this hard," Mark replied, his weariness overcome by his desire to retrieve the gold. "Can you make it? You look like your shoulder's bothering you."

"It's sore, that's all. I guess from the explosion." Jim rubbed his aching shoulder. "I'm all right."

"Let's go, then." Worrying that the rain would totally obliterate the tracks, Mark decided to ride on. It was that fateful choice that took them up that last rise and into the sights of Matt Carson's waiting rifle.

They had no idea they were that close to the Rebels, and they were caught totally by surprise when Matt fired. The sound of the gunshots spooked their mounts, and, as the bullets found their targets, the horses reared. Twisting violently in fright, they plunged off into the underbrush, leaving Jim and Mark sprawled, unconscious, in the mud.

Delight was chilled to the bone. Despite the fact that Marshall had given her both the slicker and his hat, she was drenched. Rivulets of icy water ran down her back, and her teeth chattered uncontrollably as she followed them along the narrow trail through the still, leafless trees.

They were surrounded by a silence that was broken only by the constant pounding of the rain. In the long hours that they'd been riding, there had been no sign of man or beast. The cloud-enshrouded sun continued its struggle to brighten the Missouri countryside, but the landscape was as desolate as the mood she was in. Spring had not yet renewed the face of the earth. Everything looked dead . . . the trees, the bushes, the ground, covered as it was by the fallen leaves . . . and she shivered, hoping that this feeling of death that gripped her wasn't an omen.

"Marsh!" George's tone was soft and urgent as he waved for his son to come up beside him. "Look!"

Ahead, standing nervously in a small protected copse of trees, was a horse.

"I'll get him." Marshall rode on slowly, taking care not to frighten the already jittery beast. Dismounting, he approached on foot, talking softly to soothe it. With relative ease, he grabbed the reins and rubbed the horse's wet neck with strong, reassuring strokes. "Come on," he called, and George and Delight rode forward as he tied the horse to a strong tree limb.

"Well?"

"He's pretty banged up . . . looks like he was running out of control through all the brush. There's . . ." Marshall stopped as he spotted the bloodstain on the pommel.

"What is it?" Delight asked quickly.

"Blood," he said. "Do you recognize this as one of the mounts Jim and Mark were riding?"

"I can't say. It's possible, but things were so confused last night . . ."

"It's not a Union saddle," George remarked hopefully.

"They used the ones in the stable at the landing," Delight supplied.

"But it is a Union gun," Marshall said, pulling the rifle from its scabbard.

They fell silent again as he loosened the reins and walked back to his own horse. "We'll take him with us, just in case."

"Just in case of what?" Delight asked innocently.

"In case we find out that he did belong to Mark or Jim."

They pressed on, constantly on watch now.

Jim opened his eyes slowly. Overhead, the scrawny, naked branches of the trees met in a ghoulish arbor that offered him no protection from the still driving rain. His first instinct was to try to get to safety . . . but he didn't move. Fear gripped him. Were they still close, watching him? He had no idea how long he'd been out, so it was impossible for him to know.

Jim waited long, chilling minutes until he was certain that he'd heard no sounds nearby, before finally deciding to make a move. Rolling slowly to his side, he was suddenly assaulted by a searing pain shooting up his left leg. He couldn't stop the groan that escaped him as he clutched at his thigh and his own blood, hot and sticky, stained his hands.

Wrestling himself into a sitting position, he examined his leg. The blood was flowing freely from the wound, and he was disturbed to find that the bullet had not passed completely through. Cursing under his breath, he used his belt as a makeshift tourniquet and tied it around his upper leg in hopes of controlling the bleeding. When it slowed, Jim stripped off his coat and shirt and used his shirt as a bandage. Applying it to the wound, he tightened it in place with his belt.

With the bleeding under control, Jim pulled his coat back on and looked around for Mark. He spotted him lying in the underbrush and crawled painfully through the mud to his friend's side.

"Mark . . ." Jim rolled him over and shook him, his voice a hoarse croak as he saw all the blood on his face. "Mark, for God's sake . . ."

"Jim?" Mark groaned as his hand went to his head as he came to. He sat up and immediately regretted his action as the world spun crazily before his eyes. Drawing his knees up to his chest, he rested his forearms on them while cradling his head. "What happened?"

"I think we were closer than we thought." Jim knew it was the only explanation. And, as he felt his strength fading, he leaned back shakily against a nearby tree trunk.

"Damn . . ." It was hard for Mark to think coherently, but he forced himself to try. "Are you all right?"

"No . . . I think I've lost too much blood. My leg . . ." Jim tried to talk, but a light-headed weakness assailed him.

With all the strength he could muster, Mark went to Jim's aid, cursing all the while the desperate situation they found themselves in.

"We have to get to some shelter . . ." Mark was thinking out loud as he remembered the farmhouse; but how could he get Jim there? The wound looked nasty even to his untrained eye, and he knew there was no way Jim could walk on. Standing up, he cursed his own dizziness and leaned against the tree for a moment until the world had righted itself. Then, he bent to help Jim up.

"We'll head for that old farmhouse," Mark told him, slipping an arm about his waist to support him.

"That's pretty far, isn't it?"

"Don't worry. We'll make it." Mark tried to sound confident, but he knew his own strength was fading. "Don't put any pressure on your leg. It looks pretty bad. I don't want you using it," he told him as they started off.

Jim was silent and deathly pale as he leaned heavily against Mark. And Mark tried to take it as easy as possible, but he was staggering under Jim's weight and struggling to keep his own balance. With faltering steps, Mark headed back in the direction they'd come, hoping that he could hold out until they reached the farmhouse.

Chapter Thirty-five

Marshall reined in as they came upon the farmhouse situated in the small clearing. "What do you think?"

"It looks empty, but be careful," George warned. "If there's been any guerrilla activities around here, folks might be inclined to shoot first and ask questions later."

"I will." He glanced quickly at Delight, who sat stoically on her horse. He'd been amazed at her tolerance during the last long, wet hours, for not once had she uttered a complaint. "Wait here."

Too chilled to speak, Delight could only nod. The ride had been long and miserable, but she had every intention of stiffing it out. She would do whatever they told her to do, and she would do it without argument.

Marshall rode away from them and slowly skirted the overgrown yard of the deserted cabin. When he found no sign of anyone nearby, he approached the front of the house. As he neared the old structure, he could see that it had been deserted for some time. Dismounting, he tied his horse and climbed the steps to the dilapidated front porch.

When the front door stuck, Marshall put his shoulder to it

and shoved it open. One look inside convinced him that no one had lived here for years. The windows were broken, the roof was leaking, and, except for a single bed, the other few pieces of furniture that had been left behind were useless. Turning back to where Delight and George waited for his signal, he waved for them to come forward.

"Deserted?" George asked as he reined in at the hitching rail.

Marshall nodded. "It has been for quite a while. Do you want to rest?"

"Delight?" George looked expectantly at her.

"No. The longer we delay, the longer it's going to take us to find them," she managed, her chin tilted with determination.

Marshall's respect for her grew, but he wondered if she might not be pushing herself too hard. "All right. If you're sure you can make it."

"I'm sure," she told him, gritting her teeth against the biting cold of the wind and rain. "Let's go."

When Marshall mounted, they headed out slowly again, trying to follow the washed-out trail. They hadn't ridden far when George spotted someone in the woods.

"Marsh—" His tone was soft as he pulled back on his reins, halting their progress. "I thought I saw something."

"Where?" Marshall asked anxiously as his father pointed toward the figure in a distance. Fear clutched at Marshall as he recognized Mark and realized that he was carrying someone. Putting his heels to his mount, he quickly covered the distance between them, with George and Delight racing along behind.

"Mark!" he shouted. Jumping from his horse, he ran to Mark's aid.

"Marshall?" Mark, who'd been struggling just to keep moving, was shocked out of his lethargy when he saw him. "Jim's leg . . ."

"Delight, get back to the house and fix up a place for them . . . use my bedroll," Marshall ordered, and she rushed to follow his directions as he lifted his unconscious brother in his arms. Careful of Jim's injured leg, he carried him toward the farmhouse.

"It was the guerrillas," Mark tried to explain, as George helped him to get on Marshall's horse.

"Don't try to talk now. Let's get you back to the cabin where it's dry so we can take a look at your head."

Delight reached the house first and quickly spread the blanket on the one filthy bed. By the time Marshall kicked the door fully open and came in carrying Jim, Delight had already begun gathering up odd pieces of wood for a fire. Piling the wood on the hearth, she waited nervously as he laid Jim down on the hastily made bed. Kneeling beside him, she took his hand.

"Jim—" She breathed his name in desperation, as she realized for the first time how pale he was. His coloring was almost gray, and Delight looked up at Marshall, her eyes wide with worry.

"It's his leg."

It was then that Delight saw the bloody makeshift bandage tied around his thigh. "He was shot? Oh, God . . ."

"Get him out of those wet clothes while I get a fire going. Have you ever tended a bullet wound before?" Marshall asked as he started a small blaze.

"No, but teach me," she said firmly.

"All right. The first thing we have to do is find out if the bullet's still in there or not."

"What do you want me to do?"

"For right now, make him as comfortable as you can, while I'll bring in some water."

Marshall started back outside as Mark and George were coming through the door. "Mark . . . how's your head?"

"I'll make it. Don't worry about me. Take care of Jim," Mark told him as George helped him over to the hearth.

As Delight began to strip Jim's wet, clinging clothes from him, he groaned and slowly regained consciousness.

"Jim!" She stopped what she was doing and grasped his hand. "Thank heaven!"

George rushed to the bed, "Jimmy . . ." His voice was hoarse with emotion.

Jim frowned as he looked up at them. "Delight . . . Father . . . where am I?" With his free hand, he covered his eyes, trying to remember all that had happened.

"You're in an old, abandoned farmhouse right now," His father told him. "Mark carried you . . ."

"Mark!" Jim looked up at them quickly, his eyes clouded with concern. "How's Mark?"

"I'm all right, Jim." Mark's voice came to him and he visibly relaxed.

"Your head?"

"The bullet just grazed me . . ."

"Good . . . Good . . ." The effort to talk cost him much, and all his strength seemed to drain out of him. His eyes closed in exhaustion, and Delight, thinking the worst, looked up at George, her expression one of panic.

"He'll be all right, once we get that leg taken care of," George reassured her, and she managed a weak smile.

"I'd better get another blanket to keep him warm." She started to rise, but Jim's hold on her hand stopped her.

"Don't go," he muttered, and she quickly gave up the idea.

"I'll get it," George offered.

"Thanks." She gave him an appreciative look.

"How's he doing?" Marshall asked solemnly as he came back in with a bucket of water.

"He's conscious, but weak."

"Marsh?" Jim looked up to see his brother. Smiling faintly, he managed to quip, "What is this, a family reunion?"

"We thought it was going to be a wake." Marshall couldn't stop the grin that threatened. "But from the sound of you, I don't think you're dying . . ."

Jim moaned as he tried to shift positions. "You may not think so, but . . ."

"Lie still, darling," Delight entreated, and he rested quietly.

George returned and handed her another blanket. "Let's

get the rest of those wet clothes off of him," he said as he pulled off Jim's boots, and with Marshall's help they cut away his pants.

Jim lay motionless throughout the ordeal, the only sign of his distress the tightening of his jaw as they lifted his hips to pull the remains of his pants from him. After covering him with the other blanket, Marshall hurried to heat the water.

Delight never left Jim's side as George carefully folded back the cover from his leg and removed the makeshift bandage.

"Marshall?" he called softly to his older son.

Marshall looked up from where he'd been heating water on the fire. "What?"

"In my saddlebags there's an extra shirt. Tear it up, we're going to need it for bandages . . ."

He looked down at Jim's thigh. The flesh was torn and raw, and a quick examination revealed, to George's disgust, that the bullet had not passed through his leg. As gently as possible, he probed the wound, drawing a guttural growl from Jim.

"The bullet's still in there, Jimmy." George was serious.

Jim met his father's concerned gaze. "Do what you have to do."

"Do you want a drink first?"

He nodded, and George went quickly to get the whiskey from his saddlebag. Handing it to Delight, he waited patiently while she held the flask to Jim's lips. He drank deeply of the potent liquor, and its burning warmth brought some of the color back to his face. When he finished, he glanced up at his father.

"All right. I'm ready." He brought Delight's hand to his lips, kissing it softly as he prepared himself for the trauma to come. Though the pain in his leg was bad now, Jim knew what had to be done to probe for a bullet. Girding himself, he glanced up at Delight. "Don't look so worried. It'll all be over soon."

She smiled tremulously at him and leaned forward to kiss him.

George moved to the fire and held the blade of his knife

directly in the flames while Marshall carried the hot water to the bedside, and in minutes they were set.

"Jimmy. Marsh's going to hold your leg for me."

"Do you need my help?" Mark offered, knowing that although he was injured and weak he could still help hold Jim immobile.

"It's all right, Mark." Jim nodded, "I'll hold still for them." His eyes met Delight's, and she recognized for the first time the power of his inner strength. As she held tightly to his hand, they began.

As quickly and efficiently as he could, George delved into the damaged flesh, trying to locate and remove the bullet. Jim's grip on Delight's hand was bruising, and the muscles in his neck stood out as he strained in silent agony. Turning away, his jaw clenched, he refused to give in to the scream that threatened as the hot blade cut into his leg.

Delight could almost feel his torment and her tears fell freely as Jim lay motionless, controlling himself even as the wracking pain tore at his body.

George exchanged a worried look with Marshall. The bullet was in deeper that he'd thought. In one final, desperate attempt, he probed again, and this time Jim could not stop the groan of anguish that escaped him as he lapsed into unconsciousness. Working quickly, George at last located the elusive piece of metal and pried it loose from his son's leg.

"Oh, thank God," Delight cried, when he extracted the bullet. Watching Jim suffer had been almost more than she could bear, and she felt faint from the horror of it.

The wound was bleeding freely again, and, concerned about a further blood loss, George quickly prepared to cauterize it. Delight remained steadfastly by Jim's side as George finished doctoring Jim's leg, even though the smell of the burned flesh was nauseating. She was glad that Jim had been unconscious during the last part, for the pain surely would have been more than he could have borne. When George was satisfied that the bleeding was stopped and that he'd done everything he could for Jim, he bound his leg with the clean, soft cloths.

"Will he be all right now?" Delight asked, her face pale from the strain she'd been under.

"He should be, as long as no infection sets in," Marshall started to explain, and then, realizing that she wasn't looking well, he handed her the whiskey. "Take a drink. You look like you could use one."

"Thanks." Without any hesitation, she took it from him, and, remembering Ollie's drinking lesson, she took a deep swallow. At George's amazed expression, she grinned. "Ollie taught me."

"Ollie—" George paused. "I hope he's all right . . . he didn't look too good when they took him on board Henry's boat."

"If Rose has anything to do with it, I'm sure he'll be fine," Delight reassured him.

George smiled at her answer and then realized that he hadn't taken care of Mark's wound yet. "Mark . . . let me take a look at your head . . ."

Marshall handed him the liquor as George gently examined his head.

"How's it look?" Mark asked, cringing as he touched a particularly sensitive spot.

"Not bad," George told him as he cleaned the scalp wound. "It's just a graze, but I'm sure you'll have a headache for the next few days."

"I already do." Mark tried to grin, but the throbbing in his head stifled his good humor.

As Jim stirred, all attention turned back to him. Groaning softly, he opened his eyes to see Delight hovering over him, her face reflecting her love and concern for him.

"Hello." His tone was gruff.

"Hello." Her voice was a caress, and she reached out to touch his cheek with gentle fingers.

"Did he get it out?" Jim asked.

"Yes. You'll be fine."

Trusting her completely, he relaxed, the tension flowing from him. "How long was I out?"

"Just a few minutes."

He nodded and closed his eyes. His entire body ached, but the center of the pain was the throbbing in his thigh. "Got any more of that whiskey left?"

"Sure do." Mark handed her the now half-empty bottle. Slipping her arm under his shoulders, she helped Jim up a little so he could drink more easily.

"Thanks." He lay back, exhausted.

"How do you feel?" Marshall asked.

"You don't want to know," Jim answered flatly, resting his forearm across his brow.

"That bad?"

"That bad," he confirmed.

"Try to rest, then. Sleep is probably the best thing for you."

Jim nodded wearily and turned to look at Delight. "Stay with me?"

"As long as you want me to," she answered softly, taking his hand.

He squeezed hers gently and closed his eyes.

Mark, relieved that Jim was doing better, stood up and moved around the room, testing himself. The dizziness had passed, and, physically, he was feeling much improved.

"I'll head out again in the morning. Now that you're here to take care of Jim . . ." Mark began, and Marshall and George gave him a disbelieving look.

"You can't be serious."

"Absolutely." His expression was grave. "It's my duty."

George snorted in disbelief. "It's not your duty to get killed!"

"What choice do I have? I have to go after them!"

"By yourself? Injured? That's suicide, Mark." Marshall told him angrily.

"But the gold . . ."

"Is it worth your life?" The unexpected question from Jim

stopped the entire conversation. "Better we should go back and find out who's behind it all." His breathing was ragged as he closed his eyes again.

Mark fell silent as he realized that Jim was right. He had been so obsessed with getting the gold back that he hadn't realized the danger that the spies still represented. "You're right."

"I'm glad to hear you talk sense," George told him gruffly as he put a comforting arm about his shoulders.

Mark's expression was grim, and the look in his eyes cold and hard. "I'll find them, and when I do . . . they're going to pay for what they did."

It was much later that night when the rain finally stopped. The cabin was dark, save for the glow of the small fire they'd managed to keep going all afternoon. Sitting before its warmth, they relaxed in silent companionship. The worst was over.

Jim had been sleeping off and on all the afternoon. The rest and the liberal doses of the whiskey seemed to have taken the edge off his pain. And he lay now, awake, comfortable and content.

"You two have never really told us what happened," George said, wanting to know the whole story.

"Did Delight tell you about the attack?" Mark asked.

"Not in detail, no."

"They ambushed us at the wooding station. They must have planted explosives on board, because just as we were pulling out there was an explosion. Jim was blown overboard by the blast, and I was buried under some timbers. Jim managed to rescue me and the others, but there were sharpshooters up on the hillside, and as my men tried to escape they cut them down." Mark's tone was bitter, and George offered him the whiskey bottle. After taking a deep swallow, he went on. "There was nothing more we could do there. The Rebs had gotten on the ship and stolen the gold. So when I was able to find the horses, we went after them."

"But there were only two of you," Marshall argued. "Didn't you realize that you were hopelessly outnumbered?"

"Yes, but it didn't seem to matter at the time. My men were all dead. And I thought if we could catch the guerrillas by surprise, we might have a chance to get the gold back."

"If it hadn't been raining, it would have worked," Jim added. "But it was too hard to track them in the mud. We were right on top of them and didn't even know it . . . not until it was too late."

"You're just lucky you're still alive," George told them. "Those Rebel sharpshooters don't usually miss."

"I know. Our horses shied . . . that's the only thing that saved us," Mark explained.

They were silent for long minutes.

"Tomorrow, Mark and I will go for help," George began. "I want to arrange for a wagon to come back for you. You shouldn't use that leg at all until we can get you to a doctor."

Jim nodded his agreement. "You won't get any argument out of me on that."

"Good," George smiled. "It shouldn't be too far to New Madrid. We can book passage home from there."

"The sooner we get back, the better. Mother, Dorrie, and Renee are probably going crazy by now," Marshall added.

"I'll send word upriver when we get to town tomorrow." When no one had anything else to offer, George said, "Well, let's get what sleep we can. I want to head out at first light."

Delight sat quietly on the floor at Jim's side as the men settled in and one by one fell asleep. She had thought Jim was asleep too, but when she shifted stiffly, trying to find a comfortable position, he took her arm in an easy grip and pulled her up next to him.

"I didn't know you were awake," she whispered in surprise.

"Shh . . ." Jim said, sensing her discomfort. "Lie with me. Let me feel you against me."

"But your leg . . ." she protested quietly.

"If you lie still, it'll be all right," he encouraged her.

Delight was tempted, for she wanted nothing more than to

spend the night in his arms, but she was very conscious of the other men in the room.

"Your father," she whispered, embarrassed.

"I assure you, he's asleep, and even if he wasn't he wouldn't mind." He grinned roguishly at her, and her resistance faded. "You are my wife, you know."

Smiling, she carefully stretched out beside him. "I know."

When she lay, not touching him for fear of hurting him, Jim drew her closer, pressing her head down on his shoulder. "That's better."

She sighed, at peace for the first time that day. "I love you, Jim. I don't think I could live without you."

His hand lifted to caress her cheek, and he paused when he felt the dampness of her tears. "You're crying? Don't." His voice was soft and hoarse with emotion.

"I'm sorry." Delight raised her head to really look at him. "I'm just so relieved that you're all right . . ." She studied the male beauty of him, his firm features, his dark eyes warm now with his love for her, the overnight growth of beard that added to his total masculinity.

Feeling the depth of her love, he pulled her toward him and kissed her, but as he tried to nestle closer to her soft, womanly curves he forgot about his leg and the pain exploded in a white-hot flash. "Damn!" He hissed under his breath as he released her abruptly.

"What's wrong?" Her eyes widened with worry.

He chuckled softly, lying back in agony and ecstasy. "You're so totally captivating that I forgot all about my damn leg."

"Did you hurt it again? Should I check the bandage?" She started to panic.

"No, it wasn't that bad. But why don't you bring me the whiskey?"

Delight hurried to get the bottle, and when she gave it to him, he took several big gulps.

"I thought you didn't like whiskey," Delight remarked, keeping her voice low as he swallowed the burning liquid eagerly.

"I don't like it, but believe me, it takes the edge off my leg." He grimaced, handing the liquor back to her. When she'd put it away, she wasn't certain whether she should lie down by him again. "Come on," he coaxed, patting the blanket next to him.

"Are you sure?" Delight sat on the edge of the bed.

"I'll try to control myself, but for some reason when I get this close to you there's only one thing on my mind."

She smiled as she lay beside him. "Think of me as only your cabin boy."

Jim stifled a laugh. "I'll try."

"That was a wonderful night . . ." she sighed.

"Tease. It's not fair to tempt me with memories like those when I'm not in a position to do anything about it."

Delight grinned. "As long as you don't forget."

"Ah, my love. If only we were alone . . ." Knowing that he would not enjoy the pleasures of her body this night, he held her as close as he could. "Now go to sleep."

"Yes, Captain," she murmured, safe in the haven of his arms. "Good night."

Chapter Thirty-six

Renee was home alone when she received word that the *Enterprise* had been destroyed by a Rebel attack and that the survivors had just returned to town aboard the *Belle of Memphis*. Without a second thought, she called for the carriage to be brought around and rushed down to the levee. She located the steamer without any trouble and immediately went on board in search of Jim, Mark, and Ollie.

"Excuse me." She stopped one of the clerks. "I was wondering if you could tell me which cabin Captain Westlake is in."

The man looked at her questioningly. "There was no Captain Westlake traveling with us this trip."

"Surely there must be some mistake. He was on the *Enterprise*."

The clerk gave her a pitying look. "It was a terrible tragedy, ma'am. All those people killed . . ."

Renee was growing more upset by the minute. Surely, Jim couldn't have been hurt. "What about Captain Clayton? He's a Union officer."

"No, ma'am. We picked up the survivors, but there weren't any soldiers with them."

She paled at the news. "Where are they?"

"On the promenade deck. The first eight staterooms as you come out of the companionway." He pointed her in the right direction.

"Thank you." Renee held her breath as she went in search of the survivors. No Jim and no Mark! Surely nothing could have happened to them. They were so young . . . so vibrant . . . so alive. . . . She fought down the painful possibility that they could have been lost. She wouldn't think of that now. Steeling herself, she headed up the companionway, grateful that Dorrie and Martha weren't with her.

Rose was just coming out of Ollie's stateroom on the promenade deck when she saw Renee, and she rushed to her.

"Mrs. Westlake!" Her call immediately drew Renee's attention. "Mrs. Westlake, I'm Rose O'Brien." She introduced herself, but when she saw no flicker of recognition, she explained further, "I work for Delight de Vries."

"Oh." Renee was instantly contrite and took her hand in a warm gesture. "Rose. Of course. I'm sorry. I was just so worried . . . I'm trying to locate the people who were on the *Enterprise*."

"I know . . . Ollie's right in here." She ushered Renee toward the cabin.

"Were you on board?" she asked, surprised.

"Yes, I was. Delight, too."

"Delight? I didn't know she was going to travel with Jim. . . ."

"It was a spur of the moment decision," Rose answered.

"Where is she? She wasn't hurt, was she? And what about Jim and Mark Clayton?" Renee demanded, pausing outside Ollie's cabin door.

"They're all fine," Rose assured her. "At least, they were the last time I saw them."

"You mean they didn't come back with you?"

"No. Jim and Captain Clayton took off after the Rebs. They wanted to try to get the gold back."

"Oh . . . and Delight?"

"She stayed with me and helped me with Ollie until your husband and father-in-law showed up. Once they got everything all straightened out and the rest of us on our way back home, she rode with them to find Jim."

"Marshall took Delight with them?" Renee was amazed.

"Yes. She went along."

"But what was she doing on this trip to begin with?" Renee was confused. The last she'd heard Jim was making the run and Delight was going to wait for him at home.

"I don't know if I should be the one to tell you all this . . ."

"I won't repeat anything, Rose. I just want to know what happened."

From all that Delight had told her about Renee, she knew she could trust her. "Did you know about Delight's disguise?" she asked.

"I did," Renee confirmed.

"Did you know why she did it?"

"No. Jim never told us the real reason."

As delicately as she could, Rose explained. "Martin Montgomery wanted Delight for his own. . . ."

"Her own stepfather?!" Renee's outrage was real.

Rose nodded. "She ran away from him that first night and knew that she had to hide. That's why she dressed like a boy."

"If she knew that's what he wanted, why did she go back?"

"She thought she could keep him at bay by threatening to tell her mother the truth. And it worked, for a while, but Wednesday night Martin tried to force himself on her again."

"She wasn't hurt, was she?"

"Not physically. Clara stopped him in time."

"Oh, no!" Renee gasped sympathetically. She knew how much Clara had cared for her younger husband. "Poor Clara."

"I wouldn't feel too sorry for her. It's a good thing she found out the truth about him. Anyway, she sent us to find Jim, because she knew Delight would be safer under his protection."

"Good. I'm glad she's safe. But something's not right here. . . ." Renee frowned.

"What do you mean?"

"Martin is the one who warned Marshall about the plan to attack the *Enterprise*."

Rose looked surprised. "That doesn't sound like Martin Montgomery . . . unless . . . did he demand any money?"

"No . . . but he did say that he had to get out of town because the spies were after him."

"The weasel! He only needed the money because Clara threw him out."

"But how did he find out about the attack?" Renee looked at her worriedly.

Both women fell silent for a moment as they realized that Martin might have been a spy.

"How is Ollie?" Renee finally asked, breaking the tense silence.

"He's much better now. I have to admit I was worried. He was unconscious for quite a while."

"Well, let's get him back to the house and taken care of."

"Are you sure?"

"Of course. Ollie's family. Do you have a place to stay?"

"I can go back to Clara's, since Martin is gone."

"All right, but why don't you come with me for now? We can get in touch with Clara later."

"I'd like that."

Renee followed Rose into the cabin then, and she gasped when she first saw Ollie. He still lay in bed, his head swathed in white bandages.

"Ollie?" At the sound of Renee's voice, he opened his eyes and smiled at her, and her fears dissolved.

"Renee. Did Rose tell you what happened to the *Enterprise?*" he asked.

"She did. It must have been terrible."

"I wish I could have done something to save her. . . ."

"Don't worry about that, Ollie. The important thing is that you're alive. Do you feel up to moving?" Renee asked, wanting to get him settled as soon as possible. "I want you to come back to the house with us so I can get the doctor to take a look at you."

"But I'm fine, now," he protested.

"I'll believe that when the doctor tells me so." She would brook no argument from him, and he gave up gracefully.

"Is Rose coming, too?" he asked quickly.

"Yes. She is," Renee assured him.

"Good." He was glad that Rose had not been forgotten in all the hubbub over his own injuries. Swinging his legs over the side of the bed, he rested a minute before getting slowly to his feet. Rose helped him with his coat and put an arm around him as he stood. "I guess I'm ready."

"The carriage is right at the foot of the gangplank, so you don't have far to walk."

"You haven't been up very often since the accident, so we'd better take it nice and easy," Rose told him as they started down the deck to the companionway.

They made it to the coach without mishap, and after Renee spoke briefly with Walter they were on their way. Once they arrived back at the house, Renee took Ollie into one of the guest bedrooms and with Rose's help quickly got him into bed. She sent a servant to bring a doctor and then settled in the parlor with Rose to relax and have a soothing cup of tea.

It was there that Dorrie found them a short time later when she rushed into the house, crying.

"What's wrong?" Renee rushed to her side.

"I just heard about the *Enterprise* . . . and Mark and Jim didn't come back. . . ."

Putting a comforting arm about her shoulders, Renee hugged her sister-in-law. "No they didn't, but it wasn't because they were killed. They went after the guerrillas to get the gold back."

"So, Jim and Mark were both all right?" she needed to hear the words again.

"Yes, they are. Marshall and your father, too."

Dorrie pulled herself together with an effort. "I was so upset. . . ."

"I could tell. Sit down with us for a while. Do you know Rose?"

"No. I don't believe so. . . ."

"Rose is Delight's friend and companion. She was on board with Delight."

"I didn't know that Jim was planning to take Delight along."

"It was a last-minute thing." Rose avoided repeating the tale of Martin and Delight. "I meant to tell you, Renee . . . they got married in Sainte Genevieve."

"They did?!" the other two women chorused. "That's wonderful!"

"What's wonderful?" Martha Westlake asked as she came in, having just returned from her afternoon outing.

"Delight went with Jim this trip and they were married in Sainte Gen!"

Martha smiled. "I'm so glad, but I wish they could have married here in town. . . ." She gave Renee a stern, yet teasing look. "Both my sons are married now, and I haven't been at either of their weddings!"

"Don't worry, Mother," Dorrie told her lightheartedly. "Pretty soon, you can come to Mark's and mine."

Martha looked troubled for a minute. "How did you find all this out about Jim and Delight? They're not back, are they?"

"No . . ." Renee stumbled for the right way to tell her. "Have you met Rose, Delight's friend?"

"Yes, we met before at Clara's." Martha sat down as she still tried to figure out what was going on.

"Well, Rose was with them when they got married."

"But how did she get back here so fast?" Sensing Renee's hesitation, she guessed what had happened. "It's the *Enterprise*, isn't it? Did the Rebs attack?"

"A little north of New Madrid," Rose supplied.

"And Jim?"

"He's fine, Mother. Mark and Delight, too." Dorrie hastened to confirm that bit of good news.

"Where are they?"

"They went after the Rebs to try to get the gold back. Marshall and George went with them," Renee told her.

"I see." Martha looked troubled and was about to speak when someone knocked at the door.

"It's probably the doctor." Renee hurried out into the hall to answer it and admitted Dr. Freemont. "He's upstairs, Doctor."

"Thank you, Mrs. Westlake." He followed her up the stairs. "I'll check back with you before I go," he told her as he entered Ollie's bedroom.

"I'll be in the front parlor," Renee said as she headed back to join the others.

"Why is he here?" Martha asked when Renee returned.

"Ollie was hurt, and I thought it would be best if the doctor checked him over."

"You're right, of course," Martha sighed, settling back in a chair. "When was the attack?"

"Thursday night—late." Rose told her.

Martha was pensive. "It could be quite a while before we hear anything more. We'd better pray that they're all right."

"I know," Renee and Dorrie each said, worrying about their men. They knew the hours would pass slowly until they had word from them.

Dr. Freemont came down a short time later.

"How is he?" Renee inquired, meeting him in the hall and drawing him into the parlor where the rest of the family waited.

"He'll be just fine, Mrs. Westlake. Good afternoon, ladies." He was cordial as he joined them for a cup of tea. "You did an excellent job of nursing him, Miss O'Brien."

"Thank you, Doctor." Rose was glad Ollie was going to be all right.

"Just keep him quiet for a few days . . . don't let him get too active. Within a week, he should be back to normal."

"That's good news."

Annabelle and Nathan were sharing a relaxing lunch when Wade burst into the house.

"Where are you?" he called excitedly from the front hall.

"Wade?" Annabelle rose quickly. "We're in the dining room. What's happened?"

"Our plan succeeded!" He was jubilant.

"What did you hear?" Nathan asked excitedly.

"The *Enterprise* was totally destroyed . . . she burned after the explosion."

"Did they get the gold?"

"Yes!" Wade smiled widely.

"Survivors . . . what about survivors?" Annabelle waited for the news she wanted to hear more than anything in the world.

"What few there were returned today."

"And . . ."

"And Captain Jim Westlake was·not among them."

Annabelle felt a stabbing pain in her heart, but she ignored it. Her smile was victorious as she spoke. "I think this calls for a celebration. What about you?"

"Absolutely!"

Nathan led the way to his well-stocked liquor cabinet and poured them each a drink. "To the Confederacy. May she prosper." When they had downed their liquor, he suddenly grew solemn. "There's no chance that any of this can be traced back to us, is there?"

"No." Wade was confident. "There were only two people who might have given us away . . . Martin Montgomery and Sam Wallace."

"And?"

"And I've taken care of them both."

"Good. Will you join us for dinner tonight, Wade? We'll make it a very special evening."

"I'd be honored."

As Wade started to leave, Nathan walked with him to the door for a moment of privacy. "Was it necessary to do away with Montgomery?"

Wade pinned him with a glacial stare. "Yes. The man was a fool. He knew too much and he was far too easily influenced."

"But won't he be missed?"

"No. His wife had thrown him out and he was leaving town. I just made sure that he'd never come back," Wade told him confidently. "Don't worry so much, Nathan. Everything has turned out better than we'd expected."

"Yes." Nathan paused. "Yes, it has. You're right." Clapping Wade on the back, he opened the front door for him. "We'll see you tonight."

Annabelle stood at the window and watched Wade ride away. So, it was over. Jim was dead. Her expression was pained as she remembered the time they'd had together and how much she'd desired him.

"Annabelle, darling, is something wrong?" Nathan came

into the room unannounced and was surprised by the look on her face.

Quickly masking her feelings, she forced a smile. "Of course not. We've gotten everything we wanted."

"Yes, we have, haven't we?" Nathan returned her smile as they went back in to finish their lunch.

Annabelle sat next to Wade on the sofa in the parlor savoring an after-dinner brandy. Their meal had been a feast in celebration of the success of their venture, and they had eaten their fill of the sumptuous fare.

"Have you heard any more news of the explosion, Wade?" Nathan asked as he sat in a wing chair opposite them.

"Nothing substantial, but then I was off duty all afternoon."

"Is it true the entire Union guard was killed?"

"Yes. A pity, isn't it?" Wade sneered, smiling. "Even our dear Captain Clayton didn't make it back."

"I'm so glad our plan worked out," Annabelle told him proudly. "What can we do next? Surely there is something more we can do to help. . . ."

"We'd better lie low for now and play the part of concerned citizens."

"It might do well for you to go to the Westlakes and offer your sympathies," Nathan suggested.

Annabelle paused, thinking seriously about the possibility. "That would prove interesting . . . and as the ex-fiancée, I do have an interest—however obscure—in Jim. I think I just might do that tomorrow. Maybe I'll even pay a call on Miss Delight de Vries. It would give me great pleasure to see her reaction to my sympathy call. . . ."

"My dear, I didn't know you could be so . . ." Wade paused, trying to think of the right word.

"So cruel? So vicious?" She gave him a smug look. "After what Jim Westlake and Delight de Vries did to me, I will take great pleasure in paying those calls."

"Just be careful not to be too happy about it," Nathan warned.

"Oh, don't worry. I'll be suitably upset and definitely overcome by the tragedy of Jim's death. You know how convincing I can be." She gave him a mournful look. "Why it's all so tragic. . . ." Annabelle smiled again in anticipation of her visit with Jim's family and fiancée. It would be interesting to witness the aftermath of all their careful plotting.

Chapter Thirty-seven

Marshall stood with Delight on the rickety front porch of the farmhouse, gazing out at the sun-drenched forest that surrounded them. Overnight, it seemed, the buds on the trees had burst forth, clouding the dark limbs and trunks in a haze of bright green. The grass, too, had come alive; its vibrant color was a lush contrast to the dull browns of yesterday.

"It's really beautiful, isn't it?" she said with soft amazement.

"You sound so surprised . . ." he grinned at her.

"I am. Yesterday the woods seemed dark and foreboding, but today they seem so fresh, so new . . . there's a certain feeling of serenity about it . . ."

"If you hadn't been so worried and so wet yesterday, you would have noticed it then, too," he teased.

"I guess," Delight sighed. "You know, in a way, I wish we didn't have to go back."

"Why?"

"It's idyllic here. You can almost let yourself forget . . ."

"You're worrying about Jim?"

"Of course . . . you know he and Mark aren't going to stop until they find out who was behind the whole thing."

"They're men, Delight. They have to know," Marshall replied obliquely.

"Couldn't they let the authorities do it?" Delight didn't want them to put themselves in any further danger, for she had come too close to losing Jim this time.

"Somebody we know not only destroyed our best steamer but they also set Jim and Mark up to be attacked, robbed, and killed. Do you think we can just turn that over to the military or the sheriff and let them try to solve it?"

Delight realized that there was no use in protesting any further. Their course was set. Now the best thing she could do was to support them fully. "I understand," she reluctantly agreed, realizing that Marshall was as determined as Jim and Mark.

"Good. I know it's hard for you, but this is something we have to do."

The sound of Jim's call interrupted their conversation, and Delight went back inside to check on him.

"Where were you?" he asked as he tried to push himself into a sitting position.

"Just on the porch with Marshall. Here, let me help you." She hurried to aid him in his struggle to brace himself against the wall.

"How long did I sleep?"

"A few hours. It's almost four," she told him as she straightened his covers. "Do you feel any better?"

"I think so. But I'll let you know for sure after I sit here a while."

"All right." Delight started to step back, but he caught her wrist and drew her to him.

"I'm glad you're here," he said quietly as his lips sought hers in a soft caress.

"So am I." She returned his kiss with restraint, not wanting to chance hurting his leg.

"I thought that night on the *Enterprise* when Rose was in the next room was bad, but this is ridiculous," Jim growled as he released her, his hand automatically going to his injured thigh.

"That bad?" She frowned in concern.

He nodded, grimacing, "It's bound to get better, though, right?"

"I certainly hope so. We can't have our honeymoon until it does," she said saucily, hoping to distract Jim from the pain that was throbbing in his injured limb.

"With that to look forward to, there is no doubt in my mind that I'm going to make a miraculous recovery." He grinned at her, and she was warmed by the heat of his eyes upon her.

"I can hardly wait." She leaned forward, resting lightly against his chest, and kissed him, this time with a slow, sensuous promise that stirred them both.

"Marry me?" he asked huskily.

"I already did," she laughed, getting up before she gave in to the impulse to kiss him again. "Now, what can I do to make you more comfortable?" The question was innocently put.

Jim gave her a teasing, lecherous look, "Darling . . ."

"I'm talking about food or drink . . ."

"Oh." He looked disappointed. "You're sure?"

"I'm positive," she told him firmly. "Are you hungry?"

"Only for you, sweetheart. But there's not much I can do about that right now." His tone was regretful. "Is there any whiskey left?"

Delight brought him what was left of the liquor.

"Thanks." Jim was taking a swig out of the bottle when Marshall came back inside.

"Still hurts?" he asked, already knowing the answer.

"Yes." Jim handed the bottle back to Delight.

"Let me take a look at it. I don't want to risk moving you too soon." Marshall turned back the blanket to expose his brother's leg.

Jim grabbed Marshall's arm, stopping him abruptly. Their eyes met in serious understanding. "You can't get me out of here soon enough . . ."

"I know," Marshall nodded, and, as Jim released his arm, he turned back to examine the wound.

When he stripped off the soft wrappings, the injured flesh looked vastly improved over the previous afternoon, and there was no sign of infection.

"How does it look?" Delight asked.

"Better, but he's still going to have to take it easy. I don't want him jarring it." Marshall carefully replaced the bandages with the clean ones that Delight brought to him.

"Don't worry. I have no intention of taking any chances." Jim told him. "The sooner I'm up and moving, the better."

"Good."

They passed the rest of the day quietly. Jim fell asleep at dusk, his afternoon of sitting up having sapped his energy, leaving Delight and Marshall sitting alone before the low-burning fire.

Delight glanced at Marshall. "How much do you think Martin really had to do with all of this?"

He looked at her quickly. "I wish I knew." Pausing to think, he added. "After what you told me, I don't believe his story at all, but how did he know?"

"I've been wondering the same thing."

"Martin was involved in this?" Jim's voice cut through the sudden silence, startling them.

"I didn't know you were awake . . ."

"Why didn't you tell me about Martin?"

"You've hardly been in condition to worry about it," Marshall said calmly.

"What did he do?" Jim demanded.

"Thursday morning, he came to me with the news that your boat was going to be attacked."

"He what?" Jim levered himself up on his elbow, his expression thunderous.

"He said that he'd overheard it being planned and that he wanted me to know . . ."

"Who did he hear it from?"

"He didn't say. He was worried about getting out of town because they, supposedly, were after him."

"The only person who would have been after him was me," Jim snarled, lying back heavily on the bed. "He more than overheard the damn plot . . . he probably helped to arrange it!"

"But, Jim," Delight spoke up. "How would he have found out about the gold unless he was involved with the spies? We never made mention of it in public. All he knew was that you were scheduled to leave Thursday morning."

"When we get back, I'm going to start with Martin Montgomery. Maybe he's the connection we need to unravel this whole damn thing!"

"Mark's already on it," Marshall informed him. "We told him everything before he left with Father this morning."

Jim nodded, resting his arm across his forehead, "I hope Sam Wallace has shown up . . ."

"Sam? What does he have to do with this?"

"Mark hired him to keep an eye on Wade MacIntosh, but he never reported in with any information. We looked for him, but it was almost as if he'd disappeared from the face of the earth."

Marshall frowned. "MacIntosh? Why was Mark having him followed?"

"He was working on a hunch . . . MacIntosh had told Dorrie that he'd served with Paul and a few other things that Mark later found out were lies. Something about him didn't ring true, so Mark didn't want to take any chances. Especially after Wade was promoted."

"And you didn't hear anything from Sam at all?"

"Nothing."

"If MacIntosh is involved in this, we've got our work cut out for us." Marshall considered the possibility that the spies had infiltrated the paymaster's corps. They would know every move Mark was going to make before he made it.

"I know." Jim agreed tiredly.

"Well, there's nothing we can do right now. Let's just try to get a good night's sleep. Tomorrow, we'll be on our way back to town."

Marshall stood up, drawing a curious look from Delight, "Where are you going?"

"I thought I'd sleep upstairs tonight." He smiled at her tenderly. He knew Jim and Delight had had precious little time alone since they'd married, and he wanted to give them some privacy.

"But . . ." she started to protest, but he cut her off gently.

"Don't worry. It's not nearly as cold as it was last night." He got his blanket and headed up the dilapidated steps.

"Thanks," Jim called as his brother disappeared from view, and the only answer he got was a distant chuckle.

Delight stood in front of the fire, gazing after Marshall. "He didn't have to do that."

"I know, but aren't you glad that he did?" Jim teased, holding out a hand to her.

She wasted no time in going to him, but as she started to join him on the bed, he stopped her. "Wait . . ."

Delight looked at him questioningly.

"Undress for me. Tonight, I won't have you sleeping on top of the covers," he grinned.

Without hesitation, she stripped off her boy's clothes and slipped easily under the blanket. The coolness of her slim body pressed so sweetly to the heat of his own sent a shudder through Jim, and his arm came possessively around her.

"That's better," he sighed raggedly as his hand rested on her rounded hip.

"I think so, too. You're so nice and warm." She cuddled instinctively against him.

Jim bit back a groan as he realized how impossible it was for him to hold her and still keep himself under restraint. With unsteady hands, he pulled her higher until she lay on his chest. "Kiss me."

She purred in contentment as they ended the kiss, and she rested her head on his shoulder. "How's your leg?"

"It's fine, don't worry."

"Good," she sighed.

And sleep overtook them as they lay in each other's arms.

It was midafternoon when the rumbling sound of a wagon brought Delight and Marshall excitedly from the house.

"It's about time you got back," Marshall called out in greeting as George appeared at the end of the overgrown drive in a buckboard.

"These back roads aren't exactly passable after the rain we just had," George complained as he reined in at the hitching rail. "I got stuck twice on the way back."

"How far of a ride to town is it?"

"By wagon, about six hours, if we don't get stuck," he told them as he stepped carefully up the stairs. His expression turned serious as he asked, "How's Jimmy?"

"He's doing fine," Delight assured him. "He's sleeping right now, but we changed his bandage this morning and his leg is healing nicely."

"Good. I'd like to head back tomorrow morning."

"He should be up to it," Marshall agreed. "In fact, I think we'd have trouble making him wait any longer."

George noted the concern in his voice. "He's not going to rest until he knows who was behind this, is he?"

"No."

"I had thought as much. Mark's the same way. He's going to track down Sam Wallace as soon as he gets back to town. Did Jim tell you about that?"

Marshall nodded. "At least we've got two leads. Between Martin Montgomery and Sam Wallace we should be able to find out something."

"I hope so." George's eyes were cold at the thought of the death and destruction the spies had caused. They would find whoever was responsible, and, when they did, they were going to pay.

* * *

"What do you think, Father?" Annabelle asked as she modeled the dress she was going to wear to the Westlakes'.

"You're a vision, darling." He smiled indulgently. "I take it you're going to pay your respects now?"

"I thought it would be appropriate . . ." Her eyes were alight with devious pleasure. "I'm sure they're just beside themselves with grief . . . no Jim and no boat . . ."

"Remember what I told you." He came to help her with her coat.

"I know. I'll be very careful of what I say. No matter how much I'm enjoying myself." She smiled up at him. "Don't worry. I'll be back as soon as possible."

With a last quick glance in the hall mirror, Annabelle left the house and went to visit Renee and Martha. The maid answered her knock, and she swept into the hall of the Westlake home.

"Tell Renee that I've come, please," she ordered regally as she handed the maid her coat.

"Yes ma'am, Miss Annabelle."

Annabelle stood for a moment in the hall foyer before walking casually into the parlor.

Dorrie, who'd been at the back of the house, heard the door and went to investigate. She came face-to-face with Annabelle before Renee came downstairs.

"Dorrie . . . my poor child." Annabelle hugged her, leaving Dorrie totally stunned. "I'm so sorry to hear about your loss," she claimed dramatically. "And I am just so upset . . . Jim . . . why did this have to happen to him?"

"Annabelle . . ." Dorrie tried to interrupt her to find out what she was talking about.

"No, don't say a word. I know Jim was engaged to another, but I loved him so . . ." Annabelle's eyes filled with tears that were most convincing, and for a moment Dorrie almost believed that she had really cared for her brother. "How could this have happened?"

"Annabelle?" Renee's voice came to them as she started down the staircase.

"Oh, Renee . . . darling, I'm so sorry. I know that you loved him almost as much as I did . . ." She embraced her.

"Annabelle . . ." Renee didn't understand what was going on. "Annabelle, dear, what are you talking about?"

"You mean you haven't heard?" Annabelle was suddenly cautious. How could they not have been told?

"Heard what?" Dorrie asked, confused.

"The *Enterprise* . . . and Jim . . . we just found out this morning. It's all so tragic . . . so unnecessary . . ." she sobbed.

Renee put an arm about her shoulders and seated her on the sofa. "Annabelle. Tell me what you've heard."

Dabbing at her eyes with her lace handkerchief, Annabelle related what Wade had told them. "The word came that the *Enterprise* had burned, and that Jim and Mark had both been killed . . ."

Renee gave Dorrie a helpless look and then sat down to take Annabelle's hand. "There was an explosion on board and the boat was lost, but Jim and Mark were not killed."

"What?" A look of surprise crossed Annabelle's face . . . one that Renee mistakenly took for happiness.

"They're fine."

"But they weren't among the survivors."

"No. They haven't come back yet. The *Enterprise* was attacked by guerrillas, and Jim and Mark went after them."

"They did?" Annabelle was nervous. They were alive? "Oh, thank God, they're still alive . . ." She played the part to perfection; but all she could think of was getting the news back to Wade as fast as possible. "I just couldn't bear it when I'd heard that Jim had been killed. Even though our engagement was over . . ."

"He'll always care for you, Annabelle. You know that." Renee patted her hand. "And I'm sure he'll be grateful to know that you cared enough to come here today . . ."

"Thank you, Renee . . . Dorrie." Annabelle rose to leave. "I hope I didn't disturb you too much . . ."

"Nonsense." Renee hugged her and then walked to the door with her.

"I'm so glad he's all right," Annabelle said once more, with all the sincerity she could muster.

"I know dear. Take care." Renee watched her go and then turned back to Dorrie. "See. I told you Annabelle really loved Jim."

"Maybe." Dorrie was not totally convinced. "But then again, maybe she was just being ghoulish . . ."

"Dorrie!"

She shrugged. "I could be wrong, but there's still something about her that I don't like."

"Well, we're not going to talk about Annabelle anymore. There's no point, anyway."

"Thank heaven," Dorrie remarked, but Renee chose to ignore her.

Annabelle practically ran all the way home. She flew up the steps and threw open the front door, rushing madly inside.

"Father!" she yelled, searching frantically for him in the parlor and the study. "Father! Where are you?"

The maid came from the back of the house. "Miss Annabelle. Your father went out for a while. He said he'd be home in about an hour."

"Damn!" Annabelle cursed, standing helplessly in the middle of the hall. Then, deciding on a plan of action, she went into the study to write out a note. Giving it to the maid, she instructed, "I want this delivered to Major MacIntosh right away. Do you understand?"

"Yes, ma'am."

"Good. See to it."

Taking off her coat, she threw it on a chair and went to the liquor cabinet to pour herself a drink. Things hadn't worked out as they'd planned, and they were going to have to be very careful.

It was almost a half an hour later when Wade finally arrived. Annabelle let him in. "What is it?" he demanded, angry at having been summoned while he was on duty.

"I went to the Westlakes', just like we'd planned . . ."

"And?"

"And Jim Westlake is very much alive."

"What?"

"Your friend, Mark Clayton is, too."

"I don't understand."

"Renee told me that they didn't come back with the survivors because they were too busy chasing after the guerrillas who'd attacked the boat!"

Wade cursed under his breath. "What else did she have to say?"

"Nothing else as important as that." Annabelle was frightened. "What if they catch them? We'll be exposed . . ."

"I have to talk to your father. When is he due back?"

"Anytime now."

"I can wait a few minutes, but not much more. Fix me a drink, while I try to figure this out."

Annabelle poured him a straight bourbon and took it to him where he sat on the sofa. "What are we going to do?"

"I don't know yet. It all depends on how much Tyndale told the guerrillas. If they don't know who we are, we're safe. But if he used any names and the guerrillas reveal them, we're going to have to get out of town, and fast."

Annabelle rushed into the hall as she heard her father come in. "Wade's here, and he needs to talk to you." She drew him urgently into the parlor.

"What is it, my dear? You look positively pale."

"It's Jim, Father. He wasn't killed in the attack."

"Then where is he?" Nathan was instantly worried.

"He and Mark Clayton both went after the guerrillas," Wade finished solemnly.

"Oh, no."

"I need you to get in touch with Gordon Tyndale and find out how much those guerrillas know about us. If Westlake catches up with them and they tell everything they know, we could be in serious trouble."

"I'll go see him right away."

"Good. I've got to get back on duty, but I'll stop by later."

"Hopefully, I'll have some reassuring news for you then." Nathan tried to sound optimistic. "As any good informer knows, one doesn't reveal his sources."

"Yes," Wade said sarcastically. "But just how 'good' of an informer is Gordon Tyndale?"

And the question remained unanswered until late that night when Nathan returned from his meeting with Gordon.

"Well? What did you find out?" Wade asked anxiously. He had come back to their house after he'd gotten off duty to await Nathan's findings.

Annabelle looked up nervously. "Father?"

Nathan gave them a reassuring smile. "Everything is going to be just fine. No names were exchanged. All contact between them was handled anonymously."

"Thank God!" Annabelle breathed, and Wade looked openly relieved.

"Well, all we have to do now is play it safe. We know for a fact that Mark thought I was involved in something, but with Sam Wallace out of the way there's no proof."

"Good. Let's keep things quiet now. We don't want to give them any excuse to look in our direction. Agreed?"

"Agreed." Wade felt the tension ebb from him. "Let's have a drink. I need one. This afternoon took its toll on me."

Marshall and George carried Jim as carefully as they could out to the wagon that next morning and laid him in the back on some straw and blankets. He was wearing the same shirt he'd had on the night of the explosion, but the rest of his apparel had been greatly altered. It had been impossible for him to wear anything on his injured thigh, so Delight had cut off the leg on the extra pair of pants that Marshall had brought along. Jim had managed to get them on, but the result was a bit drafty, and he was more than a little vocal about his dislike of the new style.

Luckily, there had been no more rain, and the roads were drying out as they headed back toward New Madrid. The ride was rough, and more than once Jim had to grit his teeth against the jarring pain, but finally, by late that afternoon, they made it into town. The trip had so exhausted Jim that they decided to wait until the following day to continue their trip home. Taking rooms at the hotel for the night, everyone retired early in anticipation of catching the northbound steamer that was due in town near dawn.

Mark stood on the deck of the steamboat watching as the St. Louis riverfront came into view. He was back, at last. He'd done some serious thinking on the way home, and he knew exactly what course of action he was going to take. With a determination that was not to be denied, Mark Clayton left the ship intent on finding the responsible parties and exacting his revenge.

Chapter Thirty-eight

The day was warm and bright, and the sweet, heavy scent of spring was in the air. Walking slowly down the promenade deck with Marshall, Delight's manner was relaxed and easy.

"I want to thank you again for buying this dress for me," she told him gratefully.

"I was just glad that the seamstress in New Madrid had one close enough to your size that we could buy. I didn't think you'd want to head home in those same old boy's clothes."

"You're right about that. They served their purpose, but I definitely needed a change." After the long, hard days she'd spent wearing pants, the soft cotton day gown made Delight feel very much a woman.

"How's Jim feeling?" he inquired as they paused at the railing to enjoy the passing scenery.

"He got his first good night's sleep since the explosion last night, and it did wonders for him."

"Is he resting now?"

Delight nodded. "He was when I came out on deck."

"Well, a couple of days in bed and he'll be as good as new." Marshall was pleased with the news.

"What time are we going to be arriving in St. Louis tonight?"

"We should be there by ten or so. It just depends on how many stops we make on the way."

"Good. I know Jim is in a hurry to get back." She let the sentence drop as her eyes clouded with concern.

"Don't worry, Delight. Everything will work out."

"How can you be sure? If the spies were organized enough to plan and carry out this attack . . . won't they know that you're looking for them?"

"They may or may not know that Martin came to us. If they don't, we might be able to catch them unawares. Otherwise . . ."

"Otherwise, they'll disappear, and we'll never find out who did it." She looked determined. "We have to locate Martin and force him to tell us everything he knows."

"Mark's working on that right now," Marshall assured her. "And by the time we get back, hopefully he'll have the information we need."

"All right, Captain Clayton. Sit down." General Fields, Mark's commanding officer, looked up at him assessingly. "Now. I want to know exactly what happened."

"Yes, sir," Mark replied respectfully and sat down at the chair placed strategically in front of the massive desk.

Mark knew an accounting to his superiors was due, but he just wished it could wait until he'd had the time to locate Martin Montgomery. General Fields, however, had other ideas. He had somehow known the moment Mark had arrived back in town and had sent for him immediately. Mark hadn't even had time to clean up. He was controlling his frustration at being there with great difficulty. The last thing he wanted to do was spend the day going over everything that had happened. Montgomery was the key to the entire operation, and he had to go after him.

"I'm waiting, Captain." General Fields sat patiently as Mark gathered his thoughts.

"We shipped out on schedule, sir, early Thursday morning. As you know, there had been a slight breach of security, so we doubled the guard."

"By a breach of security, you mean the fact that it was known that the Westlake Line was carrying the gold?"

"Yes, sir."

"Go on."

"We rearranged the shipping schedules to keep everything off balance, and we sent guards on every run, so it wouldn't be obvious when the gold did go." As the general nodded, Mark continued. "We had a safe run as far as the wooding station north of New Madrid. The guerrillas, in disguise, had taken over the station. We wooded up with no problem, but as we were pulling out there was an explosion on board."

"An explosion?"

"They must have planted some explosives. Anyway, the steamer caught fire, and as my men tried to evacuate . . ." Mark choked as he remembered vividly exactly what had happened. "There were sharpshooters on the hillside."

"Where were you at this time, Captain?"

"On the main deck, I had been supervising the loading with Captain Westlake. When the blast occurred, he was thrown overboard and I was trapped unconscious under the debris."

"And who rescued you?"

"Captain Westlake, sir, and his pilot, Walter."

"Continue," the general ordered imperiously.

"After I came to, I found out that the Rebs had stolen the gold. So I took what weapons I could find and went after them."

"Did you go alone?"

"No, sir. Captain Westlake went with me."

"Why didn't you send for help, Captain?"

"There wasn't time, General. It was raining and I was afraid the trail would wash out. Besides, it seemed to me at the time that the element of surprise was on my side. I was certain that the guerrillas thought we were all dead, and I had hoped that they would not be expecting anyone to give chase." Mark paused, taking a deep breath.

"And did you find them?"

"Unfortunately, yes. It was storming so badly that they had holed up and Jim—Captain Westlake—and I weren't aware of it." Mark touched his head. "We're lucky we're still alive."

"Did you get a look at any of them?"

"No, sir."

"Where is Captain Westlake now?"

"He was more seriously wounded than I was. He had to remain behind for a few days until it was safe for him to travel. His father and brother were the ones who found us."

The general frowned. "How did they know . . . ?"

"Sir. It's my belief that someone within our own ranks is involved in this."

"Captain Clayton, you did not answer my question. How did the Westlakes know?" the general demanded.

"They were informed that the *Enterprise* was going to be attacked, and they came after us."

The general was genuinely surprised. "Who told them, Clayton? I want to know names."

"A man named Martin Montgomery, sir."

"Montgomery?" The general was pensive for a moment. "I don't believe I've ever heard of him. Is he a sympathizer?"

"Not that I know of. From what I understand, he told Marshall Westlake that he had overheard the plans being made."

"But he didn't reveal who was making those plans?"

"No, sir."

"I want Montgomery, Clayton. Are you up to the assignment?"

"Yes, sir." Mark brightened. He'd been afraid that the general was going to relieve him of his command.

"Good. Now as to these allegations that you believe there is someone connected to this within our ranks . . . I want facts and names. Not innuendo! Is that understood, Captain?" the general asked sternly.

"Yes, sir. I'll get on it right away." Mark stood and started from the room.

"And Captain?"

"Yes, General?"

"I'm glad you made it back."

"Thank you, sir."

Delight left Marshall on deck and entered the cabin quietly to check on Jim. At the sight of him standing awkwardly near the washstand, Delight gasped and demanded, "What are you doing out of bed?"

He turned to her, a proud grin on his face, "Just testing myself. We'll be home tonight, and I wanted to make sure that I'm strong enough to start moving around."

"You shouldn't be up yet," she protested uselessly as he hobbled toward her.

"And why not?" He braced himself against the wall as he stopped in front of her.

"Well—because . . ." Delight gazed up at him and couldn't help but smile. It was good to have him on his feet again, no matter how unsteadily.

"Don't I get a reward for my efforts?" His eyes raked over her, taking in all of her natural beauty. "Your hair's getting long again," he murmured, and with his free hand he reached out to toy with her silken tresses.

Delight didn't speak as his hand slid lower to the back of her neck and drew her forward. Her lips parted in anticipation of his kiss, and their mouths met in a flaming caress. Resting her hands on his chest, she could feel the thunderous poundings of his heart as she slipped her arms around him to hold him close.

As Delight pressed herself against him, Jim broke off the kiss and stared down at her, his eyes dark with passion. "I love you, sweetheart."

"Show me," she encouraged, and, keeping one arm around his waist to support him, she walked him to the bed.

Delight helped him to undress and lie down, and then, after quickly shedding her own things, she joined him.

"Someday," he promised, as he claimed her mouth for a passionate kiss, "I'm going to make love to you on a nice, soft, big bed."

Her hands moved restlessly over him, tracing teasing paths, as she met him in kiss after kiss. "I think you're doing fine right here," Delight breathed as his mouth sought the tender flesh behind her ear. She shivered as his lips explored the pulse that was beating wildly in her throat and then dipped lower to the valley between her breasts. With eager hands, she pulled him to her, wanting and needing all of him. They came together and were lost in the bliss of their rapture.

It was growing dark when Delight stirred in Jim's arms, "I think we just slept the day away," she murmured, stretching sensuously against him.

"I enjoyed every minute of it," he said, his voice husky as he pulled her to him for a quick kiss. He was about to say more when a knock sounded at the door.

"Jim? Delight?" George spoke to them through the door.

"Yes, Father?" Jim answered, and Delight tried to dive under the covers.

"Marshall and I are going in to dinner. Would you like us to have something sent to your cabin?"

"Please," Jim called out, holding her immobile and grinning at her embarrassed confusion. "Delight and I will dine in here."

"All right. I'll have them bring your dinner to you."

"Thank you, George," Delight finally managed.

"You're welcome," George answered, and they heard him move off down the deck.

"What are you grinning at?" she demanded, sitting up furiously in the bed.

"You," he chuckled. "What did you think Father was going to do? Walk in on us?"

Delight slowly returned his smile. "Well . . . yes, I guess I did," she answered sheepishly.

"Don't worry, love. We're married, and they're gentlemen enough to respect our privacy."

"They are, are they?" And she returned without hesitation to the security of his embrace. "How long will it be before they bring us our dinner?"

"I don't know. Maybe a half an hour or so. Why?"

"Don't you know?" Delight teased and she raised above Jim to meet him in a heart-stopping kiss.

Mark left the general's office anxious to be about his business. After stopping at his quarters to bathe and put on a new uniform, he was off for a quick visit with Dorrie and to deliver George's and Marshall's messages.

"Captain Clayton!" the maid greeted him excitedly. "Come in, come in. Let me get Miss Dorrie for you." Ushering him into the parlor, she went in search of Dorrie.

"Mark!" Dorrie came flying into the room and without pause into his waiting arms. "Oh, thank God you're back! We were so worried. . . ."

His kiss silenced her, and they only broke apart when they heard Martha and Renee coming down the hall.

"Mark!" They greeted him warmly. "We're so glad to see you! Are Marshall and George with you?"

"No. I came on alone."

"Was there a problem?" Martha was immediately concerned.

"Jim was injured. . . ."

Before he could finish his sentence, Renee interrupted him, "Was he hurt badly? Where is he?"

"He's going to be all right, but he was wounded in the leg and . . ."

"Wounded!?"

"We caught up with the guerrillas, but they saw us before we saw them."

"Oh. You couldn't get the gold back?"

"Unfortunately, no. They took us by surprise . . . Jim and I are very lucky to still be alive."

Dorrie hugged him tightly, terrified at the thought that she might have lost him.

"So, I came on back to report in and to let you know that everyone was all right. George and Marshall said to tell you that they'll be along as soon as they think it's safe to move Jim."

"Good." Martha was relieved.

"How's Delight?" Renee asked.

"She was doing fine."

"Can you stay for dinner? We'd love to have you."

"I have some business I have to take care of first. What time do you plan to eat?"

"Whenever is convenient for you."

"How's seven o'clock? That should give me time enough to do what I have to do."

"We'll plan on it, Mark."

He headed for the door then, his arm still around Dorrie. When he was certain that they were alone, he pulled her close and kissed her. "I'll be back," he promised, and with that he was gone.

Mark rode directly to Clara Montgomery's house. He knew this might be an awkward interview, but it was something he had to do.

Clara herself answered the door and was surprised to see Mark Clayton on her doorstep. "Mark . . . this is a pleasant surprise. Come in."

"Thank you, Clara. I was wondering if I could talk with you for a few moments?"

"Of course. Let's go into the parlor." She led him into the room and directed him to take a seat. "What is it? Is Delight all right?"

"She's fine. I take it you know everything that's happened?"

"Yes. Renee and Martha have been keeping me informed. Is there any news?"

"I just got back today. We didn't get the gold back."

"I'm sorry."

"So am I." His expression was grim as he thought of the explosion and fire. "Jim and I chased them, but they got away."

"Where is Jim now?"

"We were both wounded by the guerrillas, but his injury was more serious. He had to stay behind until it was safe for him to travel."

"And Delight's with him?"

"Yes. George and Marshall, too."

"I appreciate your coming by to tell me all this. I can rest a little easier now, knowing that Delight is safe and well."

"Clara?" His tone was determined and she looked up at him questioningly.

"Yes?"

"I need to talk to you about Martin."

Clara paled suddenly. "Why?" she whispered.

"He may have been involved in the plot to blow up the *Enterprise*."

"Martin?" Her eyes widened at the thought.

"Yes. I'm sorry. I know this is painful for you, but I need to know if you've seen him lately."

"No. Not since Wednesday night when I threw him out." There was a steely edge to her answer.

"He's made no effort to get in contact with you since then?"

"No. None."

"Do you know if he had any unusual business acquaintances?"

"He handled most of my affairs for me, but he didn't deal with anyone unsavory that I'm aware of."

Mark paused pensively. "Do you have any idea where he might have gone? Did he have any family?"

"No. Don't you understand, Mark? I don't want to hear from that man again as long as I live," she told him with fierce finality.

"But . . ."

She cut him off. "When I think of what he almost did to Delight . . ." A shudder of rage shot through her.

"I'm sorry, Clara." Mark was contrite at having upset her so much.

"So am I," she told him regally. "But it's over now. The important thing is that my daughter is safe."

"Did Renee tell you that they got married?"

"Yes, she did. And I'm so happy for Delight. I know she loves Jim very much."

"I'm sure they'll be happy together." Mark knew there was nothing more he could learn from Clara. "I'd better be going."

She sighed. "I wish I could be of more help to you."

"Well, if you do hear anything from him, I'd appreciate it if you'd let me know."

"I will, Mark." She escorted him to the door.

"Thank you, Clara. I'll be in touch."

Clara watched him ride away, the sadness in her heart lightened a little by the knowledge that Delight was well and would be coming home soon.

It was after ten when the steamer docked at the St. Louis levee. Eager to get back home, George and Marshall wasted no time hiring a carriage, while Delight waited on board with Jim. Though they kept a blanket carefully wrapped around his bare injured leg, Jim was glad for the cover of darkness when Marshall finally came to help him to the coach.

The ride home was short and sweet, and Martha was thrilled when she heard the sound of her husband's voice in the front hall.

"George!" She hurried from the parlor where they had gathered after dinner to greet him.

George was waiting for her with arms spread. "Martha, darling. It's so good to be back."

She hugged and kissed him quickly, before looking around for Jim. "Where's Jimmy?"

"Marshall is helping him in right now."

Renee, who'd followed Martha into the hall, rushed to the door to see her husband coming up the steps, his arms supportively around Jim's waist, and Delight following them both. "Hello," she greeted him, her voice husky with heartfelt emotion.

Marshall bent to give her a quick kiss as he came through the door, "Where do you want him?" he asked teasingly, and Renee and Martha turned their attention to Jim.

"Jimmy . . ."

"Hello, Mother." He accepted her kiss.

"Take him on into the parlor for now," Martha directed as she hugged Delight. "Hello, dear."

"Martha, it's good to be back. . . ." Delight returned her embrace.

"Come in. Have you had dinner?"

"Yes, we ate earlier on the steamer," George informed her as they gathered in the parlor. Then, greeting his friends warmly, he asked, "How are you, Ollie?"

"I'm doing fine." Ollie told him.

"You told everyone about Jim and me, didn't you?" Delight asked Rose.

"Yes, she told us." Martha smiled at her with open affection. "And we couldn't be happier for you."

"Does Mother know?" Delight asked quickly.

"I went to see her the day after Rose returned. She was pleased."

"Good." Delight went to sit beside Jim as Marshall helped him down onto the sofa. She noticed that he looked a bit strained and she asked him, "Do you want me to send for the doctor tonight?"

Jim took her hand and squeezed it gently. "No. There's no need. I'm just a little tired." He smiled tenderly at her and didn't release her hand when she would have moved away. "Stay here."

She settled in comfortably next to him, ready to enjoy a night of visiting.

"Papa!" Roger's excited cry echoed through the front hall as he charged down the front staircase and jumped into his father's arms. "You're back!"

"We just got here. Did we wake you?" Marshall kissed his son and hugged him tightly.

"Uh-huh, but that's all right. I wanted to see you real bad."

"Why?" Marshall asked, thinking that something was wrong.

"Because I missed you, Papa." Roger threw his arms about his father's strong neck and gave him an endearing hug. "I love you."

"I love you, too, son," Marshall told him, momentarily choked with emotion, and Renee joined in the intimate family embrace.

Jim watched the exchange and longed for the time when he would be coming home to Delight and their own children.

Delight sensed the direction of his thoughts and leaned closer to kiss his cheek and whisper, "Some day . . ."

He smiled and pulled her closer as Roger finally noticed him and his grandpa.

"Uncle Jimmy! What did you do to your leg?" Roger's eyes were round as saucers.

"I had a run-in with some bad guys, and I'm afraid they won, Roger."

"Gee, Uncle Jimmy, I thought you never lost." Roger pondered the profound revelation that his cherished uncle was, indeed, a mortal.

"But your papa and grandpa saved me."

"Did you, Papa?" Roger turned his hero worship to his father.

"Well, uh . . . yes, Grandpa and I did help out, and so did Mark."

"It's going to be lots of fun when I get to go with you, huh?" Roger couldn't wait to share in their adventures. Everything sounded so exciting.

"Right," Marshall groaned. "Lots of fun."

"Let's get you back to bed, young man." Renee tried to take him from Marshall, but Roger held on to him with a death grip.

"Will you tuck me in, Papa?"

Marshall looked down at the sweet young child who was his son and knew he could refuse him nothing. "I think I'd like that. But Roger?"

"What?"

"Can your mother come along too?"

"Sure," Roger stuck out a chubby hand to Renee. "Mama

gives great bedtime kisses. You should let her tuck you in sometime, Papa."

Marshall's eyes were twinkling as he gave her an assessing look. "Great bedtime kisses, huh? Maybe I'll just do that. . . ."

After they had disappeared upstairs to put Roger to bed, Ollie and Rose excused themselves for the night, knowing that the family would want some time alone.

Martha sighed contentedly as she handed Jim and George each a drink. "I have a feeling you both need one."

"You're right about that, dear," George acknowledged as he leaned back comfortably in an overstuffed wing chair. "It's been one long day."

"It's been a long week," Mark added sardonically.

"Have you found out anything since you've been back?" Jim had to ask.

"I talked with Clara at length this afternoon, but she hasn't seen or heard from Martin since Wednesday night. I checked with the hotels and discovered that he stayed two nights at the Planter's House before checking out Friday morning."

"Did he give any forwarding address?"

"No. Nothing."

"He could have gone anywhere."

"I plan on checking with the steamship lines tomorrow, and the stables in town, too. Just in case he bought himself a horse."

"That's a good idea." George agreed. "I'll help you all I can."

"What about Sam Wallace?"

"He hasn't been seen or heard from since the day I hired him."

"Then something must have happened to him."

"That's the only conclusion I can come up with." Mark paused. "We have got to find Montgomery . . . he's our only connection."

"We will," Jim said with grim determination. "I want those spies."

"We all do," Marshall said, as he and Renee came back into the room.

"Is Roger all tucked in?" Martha asked, pleased to have her family gathered around her.

"He's sound asleep." Renee smiled gently.

"And now we can all relax," Marshall added.

And they passed the rest of the evening in easy camaraderie, enjoying one another and the sense of peace that came from being with family.

Chapter Thirty-nine

It was well after midnight when Mark stood with Dorrie in the privacy of the dimly lighted front entry foyer. Everyone else had retired, and they were left alone to say their good nights.

Dorrie glanced up the steps to make sure everyone had disappeared from view before slipping quickly into the safe, inviting confines of Mark's embrace. "I've been waiting all day to do this," she told him as she pulled his head down for her eager kiss.

"So have I," he responded as their lips met again and again in short, passionate exchanges. "It's been hard to keep my hands off you."

"You don't have to anymore," she teased invitingly, leaning more fully against him, and Mark tightened his hold on her, crushing her to his chest.

His mouth descended to ravage hers in a plundering caress that stole her breath and left her trembling and weak. "Dorrie. . . ." His voice was a husky whisper.

"What?" she asked quietly as she pressed tender, soft kisses against his throat.

"Stop that for a minute," he growled, holding her a little away from him.

"But why?" Her eyes were round as she pretended to be unaware of the effect her touch had on him.

"Because, my love, I need to talk to you."

"You mean you can't talk while I do this?" She repeated her actions.

"I can't even think while you do that, much less talk, woman."

"Oh, Mark . . . I love you."

His mouth sought hers then in a soaring brand of total commitment. "Marry me, Dorrie."

"Oh, yes, Mark." She knew that she wanted nothing more than to spend the rest of her life loving this man.

There in the deep shadows of the hall, Mark enfolded her in his arms and sealed their pledge to each other with a single, heart-stopping kiss. Their breathing was labored as they ended the embrace and moved a little apart.

"I love you," he declared, framing her face with his hands.

"I love you," she responded, her eyes luminous with her love for him.

Gently Mark leaned toward her again, and his lips met hers in a delicate caress that left them shaken by its intimacy.

"I'd better go," he muttered in frustration as his need to know her grew unbounded.

"Do you have to?" she protested, not knowing how close he was to losing the little control he had.

"I'm afraid so, darling. But I'll come back tomorrow and we can begin to make our plans."

"We could always go to a justice of the peace." She looped her arms about his neck and kissed him lingeringly.

"The idea is tempting, but I want everything to be perfect for us. I want to see you walk down the aisle to me in a flowing white gown. The memory of our wedding should be a special gift we give ourselves . . . something we'll treasure for always." With gentle fingers he caressed her cheek.

Her face was radiant as she smiled up at him, and she turned to rub her cheek against his warm hand. "It sounds beautiful."

"It will be, just like you." He kissed her one more time and then forced himself to move away as the thought of staying longer grew far too tempting. "I'll see you tomorrow. All right?"

"All right. But I'm already looking forward to the time when you won't have to leave me."

"No more than I am, believe me." He grinned at his self-imposed exile. "Good night."

Dorrie watched as he strode from the house and closed the door softly when he turned the corner on his way back to his quarters.

"Do you realize what a torture this is?" Jim muttered from where he sat on the bed.

"A torture? Really? I was thinking it was an exquisite pleasure." Delight's laugh gurgled from her as she sank beneath the water in her bath. It seemed to her that it had been an eternity since she'd had the pleasure of a steamy, scented soak, and she was going to enjoy every moment of it. "I may just stay in here until the water turns cold. . . ." She slanted him a sideways glance, her eyes twinkling with merriment.

"If you plan on staying in there more than another five minutes, I'm going to join you." He glowered at her.

"But your leg . . ." Delight reminded him saucily; and, as she rested her head back against the tub and closed her eyes, her expression turned to one of sublime contentment.

"Since you're so worried about my physical condition . . . you'd do well to extract yourself from there right now," he threatened as he moved to the edge of the bed.

Delight opened one eye to peer at him. "Why?"

"Because I'm going to come and take you out if you don't hurry." Jim's gaze traced the water's edge where it lapped enticingly against her bosom. Unable to resist the urge to touch the creamy flesh, he stood up and walked cautiously to her.

"Jim!" she protested, sitting up quickly and splashing water on the floor. She didn't want him taking any chances with his leg. "Get back in bed."

"I intend to in a few minutes." His eyes were riveted on her breasts as he drew a chair up next to the bath. "And I don't intend to go back alone."

"Then, I guess I'd better hurry and wash." She looked up at him, her expression telling him everything he wanted to know.

A short time later she reached for the towel and stood up.

Jim took the towel from her hand as she stepped from the bath and began to dry her with quick, brisk strokes that left her flesh tingling. "You realize I've been waiting for this moment for a long time," he told her, motioning toward the bed. "Did you happen to notice how nice and big and soft it is?"

"Now that you mention it," she smiled up at him serenely, "it does look inviting."

They moved to the bed where, with Delight's help, he pulled off his nightshirt. Lying back on the bed, he drew her down beside him. She went to him eagerly, her body thirsting for a full draught of his love. Giving herself up to the headiness of his kiss, her caresses grew more bold as she sought only to please him.

Excited by Delight's uninhibited response, Jim could deny himself no longer. They came together in love's most passionate embrace.

As they clung together in the rapturous aftermath, Jim murmured treasured endearments to Delight while they rested, unaware of anything save the perfection of their joining. They loved through the night . . . each touch, each kiss a cherished enchantment, until at last, near dawn, they fell into an exhausted slumber. And even in sleep they refused to be parted, as they sought each other's warmth and lay nestled together in blissful peace.

"Where's Uncle Jimmy?" Roger asked cheerfully as he came down to breakfast the next morning.

"He decided to sleep late, today," Renee told him.

"Oh." The little boy's face fell.

"But don't worry, he'll be staying here with us for a while, and you'll have lots of time to be with him."

"He will? That's great," Roger responded, his mood brightening again.

"What are your plans for the day?" Renee asked her husband and father-in-law as the maid began serving the meal.

"We're supposed to meet Mark at his quarters around ten o'clock, so we can coordinate our efforts to locate Martin."

"I hope you find him."

"So do we." Their determination was evident.

"I'd like to come along, if you don't mind," Ollie offered.

"Are you up to it?" George worried.

"I'm fine."

"Good. We can use the extra help." With that settled, they began to eat.

When breakfast was over they went their separate ways, and Renee and Roger saw them off.

"Can I go see if Uncle Jimmy's awake yet?" he pressed, eager to spend some time with him.

"No." Renee was firm. "He needs his rest."

"Did the *Enterprise* really burn up, Mama?" Roger had overheard the general conversation of the past few days and knew that something was greatly amiss.

She looked at him quickly, realizing that it was time she told him the truth. "Yes, it did."

"But what's Uncle Jimmy going to do now that he doesn't have his boat anymore? Is he going to stay here and live with us forever?" Roger was hopeful as he voiced his most fervent wish.

"I don't think so." Renee couldn't suppress her grin. "But the first thing he's going to do is get completely well again."

"Is his leg real bad?"

"He's getting better," she assured him. "He'll probably be up and walking around today."

"Good. I don't like it when he's sick. . . ." Roger was thoughtful.

"Nobody does."

"Do you think he'll buy a new boat?"

"I'm sure they're planning on it."

"I'm glad. Uncle Jimmy wouldn't be happy without one," he said with amazing insight for one so young.

"You're right about that," Renee agreed. "Now, are you ready to go to school?"

"Do I have to? Can't I stay home with you today?"

She hid her smile when she saw his mournful expression. "No. Now get your things together. It's time for you to leave."

Amidst a string of protests, she followed him from the dining room to help him get ready to go. After Renee had seen him safely off, she sent the maid to Dr. Freemont with a note requesting that he drop by and check on Jim's leg, and she returned with the news that he would be by sometime during the morning.

It was nearly ten o'clock before Delight and Jim emerged from their room and came downstairs.

"Good morning," Renee greeted them as they came into the dining room.

"Is it too late for breakfast?" Jim asked, in good humor.

"Of course not. I'll go tell the cook to fix you both something."

"Thanks, Renee," Delight said graciously. "Can I help with anything?"

"No, You two just relax and take it easy," Renee told them as she bustled off to the back of the house.

When Renee had gone, they shared a quick passionate embrace before settling in at the table. "I think the first thing I'm going to do this morning after we eat is send word to Mother that we're back."

"Good. I'm sure she's been waiting to hear." Jim could well imagine how upsetting the past week had been for Clara.

Delight nodded, her expression reflecting her concern, "She's probably lonely . . . now that Martin and I are both gone."

"It's probably been a very difficult time for her," Jim agreed. "But now that you're back, she'll be happy."

"I hope so." Delight sounded worried, and Jim was puzzled by her attitude. He was about to question her further, but Renee returned.

"Are you talking about Clara?" Renee asked, coming into the room with a pot of steaming coffee.

"Yes. I've been concerned about her."

"Well, Martha was going to stop by your house on her way out with Dorrie and Rose this morning to let her know that you're back. I'm sure she'll be over to see you right away," she told Delight as she poured her a cup of the hot brew.

"Thank you." Delight was pleased with the news. "I have missed her, very much." Delight sighed. A few weeks ago Clara had had everything, and now it was all gone. Delight felt somehow responsible for Martin's actions, and she hoped that her mother could find it in her to forgive her.

"I know, and I'm sure she's missed you, too."

"I also took the liberty of sending word to Dr. Freemont that you needed to have your leg checked," Renee informed Jim as she efficiently fixed him a cup of coffee, too.

Jim grimaced at the thought, but he didn't protest. "What time is he coming?"

"He sent word back that he should be here sometime this morning."

"Good. The sooner he comes, the sooner I can start helping Mark."

"How is your leg this morning?" Renee asked.

"It's stiff and still sore, but it's not nearly as bad as it was those first couple of days."

Delight was relieved by his answer for she'd feared that their late-night activities might have put a strain on his leg. She smiled a bit dreamily to herself as she thought of the hours just past. It had been nothing short of heavenly, and she hoped every night for the rest of her life would be as wonderful.

Jim noticed Delight's contented smile and was tempted to take her in his arms, for the memory of that look stirred him, but Renee's presence and the untimely arrival of their meal kept him regretfully restrained. The maid served their food, and they were just about to eat when Clara arrived.

"Mother!" Delight rushed out into the hall to hug her in a tearful embrace.

"Oh, darling. I'm so glad that you're safe." Clara held her protectively, relieved that the worst was over for them both. "When I heard about the explosion I was beside myself with worry. . . ."

"I can imagine," Delight sympathized. "I'm sorry you had to go through all this because of me. . . ."

"No, Delight. Not because of you, but because I love you. Nothing is more important to me than your happiness." Clara loved her daughter with all of her heart.

"Thank you, Mother." Her mother's heartfelt words freed Delight from the guilt she had been carrying deep within her. "I know how much you cared for Martin. And I was afraid . . ."

Clara understood Delight's sentiments. "You were afraid that I would blame you for Martin's actions?"

Delight nodded.

"No, darling. In the beginning of our marriage, I cared for Martin. But as time went on, I found out what he was truly like. I could forgive his indiscretions up to a point, but I could not forgive what he tried to do to you," she said firmly. Then, smiling, she added. "But, that's all in the past. Things will be better now."

"Oh, yes, Mother. They will." Delight hugged her again.

"Where's Jim? How is he?"

"He's in the dining room with Renee. He's doing very well," she told her as they walked into the room where Renee and Jim awaited them.

"Jim. . . ." Clara went to kiss him. "It's good to see you. Are you feeling all right?"

"I'm doing much better. Thank you." It set his mind at rest to know that she was a strong enough woman to deal so well with the truth about her husband.

"I'm glad." She joined them at the table. "You have to tell me everything that's happened. I know you got married, and I think it's wonderful. I've never seen anybody more in love than you two."

Delight looked at her husband with obvious affection, and he returned her visual caress. "It hasn't exactly been a normal marriage so far," he laughed, reaching over to take his wife's hand. "But we're working on it."

"And you have the rest of your lives to do that," Renee added, smiling at the openness of their love.

"Has Mark heard anything about Martin yet?"

"No, not yet. But they're still out looking for him. Hopefully he'll turn up something soon."

"If you find him, I want to know," Clara stated with determination.

"Not if, Clara, when," Jim corrected, and she nodded as his own fierce need to discover who'd been behind the plot surfaced. "We're going to find him, and, when we do, we're going to break the spy ring that was responsible for the attack against the *Enterprise*."

"I'm afraid that won't be happening." The sound of Marshall's voice cut through their discussion, and they glanced up to see him and Mark standing in the doorway, looking ominously defeated. "At least, not right away."

"What's happened?" Jim asked, knowing by their expressions that they were the bearers of bad news.

"We found Martin."

"But that's good news," Renee started to protest, but Mark interrupted her.

"He's dead."

Clara gasped and paled at their revelation. "Dead?"

"His body was found this morning north of town," Mark supplied.

"Was he robbed?" Jim asked.

"It could have been a robbery," Mark said, frowning, "but I don't believe it." Piecing together all that had happened, he knew that Martin had been murdered to cover up the plot. He felt furious and totally frustrated. Martin had been their only possible connection. . . .

"He was murdered," Marshall stated flatly, with finality. And a heavy silence descended on the room.

Chapter Forty

Sarah was busy serving Danny and Charlie their breakfast when she heard a hoarse call. Dropping everything, she hurried with the boys into the bedroom to find the man she'd been so tenderly caring for awake at last. She paused in the doorway while her sons eagerly went forward to meet him.

"You're awake!" Danny cried out in excitement as he approached him without fear. "We were wondering when you were going to wake up."

"Hi!" Charlie spoke timidly from behind his brother, a little afraid of this stranger who'd been in their home for so long now.

"Hello." Sam's voice was gruff from lack of use, and he braced himself up weakly on his elbow to look at the two boys and the woman who stood hesitantly back.

"I'm Danny, and this is Charlie. And this is my mama."

"I'm glad to meet you, Danny and Charlie. I'm Sam Wallace." He smiled at the youngsters and then glanced over at their mother. "Does your mother have a name?"

"Sure," Danny told him easily. "Her name is Sarah, and she took real good care of you, huh?"

Sam's gaze swept to the door to look at the woman who stood there in silence.

"Yes, Danny. Your mother took care of me real good." His eyes met hers across the room. "Thank you, Sarah." His words were only for her.

"You're welcome, Sam Wallace. It's so good to have you back among the living," Sarah was saying as she came into the room. "I'm Sarah Webb, and these are my two sons."

He lay back as he felt himself weakening. "Where am I?"

"This is my home. We're on the river road a little north of town."

"How did I get here?" He frowned, trying to remember all that had happened.

"We found you in the river!" Charlie finally found his tongue.

"The river . . . ?" Sam suddenly groaned, holding his head. "Oh, God . . ."

"Are you all right?" Sarah asked worriedly, quickly moving to his side.

"No . . . yes . . ." He was confused and overcome by the memories that had just returned. "How long have I been here?"

"Almost a week, now."

"Oh, no . . ." He closed his eyes.

"What's wrong? Can I help?"

"I've got to get back to town. I've got to get to Captain Clayton . . ." He struggled to sit up, but fell back as he was overcome by dizziness.

"But Mr. Wallace, you're not strong enough. How could you possibly sit a horse, when you can't even sit up in bed? Please, try to rest. I'll send for Doc Simpson."

"Dr. Simpson?"

"He's been coming to check on you every day. You've been seriously ill." Leaving the room momentarily with the boys, she instructed them to go for the doctor.

Sam watched her leave and knew she was right, but it

didn't lessen his determination to search out Mark Clayton. He had to find out what had happened. He had to get back to town.

Looking around the room, he spotted his clothes folded neatly, lying on top of the dresser. Sitting up in bed, he swung his legs over the side and got to his feet, keeping the blanket wrapped around his waist. But after so many days of being flat on his back, he was shaky and unsteady and could manage only a few staggering steps.

Sarah heard a noise and was coming back through the door when she saw him try to cross the room. Gasping, she rushed to his aid, just as he started to lose his balance. It took all of her strength to keep him upright as she held him tightly around his waist.

"Mr. Wallace! You shouldn't be up!" She scolded, supporting him and trying to get him back into bed.

"I've got to get into town" he argued, but his voice lacked some of its original conviction as he realized now that he really was too weak to travel.

"Let's get you back in bed," she directed.

"All right," Sam finally agreed.

"Please, call me Sarah." Her voice was breathless.

"Sarah . . ." he whispered her name. "Thank you, Sarah."

"I'll go fix you something to eat, while we wait for the doctor."

Sam watched her as she came back into the room with his tray of food a short time later.

"Does anybody know I'm here besides the doctor?" he asked.

"Just the few neighbors who've been helping me," Sarah answered. "Why?"

"Because I'm sure there are people who have been looking for me." He didn't want to involve her in what he knew to be a dangerous situation.

"Would you like me to send a message to them for you?"

"Yes. Right away, if you could."

"I can send Danny as soon as he gets back."

"Good."

"You go ahead and eat, while I get you some paper and a pencil." She helped him to sit up and then placed the tray on his lap.

Sam's appetite had not yet returned, and he only picked at the food while Sarah went to find the writing materials.

"Here you are." She came back a short time later, took the tray and she handed him the stationery and pencil.

Sarah took the food back to the kitchen while he wrote out a short, concise message for Mark, and, just in case Mark was still gone on the *Enterprise*, one for Marshall Westlake, too. Stuffing them into envelopes, he sealed them tightly and addressed them.

"All finished?"

"Yes. Now all we have to do is get them delivered." He gave her the notes.

"I'll make sure Danny delivers these as soon as he gets back with the doctor."

"Thanks." Sam wanted to talk with her more, but he was growing tired. "I've got to rest for a while," he told her as he lay back down.

"Fine. If you need anything . . . I'll just be in the other room."

It was almost an hour later when Danny and Charlie returned, riding with Doc Simpson in his carriage, their horse tied to the back. She hurried out to meet him.

"Doc, thanks for coming."

"So, our mystery man has finally regained consciousness?"

"Yes. His name is Sam Wallace, and he seems quite well, considering."

"Well, let's just go see. You boys wait out here," the doctor instructed as he disappeared indoors with Sarah. "Has he eaten anything?"

"Yes. I fixed him some food about an hour ago, and he ate some of it."

He nodded silently and followed her into the bedroom. Sam stirred and opened his eyes when they entered the room.

"Hello, Mr. Wallace. I'm Dr. Simpson. I've been taking care of you since Mrs. Webb rescued you from the river."

"Thanks, Doctor. I appreciate it."

"How do you feel, young man?"

"Weak and dizzy, mostly," Sam answered honestly.

"I see. Have you gotten up?" The doctor sat down on the side of the bed and took out his stethoscope.

"Only once," Sam chuckled. "I won't try that again for a few days."

"Wise decision," the doctor agreed. "Between your head injury and the pneumonia, you've been very sick. How did you happen to end up in the river? Were you robbed?"

Sam was grateful for the way out the doctor had inadvertently provided. "Yes—I was. . . ."

"We ought to report this to the authorities, then. Do you have any idea who did it?"

"No. I don't . . . it was dark and I didn't see a thing," Sam lied. He knew exactly who'd done this to him, and he fully intended to see that they got what they deserved.

The doctor seemed to understand his reluctance to talk about the whole ordeal and let it drop. "All right," he told him as he completed his examination. "You're just about healthy again, but I don't want you up and about for at least two more days."

"Yes, sir." Sam agreed.

"I'll be back the day after tomorrow to check you over one more time. Until then, I want you to stay quiet," the doctor ordered.

He shook hands with Sam as he stood up to leave.

"Is there anyone you'd like us to contact for you?"

"I've already taken care of that for him, Doc," Sarah told him.

"Good. Well, I'll see you in a few days. Good-bye, Mr. Wallace. I'm glad you're feeling better."

Sarah walked with him to the door. "Do you really think he's going to be all right, Doc?"

"Yes, my dear. You did an admirable job nursing him. Once he gets his strength back, he'll be just fine."

"Thanks." She was pleased with the news. "I'll see you soon."

"Good-bye." He waved as he drove off.

Sarah went back inside, this time taking the boys with her.

"How is he, Mama? Is he all better?"

"Yes, Charlie, darling. He's all better." She smiled down at her youngest son.

"Is he going to leave soon?" Danny asked.

"Probably as soon as he's able," she explained. "The doctor says he's still too weak to move around yet, so he'll be here at least a few more days."

They both nodded their understanding.

"Danny?"

"Yes, Mama?"

"I've got a very important job for you to do."

"Can't I help, too?" Charlie begged.

"Not this time. This is something only a big boy can do." Charlie looked crestfallen, but Danny swelled with pride.

"What is it?" he asked, eager to please her.

"Mr. Wallace has written two notes that have to be delivered in town right away. I want you to deliver them for me."

Sarah got the letters. "This one is to be delivered to Captain Clayton in the quartermaster's office." She handed him Mark's.

"Yes, Mama," he told her solemnly, knowing that this was important.

"And this one is to be delivered to a Mr. Westlake at this address." Sarah gave him the other envelope.

"Yes, ma'am."

"Good boy. You be careful."

"I will." Danny said, with a firmness that belied his years. "And I'll hurry back."

Sarah watched as he rode off on their only horse in the direction of town before going back to check on Sam again.

"He's gone?" Sam asked, a certain tenseness reflected in his voice.

"Yes. He just left."

He nodded in relief and then slumped back as a great weariness washed over him.

"I owe you a lot."

Danny rode quickly into town and managed to find the quartermaster's office with no problem. Soldiers were swarming all over the place, and he was more than a little intimidated by them. Finally, though, he worked up enough courage and he entered the building. He stood at the front desk, and it was long minutes before anyone even noticed him.

"What is it?" a corporal finally asked, irritated by the interruption.

"I have a message for Captain Clayton, sir. Is he here?"

"No, he isn't, and we don't expect him back until late this afternoon." He dismissed the boy curtly.

"But, sir . . . I was told to give this to him. . . ." Danny held up the letter.

"He's not here, kid. Come back later."

Wade happened to be crossing the room, and he overheard the exchange. His interest was piqued by the mention of Mark's name, and he casually approached Danny.

"Son? Can I help you? I'm a friend of Captain Clayton's."

"Yes, sir. I'm trying to find him to give him this letter. It's important."

"He is out just now. Would you like to leave it with me?"

"I don't know . . . she didn't say anything about leaving it with anybody else."

"She?"

"My mama," Danny explained.

"Well, I'll be happy to give it to him for you," Wade offered silkily, anxious to know everything that Mark was involved with.

"I guess ~~it will be~~ all right," Danny finally convinced himself, and he handed Wade Mark's envelope.

"I'm just glad to be of service." He smiled as the youngster hurried from the office. When Danny was out of sight, Wade slipped the envelope safely into his breast pocket until he could find a moment to read it in private.

Delight, Clara, and Renee listened attentively to everything the men were saying. The news of Martin's death left them with no solid leads to follow, and Mark, Marshall, and Jim were trying desperately to think of some other angle they could pursue in order to catch the culprits before they struck again. Again and again they came back to Sam and his unexplained disappearance. It just didn't make sense, unless Wade was indeed part of the conspiracy. But they had no proof, only their suspicions.

"We can have him tailed again, but I don't think we'll find out anything now. The spies have accomplished what they wanted to do, and they're just going to lie low until all the uproar dies down," Jim said.

"I know," Mark agreed, disheartened. All of his men had died, and there had been nothing he could do to help them. Not then and not now.

Marshall was about to speak when someone knocked at the front door. "I'll get it," he offered, and he went out into the hall. "Annabelle!" He was surprised to find her on his doorstep.

"Marsh. It's so good to see you." She swept into the hall, and Marshall was engulfed in the heady scent of her perfume. "I just heard that Jim had gotten back and I wanted to make sure that he was all right. Is he here?"

"Yes. In the dining room. . . ." Marshall directed, a little overpowered by her assertiveness.

Annabelle gave him an endearing look and walked right

on into the room where everyone was gathered. "Hello, Renee. Why Clara, how nice . . ." Annabelle deliberately ignored Delight and went straight to Jim's side. "Oh, Jim, darling." She leaned down to embrace him. "When I heard what had happened, why I was just so upset. At first, they'd told me that you'd been killed. But Renee set me straight on that matter . . . so when I finally heard that you were back, I just had to come see with my own eyes that you were safe and sound."

"Yes. I'm going to be just fine." His voice was tight as he remembered her visit to Delight's house.

"Going to be . . . ? You mean, you were injured?"

"I was shot in the leg, but it's healing nicely," he assured her, trying to avoid her clinging presence.

But Annabelle wanted to continue her charade. They had to believe that she was seriously concerned about him. "You know, I'll always care about you. . . ." she told him.

"Thank you, Annabelle. Had you heard that Delight and I were married?" Jim offered the news politely.

"Married?" She was stunned. She had not heard any of this. Why, it made her look the fool! "When?"

"On the trip," Delight told her gloatingly as she reached out to Jim and took his hand possessively.

"She went with you on this trip?" she directed her question to Jim.

"Yes, she did," he affirmed as he lifted Delight's hand to his lips and kissed it gently.

"Well, what a shame that you didn't have time for a big wedding. But I'm most happy for you both," Annabelle lied beautifully.

"I'm sure." Delight couldn't stop the remark, and she met Annabelle's eyes with cold dignity.

"I hope we can be friends."

"Of course, Annabelle," Jim replied for them both, wanting to avoid any unpleasantness.

She was about to make a quick exit, for this encounter had

not turned out as she had hoped, but a knock at the door prevented her from making good her escape.

Danny had stood outside the big, fancy house for long minutes and had checked the address twice, before he bravely mounted the front steps and lifted the ornate brass knocker. He let it fall, and it rapped loudly against the heavy front door.

Renee was the one to answer it this time.

"Can I help you?" she asked politely when she saw the young boy standing on the porch.

"I've got a letter here for a Marshall Westlake, and I'm supposed to deliver it to him. It's important that he gets it right away."

"He's right here. Let me get him for you." Renee went to the dining room door and motioned to her husband. "There's someone here to see you."

He gave her a quizzical look as he started out of the room. "Who is it?"

"A boy. He says he has an important message for you."

Danny looked up as the tall, dark-haired man came out into the hall. "Are you Marshall Westlake?"

"Yes. I am," Marshall answered seriously, wondering who'd be sending him a message at home. Normally, he had all his correspondence directed to the office.

"I'm supposed to give this to you." Danny thrust out the envelope at him.

"Thank you." He glanced down at the handwriting but didn't recognize it. Reaching into his pocket, he drew out a coin and tossed it to the boy.

"Thanks, sir." The youngster was glowing as he left the house.

"Good-bye." Renee watched him go down the steps and out the walk, before closing the door and following Marshall back into the dining room.

"I'll be going now," Annabelle was saying as they rejoined the group.

"It was kind of you to drop by," Renee said. She started to escort her from the room as Marshall sat back down at the table and opened the letter.

"Yes. Thank you for your concern," Jim told her graciously as he watched her go, glad that the tense visit had come to an end.

"Mark! Jim!" Marshall's unexpected shout startled everyone.

"What is it?" Jim demanded.

"It's from Sam . . . Sam Wallace!" He held out the slip of paper.

Jim grabbed the note from him and read it quickly. "He's alive! And it says here that he's got the information we need. . . ."

Annabelle, who was just about to head out the door, heard his excitement and knew a true moment of panic. Wade had said he'd killed him . . . could Wade have failed? By sheer inner strength, she maintained her composure.

"Good-bye, Renee. I'll see you soon."

"Thanks for coming by." Renee closed the door as soon as she was outside and rushed back in with the others. "What is it?"

"The note's from Sam Wallace," Mark told her quickly. "He's been injured, but he's recovering, and he's staying at the Webb place, north of town."

"What are we waiting for?" Jim asked. "Let's go."

"I'll have the carriage brought around for you." Marshall rushed out of the room.

"Do you think you should go?" Delight asked worriedly. "The doctor hasn't been here yet. . . ."

"There is no way I'm going to miss this. He's our one hope of nailing the bastards who blew up the *Enterprise* and killed all those men. We've got to get there right away."

Delight knew that he was determined to go, so she dropped her protest. "You'll be careful?"

"Of course. No one else knows he's there. We'll be safe." Jim stood up gingerly, kissing her quickly.

She smiled up at him. "Good."

"We'll plan on bringing him back here, though, so we can keep him under protection," Marshall said as he returned.

"That's a good idea," Renee agreed. "Once the word gets out, there's no telling what will happen."

"The carriage is out front—" Mark saw it drive up.

"Then let's go."

Certain that they had the breakthrough they so desperately needed to help them with the investigation, the three determined men left the house; unaware that Mark's message had already been intercepted and read by Wade, who was well on his way to the Webb house.

Chapter Forty-one

Wade slapped the reins viciously against the horse's back as he headed the carriage out of town toward the Webb house. Gripped by the horror of what he'd just discovered, he wasted no time as he raced along the deserted dirt road.

Damn! How could it have happened? How could Sam Wallace have survived that night? Wade was furious with himself for not making sure Sam was dead before he had pushed him into the river, and he was determined to finish him off before he could reveal all he knew to the authorities.

Wade had not notified Nathan of the news, for he was too embarrassed to let him know that he'd failed in his first attempt. No, he would handle this himself, quickly and quietly, and no one would be the wiser. This time, Sam Wallace would die, and so would anyone else who got in his way.

Sam was sleeping when Sarah heard the carriage drive up

in front. Looking out, she saw the Union officer climbing down from his vehicle, and she went out to meet him.

"Captain Clayton?" She approached him.

"No, ma'am. I'm Major Macintosh." He introduced himself. "Are you Mrs. Webb?"

"Yes, I am."

"Captain Clayton is out of town and won't be back until late. Mr. Wallace's note sounded important, so I thought I should come in his stead."

"That's kind of you, Major. I know Sam will be glad that you're here. Come on in."

Wade followed her inside the small house, his hand hovering over his sidearm as he glanced nervously around. "How is he? He mentioned in the message that he'd met with some kind of accident?"

"It was no accident, believe me. He was robbed," she confided as they crossed the room. "He didn't regain consciousness until just this morning."

"His injuries were that serious?"

Sarah nodded, "He had a terrible head injury and then he came down with pneumonia."

"He's still very weak, then?" Wade asked conversationally.

"Very. And, according to the doctor, he's not to get out of bed for at least two more days."

"That presents a problem for me." Wade frowned, playing his part effectively.

"Why?"

"I'd been instructed to bring him back to headquarters."

"He's hardly in condition to travel . . ." Sarah protested.

"Well, I'm sure we can arrange something. May I see him now?"

"Of course. He's in the bedroom. Go on in." She directed him. "I'll wait out here."

"Thank you, ma'am." Wade walked softly into the room where Sam lay sleeping on the bed. He was glad that Mrs. Webb had chosen to give them privacy, for the next few minutes were going to be the most dangerous for him. If Sam yelled or made any violent protest . . . "Well, Sam Wallace, we meet again."

Sam had not been sleeping very soundly, and he opened his eyes at the sound of that cold, deadly voice. Paralyzed with fear, he whispered, "MacIntosh."

"Yes, it is me." Wade grinned at him evilly. "I've come to finish the job I started."

"No." How had Macintosh found out? Where was Mark or Westlake? He glanced nervously toward the door, worrying about Sarah.

"Don't worry about the woman. She's fine. She was courteous enough to leave us alone for a few minutes."

When Sam shifted on the bed to sit up, Wade rested his hand on his gun. "Don't try anything stupid or I'll shoot you right there. And the woman, too."

Sam remained perfectly still, his eyes following Wade's every move.

"I'm curious, Wallace. How did you ever survive?"

"Mrs. Webb pulled me out of the river."

"Remind me to thank her as we leave." Wade's words were sarcastic. Walking to the dresser, he picked up Sam's clothes and threw them at him. "Get dressed. We're getting out of here."

"But . . ."

"You wouldn't want me to involve her in this, would you? I'm going to tell her that I'm taking you back to town to one of the hospitals." His smile was wolfish. "But, of course, you're going to meet with an unfortunate accident along the way." When Sam didn't move, Wade stalked to the bed and hissed, "You either get moving or I'll call her in here. And you know what I'll do then."

Sam put on his shirt, buttoning it quickly, and then stood to pull on his pants. He felt dizzy and weak, but he knew he had to get out of there with Wade, before Sarah or the boys got hurt. Wade handed him his boots and stood impatiently by while he pulled them on.

"All right. Now, let's go." Wade took his arm in what looked to be a sympathetic grip. "And just remember . . . any sudden moves and I'll shoot the, woman first.

Sam nodded, as he walked with Wade from the bedroom. Sarah had been sitting at the kitchen table, and she looked up in surprise when they came into the room.

"Sam . . . you aren't supposed to be up!" She stood and came to him.

"I know, but this is important. I have to get back as soon as possible."

"It is urgent, Mrs. Webb," Wade added.

"Thank you for everything. I'll keep in touch," Sam said, as he swayed on his feet, his expression grim.

"I've got to get him out to the carriage, ma'am. Thank you for taking such good care of him." Wade supported more of Sam's weight as they started quickly out the door. "Good-bye."

Sarah watched them go with a heavy heart. She had thought she'd have more time with him, but it was not to be. As the major helped Sam into the carriage, she turned away and closed the door.

"Sit quietly, Wallace. We don't want to draw any undue attention to ourselves." Wade climbed in beside him.

Sam glared at him, but wisely made no foolish moves. And Wade, instead of starting back toward town, headed off farther down the river road.

The little house looked peaceful and quiet as Jim, Mark, and Marshall rode up in front. They had made the trip out from town in record time and were excited at the prospect of their meeting with Sam.

"This is it." Mark hurried on ahead of them and knocked on the door.

Danny, who'd returned from town, answered it. "Who are you? What do you want?"

"I'm Captain Mark Clayton, and I'm here to see Sam Wallace," Mark informed him.

"He's gone already," Danny said, as he started to close the door.

"Wait a minute. What do you mean, he's gone? You just brought a note to the Westlake house from him saying that he was staying here," Mark argued as Jim and Marshall joined him.

"Well, he isn't anymore."

"Danny? Who are you talking to?" Sarah heard the sound of voices and came to see who was at her door. "I'm Mrs. Webb. Can I help you gentlemen with something?"

"I'm Marshall Westlake, ma'am. I just received a note from Sam Wallace that said he was here."

"He was, but you just missed him."

Mark frowned. "Missed him? What do you mean?"

"Who are you?"

"I'm Captain Mark Clayton."

"But the other soldier said that you were out of town for the day and that was why he'd come for Sam . . ."

"What other soldier?" Jim asked quickly.

"The one from the quartermaster's office where Danny delivered the note Sam had written to you."

"Sam wrote a note to me?" Mark questioned.

"Yes, and one to Mr. Westlake, too. And then, just a short time ago, that major showed up and took Sam back into town to a hospital."

"Major? What was his name? Do you remember?"

"MacIntosh," she replied.

"It was Wade . . ." Mark cursed under his breath. "Is there another road back to town besides this one?"

"Why, no . . . why do you ask?"

"Because we didn't pass them on the way here."

"How long ago did they leave?"

"No more than ten minutes . . . why? Is Sam in some kind of trouble?"

"It looks that way," Jim told her grimly as they prepared to leave.

"Can I help?" She offered as they turned to rush back to their horses.

"No, ma'am. This is likely to be dangerous," Mark explained, mounting up.

"You find him!" she called as Jim drove off at breakneck speed.

"We will." came his answer.

Wade pulled his coach off onto a rutted side road and tied up in a heavily wooded area. Climbing down, he drew his pistol and waved Sam out of the carriage.

"Let's go." He pointed a way through the underbrush. "Walk."

Sam staggered forward, barely able to stay upright. He knew he had to save himself . . . there would be no one coming to the rescue. Looking around, he nervously searched for something he could use to defend himself against Wade, but it was no use, for he had little strength left. Stumbling, he fell, landing on his hands and knees on top of a rotted tree trunk.

Wade followed behind him, confident that he'd have no problems this time. He'd just take him a little deeper in the woods and shoot him. When Sam fell, Wade automatically stepped toward him to grab his arm and pull him upright.

It was at that moment that Sam struck. With a piece of rotten wood from the tree trunk, he swung upward and sideways with all the force he could muster, catching Wade unawares and knocking him to the ground.

Wade's gun went off as it flew from his hand, and Sam scrambled away, trying to get back to the carriage. Wade was stunned but unhurt by the sudden unexpected attack. Getting to his feet, he searched for and found his pistol and then gave chase, running at top speed through the prickly underbrush after the faltering Sam.

Mark and Marshall, who had galloped far ahead of Jim, heard the shot and hoped that they were not too late.

"You take the road . . . I'll cut through the brush," Mark ordered, and Marshall quickly complied.

Turning his horse off the road, Mark spurred it on through the dense undergrowth in the direction of the shot, as Marshall followed the rutted side road.

Sam groped his way forward, his breathing labored, his strength about gone. Desperation was all that drove him, and he lurched ever onward, trying to escape certain death at Macintosh's hands. He could hear Wade gaining on him, and he knew he had little time . . .

Wade was chasing after him with relative ease. Sam was in no condition to camouflage his movements, and Wade could hear him moving through the bushes. Keeping his gun ready, he followed him, waiting for the first moment when he'd have a clear shot.

Sam staggered out into a small open field and stood, swaying, as he looked around. He had lost all sense of direction since he'd fled from Wade, and now he wasn't sure which way to go. Knowing that he had to get under some kind of cover, he skirted the clearing, staying near its edge in hopes of avoiding his pursuer.

Wade smiled as he watched Sam's pitiful attempt to escape him. He had him, now, of that there could be no doubt. With a cool hand, he raised the revolver and aimed, his finger slowly squeezing the trigger.

Mark's mount burst forth into the field, startling Wade just as he fired, and the shot went off target, missing Sam, who dove quickly into the woods to escape another shot.

Mark glanced in Sam's direction, "Are you all right?"

"Yes . . ." Sam called, hiding behind some trees.

"Good. Stay there." Mark immediately raced toward Wade.

Wade drew a bead on Mark and fired, but Mark slipped lower in the saddle and the bullet whizzed harmlessly past.

Realizing that he had to get back to his carriage, Wade took off at a run, staying in the densest brush to keep Mark's horse at bay. Crashing hurriedly through the weeds, the hunter became the hunted. Terror took him, and he knew the fear of being trapped. His only hope was to get away in the carriage . . . but even so, Mark would easily be able to overtake him on horseback. He had to shoot his way out. There was no alternative.

"Hold it, Major," Mark called.

But Wade ran on, ignoring his warning. Hiding behind a tree, he shot hurriedly at Mark, not taking the time to aim, and again he missed. Turning, he ran on, dodging behind trees and whatever other cover he could find, until, at last, he made it back to the road.

Jim was pulling up next to where Marshall waited, just as Wade emerged from the forest. In one last, wild attempt to get away, Wade fired off two rounds in their direction, as they dove for cover, before running for his carriage. He never made it.

With slow precision, Mark pulled the trigger as Wade made his final desperate lunge for the vehicle. The bullet caught Wade in the shoulder, yet still he struggled on, firing in both directions until Mark's second shot found its target and he pitched forward into the dirt and lay still.

Mark rode forward slowly and dismounted, his gun still in hand. "Are you hurt?"

"No," Jim and Marshall responded together as they stood up and moved closer.

"Is he dead?" Jim asked as Mark leaned over him.

"Yes." Mark's voice was flat as he checked him.

"Where's Sam? Was he hurt?"

"He's back in the woods by the field. We got here just in time," Mark said, breathing a little more easy.

"I'll go back for him." Marshall rode back in the direction that he had just come from while Jim helped Mark lift Wade's lifeless body into the carriage.

He found the clearing without any difficulty. "Sam! It's Marshall Westlake. You can come out. We've caught MacIntosh!"

Sam crept from his hiding place just beyond the wood's edge, cautiously. "I'm over here," he managed.

Marshall rode quickly to him and gave him a hand up behind him.

"Thank you." Sam was grateful. "If you hadn't shown up when you did . . ."

"I know . . . we were lucky that we got here in time," Marshall told him as they came out of the forest where Jim and Mark awaited them.

"Sam!" Mark helped him down. "Thank God you're alive!"

Sam gave him a weak grin. "I couldn't agree with you more."

"I think you've got a lot to tell us." Jim urged.

He nodded. "I do."

"Are you up to talking?" Mark asked.

"I'm more than ready." Sam was anxious to tell them everything. "Where do you want me to start?"

"How did Wade find out about you?" Jim was curious.

"I must have made some noise in the bushes."

"Bushes? What bushes?"

"I had followed him to a meeting at Nathan Morgan's house, and I was listening outside a window. He took me by surprise, and the next thing I knew I was tied and blindfolded. MacIntosh took me down on the river somewhere. He asked me what I had been doing there, and, after I told him, he hit me over the head. That's the last thing I remember until I woke up at Sarah's."

"What kind of a meeting was it?" Mark asked.

"It was them . . . All of them. And they knew exactly when the gold was being shipped."

Jim had been stunned at the mention of Nathan Morgan's name. "The meeting was at Morgan's house?"

"Yes," Sam confirmed.

He knew then, with an almost sickening certainty, that he'd been used, and it filled him with righteous anger. "What about his daughter, Annabelle?"

"She was there."

"Damn!" he swore viciously. "And she almost got away with it, too!"

"It's a good thing Delight came along when she did, or you'd still be engaged to Annabelle," Marshall remarked.

"Yes, but Annabelle was just at the house . . ." Mark put in.

"We'd better get back to town and go after her right now. I don't know if she heard us when we read Sam's note, but if she did then she's had time enough to try to get away." Jim was ready to leave.

"First, we need the rest of the names of those involved. If we go after the Morgans without knowing who else helped in the plotting, they'll disappear without a trace before we can get to them." Mark's words stopped Jim. "If we do this right, we can synchronize our movements and arrest everybody at the same time."

Jim waited as Sam told them all he remembered. He did not like the idea that he'd been played for a fool. Allowing his thoughts to drift back over the time he'd shared with Annabelle, he realized that she had been subtly trying to get information out of him by using the pretext that she wanted to know how long he'd be in town. What a consummate actress she was . . . and no wonder she'd slapped him that day he'd broken off their engagement. He grinned as he thought of how thoroughly he'd ruined their plans by ending the betrothal.

It must have been shortly after that that Martin Montgomery had entered the picture, Jim deduced. He had been jealous and had wanted to get rid of him, so he could have Delight for himself. What better way than to provide information about his shipments to the sympathizers? Martin, undoubtedly, had figured that Jim would be killed in the attack, and his own problems would be solved.

"Let's go," Mark was saying as Sam finished. "Do you want to split up?"

"Yes," Jim said, without hesitation. "There's no time to waste."

"All right. You and Marshall go after Annabelle and Nathan, while I go to General Fields with my proof."

"Fine."

"You'll need guns."

"We can stop at the house before we go to the Morgans', and Sam can stay there."

"Good. We'll meet at headquarters later." Mark was ready to set his plan into action.

Chapter Forty-two

Annabelle rushed into the house and slammed the door behind her. "Father!"

She sounded hysterical, and Nathan hurried into the hallway to see what was the matter. "Annabelle, darling, what's wrong?"

"We've got to get out of here now!" she cried, running down the hall to him. "They know!"

"What are you talking about?"

"I was over at the Westlakes' . . . you know, I went to pay my respects. . . ."

"Yes, so?"

"So, while I was there they received a message from Sam Wallace!" Her eyes were wide with fright.

"Sam Wallace? But I thought Wade killed him!"

"I did, too, but the note said that he was alive. They're on their way to see him . . . we can't stay here! They'll be coming for us next!"

"Damn! How could Wade have bungled it so badly? It's not like him to be so careless," Nathan said angrily.

"Who cares what Wade did or did not do! We've got to think of our own safety now!" Annabelle was shaking as she thought of being captured and put in prison.

"All right. Now calm down."

"Calm down?" She looked at Nathan aghast. "We're about to be caught and thrown into jail and all you can say is 'calm down'?"

"My dear." He took a deep breath and then spoke slowly. "There is no need for you to panic. Did you think that I was so ineffectual that I wouldn't have a plan, just in case something unfortunate like this should happen?"

"You have a plan?"

"I most certainly do. You go on upstairs and put on some traveling clothes . . . something that won't draw attention to you. You may take one bag with you, but, remember, we'll be traveling light."

"Yes, Father. Thank you." Annabelle was relieved and she started upstairs feeling much more in control.

Nathan went back into his study and began methodically destroying all of his important papers. When he'd finished, he got all of his ready cash out of the wall safe and then went to his room to pack.

Within a half an hour, they were all set to leave. After helping Annabelle into the carriage, he took up the reins himself. She sat back, tense and on edge while he drove, but when he turned in the direction of the quartermaster's office Annabelle grabbed at his arm.

"What are you doing?" she hissed.

"I'm going to stop by and see if Wade's here."

"That's crazy! Do you want to get yourself killed?"

"No. But I don't want Wade to get killed, either. He's done a lot for us, and we owe him."

Annabelle thought her father had surely lost his mind, but she held her tongue.

"Be careful," she told him quietly as he pulled to a stop in front of the office.

"I will be. Don't worry." He climbed down. "Wait here for me. I won't be long."

Annabelle nodded and sat back, not wanting anyone to see her, but watched carefully while Nathan casually entered the office in search of Wade.

"Excuse me." He approached the corporal sitting at the front desk.

"Yes, sir. What can I do for you?"

"I'm looking for Major MacIntosh. Is he here?"

"I'll check for you. Just a minute." The soldier went off in search of Wade, leaving Nathan to cool his heels.

Though his manner didn't reflect it, Nathan was upset by the entire situation, and the long minutes that he spent awaiting the man's return did little to ease his anxiety.

Annabelle wanted to scream. Where was her father? And where was Wade? She'd been sitting there for over ten minutes and there was no sign of either one. Her instincts told her to run, far and fast, but she knew she couldn't leave without her father. Maintaining what little control she had, she waited, frightened and frustrated.

"I'm sorry I took so long, sir," the corporal told Nathan as he came back to his desk. "I thought the major was in a meeting, but I was mistaken. It seems he left on an errand for Captain Clayton some time ago, and he's not expected back until much later this afternoon."

"Thank you." Nathan said curtly, furious that he'd been detained so long. Leaving the office as calmly as possible, he climbed back into the carriage with Annabelle.

"Well? Where's Wade?" she demanded as he took up the reins again.

"He's gone."

"Gone? You mean he's left town?" Annabelle said, aghast.

"No. No, nothing like that. The man I talked to said that he was on an 'errand' for Captain Clayton."

"For Mark? What could he possibly be doing for Mark Clayton?"

"I don't know, but we're not going to wait around here to find out."

"Did you leave a message for him?"

"No. I don't want it known that we have been here."

Annabelle nodded. "Where are we going now?"

"We are going on a voyage, my dear."

Nathan drove straight to the offices of Mid-Rivers Steamship Company and again bade Annabelle wait in the carriage. Disappearing inside, he was gone only a few minutes before he came back outside with Micah Abernathy.

"Annabelle. It's good to see you." Micah was cordial, but nervous. "We'll have you and your father taken care of shortly. You'll be booked under the names of John White and wife."

She glanced quickly at her father, but didn't interrupt.

"That will be fine, Micah. You know we appreciate all you're doing."

"It's for the Cause, Nathan," he said proudly. "I'm glad you asked."

"We appreciate your kindness, Mr. Abernathy." Annabelle was gracious.

"You can go on aboard now, if you like. The boat will be pulling out in about twenty minutes."

"Fine." He shook hands with him and handed him an envelope stuffed with Yankee greenbacks.

"Good luck, Nathan."

They drove off to the levee and tied up near the boat on which their passage had been booked. Nathan helped Annabelle descend from the carriage, and they started toward the steamer.

"Wait. I've got an idea. . . ." Nathan paused and then called to a roustabout standing nearby.

"Yes, suh?" The burly man hurried to do his bidding.

"Do you see that carriage?" He pointed out his own vehicle.

"Yes, suh."

"I want you to drive it downtown and park it near the Westlake Law Office. All right?"

"Yes, suh. Should Ah tell anybody dat it's dere?"

"No. Just tie it up and leave it. It will be picked up later." Nathan handed the man a large bill. "Hurry now."

"Yes, suh. Ah'll hurry real good." And the man rushed off and climbed into the carriage and drove away, while Nathan and Annabelle exchanged looks.

"They'd never think to look for it there." She couldn't stop the smile that threatened, despite their precarious situation.

"I know. It could be a full day before they realize it's ours." He escorted her up the gangplank.

After being directed to their cabin, they remained in seclusion until the boat had pulled away from the levee. Only then did they venture out on deck.

"Father! We're heading north!"

Nathan smiled blandly at her. "Of course. The last place they'll expect us to go is the North. They'll have every trooper from here to Memphis on alert trying to catch us, and we'll be heading in the opposite direction. We're going to make connections at Rock Island and go on to Chicago. There are people there we can stay with until things settle down."

Annabelle beamed at her father's ingenuity. "I'm glad you had all of this figured out. I was really in a panic."

"My only concern now is Wade. He was like a son to me, and I'm worried that he's going to get caught in a hornet's nest . . ."

"He'll do fine, Father. Wade always does." Annabelle gave her lover no further thought; her own survival was her only concern.

"I know . . . I know . . . I just can't help but think that he's involved in something far more dangerous than he ever realized. . . ." Nathan sighed.

"Perhaps. But let's not worry about him. He'll catch up with us sooner or later."

She distracted him with idle chatter as they walked along the promenade deck, but still, in the back of his mind, Nathan wondered what was to become of Wade.

Delight was sitting with Renee in the parlor. The hours had passed slowly since the men had gone, and they were growing more and more concerned. Clara had long since left to return home and they were alone, waiting anxiously for word from their men.

"What do you suppose is taking so long? All they had to do was to go and meet with Sam, right?" Delight played nervously with the bit of needlepoint she was holding.

"That's what I thought, too." Renee glanced out the window again in hopes that she would see them drive up, but the street in front of the house remained empty.

They looked at each other helplessly, wondering what, if anything, they could do. It was then that they heard the sound of the carriage, and they both rushed to open the door as they saw Jim and Marshall ride up with Sam.

"Where's Mark? Did everything go all right?"

"We don't have time to explain right now," Jim said tersely as they came inside. "Sam will tell you everything. He's staying here."

"Renee, get me the key to the gun cabinet," Marshall ordered, leading the way back to his study.

"The gun cabinet? What are you planning on doing?" Renee asked, following quickly along behind him. "What do you need a gun for?"

"Jim and I are going after two spies, and we want to be prepared, just in case."

"In case of what?" Delight worried, and Jim stopped to calm her.

"We've discovered that Annabelle and Nathan are a crucial part of the spy ring. We're going for them, while Mark rounds up the others."

"Others? You mean there are more?"

Martha and Dorrie had heard the commotion and were hurrying down to greet them when Marshall came out into the hall with two revolvers and a rifle.

"They're loaded," he informed Jim as he handed him a pistol.

"Thanks. Let's go."

"Where are you going?" Martha asked.

"We know Annabelle and Nathan are spies, and we're going to get them before they have a chance to get away," Marshall explained as he headed down the hall.

"Can't you wait?" Renee pleaded. "Surely, Mark will send some soldiers to help. . . ."

"He might, but by that time Annabelle and Nathan could be miles away."

"She was here when you opened the note," Delight remarked.

"I know, and they might already be long gone."

"Be careful!" She hugged Jim quickly and then let him go.

"We will," he told her confidently as they disappeared outside to make the short trip to the Morgan house.

Marshall reined in the carriage a few houses away. "I'll check around back, while you go on up to the front."

"All right." Jim climbed down after his brother and made his way up the front steps.

He somehow knew before he even knocked that they had gone. The house had an aura of desertion about it, and his suspicions were confirmed when he knocked on the door.

"Yes, sir?" The maid answered and looked at him questioningly.

"Is Mr. Morgan or Miss Morgan at home?"

"No, sir. They're gone," she told him.

"And what time do you expect them back?" Jim asked courteously, stalling for time.

"I don't know, sir. They didn't say. They left together some time ago."

Jim cursed under his breath. If what this servant was saying was true, there was little chance that they could catch up with them now.

At the sound of hurried footsteps coming down the hall, the maid turned nervously. "What are you doing in here?" she demanded as she saw Marshall walking toward her from the back of the house.

"I'm looking for the Morgans. I'm going to check upstairs, Jim." He started up the steps.

"The maid says they left a couple of hours ago."

"Right after she left our house," Marshall supplied in disgust.

"It looks that way."

"I'm going to check upstairs, anyway. They might have left a clue of some kind." He hurried on up the staircase.

"What do you think you're doing? I'm going to call for the sheriff!" the maid threatened.

"You go right ahead. I'm sure he'd be glad to know about what's been going on here," Jim said evenly, folding his arms across his chest as he waited for his brother to come back down.

"They're gone, all right. And it looks like they left in a hurry. There's clothes thrown all over Annabelle's room," he informed Mark as he came back downstairs after searching each bedroom.

"Where did they go?" Jim turned to the maid, his expression cold and unyielding.

"I don't know," the maid replied, her manner defiant. "You get out of here now. You know they're not here, so you don't need to be rummaging through this house."

"We'll go when we get some answers out of you," Marshall threatened. "You can talk to us here. . . . or we can take you down to General Fields's office and you can talk there."

"General Fields?" She was suddenly frightened.

"That's right. And if you stall too much longer you're probably going to have a platoon of soldiers going through every inch of this house, instead of just us. Now." He softened his tone. "Tell us where Nathan and Annabelle went."

"He didn't say. They left so quickly . . . I know they did

have a few bags with them, but nothing like they would have taken if they'd planned on being gone a long time."

"Unless they planned on travelling quickly and quietly. . . ." Jim added.

"Did Nathan say anything about how they were going to travel?"

"No. Not a word." She couldn't tell them what she didn't know.

"All right. We'll be back," Marshall told her as he turned to leave, well aware that Nathan had no intention of ever returning to this house.

They walked slowly down the steps together. "Where do you want to start?" Jim asked, favoring his bad leg.

"Don't you think you ought to go back to the house and rest for a while?" Marshall suggested, seeing the lines of fatigue and pain in Jim's face.

"No. Not when we're this close!" Jim refused. "Let's check the riverfront. That would be the fastest, safest way for them to slip past us."

"Right." They drove off toward the levee, hoping to unravel the sudden and convenient disappearance of Nathan and Annabelle.

"Captain Clayton is here to see you, General. He says it's important."

"Send him right in, Corporal." General Fields ordered.

"Yes, sir." The soldier went out of his office and motioned to Mark. "He'll see you now."

"Thank you, Corporal." Mark strode into the room to face his superior officer.

"Sit down, Captain." He waved him to a nearby chair. "I hope you have something for me."

"Yes, sir. I do. But I don't think you're going to like what I have to tell you."

"Let me be the judge of that. What have you found out?"

"The traitor in our midst was Wade MacIntosh."

"Major MacIntosh? Surely you're mistaken." The general scoffed at the idea.

"I am not mistaken. I have here a list of all the Southern spies who were involved in the plot to steal the gold. At the top of the list is Major MacIntosh."

"Where is Wade? I want to hear his side of this."

"He's outside, sir," Mark told him slowly.

"Well, get him in here. I want to talk to him."

"I'm afraid that's impossible, sir."

"And why is that, Captain?" The general was growing angry.

"Because he's dead, sir."

"Dead?" He pondered that for a moment. "I think you'd better explain yourself. And start at the beginning."

"Yes, sir." Mark shifted in his seat as he related all that had happened since their last meeting. "We just received the note from Sam Wallace this morning, saying that he was still alive and had all the information we needed."

"And you had hired Sam Wallace yourself? What for?"

"To follow MacIntosh, sir. There was something about him that didn't ring true."

"And?"

"And Sam was listening in on the spies' meeting when Wade discovered him. Wade took him down to the river, knocked him out, and threw him in."

"You're saying that he tried to kill Sam Wallace in cold blood?"

"Yes, sir. Not once, but twice. You see, MacIntosh intercepted a note for me from Sam, telling me where he was and that he had the information I needed."

"And he went after him again?"

"This morning, sir. We got there—"

"We?"

"The Westlakes and I, sir," Mark explained. "Anyway, we got there just in time to prevent him from shooting Sam."

"And you shot him?"

"Yes, sir."

"Was Sam injured?" The general grew concerned.

"No, not today. In fact, he's just fine. He gave me the names of everyone in attendance that he could remember."

General Fields held out his hand. "Let me see the list."

"Yes, sir." Mark handed it over.

"Wade Macintosh—Nathan Morgan—Annabelle Morgan—Gordon Tyndale . . ." The general paused in his reading of the names. "Captain Clayton, this reads like the St. Louis social register."

"I'm aware of that, General, but it also explains how they came by the information they had." Mark carefully watched his expression as he digested this new, startling information. "May I proceed with the arrests, sir?"

"Take as many men as you need. I want everyone on that list." The general was furious.

"Jim and Marshall Westlake have already gone after the Morgans."

"Good. Keep me informed of your progress."

"I will, sir. And thank you."

"You've done a good job so far. Now, let's finish it."

Mark hurried from the office to do just that. And while he was successfully rounding up the other unsuspecting members of the spy ring, Marshall and Jim were combing the riverfront in hopes of turning up a clue to Nathan's and Annabelle's whereabouts.

"Where to now?" Marshall asked in frustration as they left the office of the Mid-Rivers Line.

"I don't know. I've been trying to figure out what I would do if I were Nathan," Jim said pensively. "And it seems to me that I would do the opposite of what everybody expected me to do."

"You think we should have been checking northbound departures?"

"It's a start. But let's face it, we don't even know for sure that they did leave by steamer."

"Let's go." Marshall and Jim went back inside the Mid-Rivers office.

Micah Abernathy looked up as Jim and Marshall reentered the room and cursed silently to himself. When he had seen them on their way in the first time, he had quickly absented himself from the office. Nathan had warned him that Clayton or the Westlakes might come looking for him, and, being a nervous man by nature, Micah had not wanted to chance talking to them. But now, he was trapped. There was no way for him to avoid them.

"Micah." Jim greeted him easily. "We didn't know you were here."

"I've been in the back. Why?" Micah took off his glasses and began cleaning them with a handkerchief.

"No reason." Marshall spoke calmly. "We just need some additional information."

"About what?"

"We just talked to the clerk a minute ago. We were checking on departures of southbound packets."

"And?" Micah sounded agitated, and Jim gave his brother a sidelong glance.

"And now we need to know about any steamers that left port northbound in the last few hours." Jim watched his reaction to their request.

"Let me check for you . . . any particular destination in mind?"

"No. We're more interested in times than places," Marshall answered.

Micah's hands were trembling as he put his glasses back on and opened his ledgers. "We had the *Liberty Bell* pull out about two hours ago and the *Sugar Blossom* departed a half an hour later."

"Where are they bound?"

"The *Belle* is heading for Rock Island and the *Blossom* is going as far north as Alton and then she's heading up the Missouri to St. Charles and then on to Kansas City."

"Do you have your passenger lists?" Marshall inquired. "We'd like to see them."

"What's going on?" Micah tried to sound casual as he turned the book around so Jim and Marshall could check the lists.

"We're trying to locate Nathan and Annabelle Morgan. Do you know them?"

"Yes. I've had some dealings with Nathan," Micah hedged. "Why are you looking for them?"

"We're not at liberty to say right now. Have you seen them today? Did they book passage on one of your steamers?" Jim pushed.

"No!" he denied, too quickly.

Marshall and Jim were instantly suspicious as they pored over the ledger. They checked the *Blossom* first, only to find that there were no women traveling on her this trip. Having successfully eliminated one of the two boats, they turned their scrutiny to the *Belle*.

"There are two couples on the *Belle*, Jim," Marshall said, keeping an eye on Micah as he spoke. "But neither one is the Morgans."

Micah tried to disguise his relief, but they both read it easily.

"Thank you for your help, Micah." Jim turned the ledger back to him.

"You're welcome." He watched them leave and sighed audibly.

Once they were outside, Marshall and Jim exchanged knowing looks. "Let's check the other three offices. I think we've got our man, but I don't want to take any chances and go on a wild-goose chase."

They retraced their steps to find that a total of four steamboats, including the *Belle* and the *Blossom*, had left town, northbound, during the last few hours. A careful check of the passenger lists narrowed it down conclusively to the *Belle*. The other two boats were primarily used for freight and had few if any accommodations. Those people who did choose to travel on them generally slept on the deck, and, knowing Annabelle, Jim and Marshall immediately eliminated them from consideration.

"What do you think?"

"I think we should go back and pay our jittery friend Micah one more visit."

Micah nearly groaned aloud when he saw them returning. "You're back."

"Yes, and we need to speak with you for a minute, in private, if you don't mind. . . ." Jim's words were cordial, but there was a certain steeliness to his tone that sent a shiver down Micah's spine.

"We can use the back room," he offered lamely, preceding them into the privacy of the smaller office and closing the door. "Now, what can I do for you?"

"We want to know the truth," Marshall said threateningly.

"I—I don't know what you mean. . . ." Micah was appalled.

"Are the Morgans on the *Belle* or not?" Jim demanded.

"I have no idea what you're talking about! If you'll excuse me . . ." He started to leave the office, but Marshall's hand on his arm stopped his progress.

"Micah . . . we can offer you a deal, but we need to know the truth, now."

"A deal . . ." Micah swallowed nervously.

"If you talk to us and tell us the truth, we won't inform the authorities of your involvement. However, if we're forced to bring Captain Clayton and General Fields into this . . . well, needless to say, the army's penalty for helping spies escape is severe."

Micah weighed his alternatives. He had had business dealings with the Westlakes before, and he knew them to be honest and fair. If he cooperated, he knew that he would be safe . . . but if he refused to tell them and he was arrested . . . in the way of a weak individual, Micah made the choice that would do the most to ensure his own well-being.

"All right. I'll tell you what I know. . . ."

Jim and Marshall smiled grimly. "Go ahead. We're listening."

"Nathan stopped here at the office shortly before the *Belle* was scheduled to leave port. He needed to get out of town fast."

"Where was he going?"

"He didn't say. He just said that he needed passage on a northbound boat for himself and his daughter."

"And the *Belle* is going to Rock Island, right?"

"Right."

"Thanks, Micah. Our deal stands, but if we ever find out that you're involved with the Rebs again . . ."

"I know. . . ."

With that, Jim and Marshall hurried from the office in search of Mark. They found him at headquarters as the last of the men identified by Sam were being brought in.

"What did you find out?" Mark asked as they joined him.

"They've left town on a packet heading for Rock Island. Do you want to go after them?"

"You know I do," he told them with determination. "I want them all."

"The *Mound City* just arrived back in town this morning. It can be ready to leave as soon as we are."

"Let me report to General Fields, and then we can go."

"We'll have to stop by the house to let everyone know we're leaving, but with our luck we should be on the river within the hour."

"How much of a headstart do they have on us?"

"Less than four hours. And since the *Belle* is on a normal run, we should be able to catch up with her in no time."

"Good. I'll be right back."

And Jim and Marshall waited patiently while Mark went to meet with his commanding officer.

Chapter Forty-three

It was late afternoon. The sun was starting to dip lower in the west, its fading presence casting long shadows wherever it touched. The Mississippi was running wide and fast, slowing the progress of the *Mound City* as she struggled upstream against the current.

Jim lay on the bunk in a cabin on board the packet trying to relax, but the throbbing in his leg and the thought of his upcoming confrontation with Annabelle was making it virtually impossible. Sitting up, he picked up the bottle of scotch that Marshall had brought him and poured himself a whiskey glass full, hoping it would take the edge off his pain. With no hesitation, he drank the whole thing and poured himself another.

Jim had no doubt that the day had been a success. Everyone involved in the robbery had been apprehended except Annabelle and Nathan, and they hoped to correct that within the next few hours.

Jim had hated to leave Delight again, but he felt this was something that he had to do. And she had been understanding about it, especially since he'd promised her their long-postponed honeymoon as soon as he got back. He smiled to himself as he sipped at his liquor. He was looking forward to that himself.

The knock at the door drew his attention, and he called for them to come on in. "It's open."

The cabin door swung wide and Marshall entered. "How's the leg?"

"The truth?"

"Of course."

"It hurts like hell." Jim grimaced. "By the way, thanks for the scotch."

"I knew you were going to need something. Do you realize what we've done today? And it was your first day back on your feet."

"I think I overdid it a bit," Jim grinned.

"I know you did."

"It'll be all right. I just have to stay off it a while."

"Why didn't you just stay home? Mark and I could have handled this."

"No. I want to be there when we catch up with Annabelle." He took a deep drink from his glass. "I don't like being used. And I'm just thankful that I didn't give her any important information."

Marshall well understood his brother's anger and disgust. "I know. She had us all fooled." He paused as he thought of all the times Annabelle and Nathan had been guests in his home.

"How soon do you figure we'll catch up with them?"

"According to the pilot, if things go well and the *Belle* makes some stops on the way, we should catch her by Alton."

"Good."

"Are you going to stay in here and rest until we get there?"

"Yes, but call me if we sight her, all right?"

"I will. You take it easy. Do you need anything else?"

"No. Not right now."

"I'll be back." And Marshall went on out to join Mark and his men in their wait to catch sight of the *Liberty Belle*.

Annabelle sipped at her glass of wine in celebration as the *Liberty Belle* neared Alton. It was true . . . they had made it! She almost laughed now when she thought of how desperate and afraid she'd been this afternoon. How could she have doubted her father? He always had a solution for everything.

Relaxing now in their cabin while Nathan made his presence known in the men's saloon, she thought of this morning and her visit to the Westlakes. What a miserable experience! It had been bad enough to find his insipid fianceé, with her ridiculous name, there with him when she'd stopped by, but to discover so unexpectedly that they'd married had really upset her. Her little ploy to break them up hadn't worked. She hadn't had time since then to think about it, but now she realized that it had hurt her more than she'd been aware.

She had cared for Jim . . . more than she'd ever truly cared for any man. And it was quite a blow to her ego to learn that he hadn't felt the same way about her.

Sighing, Annabelle placed her glass on the small table beside the bunk and curled up. The excitement of the day and the effects of the wine were making her drowsy, and she thought a short nap might help to restore her energy. She was certain that her father would wake her in plenty of time to get ready for dinner, so she fell asleep totally confident that she was safe and protected.

Marshall came barging into Jim's cabin without knocking. "We've just spotted her!"

"How far ahead is she?" Jim struggled out of bed.

"Less than a half mile."

"Where are we now?"

"We'll be in Alton in an hour."

"What's Mark decided to do? Board her at Alton?"

Marshall nodded. "We're going to pass her and dock at Alton to wait for her."

"Good. Are all the soldiers off the decks? I don't want Nathan to suspect anything if he should happen to be out walking on deck and look over at us."

"Mark's already sent the men inside."

"I want to watch this," Jim told him as he started out of the stateroom, still limping.

"Is your leg any better?" Marshall joined him on the promenade deck.

"A little. It's more stiff than anything, right now." They

walked slowly around the boat until they caught sight of the *Liberty Belle* a short distance ahead of them.

They stood poised at the railing as the *Mound City* gained and then passed the slower-moving steamer.

"Good," Jim smiled. "Now all we have to do is wait."

As soon as the boat was behind them, Mark came out on deck to join Jim and Marshall. "I've told the pilot to dock at the first wharf boat he can find, and if anyone gives him any trouble, I'll handle it."

"We'll be there within the hour," Jim told him.

"I know. And we'll have just enough time to get ready before the *Belle* docks." Mark was eager for this moment. His revenge was not quite complete.

They fell silent for a moment as they thought of the tense encounter to come.

"Our biggest problem will be to take them by surprise. I don't want any shootouts. I want them to stand trial for what they've done," Mark advised them.

And they agreed, as their steamer carried them on, ever closer to the final confrontation.

Mark had positioned his men strategically along the levee near the landing sight of the *Liberty Belle* and then had retreated with Jim and Marshall a short distance away to wait until she'd tied up. From their vantage point, they could watch as the steamboat carefully maneuvered into the place at the wharf boat. When the final line had been thrown, they moved forward cautiously.

"Let's go." Mark signaled his men. Congregating at the foot of the gangplank, he issued further orders. "I want three men here, armed and ready, just in case there is trouble. We don't anticipate any, but in situations like this, you never know."

"Yes, sir."

"The rest of you follow us. We're going on board and, if necessary, we're going to search every cabin until we find them. Ready?"

"Yes, sir."

"Then, let's go." Mark, Jim, and Marshall led the way up the gangplank.

"I know Captain Dalton. Let's see if I can find him." Jim started up the stairs on his way to the pilothouse.

Captain Dalton, having seen the soldiers approaching, was on his way down, and they met on the promenade deck. "Jim? What's the meaning of this?" he thundered, wondering at this armed invasion of his boat.

"John, do you know Captain Mark Clayton?"

"No. I don't believe I've had the honor."

"Mark Clayton, this is John Dalton." Jim introduced them and they shook hands.

"We have reason to believe, Captain Dalton, that two of the spies who were responsible for the attack and subsequent destruction of the *Enterprise* are on board your vessel."

"Who?" he demanded.

"In reality, their names are Annabelle and Nathan Morgan, but they've come aboard your ship under the names of Mr. and Mrs. White."

"Why, he was just down in the saloon a few minutes ago."

"Is he still there?" Mark asked.

"To the best of my knowledge. Let's go check." Captain Dalton led the way.

"What about the woman?" Jim questioned.

"I haven't seen her since they came on board back in St. Louis, but they're in cabin number twenty-four."

"Thanks." Jim left them and headed toward the stateroom.

"Jim?"

"You take care of Nathan. I'm going for Annabelle."

"Be careful." Marshall warned, and Jim wisely heeded his advice.

Jim didn't bother to knock, not wanting to give her time to prepare. Instead, he stealthily turned the knob and opened the unlocked door soundlessly. He had been ready for trouble, his hand resting on his revolver, but the sight that greeted him convinced him that there was no need. Annabelle was alone, and she was sound asleep.

Moving into the room, he closed and locked the door behind him and then went to stand by the bed. It amazed him that she could look so beautiful in her sleep. But he knew what kind of a treacherous woman she really was, and her beauty stirred only contempt in him.

"Are you going somewhere, Annabelle?" He spoke loudly, wanting her to awaken suddenly.

Her eyes flew open, and she looked up groggily at the man who stood over her. "Jim . . ." His name was a whisper on her lips. "What are you doing here?"

"I'm looking for you," he said solemnly.

Annabelle sat up quickly, her eyes narrowed as she tried to figure out what had happened. "Where's my father?"

"By this time, I imagine he's with Mark. They were going down to the saloon to pick him up."

"What do you mean?"

"I mean, it's over, Annabelle."

"Over?" She was trying to pull herself together . . . to figure a way out of this. Where was her father? Could he really have been taken by Mark, or could Jim be lying? How could this have happened when they were so close to getting away?

"You must have considered yourself most fortunate that you were at our house when the note from Sam Wallace arrived. That bit of advance information gave you the extra time you needed to get out of town before we came after you."

Annabelle stood up and walked across the cabin from him. She was caught, and she knew it. Turning to face him, she lifted her chin defiantly. "Yes, it did."

Jim was stunned by her brazen confession. He had expected her to deny everything . . . to play the innocent victim, not readily to admit her involvement.

His gaze hardened as he stared at her. He had never really known her at all. She had created an image for him, and he had believed what he'd seen. He wondered if she had been determined enough to have gone through with her marriage to him, just to get the information. Looking at her now, he knew that she would have done it, and the thought sickened him.

"Let's go," he told her, his tone one of disgust.

But Annabelle wasn't about to give up that easily. She was prepared to barter the only thing she had left for her freedom . . . her body.

"Jim . . ." Though she was nervous, she lowered her tone and walked toward him slowly. Her expression was openly seductive.

He didn't speak, but eyed her calmly as she began to unbutton the bodice of her dress.

"I know you found me attractive once. I can make you feel that again," she murmured, stopping directly in front of him and pressing intimately against him. "I'll do anything you want, if you'll let me go."

"Annabelle—" Jim found her behavior repulsive and he took her by her forearms and held her away from him "It's time I got you back to Mark."

"But . . ." She was totally shocked at his refusal to take her up on her offer.

"Button your dress and move." He directed her toward the door. "They're waiting."

"You'll pay for this, Jim Westlake!" she hissed, out of control in her fury. "Wade will get you for this!"

"I'm afraid not, my dear," he told her as he opened the door for her, still holding her by her arm. "You see, Wade MacIntosh is dead."

"He's dead?" Her eyes widened in shock at the news.

"He was killed this morning in a shootout with Mark."

"Oh, no!" She swayed as the reality of it hit her. It was over. . . .

Accompanied by Captain Dalton, Mark and Marshall entered the saloon and immediately spotted Nathan, still at the bar in a discussion with some other men passengers. He did not look up as they came forward, and it wasn't until Mark spoke to him that he realized his precarious situation.

"Nathan . . . your trip is over," Mark said levelly.

Turning almost in slow motion, Nathan paled as he came face-to-face with Mark and Marshall. "You! How?"

"It doesn't matter how we found you. The important part is that we did find you," Marshall told him.

"Marsh, check him for a gun," Mark instructed. When Marshall found that he was clean, Mark continued, "Now, let's move out of here nice and easy."

Nathan's mind was racing. What could he do? He thought of running, but as soon as they left the saloon and he saw the soldiers Mark had with him he gave up the idea. Worrying about Annabelle, he glanced nervously up the companion-way as they came out on deck. To his horror, Jim Westlake was bringing her down the steps.

"Annabelle! Are you all right?" His worry was real.

"Yes." Her tone was flat when she answered him.

Somehow, Nathan thought, he had to create a diversion to give Annabelle a chance to get away. Hoping that she would have sense enough to run when he did it, he gauged his distance to the railing. And then, when he knew the soldiers had relaxed their vigilance, he raced for the rail and jumped overboard. He thought the fall would never end as he tumbled the two stories into the cold, dirty water.

"Get him!" Mark shouted to his men still on the levee.

Marshall, who waited until Nathan surfaced to make his move, dove expertly into the river near him. Easily overpowering the older man, he swam the short distance back to the bank with him in tow. The three guards were there to take him from Marshall as he staggered up onto the levee.

Nathan looked up at the boat in hopes that Annabelle had taken advantage of his diversion, but Jim Westlake was still holding onto her possessively. He shook his head at the wasted effort and followed the guards off down the riverfront.

Marshall stood, soaking wet, waiting for them to leave the

steamer. "How did I do?" he asked, grinning, as Mark finally came down the gangplank.

"I didn't know you could swim so well."

"Neither did I." He laughed as Jim joined them, still keeping a hold on Annabelle.

"Sergeant!" Mark called to one of his men.

"Yes, sir?"

"Take Miss Morgan on board the *Mound City* and lock her in this stateroom." Mark handed him the key to the cabin.

"Yes, sir."

"And, Sergeant?"

The young man looked back at his captain questioningly.

"Be careful."

"Yes, sir." He took Annabelle by the arm and led her none too gently toward the other boat.

The three men stood together in silent companionship as they realized that they had accomplished what they'd set out to do. They had caught all the people responsible for the attack on the *Enterprise*. Exchanging happy looks, they clapped one another on the back and headed for home.

Chapter Forty-four

Delight sat wearily in the front parlor with Renee. Stifling a yawn, she gave her friend a helpless look. "If they don't get home pretty soon, I'm going to be sound asleep."

"I know," Renee agreed, slowly losing her own battle to stay awake. "What time is it, anyway?"

"It's after one." She glanced at the mantel clock.

"No wonder everybody else went to bed. You know, they might not make it back until tomorrow. Maybe we should go on upstairs, too."

"No. I'm going to wait down here for him. But why don't you go to bed? You know Roger's going to wake up at seven, regardless. You're going to need a little sleep."

Renee smiled as she stood up. "That's true enough. He's a regular alarm clock. I'll see you in the morning."

"Good night," Delight called softly, as Renee headed on up to bed.

Getting up, Delight picked up the lamp and carried it with her to Marshall's study. The flickering golden flame cast wavering shadows about as she entered the dark paneled room to select a book from his large library. Checking the titles of the beautiful leather-bound volumes, she finally chose a well-worn book of poems and went back to settle in on the sofa.

She had been reading for almost an hour when the words began to blur before her eyes. Wanting to stay awake, but knowing that the battle was lost. Delight curled up on the sofa and fell asleep.

"Gentlemen," General Fields was saying as he lifted his glass of bourbon. "To a job well done."

Mark, Jim, and Marshall joined him in that toast. It had been a long, dangerous day, but they had succeeded.

"Have you made any decisions concerning replacing the *Enterprise?*" the general asked.

"I've made some inquires," Marshall told him. "There is a steamer for sale in Cincinnati. We could have her refitted and ready to sail in about six weeks, I should think."

"Good. But can you fulfill your contract? There will be at least two more gold shipments in that time. Do you have a boat available?"

"We own four other packets, all of which will suit our purpose," Jim told him.

General Fields nodded. "Now that we've eliminated the informers from our midst, we should be safe."

"We'll be ready whenever the shipments come in, sir," Marshall assured him.

"Thank you for everything. We'll be in touch." He shook hands with Jim and Marshall both.

As they turned to leave, Mark started to follow.

"Captain. I'd like to speak with you for a few minutes."

"Yes, sir." Mark thought all their business had been concluded, and he was surprised by the request. "Jim—Marshall, I'll see you tomorrow. Tell Dorrie I'll be by as soon as I can."

"Okay." Good night."

When they had disappeared from the room and closed the door behind them, Mark turned to face his commanding officer.

"Yes, sir?"

"I wanted to commend you on your handling of this investigation. You alone suspected that we had an informer in our midst, and, by your perseverance, you uncovered him."

"Thank you, sir."

"You are to assume the rank of major, now, Clayton."

Mark was taken completely by surprise. "Major?"

"You've earned it. Congratulations."

"Thank you, sir!"

It was near dawn as Jim and Marshall finally got away from headquarters and started home. They rode in silence, both exhausted yet excited by the events of the day.

A single lamp burned low in the parlor window, and both men entered the house, looking forward to its warmth and shelter. Heading into the parlor, they stopped, the sight that greeted them making them smile.

"I guess Renee gave up on me," Marshall chuckled. "I'll see you sometime later today." And with that, he went up to his wife.

Jim crossed the parlor quietly and stood staring down at her gentle loveliness for long minutes before kneeling beside her. With infinite care, he leaned forward and kissed her softly.

Delight stirred at the touch of his lips and smiled sleepily. "I knew you'd be home soon."

She caressed his cheek and then slid her hand behind his

neck to pull him down for another kiss. It was a warm, loving exchange, and Delight's heart swelled with her love for him.

Without breaking off the kiss, Jim shifted his weight until he was lying beside her, and Delight turned on her side to give him more room.

"Have you been here all night?" he asked huskily as his lips explored the sweetness of her throat.

"Yes," she whispered, shivering at the force of the emotion he was arousing.

Jim's control slipped as she responded to him without restraint. He had wanted to be with her ever since his confrontation with Annabelle . . . a confrontation that had left him feeling somehow soiled. He needed to taste the splendor and peace of Delight's love again.

"Darling?" He spoke softly.

"Um?" She wriggled closer to him.

"I think we'd better go upstairs . . ." He gave a low chuckle as she murmured a protest and sought to draw him to her for a kiss.

"Do we have to?" she protested when he refused her tempting ploy; she didn't want to move from this haven.

"I'm afraid so."

"But why?"

"First, because I refuse to make love to you here on this lumpy, uncomfortable sofa. And second, because it's almost dawn, darling." He couldn't resist her any longer, and he stole a quick, passionate kiss.

"Dawn?" Delight blinked in surprise as he ended the embrace and glanced out the window to see the sky brightening to the east. She had thought it was only two o'clock in the morning. "What happened? Where have you been? I had no idea it was this late." She turned worried eyes to him as he got up awkwardly off the couch.

"It's a long story . . . let's go up to bed and I'll tell you." He held out a hand to her and helped her to her feet.

She slipped her arm about his waist as they left the room. "How's your leg? I was so worried about you . . ."

"It's better." His leg was the last thing on his mind.

"Good." She hugged him. "Did you catch up with Annabelle and her father?"

He nodded. "They're both in custody. We managed to beat their steamer to Alton, and Mark made the arrests there."

"Then it's all over?" she asked hopefully, starting up the staircase.

"Yes. Everyone Sam named has been caught."

Relief swept over her like a physical thing. Slanting him a provocative sideways glance, she asked, "Then we can start our honeymoon now?"

"I did have that on my mind." He grinned down at her as he opened the door to their bedroom.

She smiled in delight as they entered the room and locked the door behind them.

The predawn light gave their bedroom a softly muted glow as they went quickly into each other's arms. The embrace was tender and complete as they shared a moment of blissful contentment. But the emotional fires that had been stoked in the parlor were near the surface, and Delight lifted her face to accept his kiss.

"I love you," Jim said earnestly just as his lips claimed hers in a searing brand.

Delight threw her arms about his neck to hug him to her, wanting only to get as close to him as possible.

Delight smiled up at him, her desire for him glowing in her eyes. "I love you, my captain."

Willing himself to take his time, he slowly and methodically began to unbutton her dress, pausing after each button to place a soft kiss on her waiting mouth. When at last the bodice was undone, he spread the material apart and caressed the swell of her bosom so delightfully displayed above her chemise.

"You wear too many clothes," he complained sensuously as his hand dipped within the confines of the chemise.

Her breath caught in her throat at his touch, and she clung to him as he deepened the caress with a kiss. Her knees weakening under his sensual onslaught, Delight hurried to unbutton his shirt so she could run her hands over the hard muscles of his furred chest.

His already overpowering need for her grew as she boldly explored him, and finally he could stand no more of her erotic torment. With gentle hands, he stripped her gown from her and then helped her shed her petticoats and chemise.

"You are gorgeous." His voice hoarse with emotion as he stared at her slim beauty. His eyes caressed her with a heated gaze . . .

Delight held her arms out to him, inviting him to love her, and he went to her eagerly, needing to lose himself in her womanly sweetness.

Moving to the bed, Jim shed his remaining clothes and joined her on the wide expanse of softness.

"This is much better than the sofa," she told him as he came to her.

"Much," he agreed before kissing her deeply.

His hands explored her freely, touching and provoking magical responses from her as she was lost in a haze of passionate glory. His mouth plundered hers as he moved to make her his own.

They lay together as one, savoring the closeness that this, love's fullest pleasure, gave.

Replete in love's rapturous splendor, they rested, and they were soon lulled to sleep by the sense of blissful peace that overcame them.

It was a loud pounding on the door that woke them long hours later.

"Uncle Jimmy! Are you ever going to get up?" Roger's voice came to them plaintively through the heavy, locked door, followed quickly by Renee's hushed reprimand.

"Roger Westlake! You get away from there and let them rest. You know he was out late last night with your father!"

"I know, Mama, but Papa's up . . . why doesn't Uncle Jimmy get up?" His protest faded as he walked dejectedly away from the bedroom door.

Delight and Jim exchanged mischievous looks as they lay in each other's arms.

"Why don't I get up?" he asked, leaning over to kiss her good morning. "It must be near noon . . ."

"I can think of one good reason why not," she teased.

"That's a good reason," he growled, before once more claiming her in love's play.

It was nearly an hour later that they finally left the privacy of their room and went downstairs to eat.

"Good afternoon," Renee greeted them smilingly as they came into the dining room. "We're just having lunch, but I'm sure I can come up with breakfast for you, if you'd prefer."

"Lunch will be fine," Jim said as they joined her and Marshall at the table. "Where is everybody?"

"I sent Roger out to play. He was anxious to see you and he probably would have camped outside your bedroom door if I hadn't . . ." She grinned.

"I know, we heard," Jim laughed.

"Mother and Father went out, Dorrie is up in her room, and Sam went to report in," Marshall finished.

"Has Mark been by yet?"

"No. I don't look for him until later this afternoon."

"No word on how his meeting with the general went?"

"Haven't heard a thing yet."

It was then that the knock came at the front door, and Renee went to answer it.

"Mark! We were just talking about you. Come in." She held the door wide to admit him. "Marshall, Jim and Delight are in the dining room. Go ahead in, and I'll get Dorrie."

"Thanks, Renee."

He went to join the others. "Good afternoon." He smiled, pleased with the news he was about to impart.

"You look quite satisfied with yourself today. How did your meeting with Fields go last night?" Jim asked as Mark sat down at the table.

"It went just fine . . . I'm Major Clayton, now." He beamed, proud of himself.

"Well, well. That's impressive. Congratulations," they lauded him.

"Mark?" Dorrie hurried into the room, anxious to see him after a long night of worry.

He met her halfway across the room and embraced her. Uncaring that everyone was looking on, he kissed her.

"I'm so glad you got back safely. We were all so worried."

"Everything worked out perfectly. All the arrests were made with a minimum of violence . . . and we had only one small bit of excitement ourselves." He looked at Marshall, his eyes twinkling.

"You didn't tell me there was any danger," Renee said accusingly as she witnessed the exchange between her husband and Mark.

"Neither did you," Delight added to Jim.

"Well, it wasn't dangerous . . . not really."

"What wasn't dangerous?" Renee demanded of Marshall.

"Nathan tried to get away . . . that's all. He tried to shrug it off.

"And? I know there must be more to it or Mark wouldn't have brought it up."

"I had to jump in the river to get him," he answered blandly.

"From the promenade deck!" Jim embroidered.

"From the promenade deck?"

"I had to hurry or he might have gotten away. Besides, I figured if Nathan could live through the fall, so could I." He grinned at her, and then said, for her ears only, "I wasn't taking any chances. You know what a good swimmer I am."

Renee softened. "I'm just glad it's over and done with."

"You're not the only one," Delight admitted.

"Mark. Tell Dorrie your good news," Jim prompted.

"Good news?"

"I've been promoted. I am now Major Clayton."

"How wonderful!" She threw her arms around him and kissed him again. "Now, how soon are we having the wedding?"

"As soon as you can arrange it. I want us together as soon as possible."

"Is anyone going up to Cedarhill anytime soon?" Jim asked conversationally.

"Not that I know of. Mother and Father are planning on staying in town for the Bradford ball in two weeks. Why?" Marshall responded.

"I want to spend some time alone with my wife." He took her hand. "We really haven't had a honeymoon yet."

"That sounds romantic . . ." Renee sighed, giving them a gentle smile.

"I hope so. Of course at this point, anyplace alone with Delight would sound romantic to me." Jim laughed in good-natured frustration and then turned to her. "We'll leave in the morning, then."

"I'll be ready whenever you are."

"Uncle Jimmy!" Roger's loud call reverberated throughout the room as he rushed back in from playing.

"Hello, Roger. I understand that you've been looking for me?"

"Yes. I've been waiting all morning for you to get up. How come you slept so long?"

"I guess I was just tired," Jim replied, giving Delight a special look.

"Oh." He found his uncle's answer evasive, but let it go. "Anyway, are you really going out to Cedarhill tomorrow? Can I go along this time, too?"

"Not this trip, I'm afraid." Jim's eyes gleamed as he looked at his wife. "I just want to go out to the country to rest and relax for a while. But I promise you I'll take you next time. All right?"

"All right."

"Rest and relax?" Marshall queried, his eyebrows raised mockingly.

Leaning toward Delight to kiss her gently, Jim smiled widely. "Well, I will need to rest and relax . . . afterward."

His eyes met hers in perfect understanding as their love flowed around them, encircling their lives and guiding them to life's greatest joys.